sail away

also edited by **lena lenček** and **gideon bosker**

BEACH: STORIES BY THE SAND AND SEA

sail away

STORIES OF ESCAPING TO SEA

EDITED AND WITH AN INTRODUCTION

BY **lena lenček** AND **gideon bosker**

PHOTOGRAPHS BY MITTIE HELLMICH, LENA LENČEK AND GIDEON BOSKER

marlowe & company • new york

Published by
Marlowe & Company
An Imprint of Avalon Publishing Group Incorporated
841 Broadway, 4th Floor
New York, NY 10003

SAIL AWAY: *Stories of Escaping to Sea*
Compilation and introduction copyright © 2001
by Lena Lenček and Gideon Bosker
Photographs copyright © 2001 by Mittie Hellmich, Lena Lenček and Gideon Bosker
Page 329 represents a continuation of the copyright page.

LIBRARY OF CONGRESS CATALOGING-IN-PUBLICATION DATA
Sail away: stories of escaping to sea/edited by Lena Lenček and Gideon Bosker.
p. cm.
ISBN 1-56924-584-3
1. Sea stories. 2. Sailing—Fiction. I. Lenček, Lena. II. Bosker, Gideon.
PN6120.95.S4 S25 2001
808.83'932162—dc21
2001030024

9 8 7 6 5 4 3 2 1

DESIGNED BY PAULINE NEUWIRTH, NEUWIRTH & ASSOCIATES INC.

Printed in the United States of America
Distributed by Publishers Group West

In memory of Chuck Isenberg,

who navigated the prose of Osip Mandelshtam

and the Gulf of Maine with equal relish,

elegance, and ease.

"sailboat" (1832)

A solitary sail gleams white

Against the blue haze of the sea . . .

What does it seek on the horizon?

What does it want to leave behind?

The waves rear up, a shrill wind whistles,

The straining mast contorts and creaks . . .

No, happiness is not the object,

Nor flight from happiness the end.

Below: the brilliance of an azure current,

Above: a stream of golden light . . .

Rebellious, it needs the tempest,

As if in tempests rest resides.

—BY MIKHAIL LERMONTOV, TRANSLATED BY LENA LENČEK

contents

introduction

it takes trust to leave land for the unpredictable shimmy of a boat. I was three the first time my father took me sailing on a glacial lake high in the Julian Alps of northern Italy. I can still feel the terror spreading from my eyes down through my spine to the tips of my toes. Imagine: massive peaks, black stands of pine, water a searing shade of green, and, impossibly high overhead, a scramble of white cloud on a thin blue sky. My father ran up the sails. I sat stiff in my red-and-white pinafore and kept my eyes fixed on shore. The boat rocked. The mast creaked. By slight jerks, the hotel and the dock and the people on it got smaller and smaller, and the sounds of land grew clearer, somehow more distinct. I took a deep breath and looked down into those clear depths with their mangled stumps of giant trees vanishing into an even deeper murk, and saw silvery, flickery ghosts rising up to meet the oars. Trout broke the surface. A dense cold rose all around, sending shivers across my sun-warmed skin. A gust of wind filled the sail: We flew across the lake and the joy of being on water took hold of me for good.

Being on a vessel does remarkable things to your soul. We found this out over the years as we sailed away on everything from sailboats, canoes, and ferries, to ocean liners, rafts, and submersibles. Nomadic by necessity as much as inclination, we are ever ready to balance on a floor that pitches and rolls, to gaze at a flat horizon that, at any moment, a sudden wind might whip into a heaving mountain. We've heard it said that, "on a ship, there is a fate in every plank." This is no cliché; no two voyages, no two excursions, are ever alike. That every journey on water is unique isn't just a matter of different times, different places, but something much more fundamental. On a purely physical level, being on water is literally the closest thing we have to inhabiting a parallel universe—at least until space travel becomes practicable.

At sea, the landlubber eye instantly adjusts, capable of reading the cryptic language of natural phenomena for which there is no exact counterpart on shore. The surface texture of water, the smoothness or the chop of the seas, the feel of the wind, the smell of the air, even the color and shape of the foam flecking the cresting waves—these are all signs that the eye must learn to read. For most of us, that elementary foreignness of being at sea turns us into visionaries. After all, you may take the same pair of eyes to sea, but what—and even more important, how—you see through them will be totally different. Instead of fixed verticals and horizontals, there is a constantly shifting visual field that oscillates, swings, rises, and falls in a rhythm far more complex and unpredictable than anything on earth.

With no warning and no obvious pivot points, the sometimes ethereal, sometimes violent seascape opens doors to the inner self in a way that only meditating or listening to the most complex music approximates. After all, waves and wind are the music of the planetary spheres as they exert their influence on air and water. Their sounds enter the soul and fill it with fear and strength, soaring aspirations, sorrow, hope; above all, they stir in us an ecstatic engagement with life. Mere specks on a vast, powerful element controlled by the pull of the moon, we are always a miscalculation away from sinking into the oceanic depths. The sea voyage, after all, is the original stage for hubris, for a never-ending drama of titanic will pitted against nature, destiny, God—whatever your *nom de jour* for the everything over which we have no control.

VOYAGING ON THE sea has the power to crystallize an emotion or an understanding so obscure, so subtle, and so ephemeral, that on land— where we can order life with some illusion of control and predictability—it never has a chance to show up on the radar screen of our consciousness. Only at sea, where we abandon the assumptions and routines to which we cling as long as we walk on stable ground, do we begin to see lucidly into our innermost depths. Sailors often talk about the way the sea alters their sense of time, their diurnal rhythms, the texture of their self-awareness. Under the spell of solitude and the erratic pace of weather, the soul unfurls like a sail and lets the wind carry it where it will. Ann Davison, the most philosophical of a rugged breed of solo ocean sailors, gets it right when she writes in *My Ship is So Small* that beyond the "travelogue superficiality" of her journey, the experience in fact went "much deeper than it appeared."

The stories in this collection will take you into these depths. Whatever their tack—lyrical, ironic, humorous, or sardonic—these nautical narratives reveal that every sail away is a pilgrimage into the unknown. Hauling, tacking, and veering across the planet's seas, these writers report on how it feels to traverse a certain stretch of water, what thoughts come to mind in the face of marine misadventure, what hopes and trepidations accompany embarkation. For some, the nautical journey reveals character and defines destiny. For others, it crystallizes a crucial moment in the life of the soul. For still others, it catalyzes extreme psychic states and brings into play every note in the deadly and sinful scale of passions, from lust and envy to murderous rage. Whatever their immediate focus, however, all of these writers are obsessed with the idea that just as the sea is defined by its terrestrial borders, so is escape by sea bounded by what lies on either figurative shore. After all, the ship is nothing more than a needle threading its way through a richly variegated tapestry of life.

A boat, Migael Scherer writes in *Sailing to Simplicity*, "revolves like a planet around the fixed pole of the anchor. There's the sea, below and around, and the sky and the land which seem to grow from the sea. There's the boat suspended between, and me in the boat, dreaming shallow dreams, still listening." This hovering of the mind, between dream and waking, is the crux of the nautical frame of mind. That, plus the enforced proximity of a ship's tight quarters, breeds intimacies unthinkable on land. Maybe that's why romances click so much faster onboard a ship, and why ailing marriages heal on the tilting deck of a sailboat. That, at least, has been our experience, from the time many years ago that we sealed our friendship aboard a fishing boat in the Adriatic, sharing a bottle of wine and a dozen tomatoes. Even now, at the first sign of the doldrums of the soul, we make our escape: from the ordinary, the predictable, the safe, and the painful.

Until the mid-19th century only dire necessity or wanderlust prompted travelers to board cramped, unreliable wooden vessels for voyages of uncertain duration—and even more uncertain outcome. To venture on the sea was to put oneself at risk, not only physically, but psychologically. For centuries the consciousness of this risk formed the core of nautical tales, even when covered over with humor, metaphysics, or allegory. One would have expected that once technological innovations made sailing the most predictable of journeys, the element of fear would have been banished from sea stories. After all, with the rare exception of a *Titanic* or an *Andrea Dorea*, ocean liners such as the *Queen Elizabeth* and the *Queen Mary* have made once perilous crossings so safe and so comfortable that now many of us have come to view them as bland and self-indulgent cocoons from experience. In fact, nothing could be farther from the truth. Even with global positioning systems and sea-lanes, these stories make it clear that the sea remains unpredictable and ruthless.

It was in the spirit of the great escape that we selected the narratives in this collection to illuminate the entire gamut of navigational experiences—to distill the very best accounts of the magic of sailing, in the broad sense of traversing water, in all its inflections, moods, and registers. To do this we "trawled" a veritable sea of nautical narratives—including all *Eighty-Nine Good Novels of the Sea, the Ship, and the Sailor* listed by book collector and pharmacist J.K. Lilly—as well as hundreds of other novels, stories, memoirs, and other miscellaneous pieces. Completeness, however, was no more our goal for this collection than was an academic procession of well-known pieces. That is why we resisted the lure of such obvious choices as Homer, Melville, Poe, Conrad, Crane, E.M. Forster, Hemingway, Lawrence Durrell, or Patrick O'Brian. A historical "survey" was equally off course, which explains why we've avoided an orderly progression from, say, Sebastian Brant's *Das Narrenschiff* to Katherine Anne Porter's *A Ship of Fools* and Julio Cortázar's *The Winners*. Much as we savor the language and plotting of classics such as Mark Twain's *The Innocents Abroad* or Robert Louis Stevenson's *The Amateur Emigrant*—not to mention Joshua Slocum, that granddaddy of solo circumnavigational writers—we decided against including pieces whose patina of age, of another era, was too bright.

Much contemporary sailing literature is of the "dirty weather" variety, with its adrenaline-surging focus on surviving the rage, inconstancy, and power of open water. So inherently challenging are the physical demands of survival on water that stories about being at sea tend to focus on the sheer ordeal of the experience: the courage, endurance, and loneliness; the need for constant vigilance; the dangers that always lurk over the horizon in the form of weather and wind and passing ships. To be sure, reading about trials such as these is immensely satisfying, and we made sure to spike our collection with such masterful, harrowing accounts—Bryan Burrough's "Storm Warning" and an excerpt from Pete Goss' *Close to the Wind*. But we wanted to come up with something more than the voyeuristic charge of looking over someone else's shoulder into the maw of destruction. We wanted to capture the comical, the tragic, the sublime, the banal, the mysterious, the predictable.

Like Freya Stark, described by Laurence Durrell as a great traveler who "covers the ground outwardly, so she advances inwardly," we were as intrigued by the inner journeying of the navigator as the outer, as curious about the consciousness shaped by the sea as the shape of the seascape itself. This double focus took us to stories that reveal what being on water allows to happen, what is catalyzed in the depths of our emotional life when we insert ourselves into a natural realm that is thoroughly alien to our species. *Sail Away* offers the opportunity to look at all kinds of "sea-faring" expeditions—from scientific submersions to recreational excursions, from solitary adventures to mass market and luxury cruises—as a way of charting the intricacies of aquatic navigation and the human reactions to venturing into the unknown. Each of the stories presented here unfolds from the basic premise that by the simple act of putting a plank between ourselves and water and letting go of the certitudes of terra firma, we open ourselves up to novel insights, deep experiences, and startling encounters.

A word about the sequence (which you're welcome, of course, to blithely ignore). We've arranged the stories to progress by degrees from a tight focus on the material circumstances of being at sea, to an increasingly abstract exploration of its psychological, social, developmental, and finally, spiritual dimensions. In this respect, the stories reflect the full spectrum of navigational plots: from the quest for the exotic and escape from the ordinary to the rite of passage; from epiphany to the mordant send-up of human foibles. As a trip on the sea does, may it catalyze a magical, life-affirming epiphany, or launch your spirit on new trajectories.

Happy sailing!

—LENA LENČEK AND GIDEON BOSKER

reading the weather

MIGAEL SCHERER

TO ONE UNFAMILIAR with the technicalities of sailing, Migael

Scherer's "Reading the Weather" (2000) is a revelation, a prose haiku of

two hundred or so words that encapsulate the wisdom of sailors since

time immemorial. Beyond this practical dimension, however, Scherer's

seemingly simple checklist of questions invites us to understand that nav-

igating on water lets us take our bearings in the cosmic scheme of things.

morning.a halyard is slapping, "Let's go, let's go." The rigging creaks, "Stay."

First, look out the hatch. What color is the water? Is it pale blue, deep navy, pearl gray, or charcoal? Is the surface rippled, ruffled, flecked with white, dimpled, or polished? What's happening above? Does the sky seem washed with light or scrubbed by wind? Are the clouds high or low, dawdling along or racing by?

Feel the air on your face, feel it cooling or warming.

Now check the barometer. Consider it another sense, delicate as touch. Is the pressure rising or falling? A lot or a little? Before you decide that the weather is stable or changing, turn on the radio and listen, beyond the forecast. What are conditions five miles away? twenty miles away? How high are the seas in the channels and straits and in the open ocean? Spread out a chart that encompasses your entire cruising area—larger than that if you have one. Your anchorage is no bigger than the end of your thumb, your boat the point of a pencil. Imagine yourself flying high overhead, looking down. You may be in a pocket of calm while all around a gale is brewing. Or the wind that woke you may be entirely local, a dropping of cold air off a mountain, a funneling of air through a narrow entrance.

What do the trees on shore know? Are their boughs swaying? Or are the tops of the evergreens upright and still? If they are stunted and frozen, all the branches leaning inland, pay attention; they have been anchored here longer than you. Think of the weather that taught them to grow like that.

YOU'VE FOUND A cove that will protect you from wind and wave. You've dropped the anchor and let out plenty of chain and then backed down to set the flukes deep into the mud. You've checked the tide tables to make sure you have enough scope so that even if the wind were to find you, the anchor would hold. You've taken bearings against the shore and determined that, no, you're not drifting, just swinging and recoiling a bit. And the engine finally is silent.

I love those first moments, when the silence is like a sound in itself. Suddenly I realize that all I've really been listening to under way was the boat's rumbling engine, thrumming sails, and turning propeller. The boat still speaks—every now and then the anchor chain moves against the bobstay with a dull clunk, or a loose halyard slaps the mast—but now my ears are tuned beyond the gunwale and the bowsprit, higher than the masthead. Birds cry, or caw, or whistle musical scales across the water. Wavelets whisper to the beach.

No longer checking the instruments or reading a chart, watching the leech of the sail or the telltales near the luff, I notice other details. Shadows of the evergreens move over the rocks, down the beach, and reach for us across the water. A rippled circle spreads outward where a grebe just dove, or a fish just leapt, or a seal slipped, nose last, beneath the surface. A tree branch sags where a large bird—an eagle? a raven?—has just perched.

No longer navigating the boat, I watch the course of objects in the sky. The sun tracks westward, gathering gold as it drops. When it sets, color goes with it, until what was fuchsia is pink and what was pink is violet, then gray, then black. The stars that had been there all along come forward quietly until the sky is a riot of light. When the moon rises, it dims the stars.

I will sleep lightly at anchor, for the boat is still moving, gently swaying, slowing, swinging with the current. It rocks freely to a passing wake, unrestrained by dock lines and fenders. It revolves like a planet around the fixed pole of the anchor. There's the sea, below and around, and the sky and the land which seem to grow from the sea. There's the boat suspended between, and me in the boat, dreaming shallow dreams, still listening.

And when the anchor is raised and the boat is under way once more, for a moment I'll feel that a part of me was left behind and is rushing to catch up.

from twenty thousand
leagues under the sea

JULES VERNE

DECADES BEFORE THE world's navies built and sailed sub-

marines, Jules Verne launched the amazing *Nautilus* in his science fic-

tion novel *Twenty Thousand Leagues under the Sea* (1869–70). Filled

with scrupulously researched scientific and geographical data, Verne's

morality tale of the misanthropic Captain Nemo has the universal

appeal of myth. In this section, we literally catch our breath along with

the survivors of the shipwreck caused by Captain Nemo as they dis-

cover, for the very first time, the fantastic marvels of the deep.

the portion of the terrestrial globe which is covered by water is estimated at upward of eighty millions of acres. This fluid mass comprises two billions, two hundred and fifty millions of cubic miles, forming a spherical body of a diameter of sixty leagues, the weight of which would be three quintillions of tons. To comprehend the meaning of these figures, it is necessary to observe that a quintillion is to a billion as a billion is to unity; in other words, there are as many billions in a quintillion as there are units in a billion. This mass of fluid is equal to about the quantity of water which would be discharged by all the rivers of the earth in forty thousand years.

During the geological epochs, the igneous period succeeded to the aqueous. The ocean originally prevailed everywhere. Then by degrees, in the silurian period, the tops of the mountains began to appear, the islands emerged, then disappeared in partial deluges, reappeared, became settled, formed continents, till at length the earth became geographically arranged, as we see in the present day. The solid had wrested from the liquid thirty-seven million, six hundred and fifty-seven square miles, equal to twelve billions, nine hundred and sixty millions of acres.

The shape of continents allows us to divide the waters into five great portions: the Arctic or Frozen Ocean, the Antarctic or Frozen Ocean, the Indian, the Atlantic, and the Pacific Oceans.

The Pacific Ocean extends from north to south between the two polar circles, and from east to west between Asia and America, over an extent of 145 degrees of longitude. It is the quietest of seas; its currents are broad and slow, it has medium tides and abundant rain. Such was the ocean that my fate destined me first to travel over under these strange conditions.

"Sir," said Captain Nemo, "we will, if you please, take our bearings and fix the starting-point of this voyage. It is a quarter to twelve and I will now go up again to the surface."

The captain pressed an electric clock three times. The pumps began to drive the water from the tanks; the needle of the manometer marked by a different pressure the ascent of the *Nautilus*, then it stopped.

"We have arrived," said the captain.

I went to the central staircase which opened on to the platform, clambered up the iron steps, and found myself on the upper part of the *Nautilus*.

The platform was only three feet out of water. The front and back of the *Nautilus* was of that spindle-shape which caused it justly to be compared to a cigar. I noticed that its iron plates, slightly overlaying each other, resembled the shell which clothes the bodies of our large terrestrial reptiles. It explained to me how natural it was, in spite of all glasses, that this boat should have been taken for a marine animal.

Toward the middle of the platform the long-boat, half buried in the hull of the vessel, formed a slight excrescence. Fore and aft rose two cages of medium height with inclined sides, and partly closed by thick lenticular glasses; one destined for the steersman who directed the *Nautilus*, the other containing a brilliant lantern to give light on the road.

The sea was beautiful, the sky pure. Scarcely could the long vehicle feel the broad undulations of the ocean. A light breeze from the east rippled the surface of the waters. The horizon, free from fog, made observation easy. Nothing was in sight. Not a quicksand, not an island. A vast desert.

Captain Nemo, by the help of his sextant, took the altitude of the sun, which ought also to give the latitude. He waited for some moments till its disk touched the horizon.

While taking observations not a muscle moved; the instrument could not have been more motionless in a hand of marble.

"Twelve o'clock, sir," said he. "When you like—"

I cast a last look upon the sea, slightly yellowed by the Japanese coast, and descended to the saloon.

"And now, sir, I leave you to your studies," added the captain; "our course is E. N. E., our depth is twenty-six fathoms. Here are maps on a large scale by which you may follow it. The saloon is at your disposal, and with your permission I will retire." Captain Nemo bowed, and I remained alone, lost in thoughts all bearing on the commander of the *Nautilus*.

For a whole hour was I deep in these reflections, seeking to pierce this mystery so interesting to me. Then my eyes fell upon the vast planisphere spread upon the table, and I placed my finger on the very spot where the given latitude and longitude crossed.

The sea has its large rivers like the continents. They are special currents known by their temperature and their color. The most remarkable of these is known by the name of the Gulf Stream. Science has decided on the globe the direction of five principal currents: one in the North Atlantic, a second in the South, a third in the North Pacific, a fourth in the South, and a fifth in the Southern Indian Ocean. It is even probable that a sixth current existed at one time or another in the Northern Indian Ocean, when the Caspian and Aral Seas formed but one vast sheet of water.

At this point indicated on the planisphere one of these currents was rolling, the Kuro-Scivo of the Japanese, the Black River, which, leaving the Gulf of Bengal where it is warmed by the perpendicular rays of a tropical sun, crosses the Straits of Malacca along the coast of Asia, turns into the North Pacific to the Aleutian Islands, carrying with it trunks of camphor-trees and other indigenous productions, and edging the waves of the ocean with the pure indigo of its warm water. It was this current that the *Nautilus* was to follow. I followed it with my eye; saw it lose itself in the vastness of the Pacific, and felt myself drawn with it, when Ned Land and Conseil appeared at the door of the saloon.

My two brave companions remained petrified at the sight of the wonders spread before them.

"Where are we—where are we?" exclaimed the Canadian. "In the museum at Quebec?"

"My friends," I answered, making a sign to them to enter, "you are not in Canada, but on board the *Nautilus*, fifty yards below the level of the sea."

"But, M. Aronnax," said Ned Land, "can you tell me how many men there are on board? Ten, twenty, fifty, a hundred?"

"I cannot answer you, Mr. Land; it is better to abandon for a time all idea of seizing the *Nautilus* or escaping from it. This ship is a masterpiece of modern industry, and I should be sorry not to have seen it. Many people would accept the situation forced upon us, if only to move among such wonders. So be quiet and let us try and see what passes around us."

"See!" exclaimed the harpooner, "but we can see nothing in this iron prison! We are walking—we are sailing—blindly."

Ned Land had scarcely pronounced these words when all was suddenly darkness. The luminous ceiling was gone, and so rapidly that my eyes received a very painful impression.

We remained mute, not stirring, and not knowing what surprise awaited us, whether agreeable or disagreeable. A sliding noise was heard: one would have said that panels were working at the sides of the *Nautilus*.

"It is the end of the end!" said Ned Land.

Suddenly light broke at each side of the saloon, through two oblong openings. The liquid mass appeared vividly lit up by the electric gleam. Two crystal plates separated us from the sea. At first I trembled at the thought that this frail partition might break, but strong bands of copper bound them, giving an almost infinite power of resistance.

The sea was distinctly visible for a mile all round the *Nautilus*. What a spectacle! What pen can describe it? Who could paint the effects of the light through those transparent sheets of water, and the softness of the successive gradations from the lower to the superior strata of the ocean?

We know the transparency of the sea, and that its clearness is far beyond that of rock water. The mineral and organic substances which it holds in suspension heighten its transparency. In certain parts of the ocean at the Antilles, under seventy-five fathoms of water, can be seen with surprising clearness a bed of sand. The penetrating power of the solar rays does not seem to cease for a depth of one hundred and fifty fathoms. But in this middle fluid traveled over by the *Nautilus* the electric brightness was produced even in the bosom of the waves. It was no longer luminous water, but liquid light.

On each side a window opened into this unexplored abyss. The obscurity of the saloon showed to advantage the brightness outside, and we looked out as if this pure crystal had been the glass of an immense aquarium.

"You wished to see, friend Ned; well, you see now."

"Curious! Curious!" muttered the Canadian, who, forgetting his ill-temper, seemed to submit to some irresistible attraction; "and one would come further than this to admire such a sight!"

"Ah!" thought I to myself, "I understand the life of this man; he has made a world apart for himself, in which he treasures all his greatest wonders."

For two whole hours an aquatic army escorted the *Nautilus*. During their games, their bounds, while rivaling each other in beauty, brightness, and velocity, I distinguished the green labre; the banded mullet, marked by a double line of black; the round-tailed goby, of a white color, with violet spots on the back; the Japanese scombrus, a beautiful mackerel of these seas, with a blue body and silvery head; the brilliant azurors, whose name alone defies description; some banded spares, with variegated fins of blue and yellow; some aclostones, the woodcocks of the seas, some specimens of which attain a yard in length; Japanese salamanders, spider lampreys, serpents six feet long, with eyes small and lively, and a huge mouth bristling with teeth; with many other species.

Our imagination was kept at its height; interjections followed quickly on each other. Ned named the fish, and Conseil classed them. I was in ecstasies with the vivacity of their movements and the beauty of their forms. Never had it been given to me to surprise these animals, alive and at liberty, in their natural element. I will not mention all the varieties which passed before my dazzled eyes, all the collection of the seas of China and Japan. These fish, more numerous than the birds of the air, came, attracted, no doubt, by the brilliant focus of the electric light.

Suddenly there was daylight in the saloon, the iron panels closed again, and the enchanting vision disappeared. But for a long time I dreamed on till my eyes fell on the instruments hanging on the partition. The compass still showed the course to be E. N. E., the manometer indicated a pressure of five atmospheres, equivalent to a depth of twenty-five fathoms, and the electric log gave a speed of fifteen miles an hour. I expected Captain Nemo, but he did not appear. The clock marked the hour of five.

Ned Land and Conseil returned to their cabin, and I retired to my chamber. My dinner was ready. It was composed of turtle soup made of the most delicate hawks-bills, of a surmullet served with puff paste (the liver of which, prepared by itself, was most delicious), and fillets of the emperor-holocanthus, the savor of which seemed to me superior even to salmon.

I passed the evening reading, writing, and thinking. Then sleep overpowered me, and I stretched myself on my couch of zostera, and slept profoundly, while the *Nautilus* was gliding rapidly through the current of the Black River.

from kon-tiki

THOR HEYERDAHL

PART MEMOIR, PART scientific treatise, and part adrenaline-

churning adventure story, *Kon-Tiki: Across the Pacific by Raft (1948)*

tracks the Norwegian Thor Heyerdahl as he sets out to prove a star-

tling hypothesis: that Polynesia may originally have been settled by

stone age Peruvians making the 4,000-mile ocean crossing in light

balsa rafts. The opening leg of the journey, from Peru to the

Galapagos Islands, introduces us to an adventurer whose audacity,

inventiveness, and wonder at the resourcefulness of the sea put him

squarely in the tradition of *Robinson Crusoe.*

there was a bustle in Callao harbor the day the *Kon-Tiki* was to be towed out to sea. The minister of marine had ordered the naval tug *Guardian Rios* to tow us out of the bay and cast us off clear of the coastal traffic, out where in times gone by the Indians used to lie fishing from their rafts. The papers had published the news under both red and black headlines, and there was a crowd of people down on the quays from early in the morning of April 28.

We six who were to assemble on board all had little things to do at the eleventh hour, and, when I came down to the quay, only Herman was there keeping guard over the raft. I intentionally stopped the car a long way off and walked the whole length of the mole to stretch my legs thoroughly for the last time for no one knew how long. I jumped on board the raft, which looked an utter chaos of banana clusters, fruit baskets, and sacks which had been hurled on board at the very last moment and were to be stowed and made fast. In the middle of the heap Herman sat resignedly holding on to a cage with a green parrot in it, a farewell present from a friendly soul in Lima.

"Look after the parrot a minute," said Herman, "I must go ashore and have a last glass of beer. The tug won't be here for hours."

He had hardly disappeared among the swarm on the quay when people began to point and wave. And round the point at full speed came the tug *Guardian Rios*. She dropped anchor on the farther side of a waving forest of masts which blocked the way in to the *Kon-Tiki*, and sent in a large motorboat to tow us out between the sailing craft. She was packed full of seamen, officers, and movie photographers, and, while orders rang out and cameras clicked, a stout towrope was made fast to the raft's bow.

"*Un momento*," I shouted in despair from where I sat with the parrot. "It's too early; we must wait for the others—*los expedicionarios*," I explained, and pointed toward the city.

But nobody understood. The officers only smiled politely, and the knot at our bows was made fast in more than exemplary manner. I cast off the rope and flung it overboard with all manner of signs and gesticulations. The parrot utilized the opportunity afforded by all the confusion to stick its beak out of the cage and turn the knob of the door, and when I turned round it was strutting cheerfully about the bamboo deck. I tried to catch it, but it shrieked rudely in Spanish and fluttered away over the banana clusters. With one eye on the sailors who were trying to cast a rope over the bow I started a wild chase after the parrot. It fled shrieking into the bamboo cabin, where I got it into a corner and caught it by one leg as it tried to flutter over me. When I came out again and stuffed my flapping trophy into its cage, the sailors on land had cast off the raft's moorings, and we were dancing helplessly in and out with the backwash of the long swell that came rolling in over the mole. In despair I seized a paddle and vainly tried to parry a violent bump as the raft was flung against the wooden piles of the quay. Then the motorboat started, and with one jerk the *Kon-Tiki* began her long voyage.

My only companion was a Spanish-speaking parrot which sat glaring sulkily in a cage. People on shore cheered and waved, and the swarthy movie photographers in the motorboat almost jumped into the sea in their eagerness to catch every detail of the expedition's dramatic start from Peru. Despairing and alone I stood on the raft looking out for my lost companions, but none appeared. So we came out to the *Guardian Rios*, which was lying with steam up ready to lift anchor and start. I was up the rope ladder in a twinkling and made so much row on board that the start was postponed and a boat sent back to the quay. It was away a good while, and then it came back full of pretty *señoritas*, but without a single one of the *Kon-Tiki's* missing men. This was all very well but it did not solve my problems, and, while the raft swarmed with charming *señoritas*, the boat went back on a fresh search for *los expedicionarios noruegos*.

Meanwhile Erik and Bengt came sauntering down to the quay with their arms full of reading matter and odds and ends. They met a whole stream of people on its way home and were finally stopped at a police barrier by a kindly official who told them there was nothing more to see. Bengt told the officer, with an airy gesture of his cigar, that they had not come to see anything; they themselves were going with the raft.

"It's no use," the constable said indulgently. "The *Kon-Tiki* sailed an hour ago."

"Impossible," said Erik, producing a parcel. "Here's the lantern!"

"And there's the navigator," said Bengt, "and I'm the steward."

They forced their way past, but the raft had gone. They trotted desperately to and fro along the mole where they met the rest of the party, who also were searching eagerly for the vanished raft. Then they caught sight of the boat coming in, and so we were all six finally united and the water was foaming round the raft as the *Guardian Rios* towed us out to sea.

It had been late in the afternoon when at last we started, and the *Guardian Rios* would not cast us off till we were clear of the coastal traffic next morning. Directly we were clear of the mole we met a bit of a head sea, and all the small boats which were accompanying us turned back one by one. Only a few big yachts came with us out to the entrance to the bay to see how things would go out there.

The *Kon-Tiki* followed the tug like an angry billy goat on a rope, and she butted her bow into the head sea so that the water rushed on board. This did not look very promising, for this was a calm sea compared with what we had to expect. In the middle of the bay the towrope broke, and our end of it sank peacefully to the bottom while the tug steamed ahead. We flung ourselves down along the side of the raft to fish for the end of the rope, while the yachts went on and tried to stop the tug. Stinging jellyfish as thick as washtubs splashed up and down with the seas alongside the raft and covered all the ropes with a slippery, stinging coating of jelly. When the raft rolled one way, we hung flat over the side waving our arms down toward the surface of the water, until our fingers just touched the slimy towrope. Then the raft rolled back again, and we all stuck our heads deep down into the sea, while salt water and giant jellyfish poured over our backs. We spat and cursed and pulled jellyfish fibres out of our hair, but when the tug came back the rope end was up and ready for splicing.

When we were about to throw it on board the tug, we suddenly drifted in under the vessel's overhanging stern and were in danger of being crushed against her by the pressure of the water. We dropped everything we had and tried to push ourselves clear with bamboo sticks and paddles before it was too late. But we never got a proper position, for when we were in the trough of the sea we could not reach the iron roof above us, and when the water rose again the *Guardian Rios* dropped her whole stern down into the water and would have crushed us flat if the suction had carried us underneath. Up on the tug's deck people were running about and shouting; at last the propeller began to turn just alongside us, and it helped us clear of the backwash under the *Guardian Rios* in the last second. The bow of the raft had had a few hard knocks and had become a little crooked in the lashings, but this fault rectified itself by degrees.

"When a thing starts so damnably, it's bound to end well," said Herman. "If only this towing could stop; it'll shake the raft to bits."

The towing went on all night at a slow speed and with only one or two small hitches. The yachts had bidden us farewell long ago, and the last coast light had disappeared astern. Only a few ships' lights passed us in the darkness. We divided the night into watches to keep an eye on the towrope, and we all had a good snatch of sleep. When it grew light next morning, a thick mist lay over the coast of Peru, while we had a brilliant blue sky ahead of us to westward. The sea was running in a long quiet swell covered with little white crests, and clothes and logs and everything we took hold of were soaking wet with dew. It was chilly, and the green water round us was astonishingly cold for 12° south.

We were in the Humboldt Current, which carries its cold masses of water up from the Antarctic and sweeps them north all along the coast of Peru till they swing west and out across the sea just below the Equator. It was out here that Pizarro, Zárate, and the other early Spaniards saw for the first time the Inca Indians' big sailing rafts, which used to go out for 50 to 60 sea miles to catch tunnies and dolphins in the same Humboldt Current. All day long there was an offshore wind out here, but in the evening the onshore wind reached as far out as this and helped them home if they needed it.

In the early light we saw our tug lying close by, and we took care that the raft lay far enough away from her bow while we launched our little inflated rubber dinghy. It floated on the waves like a football and danced away with Erik, Bengt, and myself till we caught hold of the *Guardian Rios*'s rope ladder and clambered on board. With Bengt as interpreter we had our exact position shown us on our chart. We were 50 sea miles from land in a northwesterly direction from Callao, and we were to carry lights the first few nights so as not to be sunk by coasting ships. Farther out we would not meet a single ship, for no shipping route ran through that part of the Pacific.

We took a ceremonious farewell of all on board, and many strange looks followed us as we climbed down into the dinghy and went tumbling back over the waves to the *Kon-Tiki*. Then the towrope was cast off and the raft was alone again. Thirty-five men on board the *Guardian Rios* stood at the rail waving for as long as we could distinguish outlines. And six men sat on the boxes on board the *Kon-Tiki* and followed the tug with their eyes as long as they could see her. Not till the black column of smoke had dissolved and vanished over the horizon did we shake our heads and look at one another.

"Good-bye, good-bye," said Torstein. "Now we'll have to start the engine, boys!"

We laughed, and felt the wind. There was a rather light breeze, which had veered from south to southeast. We hoisted the bamboo yard with the big squaresail. It only hung down slack, giving *Kon-Tiki*'s face a wrinkled, discontented appearance.

"The old man doesn't like it," said Erik, "There were fresher breezes when he was young."

"It looks as if we were losing way," said Herman, and he threw a piece of balsa wood overboard at the bow.

"One-two-three . . . thirty-nine, forty, forty-one."

The piece of balsa wood still lay quietly in the water alongside the raft; it had not yet moved halfway along our side.

"We'll have to go over with it," said Torstein optimistically.

"Hope we don't drift astern with the evening breeze," said Bengt. "It was great fun saying good-bye at Callao, but I'd just as soon miss our welcome back again!"

Now the piece of wood had reached the end of the raft. We shouted hurrah and began to stow and make fast all the things that had been flung on board at the last moment. Bengt set up a primus stove at the bottom of an empty box, and soon after we were regaling ourselves on hot cocoa and biscuits and making a hole in a fresh coconut. The bananas were not quite ripe yet.

"We're well off now in one way," Erik chuckled. He was rolling about in wide sheepskin trousers under a huge Indian hat, with the parrot on his shoulders. "There's only one thing I don't like," he added, "and that's all the little-known crosscurrents which can fling us right upon the rocks along the coast if we go on lying here like this."

We considered the possibility of paddling but agreed to wait for a wind.

And the wind came. It blew up from the southeast quietly and steadily. Soon the sail filled and bent forward like a swelling breast, with *Kon-Tiki*'s head bursting with pugnacity. And the *Kon-Tiki* began to move. We shouted westward ho! and hauled on sheets and ropes. The steering oar was put into the water, and the watch roster began to operate. We threw balls of paper and chips overboard at the bow and stood aft with our watches.

"One, two, three . . . eighteen, nineteen—now!'

Paper and chips of wood passed the steering oar and soon lay like pearls on a thread, dipping up and down in the trough of the waves astern. We went forward yard by yard. The *Kon-Tiki* did not plough through the sea like a sharp-prowed racing craft. Blunt and broad, heavy and solid, she splashed sedately forward over the waves. She did not hurry, but when she had once got going she pushed ahead with unshakeable energy.

At the moment the steering arrangements were our greatest problem. The raft was built exactly as the Spaniards described it, but there was no one living in our time who could give us a practical advance course in sailing an Indian raft. The problem had been thoroughly discussed among the experts on shore but with meager results. They knew just as little about it as we did. As the southeasterly wind increased in strength, it was necessary to keep the raft on such a course that the sail was filled from astern. If the raft turned her side too much to the wind, the sail suddenly swung round and banged against cargo and men and bamboo cabin, while the whole raft turned round and continued on the same course stern first. It was a hard struggle, three men fighting with the sail and three others rowing with the long steering oar to get the nose of the wooden raft round and away from the wind. And, as soon as we got her round, the steersman had to take good care that the same thing did not happen again the next minute.

The steering oar, nineteen feet long, rested loose between two tholepins on a huge block astern. It was the same steering oar our native friends had used when we floated the timber down the Palenque in Ecuador. The long mangrove-wood pole was as tough as steel but so heavy that it would sink if it fell overboard. At the end of the pole was a large oar blade of fir wood lashed on with ropes. It took all our strength to hold this long steering oar steady when the seas drove against it, and our fingers were tired out by the convulsive grip which was necessary to turn the pole so that the oar blade stood straight up in the water. This last problem was solved by our lashing a crosspiece to the handle of the steering oar so that we had a sort of lever to turn. And meanwhile the wind increased.

By the late afternoon the trade wind was already blowing at full strength. It quickly stirred up the ocean into roaring seas which swept against us from astern. For the first time we fully realized that here was the sea itself coming to meet us; it was bitter earnest now—our communications were cut. Whether things went well now would depend entirely on the balsa raft's good qualities in the open sea. We knew that, from now onward, we should never get another onshore wind or chance of turning back. We were in the path of the real trade wind, and every day would carry us farther and farther out to sea. The only thing to do was to go ahead under full sail; if we tried to turn homeward we should only drift farther out to sea stern first. There was only one possible course, to sail before the wind with our bow toward the sunset. And, after all, that was the object of our voyage—to follow the sun in its path as we thought *Kon-Tiki* and the old sun-worshippers must have done when they were chased out to sea from Peru.

We noted with triumph and relief how the wooden raft rose up over the first threatening wave crests that came foaming toward us. But it was impossible for the steersman to hold the oar steady when the roaring seas rolled toward him and lifted the oar out of the tholepins, or swept it to one side so that the steersman was swung round like a helpless acrobat. Not even two men at once could hold the oar steady when the seas rose against us and poured down over the steersman aft. We hit on the idea of running ropes from the oar blade to each side of the raft; and with other ropes holding the oar in place in the tholepins it obtained a limited freedom of movement and could defy the worst seas if only we ourselves could hold on.

As the troughs of the sea gradually grew deeper, it became clear that we had moved into the swiftest part of the Humboldt Current. This sea was obviously caused by a current and not simply raised by the wind. The water was green and cold and everywhere about us; the jagged mountains of Peru had vanished into the dense cloud banks astern. When darkness crept over the waters, our first duel with the elements began. We were still not sure of the sea; it was still uncertain whether it would show itself a friend or an enemy in the intimate proximity we ourselves had sought. When, swallowed up by the darkness, we heard the general noise from the sea around us suddenly deafened by the hiss of a roller close by and saw a white crest come groping toward us on a level with the cabin roof, we held on tight and waited uneasily to feel the masses of water smash down over us and the raft.

But every time there was the same surprise and relief. The *Kon-Tiki* calmly swung up her stern and rose skyward unperturbed, while the masses of water rolled along her sides. Then we sank down again into the trough of the waves and waited for the next big sea. The biggest seas often came two or three in succession, with a long series of smaller seas in between. It was when two big seas followed one another too closely that the second broke on board aft, because the first was still holding our bow in the air. It became, therefore, an unbreakable law that the steering watch must have ropes round their waists, the other ends of which were made fast to the raft, for there were no bulwarks. Their task was to keep the sail filled by holding our stern to sea and wind.

We had made an old boat's compass fast to a box aft so that Erik could check our course and calculate our position and speed. For the time being it was uncertain where we were, for the sky was overclouded and the horizon one single chaos of rollers. Two men at a time took turns as steering watch and, side by side, they had to put all their strength into the fight with the leaping oar, while the rest of us tried to snatch a little sleep inside the open bamboo cabin.

When a really big sea came, the men at the helm left the steering to the ropes and, jumped up, hung on to a bamboo pole from the cabin roof, while the masses of water thundered in over them from astern and disappeared between the logs or over the side of the raft. Then they had to fling themselves at the oar again before the raft could turn round and the sail thrash about. For, if the raft took the seas at an angle, the waves could easily pour right into the bamboo cabin. When they came from astern, they disappeared between the projecting logs at once and seldom came so far forward as the cabin wall. The round logs astern let the water pass as if through the prongs of a fork. The advantage of a raft was obviously this: the more leaks the better. Through the gaps in our floor the water ran out but never in.

About midnight a ship's light passed in a northerly direction. At three another passed on the same course. We waved our little paraffin lamp and called them up with flashes from an electric torch, but they did not see us and the lights passed slowly northwards into the darkness and disappeared. Little did those on board realize that a real Inca raft lay close to them, tumbling among the waves. And just as little did we on board the raft realize that this was our last ship and the last trace of men we should see till we had reached the other side of the ocean.

We clung like flies, two and two, to the steering oar in the darkness and felt the fresh sea water pouring off our hair while the oar hit us till we were tender both behind and before and our hands grew stiff with the exertion of hanging on. We had a good schooling those first days and nights; it turned landlubbers into seamen. For the first twenty-four hours every man, in unbroken succession, had two hours at the helm and three hours' rest. We arranged that every hour a fresh man should relieve the one of the two steersmen who had been at the helm for two hours.

Every single muscle in the body was strained to the uttermost throughout the watch to cope with the steering. When we were tired out with pushing the oar, we went over to the other side and pulled, and when arms and chest were sore with pressing, we turned our backs while the oar kneaded us green and blue in front and behind. When at last the relief came, we crept half-dazed into the bamboo cabin, tied a rope round our legs, and fell asleep with our salty clothes on before we could get into our sleeping bags. Almost at the same moment there came a brutal tug at the rope; three hours had passed, and one had to go out again and relieve one of the two men at the steering oar.

The next night was still worse; the seas grew higher instead of going down. Two hours on end of struggling with the steering oar was too long; a man was not much use in the second half of his watch, and the seas got the better of us and hurled us round and sideways, while the water poured on board. Then we changed over to one hour at the helm and an hour and a half's rest. So the first sixty hours passed, in one continuous struggle against a chaos of waves that rushed upon us, one after another, without cessation. High waves and low waves, pointed waves and round waves, slanting waves and waves on the top of other waves.

The one of us who suffered most was Knut. He was let off steering watch, but to compensate for this he had to sacrifice to Neptune and suffered silent agonies in a corner of the cabin. The parrot sat sulkily in its cage, and hung on with its beak and flapped its wings every time the raft gave an unexpected pitch and the sea splashed against the wall from astern. The Kon-Tiki did not roll so excessively. She took the seas more steadily than any boat of the same dimensions, but it was impossible to predict which way the deck would lean next time, and we never learned the art of moving about the raft easily, for she pitched as much as she rolled.

On the third night the sea went down a bit, although it was still blowing hard. About four o'clock an unexpected deluge came foaming through the darkness and knocked the raft right round before the steersmen realized what was happening. The sail thrashed against the bamboo cabin and threatened to tear both the cabin and itself to pieces. All hands had to go on deck and secure the cargo and haul on sheets and stays in the hope of getting the raft on her right course again, so that the sail might fill and curve forward peacefully. But the raft would not right herself. She would go stern foremost, and that was all. The only result of all our hauling and pushing and rowing was that two men nearly went overboard in a sea when the sail caught them in the dark.

The sea had clearly become calmer. Stiff and sore, with skinned palms and sleepy eyes, we were not worth many rows of beans. Better to save our strength in case the weather should call us out to a worse passage of arms. One could never know. So we furled the sail and rolled it round the bamboo yard. The Kon-Tiki lay sideways on to the seas and took them like a cork. Everything on board was lashed fast, and all six of us crawled into the little bamboo cabin, huddled together, and slept like mummies in a sardine tin.

We little guessed that we had struggled through the hardest steering of the voyage. Not till we were far out on the ocean did we discover the Incas' simple and ingenious way of steering a raft.

We did not wake till well on in the day, when the parrot began to whistle and halloo and dance to and fro on its perch. Outside the sea was still running high but in long, even ridges and not so wild and confused as the day before. The first thing we saw was that the sun was beating down on the yellow bamboo deck and giving the sea all round us a bright and friendly aspect. What did it matter if the seas foamed and rose high so long as they only left us in peace on the raft? What did it matter if they rose straight up in front of our noses when we knew that in a second the raft would go over the top and flatten out the foaming ridge like a steam roller, while the heavy threatening mountain of water only lifted us up in the air and rolled groaning and gurgling under the floor? The old masters from Peru knew what they were doing when they avoided a hollow hull which could fill with water, or a vessel so long that it would not take the waves one by one. A cork steam roller—that was what the balsa raft amounted to.

Erik took our position at noon and found that, in addition to our run under sail, we had made a big deviation northward along the coast. We still lay in the Humboldt Current just 100 sea miles from land. The great question was whether we would get into the treacherous eddies south of the Galapagos Islands. This could have fatal consequences, for up there we might be swept in all directions by strong ocean currents making toward the coast of Central America. But, if things went as we calculated, we should swing west across the sea with the main current before we got as far north as the Galapagos. The wind was still blowing straight from southeast. We hoisted the sail, turned the raft stern to sea, and continued our steering watches.

Knut had now recovered from the torments of seasickness, and he and Torstein clambered up to the swaying masthead, where they experimented with mysterious radio aerials which they sent up both by balloon and by kite. Suddenly one of them shouted from the radio corner of the cabin that he could hear the naval station at Lima calling us. They told us that the American Ambassador's plane was on its way out from the coast to bid us a last good-bye and see what we looked like at sea. Soon after we obtained direct contact with the operator in the plane and then an completely unexpected chat with the secretary to the expedition, Gerd Vold, who was on board. We gave our position as exactly as we could and sent direction-finding signals for hours. And the voice in the ether grew stronger and weaker as ARMY-119 circled round near and far and searched. But we did not hear the drone of the engines and never saw the plane. It was not so easy to find the low raft down in the trough of the seas, and our view was strictly limited. At last the aircraft had to give it up and returned to the coast. It was the last time anyone tried to search for us.

The sea ran high in the days that followed, but the waves came hissing along from the southeast with even spaces between them and the steering went more easily. We took the sea and wind on the port quarter, so that the steersman got fewer seas over him and the raft went more steadily and did not swing round. We noted anxiously that the southeast trade wind and the Humboldt Current were, day after day, sending us straight across on a course leading to the countercurrents round the Galapagos Islands. And we were going due northwest so quickly that our daily average in those days was 55 to 60 sea miles, with a record of 71 sea miles in one day.

"Are the Galapagos a nice place to go to?" Knut asked cautiously one day, looking at our chart where a string of pearls indicating our positions was marked and resembled a finger pointing balefully toward the accursed Galapagos Islands.

"Hardly," I said. "The Inca Tupac Yupanqui is said to have sailed from Ecuador to the Galapagos just before the time of Columbus, but neither he nor any other native settled there because there was no water."

"O.K.," said Knut. "Then we damned well won't go there. I hope we don't anyhow."

We were now so accustomed to having the sea dancing round us that we took no account of it. What did it matter if we danced round a bit with a thousand fathoms of water under us, so long as we and the raft were always on top? It was only that here the next question arose—how long could we count on keeping on top? It was easy to see that the balsa logs absorbed water. The aft crossbeam was worse than the others; on it we could press our whole finger tip into the soaked wood till the water squelched. Without saying anything I broke off a piece of the sodden wood and threw it overboard. It sank quietly beneath the surface and slowly vanished down into the depths. Later I saw two or three of the other fellows do exactly the same thing when they thought no one was looking. They stood looking reverently at the waterlogged piece of wood sinking quietly into the green water.

We had noted the water line on the raft when we started, but in the rough sea it was impossible to see how deep we lay, for one moment the logs were lifted out of the water and the next they went deep down into it. But, if we drove a knife into the timber, we saw to our joy that the wood was dry an inch or so below the surface. We calculated that, if the water continued to force its way in at the same pace, the raft would be lying and floating just under the surface of the water by the time we could expect to be approaching land. But we hoped that the sap further in would act as an impregnation and check the absorption.

Then there was another menace which troubled our minds a little during the first weeks. The ropes. In the daytime we were so busy that we thought little about it, but, when darkness had fallen and we had crept into bed on the cabin floor, we had more time to think, feel, and listen. As we lay there, each man on his straw mattress, we could feel the reed matting under us heaving in time with the wooden logs. In addition to the movements of the raft itself all nine logs moved reciprocally. When one came up, another went down with a gentle heaving movement. They did not move much, but it was enough to make one feel as if one was lying on the back of a large breathing animal, and we preferred to lie on a log lengthways. The first two nights were the worst, but then we were too tired to bother about it. Later the ropes swelled a little in the water and kept the nine logs quieter.

But all the same there was never a flat surface on board which kept quite still in relation to its surroundings. As the foundation moved up and down and round at every joint, everything else moved with it. The bamboo deck, the double mast, the four plaited walls of the cabin, and the roof of slats with the leaves on it—all were made fast just with ropes and twisted about and lifted themselves in opposite directions. It was almost unnoticeable but it was evident enough. If one corner went up, the other corner went down, and if one half of the roof dragged all its laths forward, the other half dragged its laths astern. And, if we looked out through the open wall, there was still more life and movement, for there the sky moved quietly round in a circle while the sea leaped high toward it.

The ropes took the whole pressure. All night we could hear them creaking and groaning, chafing and squeaking. It was like one single complaining chorus round us in the dark, each rope having its own note according to its thickness and tautness.

Every morning we made a thorough inspection of the ropes. We were even let down with our heads in the water over the edge of the raft, while two men held us tight by the ankles, to see if the ropes on the bottom of the raft were all right. But the ropes held. A fortnight the seamen had said. Then all the ropes would be worn out. But, in spite of this consensus of opinion, we had not so far found the smallest sign of wear. Not till we were far out to sea did we find the solution. The balsa wood was so soft that the ropes wore their way slowly into the wood and were protected, instead of the logs wearing the ropes.

After a week or so the sea grew calmer, and we noticed that it became blue instead of green. We began to go west-northwest instead of due northwest and took this as the first faint sign that we had got out of the coastal current and had some hope of being carried out to sea.

The very first day we were left alone on the sea we had noticed fish round the raft, but we were too much occupied with the steering to think of fishing. The second day we went right into a shoal of sardines, and soon afterwards an eight-foot blue shark came along and rolled over with its white belly uppermost as it rubbed against the raft's stern, where Herman and Bengt stood barelegged in the seas, steering. It played round us for a while but disappeared when we got the hand harpoon ready for action.

Next day we were visited by tunnies, bonitos, and dolphins, and when a big flying fish thudded on board we used it as bait and at once pulled in two large dolphins (dorados) weighing from twenty to thirty-five pounds each. This was food for several days. On steering watch we could see many fish we did not even know, and one day we came into a school of porpoises which seemed quite endless. The black backs tumbled about, packed close together, right in to the side of the raft, and sprang up here and there all over the sea as far as we could see from the masthead. And the nearer we came to the Equator, and the farther from the coast, the commoner flying fish became. When at last we came out into the blue water where the sea rolled by majestically, sunlit and sedate, ruffled by gusts of wind, we could see them glittering like a rain of projectiles which shot from the water and flew in a straight line till their power of flight was exhausted and they vanished beneath the surface.

If we set the little paraffin lamp out at night, flying fish were attracted by the light and, large and small, shot over the raft. They often struck the bamboo cabin or the sail and tumbled helpless on the deck. Unable to get a take-off by swimming through the water, they just remained lying and kicking helplessly, like large-eyed herrings with long breast fins. It sometimes happened that we heard an outburst of strong language from a man on deck when a cold flying fish came unexpectedly, at a good speed, slap into his face. They always came at a good pace and snout first, and if they caught one full in the face they made it burn and tingle. But the unprovoked attack was quickly forgiven by the injured party, for, with all its drawbacks, we were in a maritime land of enchantment where delicious fish dishes came hurtling through the air. We used to fry them for breakfast, and whether it was the fish, the cook, or our appetites, they reminded us of fried troutlings once we had scraped the scales off.

The cook's first duty, when he got up in the morning, was to go out on deck and collect all the flying fish that had landed on board in the course of the night. There were usually half a dozen or more, and once we found twenty-six fat flying fish on the raft. Knut was much upset one morning because, when he was standing operating with the frying pan, a flying fish struck him on the hand instead of landing right in the cooking fat.

Our neighborly intimacy with the sea was not fully realized by Torstein till he woke one morning and found a sardine on his pillow. There was so little room in the cabin that Torstein had to lie with his head in the doorway, and, if anyone inadvertently trod on his face when going out at night, he bit him in the leg. He grasped the sardine by the tail and confided to it understandingly that all sardines had his entire sympathy. We conscientiously drew in our legs so that Torstein should have more room the next night, but then something happened which caused Torstein to find himself a sleeping place on the top of all the kitchen utensils in the radio corner.

It was a few nights later. It was overcast and pitch dark, and Torstein had placed the paraffin lamp just by his head, so that the night watches could see where they were treading when they crept in and out over his head. About four o'clock Torstein was awakened by the lamp tumbling over and something cold and wet flapping about his ears. "Flying fish," he thought and felt for it in the darkness to throw it away. He caught hold of something long and wet, that wriggled like a snake, and let go as if he had burned himself. The unseen visitor twisted itself away and over to Herman, while Torstein tried to get the lamp lighted again. Herman started up, too, and this made me wake, thinking of the octopus which came up at night in these waters.

When we got the lamp lighted, Herman was sitting in triumph with his hand gripping the neck of a long thin fish which wriggled in his hands like an eel. The fish was over three feet long, as slender as a snake, with dull black eyes and a long snout with a greedy jaw full of long sharp teeth. The teeth were as sharp as knives and could be folded back into the roof of the mouth to make way for what was swallowed. Under

Herman's grip a large-eyed white fish, about eight inches long, was suddenly thrown up from the stomach and out of the mouth of the predatory fish, and soon after up came another like it. These were clearly two deep-water fish, much torn by the snakefish's teeth. The snake-fish's thin skin was bluish violet on the back and steel blue underneath, and it came loose in flakes when we took hold of it.

Bengt too was awakened at last by all the noise, and we held the lamp and the long fish under his nose. He sat up drowsily in his sleeping bag and said solemnly:

"No, fish like that don't exist."

With which he turned over quietly and fell asleep again.

Bengt was not far wrong. It appeared later that we six sitting round the lamp in the bamboo cabin were the first men to have seen this fish alive. Only the skeletons of a fish like this one had been found a few times on the coast of South America and the Galapagos Islands; ichthyologists called it *Gempylus*, or snake mackerel, and thought it lived at the bottom of the sea at a great depth because no one had ever seen it alive. But, if it lived at a great depth, it must have done so by day when the sun blinded its big eyes. For on dark nights *Gempylus* was abroad high over the surface of the seas; we on the raft had experience of that.

A week after the rare fish had landed in Torstein's sleeping bag, we had another visit. Again it was four in the morning, and the new moon had set so that it was dark but the stars were shining. The raft was steering easily, and when my watch was over I took a turn along the edge of the raft to see if everything was shipshape for the new watch. I had a rope round my waist, as the watch always had, and, with the paraffin lamp in my hand, I was walking carefully along the outermost log to get round the mast. The log was wet and slippery, and I was furious when someone quite unexpectedly caught hold of the rope behind me and jerked till I nearly lost my balance. I turned round wrathfully with the lantern, but not a soul was to be seen. There came a new tug at the rope, and I saw something shiny lying writhing on the deck. It was a fresh *Gempylus*, and this time it had got its teeth so deep into the rope that several of them broke before I got the rope loose. Presumably the light of the lantern had flashed along the curving white rope, and our visitor from the depths of the sea had caught hold in the hope of jumping up and snatching an extra long and tasty tidbit. It ended its days in a jar of Formalin.

The sea contains many surprises for him who has his floor on a level with the surface and drifts along slowly and noiselessly. A sportsman who breaks his way through the woods may come back and say that no wild life is to be seen. Another may sit down on a stump and wait, and often rustlings and cracklings will begin and curious eyes peer out. So it is on the sea, too. We usually plough across it with roaring engines and piston strokes, with the water foaming round our bow. Then we come back and say that there is nothing to see far out on the ocean.

Not a day passed but we, as we sat floating on the surface of the sea, were visited by inquisitive guests which wriggled and waggled about us, and a few of them, such as dolphins and pilot fish, grew so familiar that they accompanied the raft across the sea and kept round us day and night.

When night had fallen and the stars were twinkling in the dark tropical sky, the phosphorescence flashed around us in rivalry with the stars, and single glowing plankton resembled round live coals so vividly that we involuntarily drew in our bare legs when the glowing pellets were washed up round our feet at the raft's stern. When we caught them, we saw that they were little brightly shining species of shrimp. On such nights we were sometimes scared when two round shining eyes suddenly rose out of the sea right alongside the raft and glared at us with an unblinking hypnotic stare. The visitors were often big squids which came up and floated on the surface with their devilish green eyes shining in the dark like phosphorus. But sometimes the shining eyes were those of deep-water fish which only came up at night and lay staring, fascinated by the glimmer of light before them. Several times, when the sea was calm, the black water round the raft was suddenly full of round heads two or three feet in diameter, lying motionless and staring at us with great glowing eyes. On other nights balls of light three feet and more in diameter would be visible down in the water, flashing at irregular intervals like electric lights turned on for a moment.

We gradually grew accustomed to having these subterranean or submarine creatures under the floor, but nevertheless we were just as surprised every time a new version appeared. About two o'clock on a cloudy night, when the man at the helm had difficulty in distinguishing black water from black sky, he caught sight of a faint illumination down in the water which slowly took the shape of a large animal. It was impossible to say whether it was plankton shining on its body, or whether the animal itself had a phosphorescent surface, but the glimmer down in the black water gave the ghostly creature obscure, wavering outlines. Sometimes it was roundish, sometimes oval, or triangular, and suddenly it split into two parts which swam to and fro under the raft independently of one another. Finally there were three of these large shining phantoms wandering round in slow circles under us.

They were real monsters, for the visible parts alone were some five fathoms long, and we all quickly collected on deck and followed the ghost dance. It went on for hour after hour, following the course of the raft. Mysterious and noiseless, our shining companions kept a good way beneath the surface, mostly on the starboard side where the light was, but often they were right under the raft or appeared on the port side. The glimmer of light on their backs revealed that the beasts were bigger than elephants but they were not whales, for they never came up to breathe. Were they giant ray fish which changed shape when they turned over on their sides? They took no notice at all if we held the light right down on the surface to lure them up, so that we might see what kind of creatures they were. And, like all proper goblins and ghosts, they had sunk into the depths when the dawn began to break.

We never got a proper explanation of this nocturnal visit from the three shining monsters, unless the solution was afforded by another visit we received a day and a half later in the full midday sunshine. It was May 24, and we were lying drifting on a leisurely swell in exactly 95° west by 7° south. It was about noon, and we had thrown overboard the guts of two big dolphins we had caught earlier in the morning. I was having a refreshing plunge overboard at the bow, lying in the water but keeping a good lookout and hanging on to a rope end, when I caught sight of a thick brown fish, six feet long, which came swimming inquisitively toward me through the crystal-clear sea water. I hopped quickly up on to the edge of the raft and sat in the hot sun looking at the fish as it passed quietly, when I heard a wild war whoop from Knut, who was sitting aft behind the bamboo cabin. He bellowed "Shark!" till his voice cracked in a falsetto, and, as we had sharks swimming alongside the raft almost daily without creating such excitement, we all realized that this must be something extraspecial, and flocked astern to Knut's assistance.

Knut had been squatting there, washing his pants in the swell, and when he looked up for a moment he was staring straight into the biggest and ugliest face any of us had ever seen in the whole of our lives. It was the head of a veritable sea monster, so huge and so hideous that, if the Old Man of the Sea himself had come up, he could not have made such an impression on us. The head was broad and flat like a frog's, with two small eyes right at the sides, and a toadlike jaw which was four or five feet wide and had long fringes hanging drooping from the corners of the mouth. Behind the head was an enormous body ending in a long thin tail with a pointed tail fin which stood straight up and showed that this sea monster was not any kind of whale. The body looked brownish under the water, but both head and body were thickly covered with small white spots.

The monster came quietly, lazily swimming after us from astern. It grinned like a bulldog and lashed gently with its tail. The large round dorsal fin projected clear of the water and sometimes the tail fin as well, and, when the creature was in the trough of the swell, the water flowed about the broad back as though washing round a submerged reef. In front of the broad jaws swam a whole crowd of zebra-striped pilot fish in fan formation, and large remora fish and other parasites sat firmly attached to the huge body and travelled with it through the water, so that the whole thing looked like a curious zoological collection crowded round something that resembled a floating deep-water reef.

A twenty-five-pound dolphin, attached to six of our largest fishhooks, was hanging behind the raft as bait for sharks, and a swarm of the pilot fish shot straight off, nosed the dolphin without touching it, and then hurried back to their lord and master, the sea king. Like a mechanical monster it set its machinery going and came gliding at leisure toward the dolphin which lay, a beggarly trifle, before its jaws. We tried to pull the dolphin in, and the sea monster followed slowly, right up to the side of the raft. It did not open its mouth, but just let the dolphin bump against it, as if to throw open the whole door for such an insignificant scrap was not worth while. When the giant came right up to the raft, it rubbed its back against the heavy steering oar, which was just lifted up out of the water, and now we had ample opportunity of studying the monster at the closest quarters—at such close quarters that I thought we had all gone mad, for we roared stupidly with laughter and shouted overexcitedly at the completely fantastic sight we saw. Walt Disney himself, with all his powers of imagination, could not have created a more hair-raising sea monster than that which thus suddenly lay with its terrific jaws along the raft's side.

The monster was a whale shark, the largest shark and the largest fish known in the world today. It is exceedingly rare, but scattered specimens are observed here and there in the tropical oceans. The whale shark has an average length of fifty feet, and according to zoologists it weighs fifteen tons. It is said that large specimens can attain a length of sixty feet; one harpooned baby had a liver weighing six hundred pounds and a collection of three thousand teeth in each of its broad jaws.

The monster was so large that, when it began to swim in circles round us and under the raft, its head was visible on one side while the whole of its tail stuck out on the other. And so incredibly grotesque, inert, and stupid did it appear when seen fullface that we could not help shouting with laughter, although we realized that it had strength enough in its tail to smash both balsa logs and ropes to pieces if it attacked us. Again and again it described narrower and narrower circles just under the raft, while all we could do was to wait and see what might happen. When it appeared on the other side, it glided amiably under the steering oar and lifted it up in the air, while the oar blade slid along the creature's back.

We stood round the raft with hand harpoons ready for action, but they seemed to us like toothpicks in relation to the heavy beast we had to deal with. There was no indication that the whale shark ever thought of leaving us again; it circled round us and followed like a faithful dog, close to the raft. None of us had ever experienced or thought we should experience anything like it; the whole adventure, with the sea monster swimming behind and under the raft, seemed to us so completely unnatural that we could not really take it seriously.

In reality the whale shark went on circling us for barely an hour, but to us the visit seemed to last a whole day. At last it became too exciting for Erik, who was standing at a corner of the raft with an eight-foot hand harpoon, and, encouraged by ill-considered shouts, he raised the harpoon above his head. As the whale shark came gliding slowly toward him and its broad head moved right under the corner of the raft, Erik thrust the harpoon with all his giant strength down between his legs and deep into the whale shark's gristly head. It was a second or two before the giant understood properly what was happening. Then in a flash the placid half-wit was transformed into a mountain of steel muscles.

We heard a swishing noise as the harpoon line rushed over the edge of the raft and saw a cascade of water as the giant stood on its head and plunged down into the depths. The three men who were standing nearest were flung about the place, head over heels, and two of them were flayed and burned by the line as it rushed through the air. The thick line, strong enough to hold a boat, was caught up on the side of the raft but snapped at once like a piece of twine, and a few seconds later a broken-off harpoon shaft came up to the surface two hundred yards away. A shoal of frightened pilot fish shot off through the water in a desperate attempt to keep up with their old lord and master. We waited a long time for the monster to come racing back like an infuriated submarine, but we never saw anything more of him.

We were now in the South Equatorial Current and moving in a westerly direction just 400 sea miles south of the Galapagos. There was no longer any danger of drifting into the Galapagos currents, and the only contacts we had with this group of islands were greetings from big sea turtles which no doubt had strayed far out to sea from the islands. One day we saw a thumping big sea turtle lying struggling with its head and one great fin above the surface of the water. As the swell rose, we saw a shimmer of green and blue and gold in the water under the turtle, and we discovered that it was engaged in a life-and-death struggle with dolphins. The fight was apparently quite one-sided; it consisted in twelve to fifteen big-headed, brilliantly colored dolphins attacking the turtle's neck and fins and apparently trying to tire it out, for the turtle could not lie for days on end with its head and paddles drawn inside its shell.

When the turtle caught sight of the raft, it dived and made straight for us, pursued by the glittering fish. It came close up to the side of the raft and was showing signs of wanting to climb up on to the timber when it caught sight of us already standing there. If we had been more practiced, we could have captured it with ropes without difficulty as the huge carapace paddled quietly along the side of the raft. But we spent the time that mattered in staring, and when we had the lasso ready the giant turtle had already passed our bow. We flung the little rubber dinghy into the water, and Herman, Bengt, and Torstein went in pursuit of the turtle in the round nutshell, which was not a great deal bigger than what swam ahead of them. Bengt, as steward, saw in his mind's eye endless meat dishes and the most delicious turtle soup.

But the faster they rowed, the faster the turtle slipped through the water just below the surface, and they were not more than a hundred yards from the raft when the turtle suddenly disappeared without trace. But they had done one good deed at any rate. For when the little yellow rubber dinghy came dancing back over the water, it had the whole glittering school of dolphins after it. They circled round the new turtle, and the boldest snapped at the oar blades which dipped in the water like fins; meanwhile, the peaceful turtle escaped successfully from its ignoble persecutors.

from caught inside

DANIEL DUANE

THE SURFBOARD IS to sailing what the phoneme is to language: the minimal "rig" for negotiating waves of sound or water. With nothing but a few inches of Plexiglas between feet and ocean, surfers crystallize the involved physics of navigation into an art form of split-second reflexes, gestural minimalism, and pure guts. Daniel Duane, the Jack London of Generation X surfers, studies the macho cult of bronzed board-warriors who see themselves as the last of a vanishing breed of noble savages. Dude-cool and ironic, Duane's surfers cruise an aquatic niche that most sailors avoid as frightening, dangerous, and hostile. Here Duane gears up for the ride of his life as he tackles his first "tube."

the wave, ruler-edged in the bright winter dawn, feathered ahead as I flew; cold, wet speed as the lip thinned to ten yards of spray, ready to break. Two toes off the tip trimming toward that shaking fringe, then carving high and, just as the whole wave leapt forward, soaring along the breaking back. And, in that instant's tableau—a telescopic view down a glimmering glass wall below a snowcapped green mountain and a morning rainbow—I became airborne just as a truly enormous dolphin (perhaps nine feet long) exploded from the wave ahead, its shining gray body for a moment in flight. We both hung in the rising sun long enough for me to shout out loud in astonishment and lose all balance, tumble into the foam as the dolphin speared the surface and vanished. I bobbed about on my back, stared at the dark blue sky and tried to think of a God to whom I might say thanks.

But such moments are a dime a dozen in a life by the water, and serve mostly to deflate the day's anxieties. Which was just as well, because as I stripped off the rubber at this secluded longboarding break, Skinny pulled his truck over for a chat, smiled, shook hands, and we swapped details about where we'd been surfing. We made plans for the next morning that led to yet another hello from the man in the gray fish-leather suit. Skinny certainly shuffled through the seasonal shift in surf spots, and since I hadn't seen him since the muddy-socks debacle, I was happy to catch up. He'd absolutely sworn off the Point, but was happy to take me on a search farther afield; and he made good company, with just the right irony around his relentless surfer chatter to make it more pleasant than ridiculous. I'd finally improved sufficiently to avoid embarrassing either of us—all that time at the Point without competition for resources. The next morning, the air fifty-five degrees in predawn light, Skinny worked through a power breakfast of four Advil, a cup of coffee, and an Indica bong hit while that feline grin of his split his tanned face under black sunglasses.

"Sooooo," he said, exhaling, "good morning, my son. Where we go?"

Sun not yet up, high clouds in the eastern sky reddening with the dawn, he sat in the open door of his tiny trailer and cracked his knuckles. Slipped his toes into worn-out flip-flops. Sipped at the coffee.

"Sharkenport?" he asked. "Shark's creek? Lane? Oooooooh. Indicator's, ya?" I finally got a glimpse inside that trailer, saw more or less what you'd expect: clothes everywhere, a mattress filling most of it, walls papered with cutouts from surf magazines, particularly the ubiquitous islander-woman-in-thong-bikini. We drove fifteen miles north to check his favorite spot—a remote beach also favored for male-male trysts-in-the-trees.

"No good," Skinny said. "Seen it better. See that little morning sickness bump?"

Didn't, but didn't argue. Where to? Ortegas?

"The Lane could be sick." So, about-face and back to town, sun now rising over the Gabilan Mountains, two women in black tights jogging the sidewalk . . .

"Dude," Skinny said suddenly.

Yeah?

"If we're surfing the Lane together, you gotta be cool."

Howzat?

"You just get aggro. Like, I don't want to be associated with you, necessarily. I mean, just don't hoot and shit, all right? Don't hoot at me."

Ever? Why the hell not? Had he heard about my day with the kayaker? My explosion at Apollo?

"It's just," he said, "you got to keep a low profile. I don't think you realize." Skinny surfed crowded breaks, generally speaking, which means he surfed breaks with well-established local pecking orders. And as a guy who spent much of his energy dodging the world's imaginary blows and avoiding perceived grudges, he'd never fought his way into those pecking orders—just accepted his peripheral caste in the surf world.

A little rubber shark lay on the dashboard. Its mouth was all teeth. While he rattled off the breaks we were passing—Chicos, Fresnos, Gas Chambers, Electric Chairs—I staged upward surges on my finger from the deep, imagined the angle of approach that would get that mouth high enough to hit a surfer. The little rubber toy dangled tenaciously off my finger.

At Steamer Lane, cars and trucks already gathering: carpenters, roofers and painters, doctors, lawyers and professors, all having a look before work, sipping coffee, windows up against the cold. A railing separated the sidewalk from the cliff along which the waves peeled. In the diffuse light, sun still behind clouds, someone tore along a clean green wall, breezing along in the dawn—looked great.

"Don't think so."

Huh?

"It's lost the sand it had over the reef last spring, racetrack's not lin-
ing. I want zip today. High performance. Something I can slam."

Wherezit?

"Oooooh, don't know. Need something I can shrack, you know? Like
that feeling when you just blow, like the whole . . . "—gritted his teeth,
looked tense—"the whole, fucking lip off the entire, just, you know, separate . . . like remove . . . literally, the whole top of the wave?"

How about surfing Cowdoodies? A ripping left beach-break that
required a hike over pasture.

"Local scene's too heavy."

"Nobody's ever there."

"But you still don't want them to catch you out there—those guys
took a dump in my buddy's pack."

Protected plover habitat anyway—little sand-nesting birds.

Skinny, Skinny, Skinny. He'd been at Berkeley High School just before
me, in the late seventies and early eighties. Basketball, weight lifting,
petty theft, and green buds. Lots of black speech inflections—the home-
town idiom. Dad a poverty lawyer, brothers going the same route,
Skinny was hiding out. Even Berkeley'd gotten too heavy: no waves, for
one thing, but also too many enemies. With a fierce little-guy complex,
he'd fought his way through twelve grades. Still did a hundred daily
push-ups and sit-ups.

"To stay in shape for surfing?" I'd asked.

"Nah," he'd said with admirable irony. "I figured out early I was a
shrimp, so I figured I'd be a huge shrimp." And he was.

"Look, let's just rush it," I said, looking down at Steamer Lane, hoping Apollo had an early math class. "Looks killer! Totally surfable. Little
inside nuggets doing the shuffle, maybe a big drop or two outside."

"Dude, look how many guys are out. Fuckin', probably be all the local
heavies: Floater Brothers, Slacker Brothers, Peepee, Batboy . . . ." Two
guys with wafer-thin boards scrambled down a concrete stairway to the
water.

"Don't let 'em faze you, dude," I said. "Just do your thing."

"It ain't like that." He looked pained by my ignorance. "But where're
we going to surf?"

"The Point?"

"Read my lips. I DO NOT SURF THE POINT. Boring and lame.
HP. High Performance. That's what's needed."

The Steamer Lane lifers were starting to show up, guys with reputations for spending their disability checks on beer and whole days screaming obscenities at the action in the water. They'd obviously known each other much of their lives, gathered daily on that cliff like farmers coming in to market—mostly for the joy of bullshitting in a pretty place.

Then it struck Skinny.

"Ooooooh," he said, "see way in the middle of the bay? The Dunes, buya! See those two smokestacks?"

Against the agricultural haze of the Salinas Valley hung two thin lines of smoke.

"Which way's the smoke going?" He asked this quickly, quizzing.

Uuuuuhh . . .

"Offshore. Let's go. It'll be shacking."

"Shacking?"

"Green rooms, shelter sheds," he said with a smile, loving the talk. "You know, tubulation."

But . . . hut . . . we'd already wasted an hour and a half . . . tide coming up . . . the Dunes a solid forty minutes away.

"You want speed or not?"

Unbelievable. I really took that shark at my finger while we tore south through the beach towns of Capitola, Aptos, then Salinas Valley farmland, Steinbeck country-surfer as existential wanderer consumed by angst. I mean, life on the road, following the waves—it's all a load of fun, but this driving and indecision and compromising, not to mention this dereliction of worldly obligation . . . although, if there were indeed barrels, I mean, I'd been *dreaming* of tubes lately. Usually, my dreams were collages of anxieties and memories, but surfing inspired wish-fulfillment fantasies in which I launched aerials at will, took off on gargantuan, open-ocean monsters with ease. And the night before, in fact, the shimmering blue sheet of the wave's lip started to throw over me and, instead of straightening out and fleeing, I ducked under. Suddenly, I was in a sparkling, roaring cave, a palimpsest of all the tube-ride photos I'd ever seen. As I shot out unhurt, a Hawaiian surfer in a yellow neoprene tank top—and he was an important part of the dream—made smiling eye contact with me; I stuck out my tongue in stoke and thought, in the dream, "That guy has no idea what just happened to me. He doesn't realize that was my first legitimate tube ride." Tube riding is counterintuitive, except on the most perfect of waves. You're shooting along, you see the wave "go square"—lurching over to break so hard the lip throws out well past the bottom of the wave—and instinct demands getting the hell out of the way. In photographs it always looks like that most peaceful of places, the ultimate mellow; but really, it's the eye of the storm.

Small highway, farms, somebody's kooky castle with a fake train engine in the front yard. Skinny said the Dunes faced due west toward this gargantuan underwater canyon, so northwest swell got less watering down by continental shelf than outside the bay. Then he brought up our mutual acquaintance Orin—now rumored to have a hundred thousand dollars in the bank from those three years in New York.

"I'm not sure I'd trade for a hundred gees," Skinny said. "I don't know. Maybe I would. But . . . ten years of surfing? Nah. No way. Yeah. No way would I trade." Skinny's girlfriend had been worried about him, thought he ought to get a life. His guru at the local baseball-card store told him just to let her know he was capable of physical violence—solve everything. Hadn't worked. Parents? Simpatico: Oregon Summer Trail Crew didn't wash.

"I told them I'd *love* to get a career going," he said, "and I really would, but the problem is, and I told them, I'm really busy surfing. I don't have time. And, anyway, I told them, like, I've accomplished a lot. I mean, shit, I can surf! That ain't easy. People don't realize that." Making the summer's earnings stretch, he never ate out, ever. Not even a bagel. Never a burrito. A true ascetic, though a patently unspiritual one. He'd even salvaged his TV from a friend's garbage pile. "And my girlfriend's moving to Hawaii to teach," Skinny said. "It'd be so killer to get back over there. She'd have like her own place where I could stay, probably no rent. I think she wants to get married, but shit, she says I'd have to get a job. I've got the money to go and everything, and it sounds killer to be in the islands with her, but I'm thinking, damn, for the same amount I could get a new board and wetsuit."

Past beautiful farms in the alluvial plains of the inner bay, Skinny talked recession, how the guys in the high-school class before us got in on the economy before it soured. "After our year," he said, "I swear it all dried up—no jobs." Affirmative action, he explained, kept the Forest Service from hiring white men more than part-time. They laid him off each fall, rehired him each summer. "And that's my chosen career," he said, shaking his head and watching a semi pass on the right, "so I'm screwed. That's it. Twenty-eight years old, and it's over. There's honestly nothing for me to do nine months out of the year but surf and collect unemployment."

When we got to the Dunes, a harbor seal splashed in the lagoon, and broad Elkhorn Slough—a sort of swampy river of lush bottom land—

wound back inland with its rusty grasses now turning quite green. A few pickups were parked where a trail led up the dunes. Skinny parked about fifty yards away.

"Why the hike?" I asked.

"Locals Only parking up there. Trust me. And don't go dropping in on anybody."

The sand path was riprapped with dowels; about twenty yards up, we got a view: from a harbor jetty, the beach stretched clear north to Santa Cruz and there were peaks everywhere, shoulder to head-high and peeling very, very quickly. Just offshore bobbed a ring of white buoys marking the border of the Monterey Bay Canyon, a colossal, submerged rift every bit as big as the Grand and of unclear origin. (Three rivers emptying into the bay—and more or less matching arms of the canyon—suggested old river gorges, like the Colorado's. But lately the theory had been that it was cataclysmic in origin, a function of shifting tectonic plates.) Regardless, deep water unsettles, and the proximity of profoundly deep water unsettles more—one heard of enormous, amorphous life forms populating its lightless depths, vast, drifting jellyfish. We jogged up the beach, boards in arms, and swarms of little sanderlings scurried in and out with the ebbing and flowing foam, legs too skinny to be visible, their bodies appearing to float about like fish. Farther along, near the peak we'd chosen, another swarm flew in the breeze—dark on top, white below, and flying in such tight formation that when they banked as a group, their white underfeathers flashed like a school of tropical fish catching the sun. As we paddled out, three seals took a good long look from about ten feet away. Then one went under and swam right toward us. A creepy feeling: you realize your mobility is in two dimensions, a slug in a field of snakes.

Beach-break peaks shift as sandbars flow with swell and tide; very unlike a reef break, where you always wait over the same submerged stone. We paddled left, then right, then outside, and the waves had an exquisite uniformity to their peel—also unlike reef waves, since even the most symmetrical of local rock reefs suck out here or mush there as the depth changes. But sand under water settles into smooth, organized form, like a denser liquid within a liquid. Skinny kept hooting at me to "pull in," to duck under the heaving sections and go for coverage. At first I just couldn't find the tube, or bring myself to get in its way. But then Skinny screamed at me to go late on an overhead peak, to stand up just as it broke. I took off at an angle, and as the wave screamed right, I got the oddest feeling that the light around me had changed, perhaps even that time had slowed, and then I'd been double-flipped and body-slammed onto the sand bottom. Came up coughing, but thrilled—tried again and again and started to understand; I never made it out of a tube, but each time I ducked under, I got that same peculiar phase-shift sensation. Waves are, after all, forms moving through mass, bundles of energy expressed as curves: when a curve can't maintain shape because of a shoaling sandbar, its energy hunches higher and tighter until it reaches up over itself, remaking the wave form by pushing water out to close the curve; expressing the original arc, but with a hollow, spinning core. In which the surfer stands. The climber never quite penetrates the mountain, the hiker remains trapped in the visual prison, but the surfer physically penetrates the heart of the ocean's energy—and this is in *no sense* sentimentality—stands wet in its substance, pushed by its drive inside the kinetic vortex. Even riding a river, one rides a medium itself moved by gravity, likewise with a sailboard or on skis. Until someone figures out how to ride sound or light, surfing will remain the only way to ride energy.

Then a very big guy—he looked like James Dean on steroids—paddled near and, with great effort not to sound patronizing, asked if I'd like a tube-riding tip.

"Absolutely," I answered.

"Keep your eyes open." He laughed out loud with me, then introduced himself in a warm, vulnerable way quite at odds with his commandolike appearance. He explained that he'd just moved to the area from down south. "You know what?" he said, smiling again.

"What?"

"I'm so stoked, dude." He had a square-cut jaw and perfect teeth.

"Why?"

"Dude. I'm stoked. Because, just being here in Santa Cruz, I can tell I'm turning a corner. I can tell it's going to change."

"What is?" We'd drifted closer together, both sitting on our boards.

"Just the whole way I been living."

"How you been living?" I asked.

"Oh, dude. Just not dealing. Not doing school. I was really good in school, too. I'm going to be a doctor."

"An M.D.?"

"Yeah. I'm really good at that stuff. I'm going to go to Community College for a couple of years, then to UC and get my shit together. Then go to medical school. Five years and I'll be done and I'll be stoked!" He giggled at the thought as though it were a dead certainty, as though saying it could make it true, in advance. And perhaps it could. He told me his sister had inspired him to come up here. She just had her shit together, that's all. A geography teacher in Florida now, she'd gotten the hell out of southern California. He said it was going to be so great supporting just himself.

"How do you mean?"

"My dad's just like lost everything," he said, lying down on his board to paddle toward a set. His arms were comically muscular, with bricklike triceps. The waves didn't materialize, and he sat up again. "Dad's just a mess," he said. "It's like all he does is watch TV and sit on the couch. He freaks me out. It like kind of grosses me out how he just like gave up on everything. He doesn't even go looking for a job and I've been paying his rent. That's why I had to drop out of junior college down south. So I could do construction full-time to pay for my dad's life too." Then his face turned from upbeat denial to a downcast admission of his own role in it all; he said he hadn't been doing all that well in school anyway—got real distracted. "I'd go to the library to study," he said. "Honestly, but then I'd get into studying my own thing and spend *five hours* in the library just reading. Reading whatever books looked cool. But I did pretty badly in my classes."

He spun and took off on a hollow, spinning right, ducked into its tube with fearless poise, and then I saw a big fin surface directly before me, held up by a long gray body. Even as I converted the sight into terror, three more fins appeared and they all turned enough for their raked curves to be visible: dolphins. Then, three more, and two more after that—a parade left and right, behind and before, watery-slick and so humanoid in size. A small wave rolled toward me with three warping dark forms submerged inside it, dolphins giving us all a show by riding the constant pressure surfaces deep inside. And one shot along a perfect wall (dolphins, by the way, *only* ride the good set waves) toward the crowd, only high enough for the top inch of its dorsal fin to break the surface and draw a speeding, razorlike line across the wave. Then wave and rider passed under me; I turned to watch the rolling water's back, and suddenly that six-foot body erupted into the air above, scattering golden drops before the sun . . . Showing off? Oblivious?

"Dude," Skinny said, paddling near, "be cool, all right?"

Huh?

"Those guys are giving you stink-eye."

Who?

"Locals over there. Talking a little shit about you."

Four more dolphins, with something even and paced about their fins arcing into the air and down again, like the inexorable sine curve of the swell.

"Dude," Skinny said, intent, looking furtively over his shoulder, "remember, as long as we live, we're kooks 'cause we're not really from here."

from land's edge

TIM WINTON

AWARD-WINNING AUSTRALIAN novelist Tim Winton is the

best kind of beach bum: brainy, articulate, and mystical. In *Land's Edge*

(1993), a biography structured around the seven days of (self) creation,

Winton alternates between moods of escapism and self-confrontation

catalyzed by various marine experiences. Here he brings to life the sen-

sation of the fine line between recreational heroics and idiotic tragedy

that runs through aquatic ventures, and evokes the mariner's constant

awareness of the sea as a sustained, indefinable menace.

the dinghy *skims across the glass of a lagoon one long weekend Saturday in the early autumn. My two cousins sit up in the bow, my dad behind them obscured red by cane craypots, while I sit at the transom seat by my uncle who steers the outboard. I am nine years old and consumed by the sight of the reef running so lucidly beneath me. I trail my hand in the water and a little rooster tail lifts behind it.*

Out at the Hole in the Wall we idle about, looking for a likely bit of reef, and then the pots and all their rope tumble out into the green hole, leaving a train of babbles to mark their descent. The floats snug up on the surface and we curve away lighter. The sky is calm as the sea, as unblemished and endless. At the shore, the flat little town has an army of white dunes advancing on it and the island seems to have broken its moorings and come free of the land just this minute because it tilts and bobs at the edge of my vision.

Suddenly the boat swerves and the pitch of the motor rises. I lurch into the gunwale and scramble for a grip and look up to see a great glossy wave bearing down on us. It trundles along silently, lumping the dappled reef in its path, and we begin the long dry-mouthed climb up its face and launch free into the air at the crest, hanging in a gale of nervous laughter for a second, before crashing down into the trough and the veil of spray behind. But there is another one coming; there will always be another one coming. The aluminium hull vibrates. My uncle swears and steers full throttle. This wave is feathering, getting ready to break, and we tear up its dizzy front and blast sickeningly out the other side into the path of something much bigger. There is shouting and contradictory pointing of fingers. The prop cavitates, trying to get a grip on the sea. The wave blots out the sky, its lip falling already, like a detonated factory wall, and we turn hopelessly to run before it, to beat it to deeper, safer water. I feel the foam at my back and see the long horrendous downhill run before us as the wave gathers us up and propels us on.

'Hangin' five!' yells my jaunty cousin in the bow.

Then it's just bubbles, silence and a corona of bubbles that billows blue about my head. I gaze about dreamily until I understand. I am underneath the upturned boat with thirty kilogram line floating around my legs and I am drowning. My head butts against the seats. Out in front of me my fingernails are pearly and beautiful. From under the gunwale comes an arm. I watch it with grave disinterest and the fat glossy bubbles part before my rushing face.

I love the sea but it does not love me. The sea is like the desert in that it is quite rightly feared. The sea and the desert are both hungry, they have things to be getting on with so you do not go into them lightly. Never turn your back on the sea, my father told me when we fished the rocks at Parry Beach or Greenough or Gull Rock. I never go to sea, fishing wide for jewfish or pelagics, without that frisson of concern that makes my fingertips electric for a few moments every day. I often fish alone so I'm conscious of how vulnerable I am, what a speck I am out there. I am not superstitious but some days I just don't press my luck.

Out on my own last autumn, with a busted finger and no gaff, I worried a sixteen kilo jewfish to the surface on eight kilo tackle. After half an hour it lay exhausted on its side ten metres out from the boat. I tickled it toward me with forensic care, saw the frayed and savaged trace and reached for its gills. I hesitated a moment and looked seaward, out of reflex, then heaved it over the side, almost tipping myself out, and headed for home without delay. It was almost too good to claim without retribution; I went back with an open throttle.

The ocean is the supreme metaphor for change. I expect the unexpected but am never fully prepared. Suddenly, from a mirror-smooth sea, a pod of randy humpbacks starts leaping and crashing around you. Out in the channel you feel the cold grip of cramp as you swim for shore. Climbing up a slick granite slope with your fins in your hand and the dive weights slung over your shoulder you hear the terrible surge of the freak swell behind you. Beyond the flags and the laughing families, with the city spiking behind them, you labour in the rip, feeling your calm, your cool, ebb away.

Australians do not go to 'the seaside' the way the English do. We go to the beach with a mixture of gusto and apprehension, for our sea is something to be reckoned with. We are reared on stories of shark attacks, broken necks from dumpings in the surf, and the spectre of melanoma. I suspect we go because of these warnings, at times, and not simply despite them. The sea is one rare wild card left in the homogenous suburban life. Deep down we still see ourselves as goers. Being last out of the water after the shark siren, taking the biggest wave of the set, coming home with the meanest sunburn, right to the bikini line—these are still badges of honour.

There are times when the size of the ocean and its overwhelming ambivalence become dispiriting. You look up from the sink of dishes and your mild, happy thoughts and glance at the sea, sometimes, to have your mind go suddenly, unpleasantly blank. Whatever you were thinking. Just doesn't stack up against the sight of that restless expanse out there. It's like the soundless television, the windbent tree, the campfire, in that it draws you away, divides your attention. At certain moments it's like a memory you are trying to avoid. You stand there, hands dripping suds, looking for whatever it was your eye sought at first glance, but there's nothing there. Just the chafing movement and the big blue stare coming right back at you.

When I think of sleep or coma or fever or death, the ocean comes to mind. Is what we look out at from our retirement deckchairs and our corporate rooms-with-a-view the prospect of unconsciousness, rest, annihilation? Are we longing for release or anxious about being taken? Or are we stuck somewhere between? Would we be more comfortable at the sight of roads, fences, buildings, billboards, cultivated paddocks? A glance up at signs of our terrible success does not divide us so from our train of thought. For every moment the sea is peace and relief, there is another when it shivers and stirs to become chaos. It's just as ready to claim as it is to offer.

Twenty years after my experience out on the reef under the capsized boat, I came to live in that same flat little town. A glutton for punishment, I suppose.

One summer my youngest son, who didn't swim yet, played in the coral lagoon behind the island while the rest of us lay on the hot sand watching the sea lions. He saw a nudibranch float by, tiny, crimson and purple, just wallowing as they do, in the current. Nearby, hanging off its anchor over the edge of the reef, was the boat. The toddler's sunbleached head bobbed and turned, following the nudibranch toward the big hole in the reef. Before the edge of the deep, he stopped, as taught, but behind him a new current yawed the boat on its anchor. I looked up to see the leg of the outboard shunting him silently and irrepressibly toward the edge. By the time I got to him he was over the dropoff, pedalling in freefall, his blonde hair just in reach. In the sunniest family moment, a silent change; death waiting.

The same summer a deckhand found a friend of ours floating face down in the bay. A fortnight before this he had told me he 'swam like a stone'.

To complete my ragged little life circle . . . Last summer I was heading out with my neighbour, Charlie Youngs, with a boatful of pots in a choppy sea when a lumpy, windblown wave reared up before us. We ground into it and out the other side to confront the inevitable follower, which broke just as we reached it and took me and the windscreen with it. I saw that same haze of bubbles, heard that same sudden quiet and then I popped up in time for the third wave to come down on my head and send me bouncing across the reef.

When I finally surfaced and got my bearings, I saw Charlie out beyond the surf, madly bombing pots off left and right to save the boat. He was shin-deep in water and, miraculously, the outboard still ran. The boat was half submerged and the sea was running against the bare barrier of the reef just behind it. For a while I swam in my tee-shirt and shorts till the shirt began to drag on me, so I shrugged out of it, dodging breakers as I did, and balled it up in my fist to swim on. After a couple of minutes of one-handed swimming I thought about the value of the shirt, which cost me one pound on London's Oxford Street some time ago, and hadn't been much of a bargain at that. The pain of my cuts and bruises came upon me. My coccyx burned and throbbed where I had clipped the cowling of the outboard—narrowly spared the horror of the prop. I threw that damn shirt as far as I could and struck out through the surf to the wallowing boat.

That night I dreamed and sweated. I was under a boat in blue bubbles, and there was no God-like hand to haul me free.

from close to the wind

PETE GOSS

THE 1996–1997 Vendée Globe Single-Handed Non-Stop Round-

the-World Race started with sixteen competitors. Among the six who

finished, Pete Goss, a professional British sailor, came in fifth. In *Close*

to the Wind (1998), his gasconading account of the nearly 127-day

journey, Goss recalls the grinding tedium, the financial strain, and the

physical and mental wear and tear of high-speed sailing. In this selec-

tion, Goss gambles on a risky course that just might give him the break

he needs to pull ahead.

the big day dawned on 5 December. The start of the Southern Ocean. We had dawdled through a South Atlantic high and came out the other side into wind generated by Southern Ocean depressions that were driving across our path. Appropriately, this was the wind that carried us across the 40th parallel and we officially entered the notorious Roaring Forties. I saw my first albatross gliding gracefully across the water. These birds bring life to a desolate region.

The temperature dropped like a stone over the next few days and I found myself wearing my Musto thermals throughout the day to keep warm. It was also wet on deck as the boat gathered up her skirts in the ever-increasing winds and pushed out big speeds. I decided that I would go far south and get right into the depths of the Southern Ocean—not only did I believe that that was where we would perform at our best but it would also reduce the number of miles that we had to sail. I watched our first depression tracking in on the weatherfax and felt a tingle of anticipation as the pressure fell, the wind increased and the swell built up. I ate, checked the boat once more and reduced sail as we pressed further south in a rising wind.

The boat had a feel of impending action. The air became heavier, the cloud base thickened and the heaving ocean took on an oppressive grey hue. As the wind settled from the west I brought the boat up, eased the sails and let her run—and run she did, sitting up on a steady plane as she thundered down the faces of a very big swell. It was great and I stood in the cockpit for a couple of hours and savoured the sailing with Tina Turner belting through my Sony Walkman. I decided to wang up the spinnaker to see what would happen. It was a stupid thing to do really, but I had a couple of months down here so I might as well find out what the boat was comfortable with. It was blowing thirty knots and I hummed and hahed about which sail I should shove up. I set the autopilot on a very broad reach, eased the main and clambered forward to drop the number one headsail. This became a bit of a handful when it went into the water and took a good ten minutes to retrieve. I hanked on the number two—if the shit hit the fan I didn't want to be wrestling with a bigger sail. I rigged the bowsprit, made off the spinnaker lines, took a deep breath and hoisted the spinnaker in its retaining sock.

I went back to the cockpit and, uneasy, mulled over the decision once more—the boat was going well as it was and I questioned whether I should have been doing this at all. My instinct said no and yet this was my first time down here with the boat and the only way I was going to find out what it was all about was to go for it. Perhaps I was influenced by all the old-timers who talk of keeping their spinnaker up down here. There were six hours of daylight left and I decided to treat this as a training run rather than part of the race, bung it up, see what happened, fiddle about with settings and find our feet. If it all went belly up I had six hours of light to sort myself out. I checked every line and detail one last time, stripped off my heavy thermals so that I was more agile, donned my sailing gloves, made my way to the mast and clipped on. I mentally ran through everything again before I untied the sock and started to pull it up the sail. The wind immediately filled the foot, the sock ran away and the check line burned through my fingers. The spinnaker filled with a bang and we started to lay over. I ran aft as *Aqua Quorum* leapt forward and the autopilot struggled on the edge of control as we zigzagged across the wind and waves.

It was bloody hairy now and we drove down a wave at twenty knots and disappeared beneath the water. I eased the spinnaker and the sheet shuddered under the load. That was better, it was a little more comfortable now, but it was relative. We were leaping from wave to wave, the wind was thirty-five knots and gusting. We were going like buggery but I wasn't happy—trouble was just round the corner and I questioned whether I would be able to drop the spinnaker on my own. I told myself not to rush, but to stand and watch, soak up as much information as I could—it would stand me in good stead later.

I got below and made a cup of tea—I needed to get used to life down there with the boat on the edge. I had to learn to relax even when things were marginal. The boat needed to be pushed—it was a race, after all— but I had to resist the urge to leap on deck every time she felt as though she were about to go. She hadn't lost it yet and I should leave her to it. The feeling below was awful. We were screeching along on the edge of control and I had to make a cup of tea and go about daily life. Each time she rolled at speed I felt the bow coming up and I willed the autopilot to put the helm over—it seemed an eternity before it did. It played on my nerves as we yawed from side to side and I made myself shut it out, fill the kettle and get used to it.

I saw that there was a message on the satcom (satellite communication system) and called it up. It was from Amelia Lyon. I hadn't forgotten the article for so and so, had I? They were getting twitchy, the deadline was in four hours' time. Shit! The message had been sitting there for the last hour. Writing an article was the last thing I wanted to do. I bashed away at the laptop but I couldn't concentrate. *Aqua Quorum* talked to me. 'Come on, dickhead, you know you shouldn't have this amount of sail up. There are two months of this and if you push me this hard we'll never finish the race.' Bollocks, I thought. We're here to race and race we will. By the end of the Southern Ocean this will feel normal.

Suddenly we were on the back of a big wave and accelerating like fury, the wave was steep and we started to come up. The boat heeled, I could hear water rushing across the side deck as we lay over. The log climbed . . . twenty . . . one . . . two . . . three. I looked aft and saw that the helm was hard over. I marvelled at the power of the autopilot and knew that if we pulled out of this and the rudders bit, she would drive herself into a crash gybe. I braced myself and reflected on the lesson that I was about to be taught. Prat. The hull was bouncing and banging across the water. At this speed it felt as if I was driving down a dirt track in a car with no suspension. I could feel the shocks running up through my legs and bent my knees slightly to absorb the impact. The noise was deafening and the moment was bloody marvellous. The wake disappeared over the top of the wave, narrowing at the crest like a country lane over a hill; the spray off the hull cascaded out to the sides. We suddenly decelerated at the bottom of the wave, the brakes were slammed on and the boat submerged.

I braced myself for the worst and mentally ran through the setup— halyards in use, winch handle location, runner, preventer, knife in pocket and so on. We galloped off to leeward. The back of the mainsail curled, the keel was now on the wrong side and we sagged to windward. The autopilot whirred away and the helm went over. She suddenly felt dead in the water, as if she had accepted the inevitable and decided to give up. The main half gybed. I gritted my teeth, this was going to be a belter. Where was the camera? Missed the last one on the Transat, but this time it was handy in a bag by the hatch. There was a crack. I looked up from freeing the camera to see the main slam back in place. Come on *Aqua Quorum*, you can do it.

The bow lifted and it felt as if a couple of tons had been released as she bounced up and we were off again. I couldn't believe she had managed to pull out of it as I leapt on deck and eased the sheet, thinking 'I might just get away with this.' The spinnaker flogged, shaking the boat as if it were a toy. I scanned the horizon and saw a big cloud on the way. I had to get the spinnaker down before it arrived. As I ran forward the wind seemed even stronger up there. I braced myself against the mast, which was banging around like a child's fishing rod, and pulled on the spinnaker sock which snuffed out about six feet of sail before it filled again and was forced back up to the head. The rope burned my hands. A glance over my shoulder was enough—I pulled like a bastard, the cloud was looming larger by the minute. We careered off down another wave and I found myself up to my knees in rushing water. The boat lay over and started to go into another gybe—this was going to be a shitty one. The spinny suddenly collapsed behind the main. 'Go go go go!' As the sock came down hand over hand, something tugged at my feet. I glanced down and saw that the lazy line from the sock had wrapped itself round my leg. Time stopped. The boat was coming up for another run, the spinnaker was about to be slammed full of wind and I was going to be strung up with a large sail lashed to my ankle in a tidy gale. For the first time in the race I was scared. I daren't let go of the sock line. I had half the sail tamed and yet I needed both hands to untie the other end round my leg. Shit! I just couldn't free it. The main filled. I watched the brightly coloured spinny flutter gaily out from behind the shelter of the main, swallowed and waited for a lot of discomfort.

The spinnaker filled with a crash and the sock line whipped taut in my hand. I was lifted off my feet and came up short as my safety line tightened. I could feel every sinew and tendon stretching as my body took up the strain. I tensed the muscles across my back and shoulders. My duff elbow hurt but it was the thought of my shoulder coming out of its socket as I dangled in mid-air that worried me. There was no way, however much it hurt, that I was letting go of the line and unleashing the spinnaker—the consequences were unimaginable. I shut my eyes and shouted 'bastard' at the top of my voice, and started to feel breathless as the strain took its toll. My right hand fumbled for the knife I always carried in my left pocket, but I couldn't reach it. My grip was weakening and I could feel the line start to run. I had to do something. Dump the halyard—break every rule and dump the halyard. Heaven knows what would happen but it couldn't be worse. The jammer was just out of my reach. I concentrated my gaze on it, even the burning in my left hand was forgotten. The boat came up, the sail really pulled now and started to run away. I was losing the fight. The boat lurched and at last the tip of my index finger touched the jammer and I managed to hook it free.

The halyard ran—thank heavens I always flake my lines out to avoid tangles. I hit the deck and ripped the line from my leg—I had to get it off before the dumped sail filled with water. I was free. I leapt up to jam the halyard, hoping to save the sail yet. We came up to the wind and stopped with the sail filling beyond the masthead as we lay over. It shook the boat like a rag doll. I dumped the tack, ran aft and winched in on the sheet. It was enough to kill the sail. Good old *Aqua Quorum* came up and ran off downwind with ease. The spinny was sheltered behind the main now and she was quite happy with such a reduction in sail area. It was as if she was saying 'Told you so.'

I dragged the spinny in under the boom, taking care to ensure that I didn't get caught up in it. Wrapping a load of sail ties round it, I dumped it below and closed the hatch—it felt as though I had imprisoned a dangerous criminal who had been running amok. Then it was back to business, a quick stretch, nothing broken, although my shoulder would be tender for a while. I slapped a reef in, tidied the deck and checked that everything was as it should be. I rigged up the pole and prepared to goosewing the number two; I had to keep driving the boat and I now knew when the spinny was a bad idea. I hoisted the number two under the main, returned to the cockpit and winched it across to the windward side. The boat loved it and flew along. It was time for a cuppa. I had been on deck for a good eight hours and felt very tired and cold.

The warmth and light of the stove was great company. I put my heavy thermals on and stuffed a ready-cooked meal into the kettle. It's a great system. I poured the boiling water into my pint cup with four sugars in it, dragged the bag out, cut the top off and dived into a meal of beef stew with dumplings and a handful of cream crackers. Just what the doctor ordered. I polished it off quickly, food didn't stay warm down there for very long. I banged a fix on the chart and was relieved to see that we had made a good run despite the day's antics and turned in feeling pretty pleased with myself. I had learned a good deal that day. How she pulled out of some of those broaches I shall never know. Good old Ade, and well done Cetrek, was all I could say.

I lay back, braced my feet on the end of the bunk so that I didn't slide off it every time we decelerated at the bottom of a wave and wedged myself in. I had my hat, gloves, thermals and Walkman on inside my best sleeping bag. Warmth worked its way back into my bones and with it a heavy weariness. The Walkman was essential because it drowned out much of the noise of the boat as she thundered along. My tastes are varied—Tina Turner, Vivaldi, Abba, Queen, country and western, anything that grabs me. I was also very lucky to have a load of tapes made up for me by radio reporter Dennis Skillicorn. He spent hours recording his best interviews from the past forty years for me. There are thousands of them and they are fascinating. An old tramp on the Isle of Wight, Lord Mountbatten, Blondie Hasler's Cockleshell Heroes, an old farm tabourer, a poacher, the list goes on and on.

I dropped into a deep sleep and woke with a start two hours later, rolled out of my bunk and dropped into my Mustos, which were hanging nearby ready for action. It was dark, cold and wet and the prospect of going on deck wasn't at the top of my list but it was something that had to be done. I checked the voltameter, which looked good and flicked the decklight on. A burst of light opened up our little world—I patted the boat, good girl, keep it up. Clipped on with hood up, I eased my way through the hatch and into the cockpit. I glanced at the instruments and watched the waves for a few moments. It was obvious what had woken me—the wind had started to go round and a gybe would be called for some time during the night. I could have done it then but I wanted to push further south and opted to change course instead. I clambered about the deck; a sail tie had come undone but otherwise all seemed well. I shone my spotlight into the rigging, it looked great. I adjusted the course by ten degrees and spent a few minutes with her to make sure that she was happy with this new heading, taking pleasure in watching her surf off under the decklight. It seemed to heighten the experience. Wind, spray, noise, rain and waves got their moment as they swept on and off stage, entering the spotlight at random and becoming larger than life in their moment of glory. Sheets of spray, thrown up by the bow, seemed solid in the harsh light but were cut off as soon as they ventured beyond its circle. I spent an hour glorying in it as I let her settle down.

It was time for tea. I shook off my Musto jacket. *Aqua Quorum* is a wet boat and being on deck when she was really tramping was like standing under a pressure hose, and yet I always remained dry. I first used Musto gear during the *Cornish Meadow* Transat when I slept on deck all the way. I have used it ever since and feel privileged to have done my bit in passing back ideas for improvement. Keith Musto decided a few years ago that the material Gore-Tex was the way to go and, with his son Nigel, developed a new benchmark in offshore clothing, the H.P.X. System. Gore-Tex is absolutely waterproof and yet able to breathe, thus venting condensation. It is very light and supple and lets me spend my days sitting about in water while remaining dry and warm.

It was two in the morning but this meant nothing now that my twenty-four-hour body clock was up and running. I munched a slice of Mum's fruit cake, swigged back the last of a cup of tea, and pissed in the keel box, checking the colour of my urine. It is easy for a single-hander to become dehydrated at sea without realising it. Golden urine is a sure sign of this problem, which can creep up just as readily in cold climes as it can in the tropics. I drink tea as a pastime—it is a ritual, a moment for reflection or a time of contemplation before a job that needs to be done. It's no good getting to the end of the boom and finding that the job requires a tool that is sitting below. Better to think it through first and make sure you have it before starting. I have saved myself many wasted hours and energy by cups of tea.

I could make out a big squall in the distance and there was no point in going to bed. I wedged myself in front of the chart table and wrote an article for the *Daily Telegraph* back in London. I was a bit reticent when Amelia fixed up a series of articles for me to write as the race progressed. I had never written before and the prospect seemed a bit daunting. But I found I enjoyed it and could bash out a rough feature in an hour and a half. Even Tracey liked the articles, and if anyone is honest she is. The cloud passed over and I could see another coming up. I was going to have to sleep at some time and pondered whether to get my head down regardless. I tried dozing in the chair, but it just didn't work. I was still not able to relax down there as the boat thundered on.

I kept pushing south and was soon the southernmost boat in the fleet. It was bloody freezing with driving snow and became difficult to work on deck. My feet developed chilblains. Philippe Jeantot kept reminding me that it was a particularly bad year for icebergs. I was fatalistic. I hadn't seen any ice yet and my instincts told me that there was nothing to worry about. I kept a lookout but stuck to my usual laid-back approach—if a berg had my name on it then I would hit it. I was wearing full thermals, hat and gloves below by now, there was bitter snow on deck, and sail changes were particularly painful to the hands. There was a strong smell of diesel and I traced the problem to the sail locker. *Aqua Quorum* has a large diesel tank which is supplemented by plastic jerry cans. I discovered that the tops were made of a different plastic from the can itself—they were contracting at different rates in the cold and the tops had split, leaking diesel on the sails. It was these little details that I found so interesting. Like the chance discovery that pressurised canisters for inflating life rafts were unable to work in those temperatures—they froze as they decompressed—and a different gas was needed.

The race was not going to plan. I had dropped a touch too far south in my haste to get down quickly and was starting to pick up adverse winds while Raphael Dinelli and Patrick de Radigues were storming away to the north of us. I was a bit put out by this and made sure that it didn't happen again. I heard something rattle and bang along the hull. Ice! Shitty death! I was up on deck like a shot. It wasn't a big piece but it could have been the precursor to a decent-sized berg. It was hard to see in the blasts of snow. I turned on the radar but all seemed fine. It took a while for the hairs to settle down on the back of my neck, though. The desolation of that place was suddenly underlined. I couldn't see any point in slowing down—better to sail like the devil and push through the area quickly.

The longer I was away the more I missed my family. Tracey's faxes were a daily lifeline. The BT Inmarsat system was so good and immediate that we could have a written conversation. I spent a lot of time working on next year's business and sorting out details that were left undone in the frantic last-minute preparations at the start. Nick Booth and his wife Sarah were making progress with the *British Steel* refit and I felt sure that with the two boats we would be able to keep in front of the overdraft. I had managed to sell a couple of days' hospitality on *Aqua Quorum* while I had been racing. It wasn't a chore, in fact it was nice to have something to work on outside the routine of the race.

People tend to think that a race like this is an endless series of adventures. The reality is that it is eighty per cent hard graft and twenty per cent excitement. The outside world focuses on the thrills, but they don't hear about the three grinding weeks of gale after gale. Three weeks' hard work boils down to a series of plots on the chart, that's it, nothing more. A disaster becomes a highlight, a break from the routine, something to write home about.

We emerged from the cold spell one morning to be welcomed by a crisp, sunny day with a northerly breeze. My spirits soared, the headwinds were behind us and I intended to drive myself to the bone until I caught up with Raphael and Patrick, who were now many miles ahead. I knew we could do it. I spent the day working on the boat and paid particular attention to the sail locker. It took hours to clean up the mess caused by the leaks—a little diesel goes a long way. The decks were as slippery as hell and no amount of scrubbing would take off the greasy film. I just had to be careful as I moved around. It played havoc with my elbow as I slid about. No matter how hard I tried I had to use both hands to stop myself slipping over. It was starting to swell more and the relentless, throbbing pain stopped me sleeping.

I stuck my head out the forehatch with yet another bucket of dirty water, and a 'growler'—a piece of iceberg about the size of a house—quietly slipped by with the sun reflecting off its many faces and making it look like a giant jewel. I hadn't seen anything solid outside the boat for ages and I stood watching it glide away and wondered how many others I had just missed. Back to work, there was another depression on the way and I wanted the boat tiptop.

The pressure dropped and the wind rose. This felt like our first proper depression, a classic Southern Ocean version rather than the patchy things we had had to endure so far. We crossed the 50th parallel, really in among it now and feeling good. It was not so cold now; in fact, I had been through the coldest part of the race during the past few days when the jerry can caps had split. I'll not forget it either, bloody grim, the warmest place on the boat was below—and that was zero degrees.

The wind picked up and we had a steady forty knots blowing. I had been progressively shortening sail and we were down to two reefs, staysail and the number two. *Aqua Quorum* was going like a bat out of hell and felt comfortable, despite a horrible little cross sea that kept trying to throw her off course. Apart from these odd moments I felt happy with progress and was able to get on with life below. I cooked up the biggest curry yet and shovelled some sugar into it. My sugar level felt low and I knew it was going to be a long night. I threw the pan into the cockpit—it was like a dishwasher out there, water flying everywhere as we bounced our way down the waves on a permanent plane. The white spray against the darkness was fantastic and I spent a couple of minutes looking aft at the wake as we roared off into the night. Time for a kip; I had been up too long and hadn't slept for a good eighteen hours.

I hung up my Mustos in readiness—I didn't expect to be down for long—and zipped my aching body into my sleeping bag. The feeling was fantastic and I grinned into the darkness. I was really enjoying things now, loving the rough and tumble and the fact that it was all down to me and my wits. I banged some Tina Turner into my Walkman, settled down and waited for sleep to overcome the noise and motion. I woke up and checked the instruments every twenty minutes or so and popped up on deck every now and then. The wind was starting to go round and I would need to gybe the boat sometime during the night. I didn't like the cross sea, it was giving the boat a hard time, the wind had gone up a bit but I decided to hold on to what sail I had up. We were going like a rocket.

I was woken by a dull thump on the side of the hull and felt the boat yaw to the left and accelerate down a wave. Shit, shit, shit, she was going to crash gybe, I just knew it. The boat heeled to leeward as the wind came further aft and I clawed away at the zip on my sleeping bag which had jammed. I couldn't free it. I heard the battens slam back in place, they had half gybed, bending double before crashing back. We hit the bottom of the wave and round she went. I gave up on the zip, shut my eyes and gritted my teeth. Crash! Over she went, my face was pressed against the hull and I was thrown out of my bunk. It was bloody freezing. Poor old *Aqua Quorum* was flat on her side and beam on to the wind. The keel was on the wrong side and I pictured the main across the runner, pinning the boat down. It was quiet now apart from the wind whistling over us and waves breaking on to the hull.

Take your time, I told myself, we've been here before. It was familiar ground. I worked the zip free, turned on the cabin light and found that my trousers had fallen into the water. I couldn't believe my bad luck, I had managed to keep the inside of them dry for months. Still, at least they would dry out as I wore them. I threw on the decklight and began a by now well-rehearsed sequence of actions. I used the opportunity to lean well out and check the keel. I decided not to perform a jig on it as I did in the Transat—it was pitch black and I didn't feel quite so cocky down here. I flaked out the number two halyard and dumped it, threw off the main halyard and wrestled the sail down the mast. She was coming up now, reacting in the kind and predictable manner that I had come to expect. The rudders suddenly bit and we accelerated off downwind again. The autopilot caught and she settled down on course.

The wind had gone round a bit—not too much, but the combination of that and a larger than usual cross sea was enough to cause the gybe. I sorted out the runners, swung the keel over, gybed the boat properly, heaved the number two on deck and lashed it down. A couple of hanks had ripped out. I put in another reef and spent a further two hours on deck squaring everything away. Below was a mess and I sorted that out, made a cup of tea and rolled into bed absolutely exhausted. We could have had a little more sail up but the time had come for some rest. I would have a big breakfast and resume work at daybreak. We'd done enough damage for one night, thank you very much.

I had an hour's deep sleep and bounced out of bed refreshed. In normal society, everything is geared to that eight-hour sleep. Transport, shopping, radio, television—it goes on and on, ruling your life, confining you like a straitjacket. At sea my sleep pattern varies with the weather and although I feel tired for much of the time I am not debilitated. Physically I feel lean and mean. My pain barrier rises considerably and a knock that would have hurt like buggery ashore is shrugged off as if it were nothing. There is the odd day when my limbs feel heavy, my eyes are gritty and I catch myself gazing into space in a kind of exhausted trance. Then I know it's time to have a good curry and follow it up with a decent kip.

I was very tired after the capsize but I spent the day mending the damage that it caused. All the battens in the main had broken and I took the opportunity to go over the sail with a needle and thread, touching up where necessary. The number two took an hour to repair and the rest of the day was spent sorting out below and writing an article that was well overdue. I managed to keep the boat on the boil though and ended the day with a serious look at how I was running my race. It took a glance at the chart to see that we hadn't even scratched the surface of the Southern Ocean and we had already suffered a lot of damage. If I wanted to stay in the race I would have to adapt to the environment and modify my pace.

Head down, I ignored my elbow, which did a lot of work during the capsize and was aching like a bastard, and got on with the job. *Aqua Quorum* was performing like a dream: each time the race positions came in I saw that we had pulled decent miles out of the opposition. I ate, slept, worked and kept the boat up to speed, driving her hard but not so hard that we sustained damage. A sixth sense picked up the warning signals and we didn't get caught out again.

The one thing I always insist on is reassuring Tracey that all is well. However, I was very tired after the last capsize and, although I informed the race organisers of the incident during the daily chat show, I forgot to fax the news to Tracey that night. The incident quickly hit the press and sounded worse than it was. The first a worried Tracey heard of it was a call from a journalist. I was not pleased with this slip-up on my part.

We were really pulling our way up the fleet now. I was caught in a high shortly after the capsize and two records were set that day. Christophe Auguin had a record run of 375 nautical miles and I got the record for the least. Fourteen comes to mind. That was all behind us now, and we were the fastest boat in the fleet for a full seven days, which was topped by a blistering twenty-four-hour-run of just over 344 miles on 20 December. Philippe Jeantot informed me that this was a new record. I was well chuffed because I knew that the boat was capable of doing even better.

I was overjoyed to see that our wild dash had put us back up with Raphael and Patrick. I knew we could do it and spent a few hours pondering the weather information. My next target was to catch up with Eric Dumont on *Café Legal*. It was a tall order but I believed that we could do it. He had had some problems and did not seem to be on the pace as much as he should. I decided to keep pushing on—our performance hadn't cost us too much in terms of damage and I felt we had at last found our pace. The only cloud on the horizon was that Catherine had had a rough time with a bad knockdown and suffered a lot of damage. She was now a long way behind. I felt for her and hoped that she would be able to find her stride again. I was sure that she would become the first woman to finish the Vendee. She had the depth of character to overcome her problems and see it through to the end. I wished her well on the radio and acted as a link between her and the shore. It was the last radio call I would make before mine packed up.

The radio had died on me. It had received a good soaking in the capsize and, although it kept going for a couple of days, it was now silent. Never mind, I was quite happy out here and the less outside influence there was the better. It was as if the radio was my last link with society and I was unable to settle into this life of total self-reliance until my last crutch had been knocked away. The BT Inmarsat system did not have this effect—I called up its messages when I was ready for them, it was communication on my terms. Happy solitude.

The shallow bank of the Kerguelen Ridge presented a tactical dilemma. If it is blowing there the Southern Ocean waves can build up into a raging mess. I had a taste of it during the British Steel Challenge and had no wish for a repeat performance. Put simply, the bank has an island at either end, Kerguelen to the north and Heard Island to the south. My track would take me slap bang between the two. I didn't like it and decided to duck further south in order to avoid the area completely. I might lose a few miles but Raphael and Patrick were welcome to them in this case. As it happened the dogleg cost us little and I was glad to see that the others had cleared the area without mishap.

It was 22 December, my thirty-fifth birthday. I was fifty-five degrees south, the Kerguelens were well behind us and I felt great. It was time for a treat. I warmed up a bucket of water and had a shower in the cockpit under the cuddy. I put the heater on for an hour to dry the cabin, stood naked in the accommodation to let the warm air get to my skin and checked myself over. Loads of bruises, elbow hurting, but otherwise in good shape. No rashes or sores, the diet was obviously working. I slipped into a clean set of thermals—absolute luxury—and celebrated by trimming my moustache. The beard, if you could call it that, would stay because it stopped wet, salty clothing from chafing my neck.

Thirty-five years. I couldn't believe how quickly it had gone, it had been great. I had managed to fit a fair bit in so far and couldn't wait to grab the next thirty-five by the horns. Tracey and the kids sent a lovely fax, they had baked a birthday cake and eaten it for me. The race was going our way, we were catching the opposition and here I was fulfilling a lifelong dream. What a lucky man I was.

The next two days passed without a hitch and I carried out some routine maintenance and eased up on myself a little. I found that I was tired after working so hard to catch up with and pass Raphael and Patrick. I spent the odd extra hour or so in bed and made sure that I ate well. When I looked at the chart I was awed by the scale of this race—I had already packed in adventure after adventure and yet the halfway mark was still days away. Nevertheless I felt good—*Aqua Quorum* was bedded in and I knew that we would keep on improving our performance as we went on.

from a supposedly fun thing i'll never do again

DAVID FOSTER WALLACE

GRAPHOMANIAC DAVID FOSTER WALLACE turns a brilliantly caustic eye on the pieties and foibles of the current cultural scene. His "A Supposedly Fun Thing I'll Never Do Again" is easily the most obsessive, ironic, reverse snobbery piece ever written about the ersatz, cocooned, "it-never-gets-better-than-this" world of Caribbean cruising. In this selection, Wallace investigates the arcana of his accommodations on the *Nadir*, a luxury liner he inhabited March 11 to 18, 1995.

celebrity's fiendish brochure does not lie or exaggerate, however, in the luxury department. I now confront the journalistic problem of not being sure how many examples I need to list in order to communicate the atmosphere of sybaritic and nearly insanity-producing pampering on board the m.v. *Nadir*.

How about for just one example Saturday 11 March, right after sailing but before the North Sea weather hits, when I want to go out to Deck 10's port rail for some introductory vista-gazing and thus decide I need some zinc oxide for my peel-prone nose. My zinc oxide's still in my big duffel bag, which at that point is piled with all Deck 10's other luggage in the little area between the 10-Fore elevator and the 10-Fore staircase while little men in cadet-blue Celebrity jumpsuits, porters—entirely Lebanese, this squad seemed to be—are cross-checking the luggage tags with the *Nadir*'s passenger list Lot #s and organizing the luggage and taking it all up the Port and Starboard halls to people's cabins.

And but so I come out and spot my duffel among the luggage, and I start to grab and haul it out of the towering pile of leather and nylon, with the idea that I can just whisk the bag back to 1009 myself and root through it and find my good old ZnO; and one of the porters sees me starting to grab the bag, and he dumps all four of the massive pieces of luggage he's staggering with and leaps to intercept me. At first I'm afraid he thinks I'm some kind of baggage thief and wants to see my claim-check or something. But it turns out that what he wants is my duffel: he wants to carry it to 1009 for me. And I, who am about half again this poor herniated little guy's size (as is the duffel bag itself), protest politely, trying to be considerate, saying Don't Fret, Not a Big Deal, Just Need My Good Old ZnO. I indicate to the porter that I can see they have some sort of incredibly organized ordinal luggage-dispersal system under way here and that I don't mean to disrupt it or make him carry a Lot #7 bag before a Lot #2 bag or anything, and no I'll just get the big old heavy weatherstained sucker out of here myself and give the little guy that much less work to do.

And then now a very strange argument indeed ensues, me v. the Lebanese porter, because it turns out I am putting this guy, who barely speaks English, in a terrible kind of sedulous-service double-bind, a paradox of pampering: viz. the The-Passenger's-Always-Right-versus-Never-Let-A-Passenger-Carry-His-Own-Bag paradox. Clueless at the time about what this poor little Lebanese man is going through, I wave off both his high-pitched protests and his agonized expression as mere servile courtesy, and I extract the duffel and lug it up the hall to 1009 and slather the old beak with ZnO and go outside to watch the coast of Florida recede cinematically à la F. Conroy.

Only later did I understand what I'd done. Only later did I learn that that little Lebanese Deck 10 porter had his head just about chewed off by the (also Lebanese) Deck 10 Head Porter, who'd had his own head chewed off by the Austrian Chief Steward, who'd received confirmed reports that a Deck 10 passenger had been seen carrying his own luggage up the Port hallway of Deck 10 and now demanded rolling Lebanese heads for this clear indication of porterly dereliction, and had reported (the Austrian Chief Steward did) the incident (as is apparently SOP) to an officer in the Guest Relations Dept., a Greek officer with Revo shades and a walkie-talkie and officerial epaulets so complex I never did figure out what his rank was; and this high-ranking Greek guy actually came around to 1009 after Saturday's supper to apologize on behalf of practically the entire Chandris shipping line and to assure me that ragged-necked Lebanese heads were even at that moment rolling down various corridors in piacular recompense for my having had to carry my own bag. And even though this Greek officer's English was in lots of ways better than mine, it took me no less than ten minutes to express my own horror and to claim responsibility and to detail the double-bind I'd put the porter in—brandishing at relevant moments the actual tube of ZnO that had caused the whole snafu—ten or more minutes before I could get enough of a promise from the Greek officer that various chewed-off heads would be reattached and employee records unbesmirched to feel comfortable enough to allow the officer to leave; and the whole incident was incredibly frazzling and angst-fraught and filled almost a whole Mead notebook and is here recounted in only its barest psychoskeletal outline.

It is everywhere on the *Nadir* you look: evidence of a steely determination to indulge the passenger in ways that go far beyond any halfway-sane passenger's own expectations. Some wholly random examples: My cabin bathroom has plenty of thick fluffy towels, but when I go up to lie in the sun I don't have to take any of my cabin's towels, because the two upper decks' sun areas have big carts loaded with even thicker and fluffier towels. These carts are stationed at convenient intervals along endless rows of gymnastically adjustable deck chairs that are themselves phenomenally fine deck chairs, sturdy enough for even the portliest sunbather but also narcoleptically comfortable, with heavy-alloy skeletons over which is stretched some exotic material that combines canvas's quick-drying durability with cotton's absorbency and comfort—the material's precise composition is mysterious, but it's a welcome step up from public pools' deck chairs' surface of Kmartish plastic that sticks and produces farty suction-noises whenever you shift your sweaty weight on it—and the *Nadir's* chairs' material is not striated or cross-hatched in some web but is a solid expanse stretched drum-tight over the frame, so that you don't get those weird pink chairstripes on the side you're lying on. Oh, and each upper deck's carts are manned by a special squad of full-time Towel Guys, so that, when you're well-done on both sides and ready to quit and spring easily out of the deck chair, you don't have to pick up your towel and take it with you or even bus it into the cart's Used Towel slot, because a Towel Guy materializes the minute your fanny leaves the chair and removes your towel for you and deposits it in the slot. (Actually the Towel Guys are such overachievers about removing used towels that even if you just get up for a second to reapply ZnO or gaze contemplatively out over the railing, often when you turn back around your towel's gone, and your deck chair's refolded to the uniform 45° at-rest angle, and you have to readjust your chair all over again and go to the cart to get a fresh fluffy towel, of which there's admittedly not a short supply.)

Down in the Five-Star Caravelle Restaurant, the waiter will not only bring you, e.g., lobster—as well as seconds and even thirds on lobster—with methamphetaminic speed, but he'll also incline over you with gleaming claw-cracker and surgical fork and dismantle the lobster for you, saving you the green goopy work that's the only remotely rigorous thing about lobster.

At the Windsurf Cafe, up on Deck 11 by the pools, where there's always an informal buffet lunch, there's never that bovine line that makes most cafeterias such a downer, and there are about 73 varieties of entree alone, and incredibly good coffee; and if you're carrying a bunch of notebooks or even just have too many things on your tray, a waiter will materialize as you peel away from the buffet and will carry your tray—i.e. even though it's a cafeteria there're all these waiters standing around, all with Nehruesque jackets and white towels draped over left arms that are always held in the position of broken or withered arms, watching

you, the waiters, not quite making eye-contact but scanning for any little way to be of service, plus plum-jacketed sommeliers walking around
to see if you need a non-buffet libation . . . plus a whole other crew of
maître d's and supervisors watching the waiters and sommeliers and tall-
hatted buffet-servers to make sure they're not even thinking of letting
you do something for yourself that they could be doing for you.

Every public surface on the m.v. *Nadir* that isn't stainless steel or glass
or varnished parquet or dense and good-smelling sauna-type wood is
plush blue carpet that never naps and never has a chance to accumulate
even one flecklet of lint because jumpsuited Third World guys are always
at it with Siemens A.G. high-suction vacuums. The elevators are
Euroglass and yellow steel and stainless steel and a kind of wood-grain
material that looks too shiny to be real wood but makes a sound when
you thump it that's an awful lot like real wood. The elevators and stairways between decks seem to be the particular objects of the anal reten-
tion of a whole special Elevator-and-Staircase custodial crew.

And let's don't forget Room Service, which on a 7NC Luxury Cruise
is called Cabin Service. Cabin Service is in addition to the eleven scheduled daily opportunities for public eating, and it's available 24/7, and it's
free: all you have to do is hit x72 on the bedside phone, and ten or fifteen minutes later a guy who wouldn't even *dream* of hitting you up for
a gratuity appears with this . . . this *tray*: "Thinly Sliced Ham and Swiss
Cheese on White Bread with Dijon Mustard:" "The Combo: Cajun
Chicken with Pasta Salad, and Spicy Salsa," on and on, a whole page of
sandwiches and platters in the Services Directory—and the stuff
deserves to be capitalized, believe me. As a kind of semiagoraphobe who
spends massive amounts of time in my cabin, I come to have a really
complex dependency/shame relationship with Cabin Service. Since
finally getting around to reading the Services Directory and finding out
about it Monday night, I've ended up availing myself of Cabin Service
every night—more like twice a night, to be honest—even though I find
it extremely embarrassing to be calling up x72 asking to have even *more*
rich food brought to me when there've already been eleven gourmet
eating-ops that day. Usually what I do is spread out my notebooks and
Fielding's Guide to Worldwide Cruising 1995 and pens and various materials all over the bed, so when the Cabin Service guy appears at the door
he'll see all this belletristic material and figure I'm working really hard
on something belletristic right here in the cabin and have doubtless been
too busy to have hit all the public meals and am thus legitimately entitled to the indulgence of Cabin Service.

But it's my experience with the cabin cleaning that's maybe the ultimate example of stress from a pampering so extravagant that it messes with your head. Searing crush or no, the fact of the matter is I rarely even see 1009's cabin steward, the diaphanous and epicanthically doe-eyed Petra. But I have good reason to believe she sees me. Because every time I leave 1009 for more than like half an hour, when I get back it's totally cleaned and dusted down again and the towels replaced and the bathroom agleam. Don't get me wrong: in a way it's great. I am kind of a slob, and I'm in Cabin 1009 a lot, and I also come and go a lot, and when I'm in here in 1009 I sit in bed and write in bed while eating fruit and generally mess up the bed. But then whenever I dart out and then come back, the bed is freshly made up and hospital-cornered and there's another mint-centered chocolate on the pillow.

I fully grant that mysterious invisible room-cleaning is in a way great, every true slob's fantasy, somebody materializing and deslobbing your room and then dematerializing—like having a mom without the guilt. But there is also, I think, a creeping guilt here, a deep accretive uneasiness, a discomfort that presents—at least in my own case—as a weird kind of pampering-paranoia.

Because after a couple days of this fabulous invisible room-cleaning, I start to wonder how exactly Petra knows when I'm in 1009 and when I'm not. It's now that it occurs to me how rarely I ever see her. For a while I try experiments like all of a sudden darting out into the 10-Port hallway to see if I can see Petra hunched somewhere keeping track of who is decabining, and I scour the whole hallway-and-ceiling area for evidence of some kind of camera or monitor tracking movements outside the cabin doors—zilch on both fronts. But then I realize that the mystery's even more complex and unsettling than I'd first thought, because my cabin gets cleaned always and only during intervals where I'm gone more than half an hour. When I go out, how can Petra or her supervisors possibly know how long I'm going to be gone? I try leaving 1009 a couple times and then dashing back after 10 or 15 minutes to see whether I can catch Petra *in delicto*, but she's never there. I try making a truly unholy mess in 1009 and then leaving and hiding somewhere on a lower deck and then dashing back after exactly 29 minutes—and again when I come bursting through the door there's no Petra and no cleaning. Then I leave the cabin with exactly the same expression and appurtenances as before and this time stay hidden for 31 minutes and then haul ass back—and this time again no sighting of Petra, but now 1009 is sterilized and gleaming and there's a mint on the pillow's fresh new case.

Know that I carefully scrutinize every inch of every surface I pass as I circle the deck during these little experiments—no cameras or motion sensors or anything in evidence anywhere that would explain how they know. So now for a while I theorize that somehow a special crewman is assigned to each passenger and follows that passenger at all times, using extremely sophisticated techniques of personal surveillance and reporting the passenger's movements and activities and projected time of cabin-return back to Steward HQ or something, and so for about a day I try taking extreme evasive actions—whirling suddenly to check behind me, popping around corners, darting in and out of Gift Shops via different doors, etc.—never one sign of anybody engaged in surveillance. I never develop even a plausible theory about how They do it. By the time I quit trying, I'm feeling half-crazed, and my countersurveillance measures are drawing frightened looks and even some temple-tapping from 10-Port's other guests.

I submit that there's something deeply mind-fucking about the Type-A-personality service and pampering on the *Nadir*, and that the manic invisible cabin-cleaning provides the clearest example of what's creepy about it. Because, deep down, it's not *really* like having a mom. *Pace* the guilt and nagging, etc., a mom cleans up after you largely because she loves you—you are the point, the object of the cleaning somehow.

On the *Nadir*, though, once the novelty and convenience have worn off, I begin to see that the phenomenal cleaning really has nothing to do with me. (It's been particularly traumatic for me to realize that Petra is cleaning Cabin 1009 so phenomenally well simply because she's under orders to do so, and thus (obviously) that she's not doing it for me or because she likes me or thinks I'm No Problem or A Funny Thing—in fact she'd clean my cabin just as phenomenally well even if I were a dork—and maybe conceivably behind the smile does consider me a dork, in which case what if in fact I really am a dork?—I mean, if pampering and radical kindness don't seem motivated by strong affection and thus don't somehow affirm one or help assure one that one is not, finally, a dork, of what final and significant value is all this indulgence and cleaning?)

The feeling's not all that dissimilar to the experience of being a guest in the home of somebody who does things like sneak in in the A.M. and make your guest bed up for you while you're in the shower and fold your dirty clothes or even launder them without being asked to, or who empties your ashtray after each cigarette you smoke, etc. For a while, with a host like this, it seems great, and you feel cared about and prized and affirmed and worthwhile, etc. But then after a while you begin to intuit that the host isn't acting out of regard or affection for you so much as simply going around obeying the imperatives of some personal neurosis having to do with domestic cleanliness and order . . . which means that, since the ultimate point and object of the cleaning isn't you but rather cleanliness and order, it's going to be a relief for her when you leave. Meaning her hygienic pampering of you is actually evidence that she doesn't want you around. The *Nadir* doesn't have the Scotchguarded carpet or plastic-wrapped furniture of a true anal-type host like this, but the psychic aura's the same, and so's the projected relief of getting out.

I don't know how a well a claustrophobe would do, but for the agoraphobe a 7NC Luxury Megacruiser presents a whole array of attractively enclosing options. The agoraphobe can choose not to leave the ship, or can restrict herself only to certain decks, or can decline to leave the particular deck her cabin is on, or can eschew the viewconducive open-air railings on either side of that certain deck and keep exclusively to the deck's interior enclosed part. Or the agoraphobe can simply not leave her cabin at all.

I—who am not a true, can't-even-go-to-the-supermarket-type agoraphobe, but am what might be called a "borderline-"or "semi-agoraphobe"—come nevertheless to love very deeply Cabin 1009, Exterior Port. It is made of a fawn-colored enamelish polymer and its walls are extremely thick and solid: I can drum annoyingly on the wall above my bed for up to five minutes before my aft neighbors pound (very faintly) back in annoyance. The cabin is thirteen size 11 Keds long by twelve Keds wide, with a little peninsular vestibule protruding out toward a cabin door that's got three separate locking technologies and trilingual lifeboat instructions bolted to its inside and a whole deck of DO NOT DISTURB cards hanging from the inside knob. The vestibule is one-and-one-half times as wide as I. The cabin's bathroom is off one side of the vestibule, and off the other side is the Wondercloset, a complicated honeycomb of shelves and drawers and hangers and cubbyholes and Personal Fireproof Safe. The Wondercloset is so intricate in its utilization of every available cubic cm that all I can say is it must have been designed by a very organized person indeed.

All the way across the cabin, there's a deep enamel ledge running along the port wall under a window that I think is called my porthole. As are the portholes in ships on TV, this porthole is indeed round, but it is not small, and in terms of its importance to the room's mood and *raison* it resembles a cathedral's rose window. It's made of that kind of very thick glass that Drive-Up bank tellers stand behind. In the corner of the porthole's glass is this:

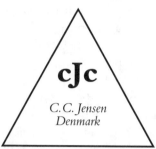

You can thump the glass with your fist w/o give or vibration. It's really good glass. Every morning at exactly 0834h. a Filipino guy in a blue jumpsuit stands on one of the lifeboats that hang in rows between Decks 9 and 10 and sprays my porthole with a hose, to get the salt off, which is fun to watch.

Cabin 1009's dimensions are just barely on the good side of the line between very very snug and cramped. Packed into its near-square are a big good bed and two bedside tables w/ lamps and an 18"TV with five At-Sea Cable® options, two of which show continuous loops of the Simpson trial. There's also a white enamel desk that doubles as a vanity, and a round glass table on which is a basket that's alternately filled with fresh fruit and with husks and rinds of same. I don't know whether it's SOP or a subtle journalistic perq, but every time I leave the cabin for more than the requisite half-hour I come back to find a new basket of fruit, covered in snug blue-tinted Saran, on the glass table. It's good fresh fruit and it's always there. I've never eaten so much fruit in my life.

Cabin 1009's bathroom deserves extravagant praise. I've seen more than my share of bathrooms, and this is one bitchingly nice bathroom. It is five-and-a-half Keds to the edge of the shower's step up and sign to Watch Your Step. The room's done in white enamel and gleaming brushed and stainless steel. Its overhead lighting is luxury lighting, some kind of blue-intensive Eurofluorescence that's run through a diffusion filter so it's diagnostically acute without being brutal. Right by the light switch is an Alisco Sirocco-brand hairdryer that's brazed right onto the wall and comes on automatically when you take it out of the mount; the Sirocco's *High* setting just about takes your head off. Next to the hairdryer there's both 115v and 230v sockets, plus a grounded 110v for razors.

The sink is huge and its bowl deep without seeming precipitous or ungentle of grade. Good C.C. Jensen plate mirror covers the whole wall over the sink. The steel soap dish is striated to let sog-water out and minimize that annoying underside-of-the-bar slime. The ingenious consideration of the anti-slime soap dish is particularly affecting.

Keep in mind that 1009 is a mid-price single cabin. The mind positively reels at what a luxury-penthouse-type cabin's bathroom must be like.

And so but simply enter 1009's bathroom and hit the overhead lights and on comes an automatic exhaust fan whose force and aerodynamism give steam or your more offensive-type odors just no quarter at all. The fan's suction is such that if you stand right underneath its louvered vent it makes your hair stand straight up on your head, which together with the concussive and abundantly rippling action of the Sirocco hairdryer makes for hours of fun in the lavishly lit mirror.

The shower itself overachieves in a big way. The Hot setting's water is exfoliatingly hot, but it takes only one preset manipulation of the shower-knob to get perfect 98.6° water. My own personal home should have such water pressure: the showerhead's force pins you helplessly to the stall's opposite wall, and at 98.6° the head's MASSAGE setting makes your eyes roll up and your sphincter just about give. The showerhead and its flexible steel line are also detachable, so you can hold the head and direct its punishing stream just at e.g. your particularly dirty right knee or something.

Toiletry-wise, flanking the sink's mirror are broad shallow bolted steel minibaskets with all sorts of free stuff in them. There's Caswell-Massey Conditioning Shampoo in a convenient airplane-liquor-size bottle. There's Caswell-Massey Almond and Aloe Hand and Body Emulsion With Silk. There's a sturdy plastic shoehorn and a chamois mitt for either eyeglasses or light shoeshining—both these items are the navy-blue-on-searing-white that are Celebrity's colors. There's not one but *two* fresh showercaps at all times. There's good old unpretentious unswishy Safeguard soap. There's washcloths w/o nubble or nap, and of course towels you want to propose to.

In the vestibule's Wondercloset are extra chamois blankets and hypoallergenic pillows and plastic CELEBRITY CRUISES-emblazoned bags of all different sizes and configurations for your laundry and optional dry cleaning, etc.

But all this is still small potatoes compared to 1009's fascinating and potentially malevolent toilet. A harmonious concordance of elegant form and vigorous function, flanked by rolls of tissue so soft as to be without the usual perforates for tearing, my toilet has above it this sign:

THIS TOILET IS CONNECTED TO A **VACUUM SEWAGE SYSTEM**.
PLEASE DO NOT THROW INTO THE TOILET ANYTHING THAN ORDI-
NARY TOILET WASTE AND TOILET PAPER

Yes that's right a *vacuum toilet*. And as with the exhaust fan above, not
a lightweight or unambitious vacuum. The toilet's flush produces a brief
but traumatizing sound, a kind of held high-B gargle, as of some gastric
disturbance on a cosmic scale. Along with this sound comes a concussive
suction so awesomely powerful that it's both scary and strangely com-
forting—your waste seems less removed than *hurled* from you, and
hurled with a velocity that lets you feel as though the waste is going to
end up someplace so far away from you that it will have become an
abstraction . . . a kind of existential-level sewage treatment.

storm warning

BRYAN BURROUGH

AUSTRALIA'S SYDNEY-TO-HOBART yacht race, one of the

top three international ocean-sailing competitions, runs through a

treacherous stretch of water in the shallow channel of the Bass Strait.

When 115 sailboats crossed the starting line of the 54th race on

Boxing Day, 1999, the brilliant blue sky gave no indication of the

deadly storm brewing about 400 miles east of Tasmania. Bryan

Burrough, special correspondent at *Vanity Fair*, tells what happened

when nature collided with blind ambition.

boom!

The little black-powder cannon's powerful report, signaling five minutes till the start of the race, could barely be heard over the cacophonous chopping of helicopters hovering above the sailboats in Sydney Harbour. It was a glorious, sun-washed Saturday afternoon, the December 26 Boxing Day holiday in Australia, and all around the harbor—from the black-wire uprights of the Sydney Harbour Bridge, which locals call "the Coat Hanger," to the scalloped hood of the famed opera house, to the multimillion-dollar mansions blanketing the hillsides above the Rushcutters Bay—more than 300,000 people had gathered to watch the start of this, the 54th Sydney-to-Hobart yacht race, one of the three jewels in the crown of international sailing.

As they inched toward the starting line, out by Shark Island, the 115 boats appeared from the air to be a swarm of vibrating gypsy moths. Down on the water, chaos reigned. Officials of the Cruising Yacht Club of Australia had elected to kick off the 630-mile run down the coast of New South Wales to Tasmania by starting all sizes of boats at once—which is not how it's done with many other ocean races. This irked Larry Ellison, who surveyed the scene from the cockpit of his gargantuan, 80-foot-long *Sayonara*, hands down the world's fastest and most advanced racing yacht; *Sayonara* was so vast that Ellison had hired the cream of New Zealand's national racing team to crew it for him. Ellison, who as the playboy chairman of the American software giant Oracle Corporation is worth more than $7 billion, was the odds-on favorite to win the multi-day race, barring a collision or other unforeseen disaster. And that was what bothered him. Looming over the 40- and 50-foot boats clogging the starting line, *Sayonara* was a great white shark hemmed in by dozens of pesky pilot fish.

Ellison had mixed feelings about the race. His arch-rival, the German software magnate Hasso Plattner, had kept his yacht, *Morning Glory*, out of the race, which took some of the fun out of things; now Ellison could only hope to beat *Morning Glory*'s race record (set in 1996), not the boat itself. His girlfriend, who had flown into Sydney with Ellison on his Gulfstream V jet the previous Thursday, had begged him not to go.

Everyone knew the Sydney-Hobart race was a rough race; Bass Strait, the shallow channel that separates Tasmania from the Australian mainland, is a notoriously treacherous swath of ocean, renowned for its steep waves and unpredictable storms. In his only other Hobart race, in 1995, Ellison had brought along News Corp. chairman Rupert Murdoch, who promptly lost a fingertip to a screaming rope in Sydney Harbour. This year Ellison had invited Murdoch's reserved 27-year-old son, Lachlan, a rising star in his father's media empire, to come along. "Lachlan came with us," Ellison said, "because his father ran out of fingertips."

Ellison ignored his girlfriend's warnings about the race, he said, because he wanted to see how good a sailor he had become. At 52, the lean, garrulous executive was popular with his crew, but like most rich yachtsmen, he was nowhere near their equal on the ocean. After 1995 he had frankly grown leery of the Hobart. "The Sydney-Hobart is a little like childbirth," Ellison liked to say. "It takes a while to suppress the pain, and then you're ready to do it again." Like Ellison, many of the other captains in the harbor that afternoon were wealthy men, some out to prove their manhood, others just hoping for a good time. Securely in the latter camp was Richard Winning, a bearded 48-year-old Sydney executive who ran his family's appliance company. Two years earlier Winning had bought a vintage wooden yacht named *Winston Churchill* and poured a quarter of a million dollars into updating it with the latest technology. Neither Winning nor any of the eight chums he invited aboard for the race, however, had any illusions about their intentions. "Gentlemen's ocean racing—that's our game," Winning told a reporter that winter.

AUSTRALIANS LIKE TO believe theirs is a classless society, and indeed, for a nation where more than half the population lives near the ocean, big-time yacht sailing has little of the snootiness that clings to the sport in America and the United Kingdom. The 1,000 or so sailors that day came from every walk of life, from the slim British Olympian Glyn Charles to schoolgirls who had won their way aboard boats in an essay contest. For every Ellison or Winning there was a bloke like 43-year-old Tony Mowbray. Mowbray was a stout, balding laborer from the coastal Australian coalmining town of Newcastle, and he had mortgaged his modest house to buy and outfit a 43-foot sailboat he hoped to take around the world. He had spent much of his savings, about $50,000, on a sparkling aluminum mast, bright new sails, and shelves of electronic equipment for his boat, which he grandly named *Solo Globe Challenger*. For Mowbray, the Hobart race was a test run, a chance to see if his boat was ready for the big water. His crew was a collection of pals, several of whom worked in the mines.

Like golf, sailing is run on a handicap system, so while everyone knew Ellison's *Sayonara* would be first to Hobart, the harbor was full of Australian captains who thought they might win the handicapped race. Groups of friends from yacht clubs all across the country, from Adelaide, Melbourne, Brisbane, Townsville, even as far as Perth, had pooled their money to prepare their boats and buy bus tickets to Sydney. The nine Tasmanian sailors aboard the 40-foot *Business Post Naiad* were typical. The boat's skipper, a meticulous 51-year-old plant manager named Bruce Guy, had won a regatta in Bass Strait earlier in the year and thought he might have the stuff to win a big race. He had gathered pals from across the island's northern coast—Steve Walker, a sailmaker, Rob Matthews, a public-housing inspector, even his back-fence neighbor, a gentle locksmith named Phil Skeggs—who had pitched in $500 apiece to get the boat ready.

As the final seconds ticked away before the one o'clock starting time, Ellison gripped *Sayonara*'s wheel and mentally went through the races. Fast minutes. It would be a difficult upwind start, forcing him to tack back and forth several times within the narrow confines of the harbor. With luck no one would hit them.

BOOOM!

The little cannon rang out again, and across the water hundreds of men, and a scattering of women, lunged forward on their boats. There were screams and curses as some of the lesser boats banged hulls, but for the most part it was a clean start beneath a brilliant blue sky. As they furiously cranked their winches and raced to and fro, no one had any idea that several of their number would not live to see Monday morning.

JUST AFTER EIGHT o'clock on Saturday morning, Peter Dunda, a 33-year-old forecaster in the Australian Bureau of Meteorology's New South Wales regional office, sat at his low-slung, L-shaped desk overlooking the busy tracks of Sydney's Central Railway Station, 16 floors below. Before him, on the wide screen of his IBM workstation, were the latest satellite photos, taken the previous night, and a computerized model of the weekend's weather generated by an NEC supercomputer at the bureau's headquarters in Melbourne. One photo showed a giant cold-air mass, a fluffy pancake of bright-white speckled clouds, moving northeast along the western shore of Tasmania toward Bass Strait. It was a classic "southerly buster," the kind that had buffeted the last several

Sydney-Hobart races, a whirring system of winds and waves that regularly shot up the coast of New South Wales. It would make for rough sailing, but nothing most skippers in the fleet hadn't encountered many times before.

What interested Dunda wasn't the front itself—forecasters had seen it coming all week—but a development in the computerized model on his screen, called the Meso Limited Area Prediction System (LAPS), which generated weather maps at three-hour intervals over the course of 36 hours. In the corner of his computer screen the model indicated a strong low-pressure system, a swirling knot of gray-white cumulus, forming by Sunday afternoon about 400 miles east of Tasmania. While it looked as if the low would be safely out of the Sydney-Hobart fleet's path, it would mean higher winds along the system's western edges.

At 9:04, Dunda issued what the bureau called a "priority gale warning" to race organizers, posted it on a special Web site for race participants, and made it available to the bureau's weather-by-fax system. In the warning he predicted winds of 30 to 40 knots off Australia's southeast coast by Sunday night. (A knot is about 1.15 miles an hour; a 40-knot wind blows about 46 miles an hour.) Down at the yacht club's modern brick building on the harbor, where the bureau had set up a booth to hand out packets of meteorological charts and predictions, a forecaster named Kenn Batt, who had given the Reefs weather briefing on Christmas Eve wearing a jaunty Santa's cap, quickly photocopied Dunda's alert and jammed it into his packets.

Three hours later, as the boats spent their final hour in Sydney Harbour, Dunda received his next set of satellite photos and LAPS models. What he saw took his breath away. In the year or so since the bureau had begun working with the new, detailed computer models, he had never encountered anything like the picture that now appeared on his screen. It showed an unusually strong low-pressure system forming not safely east of Tasmania but at the eastern mouth of Bass Strait, directly in the fleet's path. The system looked like a boxer's left hook, a forearm of white clouds jutting from the vast empty spaces of the Southern Ocean northeast into the strait, its northern end a curled fist of thunderheads. The model predicted winds of 30 to 40 knots in the area by nightfall, rising to 55 knots by Sunday afternoon, with gusts as high as 70 knots— more than 80 miles an hour.

Dunda's phone rang. It was Melbourne.

"Have you seen this?" his counterpart there asked, the alarm clear in his voice. "It certainly looks like a storm warning."

"Yes."

A STORM WARNING was highly unusual for Australia's southeast coast; the bureau had issued only one all year, on August 7, in the depths of the Australian winter. Still, at 1:58, with the fleet just clearing Sydney Harbour, the Melbourne office issued the warning. Sixteen minutes later Dunda did the same. In it he predicted that waves off Gabo Island, at the continent's southeastern tip, would average 15 to 20 feet by Sunday afternoon, with the highest waves reaching perhaps 40 feet.

Returning from the harbor, Kenn Batt, who had dozens of friends sailing in the race, grew emotional as the enormity of the situation sank in. "Those poor people are heading into a massacre," he said, taking a deep breath. After a moment he walked out onto an adjoining terrace and began to cry. Down at the yacht club, a private meteorological consultant named Roger "Clouds" Badham, who was supplying forecasts to *Sayonara* and more than a dozen other big boats, looked over his own new set of computer modes in amazement.

"Oh shit," he said to no one in particular. "This is Armageddon."

THE ENTRANCE TO Sydney Harbour is barely 1,500 yards wide, flanked by high basalt cliffs. Shaking free its lesser brethren, *Sayonara* was the first to burst through the gap, followed immediately by George Snow's streaking *Brindabella*. As the yachts wheeled to the south, surfing by the crowds baking on Sydney's famed Bondi Beach, a strong northeasterly wind billowed their sails. Aboard *Sayonara* Ellison ordered the spinnaker hoisted, and set a course due south. A spreading host of smaller boats helmed by well-known Aussie captains soon followed, led by Martin James's *Team Jaguar*, Rob Kothe's *Sword of Orion*, the mammoth 70-footer *Wild Thing*, and the Queensland yacht *B-52*. Thanks to the strong winds, by midafternoon much of the fleet was on a record pace—with the gentlemen's boats, such as Richard Winning's striking *Winston Churchill* and Tony Mobray's beloved *Solo Globe Challenger*, in the rear.

Few in the fleet were alarmed by Peter Dunda's storm warning, which was broadcast at three P.M. by the *Young Endeavour*, an Australian Navy brigantine whose radio was staffed by race volunteers. Sailing off Australian means an occasional blow of 50 knots or more, especially in Bass Strait, and few in the race expected to finish without encountering such winds. "The warning on Saturday didn't say anything more than what you could expect in any Hobart," recalls Rod Hunter, navigator on the Adelaide yacht *VC Offshore Stand Aside*. "It was for the 40s and 50s, a southerly buster. We sail in 40s and 50s all the time. It's normal. It's just a fact of life." Recalls Ellison, "There was a sense of 'Storm? Piece of cake!' Of course, no one said anything about a hurricane."

Back in the pack, the nine veteran Tasmanian sailors aboard *Business Post Naiad* greeted news of the storm warning with hearty laughter. Almost all had been sailing Bass Strait since they were boys, and they were accustomed to fighting the strait's steep, choppy waves and 50- and 60-knot winds. The skipper, Bruce Guy, speculated that the coming blow might actually give them an advantage the next day. "The guys from behind, who haven't been in Bass Strait before, they're going to get a bit of a dustup," observed Rob Matthews, the housing inspector.

THE POWERFUL WIND at their backs, Ellison would later say, should have been a warning. It was "explosive, gusty," he notes, and it quickly began to take a toll on *Sayonara*. By late afternoon, as *Sayonara* and *Brindabella* left the rest of the fleet miles behind, the gusts had blown out three different spinnaker sails aboard Ellison's boat and had snapped the brass fitting of one of the spinnaker poles, damage Ellison had never seen before. But the boat was simply going too fast for this to worry anyone. That afternoon *Sayonara* hit a boat record, 26.1 knots, and was already on pace to break *Morning Glory's* 1996 record time.

As darkness fell around nine, the wind swung around, as predicted, and began blowing hard out of the south. Raindrops pelted *Sayonara* as the boat crossed the incoming front, and the crew of 23 slipped into their bright-red heavy-weather gear. By 11, *Sayonara* was plowing into a 40-knot head wind. Waves grew to 15, then 20 feet, and almost everyone on board began to experience seasickness. "Anyone that said he didn't get sick out there is lying," recalls Ellison. "We had guys who've sailed the Whitbread [round-the-world race] puking their guts out, like five times in the first 12 hours. We were on the Jenny Craig plan—a great weight-loss experience."

By the time *Sayonara* entered Bass Strait after midnight, Ellison was having difficulty driving the boat. Heavy, dark clouds hung down, obscuring the horizon, and the flying spume and rain stung his face. A small rip developed in the mainsail, and when crewmen went to fix it they found the giant sail was tearing out the metal track that fastened it to the mast. Around three Ellison realized he couldn't take it any-more.

"You take over," he yelled to Brad Butterworth, a veteran New Zealand sailor standing to his side in the cockpit. "Get me outta here!"

Ellison went belowdecks to check the weather forecasts with his navigator, Mark Rudiger. Just as he walked up to the nav station, Ellison saw a new satellite photo downloading onto one of Rudiger's laptops. Stunned, both men looked for several seconds at the ominous doughnut of white clouds forming above Bass Strait.

"Mark," Ellison finally said, "have you ever seen anything like that before?"

Rudiger slowly shook his head. "Well, I have," Ellison said. "It was on the Weather Channel. And it was called a hurricane. What the fuck is that thing doing out here?"

WILL OXLEY, A strapping 33-year-old marine biologist, crouched on the deck of *B-52* and watched the front move in. Lightning zigzagged across the horizon to the south, and as the first raindrops wet his face, Oxley felt satisfied. He glanced at his watch. It was 12:15. As the boat's navigator, Oxley had worked with "Clouds" Badham to predict that the front would hit them at midnight.

For *B-52*, like many of the 114 boats trailing *Sayonara*, the night passed uneventfully. At 8:30 the next morning, as winds continued gusting up toward 50 miles an hour, Oxley stepped down the companionway to check the latest weather reports. He fixed the weather bureau in Melbourne for a coastal update and was surprised to see that winds off Wilson's Promontory, the southernmost point in Australia, had registered 71 knots—over 80 m.p.h.—two hours earlier. While the peninsula was well west of the racecourse, it served as an early indicator of the winds Oxley expected to blow through the strait. He guessed they might hit a 60-knot blow, which worried him. He listened to an oil-rig weather forecast and heard the same. Oxley caucused with skipper Wayne Millar, and the two men agreed that by later that day they would be in "survival mode" for several hours but should be able to begin racing again by the evening. "Looks like it's going to be a bit bouncy, mates," Oxley told the crew.

All that morning as the fleet moved briskly south, the winds picked up to 30, 40, then 50 knots. By noon some boats were already retiring from the race. At 10:30 the race's first major casualty occurred when the mast broke aboard *Team Jaguar*, a sleek 65-footer owned by the prominent Sydney attorney Martin James, forcing the boat to wait nearly 18 hours for rescue by a fishing trawler.

2:30 P.M.

Simon Clark sat on the starboard bow of *Stand Aside* and dangled his legs into the booming waves. Clark, a 28-year-old who had sailed since he was a boy, and three friends had joined up with Adelaide businessman James Hallion's eight-man crew, and Clark thought Hallion had driven a bit conservatively early in the race. Nevertheless, they had busted down the coast at an average speed of 15 knots, even hitting 18 and 19 at times.

Around noon, as winds continued to pick up, they had taken down the mainsail and put up a storm jib, expecting heavy weather. Clark wasn't too worried, nor was anyone on board. By two, winds were hitting just 35 or 40 knots, while Clark had seen only one "green wave"—that was what he called it—a rogue wall of water that looked as if it had risen straight from the mossy bottom of Bass Strait.

Suddenly he saw another. As the wave rose up before him, Clark thought it looked like a tennis court standing on end.

"Bear away!" he shouted.

Hallion was unable to steer down the wave. The boat rode high on the wave and slithered to the left. Just then the wave crested and crashed onto the deck, rolling the boat hard to port. As *Stand Aside* fell down the face of the wave, its roll continued. For a fleeting second it felt as if they were borne. Then they landed, upside down.

Slammed facedown into the roiling ocean, Clark felt a terrific pain in his left knee; his anterior cruciate ligament had snapped like a rubber band. Underwater, he unhooked his safety harness and floated to the surface just as the boat righted itself. Pulling himself back on board, Clark was stunned to see a seven-foot gash in the cabin; the mast lay draped over the side, broken. His crewmates were no better off. His friend Mike Marshman had somehow lost a chunk of his finger. Another man had broken ribs, still another a nasty cut across his forehead. Within minutes *Stand Aside* began sending out the first of what would be many Maydays that afternoon.

3:00 P.M.

As the storm system intensified, the first to encounter the full force of its lashing winds was a group of a half-dozen yachts led by *Sword of Orion* which was running seventh overall as the afternoon began. Like so many others, Rob Kothe, the boat's 52-year-old skipper, had shrugged off the storm warnings, but as he staggered down the companionway to call in *Sword*'s position at the 2:05 radio check, he realized conditions were growing far worse than anything they had been warned of. Now about

100 miles south of the sleepy port of Eden, Kothe's boat began to experience winds above 90 miles an hour. The sharp, spiking green waves towered 40 and 50 feet over the boat, crashing into the cockpit, churning his crew's bodies like laundry and stretching their safety lines to the breaking point.

In a race, weather data is a jealously guarded secret, something boats rarely share. As Kothe sat at his radio console belowdecks wiping seawater from his face, he tuned his HF dial to the race frequency and listened as boat after boat, going in alphabetical order, radioed in its position and nothing more. When it came to the *S*'s, Kothe listened to *Sayonara's* position report, then made a decision that probably saved many lives: he gave a weather report. "The forecast is for 40 to 55 knots [of wind]," Kothe announced to the fleet. "We are experiencing between 65 and 82. The weather is much stronger than forecast."

Kothe listened as the radio operator aboard *Young Endeavour*, obviously struck by news of winds approaching 100 miles an hour, repeated the warning to the fleet. Back in the pack, about two dozen boats, including the Queensland yacht *Midnight Special*, decided to quit the race and head for the port of Eden.

3:15 P.M.

Tucked away on an inland plateau two hours from the sea, the drowsy Australian city of Canberra is one of those kit-designed capitals where office workers and diplomats brown-bag their lunches around concrete fountains and sterile, man-made lakes. Downtown, the airy, third-floor war room of the Australian Maritime Safety Authority, lined with purring Compaq desktops and sprawling maps of the continent, could pass for the office of almost any government bureaucracy, a geological survey maybe, or a census bureau. But the tiny red target symbols that began popping up on Rupert Lamming's screen that afternoon weren't minerals or voters. They were distress calls.

When Lamming, a sober 41-year-old with 15 years in the merchant marine behind him, arrived for his shift at three, there was just a single target in Bass Strait, and it appeared to be a false alarm. A Thai-registered freighter, *Thor Sky*, had radioed in that it had accidentally activated its forearm-size emergency beacon, known as an Emergency Position Indicating Radio Beacon (EPIRB). Every hour, one of seven satellites in polar orbit—three Russian, four American—tracks across Bass Strait; the EPIRB'S signal bounces off these satellites, then ricochets down through ground stations in Queensland, Western Australia, and New Zealand to the computers on Lamming's pristine white countertop.

Trouble was, *Thor Sky*'s beacon broadcast at 406 megahertz; clicking his mouse on the red target on his computer screen, Lamming saw that the beacon emanated from an older, smaller model, broadcasting at 121.5 megahertz. Aware that the Hobart fleet was sailing into treacherous weather Lamming decided to take no chances. He had a colleague dial a charter air service in Mallacoota, a tiny beach town near the continent's southeastern tip. A half-hour later the plane radioed back: it had a Mayday from a yacht named *Stand Aside*.

3:35 P.M.

After finishing his impromptu weather report, Rob Kothe emerged onto the deck of *Sword of Orion* to find that the winds had suddenly fallen to 50 knots—"a walk in the park," as he later put it. Had the storm passed? Or were they merely in its eye? At 3:35—he looked at his watch—Kothe got his answer. As if a door had swung open, the winds slammed back hard, spiking up above 80 miles an hour. Kothe gave orders for everyone but two crewmen, a young bowman named Darren Senogles and the 33-year-old Olympic yacht racer Glyn Charles, to remain below. Kothe ran down the companionway, then radioed the *Young Endeavour* that *Sword of Orion* was quitting the race and heading back north, toward Eden.

Sword's decision to turn north, however, sent it back into the strongest winds wrapped around the eye of the storm. "The storm," Kothe later observed, "didn't give a rat's ass whether we were still racing or heading to port." After 15 minutes, as Kothe hunched over the radio, he felt the boat rising up an especially steep wave. Suddenly *Sword* rolled upside down and they were airborne, falling down the face of the wave for a full two seconds, until Kothe felt his boat hit the ocean with a sickening crack. Seconds later the boat rolled back over, righting itself, and he found himself facedown on the floor of the cabin, bound up with ropes and shattered equipment as if he were a broken marionette. As Kothe struggled to regain his footing, he heard Darren Senogles's waterlogged screams from above deck: "Man overboard! Man overboard! Man overboard!"

It was Glyn Charles. When the wave hit, Charles had been at the helm, attempting to muscle the seven-foot-wide wheel through oncoming waves. The force of the wave apparently swung the boom around like a baseball bat into a fastball; it struck Charles in the midsection, driving him against the spokes of the wheel and snapping his safety harness. As everyone else scrambled up onto the broken deck, Charles could be seen in the water, about 30 yards away.

"Swim! Swim!" people began shouting as Senogles frantically wrapped himself in a long rope and prepared to dive in after his friend. Charles, obviously stunned, raised a single arm, as if the other was injured. Someone threw a life ring toward him, but Charles was upwind, and the ring sailed helplessly back onto the deck.

Just then another huge wave broke and boiled onto the deck, knocking people and equipment about. By the time Kothe regained his feet, Charles was 150 yards off. The roll had actually torn the deck loose from the cabin below, and the men on deck, crouching unsteadily, were powerless to retrieve the struggling Brit. In the roiling seas Charles could be seen only when he crested a wave. Everyone watched in agony for a seemingly endless five minutes as he floated farther and farther from the boat. And then he was gone.

Kothe had already raced to the radio and began sending out an urgent Mayday. But the boat's mainmast lay broken in five places and had lost its aerial. Kothe broadcast Maydays for a solid two hours, but no one in a position to help Glyn Charles heard a word Kothe said.

4:00 P.M.

The storm system's hurricane-force winds and steep black waves had begun to engulf the rest of the fleet. Aboard *Solo Globe Challenger*, Tony Mowbray thought he was handling the mountainous seas well. In 32 years of sailing, he had never seen such conditions. The waves weren't normal waves. He thought of them as cliffs—cliffs of water—that rose to impossible heights and suddenly fell onto his boat, one after another, with a stultifyingly rhythmic Bang! . . . BANG! . . . Bang! When a large wave landed atop you, all you could do was hold on to something and twist your body away as the boat shuddered with the impact; if it struck you square in the ribs, it felt like a Mike Tyson body shot. Mowbray had pulled down all his sails a bit early, at noon, just to be safe. He had heard *Sword of Orion*'s weather warning, but thought he could still make it across the strait.

But *Solo* couldn't survive the marine equivalent of a one-two punch. Mowbray was below when the first wave socked it in the bow, swinging it around for the enormous 65-foot wave that suddenly reared up behind the boat and fell on top of it. The gleaming white yacht lurched to port and fell sideways. Then it rolled to 145 degrees and seemed to dig in as the mighty wave shoved it through the ocean, not quite face-down in the water, for what Mowbray later estimated was a full 20 seconds. The force of the "shove" shattered the interior cabin's seven-foot skylight. Seawater poured in.

When the boat finally righted itself, Mowbray charged up on deck to see what fate had befallen the four crewmen there. Glen Picasso, a 40-year-old coal miner, was in the water clinging to the stern; he had been pulled behind the boat by his safety line and had sustained broken ribs. Tony Purkiss lay on the floor of the cockpit, his head drenched in blood from a deep cut. But it was 45-year-old Keir Enderby who was in the worst shape. The mast and rigging, broken into pieces by the force of the wave, had fallen across his legs. He was screaming, "Get it off me!" Hurriedly Mowbray and others shoved the mast into the sea, then took Enderby below and tucked him into a bunk. Picasso soon followed, overcome by shock. The emergency beacon was activated.

Those uninjured bailed out the cabin, stuffed sleeping bags into the gaping hole where the skylight had been, and prayed. Mowbray spent the next few hours staring at the waves and hoping his crippled boat wouldn't founder. "I'll never look at waves the same again," he says. "Those waves were out to kill you. That was our attitude. You could see death working in that water."

5:00 P.M.

As her medevac helicopter struggled to maintain its position in the shrieking winds 50 feet above *Stand Aside*, Kristy McAlister leaned far out its right-hand door and gulped. McAlister, a trim, girlish 30-year-old paramedic with Canberra's SouthCare helicopter-ambulance service, had been working on choppers for only two months, and this was her first ocean rescue. Below was a scene unlike any she had dreamed of: evil black waves, as blocky and stout as apartment buildings, crashing this way and that. The helicopter's altimeter swung wildly, registering 60 feet one moment, 10 feet the next, as a dark wave swept up beneath its under-belly. The winds hit McAlister's face with a force she knew only from sticking her head out the window of a car speeding down the highway at 80 miles an hour. One thought crossed her mind: Oh, God . . .

Another helicopter had already winched eight sailors out of a life raft beside the boat and then, running low on fuel, had wheeled about and headed back toward land. Below, a man was in the water, floating briskly away from the raft. McAlister, wearing a black wet suit, a navy-blue life vest, and a lightweight helmet, had no time to waste. Grabbing an oval rescue strop, she held her breath—and jumped.

The water felt like concrete as she hit it, and a wave immediately drove her under, down, down, forcing seawater into her mouth and down her throat. She fought her way to the surface, coughing and hacking and found herself barely 10 feet from the man loose in the ocean.

"I'm going to put this over your head and under your armpits!" she shouted, indicating the strop.

"You must keep your arms down or you will fall out!"

The man nodded just as a wave drove both of them underwater for several seconds. When they returned to the surface, the helicopter winched them both skyward.

Within minutes McAlister had returned to the roiling ocean, this time landing beside the life raft, where two shivering sailors awaited rescue. When the last man was safely aboard, McAlister rolled to one side and began vomiting seawater. Ten minutes later she was still retching.

5:15 P.M.

As the winds swirled and howled around them, the nine Tasmanian sailors aboard *Business Post Naiad* remained in high spirits. Roughly 10 miles east of *Sword of Orion*, they had listened to Rob Kothe's weather report, but had decided to press on. Rob Matthews, like almost everyone else on board, had survived winds of more than 70 knots in Bass Strait, and had been forced down to "bare poles," with all sails lowered. A few minutes past five, Matthews was behind the wheel, attempting to drive the boat's bow through the incoming waves, when he heard Tony Guy, Bruce's nephew, pipe up behind him. "I've lit a fag, Robbie," said Guy, proudly displaying a cigarette.

"Tony reckons he's going to have a smoke in 70-knot winds," Matthews yelled to Steve Walker, the boat's helmsman. Walker grinned.

Moments later, as Matthews attempted to maneuver the boat up the face of a 50-foot wave, the boat slid sideways just as the wave crested. To the dismay of Matthews and the four other sailors on deck, *Business Post Naiad* rolled to its left and plummeted down the wave's face, then rolled still further as it fell. It landed upside down in the trough of the wave with a thunderous crack. All five men were plunged facedown, into the raging sea. Then, almost before anyone had a chance to realize what had happened, the boat righted itself. The five men, thrown over the starboard side to the end of their safety lines, popped to the surface to find the deck suddenly awash.

"Fuck, the mast is over the side!" someone yelled.

It was true. The mast had broken in half and was lying across the starboard side, its top buried in the waves. "That wasn't in the bloody brochure," Phil Skeggs said, trying to make a joke. But as the full crew of nine men struggled to pull the broken mast back on deck, their mood turned somber. For *Business Post Naiad,* the race was over. Grudgingly the crew agreed to rev up the motor and set a course toward Eden.

5:30 P.M.

"Mayday! Mayday! Mayday! Here is *Winston Churchill.* We are taking water rapidly! We can't get the motor started to start the pumps! We are getting the life rafts on deck!"

His mast and long-range aerials still intact, Richard Winning broadcast a furious Mayday even as seawater lapped onto the deck and the rest of the crew dropped the boat's life rafts over the side. Winning had been at the helm a half-hour before when a sneering green wave had slapped the old wooden yacht, knocking it flat on its side. Below, John Stanley, a taciturn 51-year-old Sydney marina manager, had been thrown into a wall as the three starboard windows imploded and foamy saltwater sprayed across the cabin. When the boat righted itself, Stanley noted with horror that a full six feet of *Churchill's* inner bulwarks was gone. "Must've sprung a plank!," Stanley yelled to Winning.

They were going down fast. As seawater began sloshing across the deck, Winning and his eight crewmates, ranging from a Sydney merchant banker to a friend's 19-year-old son, scrambled into the life rafts—Winning, the boy, and two others in one, Stanley and four friends in the other. The inflatable black rubber rafts were both topped with bright-orange canopies, which could be tied shut, though seawater still poured in, forcing the men to bail constantly. As *Churchill* sank, Winning managed to tie the two life rafts together, but the waves tore them apart barely 10 minutes later. The two boats, climbing, then falling down the faces of 50-foot waves, lost sight of each other soon after. Winning could only hope his Mayday would be answered.

6:15 P.M.

On the deck of *B-52,* Mark Vickers, a 32-year-old ceramic-tile layer, was standing at the giant, seven-foot wheel when he caught a glimpse of a mammoth wave rising up behind the boat. A wall of bluish-green water that towered over the boat's mast—Vickers later estimated its height at 60 feet or more—the wave began to crest and fall forward just as he called out to his friend Russell Kingston, who was crouched forward.

"Oh, shit, Russell!," Vickers called out. "This one's gonna hurt!"

With that the massive wave came crashing down directly onto the boat. *B-52* half rolled, half pitchpoled—an end-over-end flip—and landed upside down. The wave had hit with such force that Vickers was driven through the wheel's spokes, breaking them and badly denting the wheel. For several seconds he felt as if he were inside a blender, as the sea furiously tossed him about. Coming to his senses, he opened his eyes and at first saw only blackness. Disoriented, he glanced upward and saw light flashing through portals in the ship's hull. Only then did he realize the boat was upside down and he was beneath it.

He couldn't swim free. The rope to his safety harness was wrapped twice around the wheel. He unhooked the harness but still couldn't find a way clear of the lines and equipment swirling around him. Eventually, with his breath running out, he kicked down and swam out, coming to the surface about 10 feet from the boat's stem. He saw Kingston clinging to ropes at the overturned boat's edge.

The boat was drifting away from Vickers, and quickly. Exhausted, he began dogpaddling faster and faster, but the boat seemed only to be pulling away, eventually reaching a distance of about 100 feet. Somehow, with a helpful wave or two and the last of his energy, he reached a rope leading to the boat just as it righted itself.

The rest of the crew scrambled up the companionway to find the mast broken and deep cracks zigzagging through the deck. They activated an emergency beacon, began bailing, and prayed they could make it through what promised to be a long night.

7:00 P.M.

Peter Joubert, a wry 74-year-old engineering professor at the University of Melbourne, had quickly grown tired of fighting the waves in this, his 27th Hobart. The spume blasting his 43-foot *Kingurra* felt like a pitchfork jabbing into his face; the only way he could steer was to wear goggles. Around six he curled up in a bunk and fell into a deep sleep, leaving the driving to the group of younger men who had the energy to fight the waves.

At seven Joubert woke with a start to the sound of a "horrific crash like none I'd ever heard before." The boat pitched hard to port, and he felt a massive pain spread across his chest; a slumbering crewman in another bunk had flown across the cabin, slamming into his ribs . . .

breaking several and rupturing his spleen, Joubert later learned. As seawater gushed into the cabin, he lurched out of the bunk and crawled to the nav station, where his 22-year-old grandson helped him flip on the pumps. Glancing up the companionway, he saw three crewmen, including his friend Peter Meikle, lifting an American named John Campbell, 32, back on deck. Just then Joubert heard someone cry, "Man overboard!" It was Campbell. Halfway back onto the boat, he had slipped out of his jacket and safety harness and slid back into the ocean, wearing nothing but long underwear.

Joubert grabbed the radio. "Mayday! Mayday! Mayday! We have a man overboard!" he shouted.

As Joubert began to go into shock, Campbell floated swiftly away from the boat. *Kingurra's* motor wouldn't start; the storm jib was shredded. There was no way to retrieve him.

"Mayday! Mayday!," Joubert repeated. "We need a helicopter!"

About 7:20 P.M.

Barry Barclay, the 37-year-old winch operator on a Dauphin SA 365 helicopter operated by the Victoria Police air wing, had just finished refueling at his base in Melbourne when the call came in that racers were in trouble. Scrambling east over the mountains known as the Great Dividing Range, Barclay and his two crewmates stopped to refuel once again, at the dirt airstrip in Mallacoota, before heading out into the howling winds in Bass Strait. First ordered by the Maritime Safety Authority's war room to rescue sailors off *Stand Aside*, Barclay's crew detoured en route when word came of a man overboard off *Kingurra*. Cutting through the swirling clouds at speeds topping 200 miles an hour, the helicopter reached *Kingurra's* last reported position in 10 minutes—only to find nothing there. "I think we've overshot them!" pilot Daryl Jones shouted. "I'm heading back!"

Just then Barclay spotted a red flare arcing into the sky. Jones made for it. It was from *Kingurra*. Barclay hailed the boat on his radio. In a shaky voice Joubert told him Campbell had last been seen about 300 yards off the port bow. Jones wheeled the copter around as Barclay scanned the seas below. It was almost impossible to see. Even at an altitude of 300 feet, the waves seemed to be reaching for them, trying to suck them into the sea.

"Got something!" yelled Dave Key, another crew member. Barclay hung out of the copter's left-hand door and saw a white life ring winking among the waves; he thought he saw someone waving from inside it. But as they neared its position, the ring shot high in the air and flew off, tumbling crazily over the wave tops. There was no one inside.

Just then, out of the comer of his eye, Barclay caught a flash of movement. Peering down through the spume, he could just make out a man in the water, clad in blue long johns, waving. It was Campbell.

"I've got him! I've got him!," Barclay shouted.

Hovering above him, Barclay played out a hundred feet of wire cable and slowly lowered Key into the ocean. Three times he raised and lowered Key, like a tea bag, as the waves engulfed him and drove him under. When Key finally reached Campbell he was limp, at the edge of consciousness, and unable to help as the paramedic tried to slip the strop over his head. Eventually Key got him into the strop, and Barclay began winching them toward the helicopter.

Just as the two men were about to reach the open doorway, the winch froze. Barclay hurriedly cycled through a series of switches, trying to unlock it. It was no use. Campbell and Key hung two feet below the doorway, Campbell too exhausted to pull himself into the copter. Finally, giving up on the winch, Barclay reached down, grabbed Campbell by his underwear, and yanked him into the aircraft. Key soon followed. Campbell lay on his back, saying over and over, "Thank you thank you thank you thank you."

8:00 P.M.

By late Sunday afternoon *Sayonara* had been pushed well east of the cyclonic winds that were smashing the rest of the fleet. Eighty miles northeast of Tasmania, however, Ellison's boat suddenly began to encounter conditions worse than anything it had seen so far. A high-pressure system had developed east of Hobart, and where it brushed against the raging low the seas had taken on the character of an industrial clothes washer. *Sayonara* would surge to the top of a wave, then free-fall three, four, sometimes five seconds before landing in the trough behind it. On deck, this sent men flying up toward the rigging, then slammed them down hard each time the boat landed.

When Phil Kiely, the 44-year-old head of Oracle's Australian operation, shattered his ankle and had to be tucked into a bunk writhing in pain, Ellison began to grow worried. It wasn't just bones breaking that concerned Ellison; it was the boat. At least one of the titanium rope connectors on deck had exploded. The port-side jib winch, made of carbon fiber and titanium, had simply levitated from the deck.

Ellison had just gone belowdecks and climbed into a bunk when he noticed Mark Turner, whom everyone called Tugboat, tapping the carbon-fiber hull inside the bow.

"Tuggsy, whaddya doing?," Ellison asked.

"Trying to make sure the boat's O.K."

Ellison pulled himself out of the bunk and lurched over to where Turner stood. The constant crash of the waves, Turner discovered, had caused a section of the hull to begin delaminating, or wearing through; it was the worst thing that could happen on a carbon-hulled vessel. Turner took out a Magic Marker and drew a circle around the weakened area. There was no telling how long they had before it gave way.

"This is wacko!," Ellison shouted at Mark Rudiger, the serene navigator. "I'm not sure how much more of this the boat can take." Maybe, Ellison suggested, it was time to tack upwind, toward the shelter of the Tasmanian coastline.

"I'm not sure that's the right race decision," Rudiger averred. The move would give *Brindabella* a chance to catch them.

"Well, we can't win the race if the boat sinks," Ellison shot back. The two men talked it over with skipper Chris Dickson, who like Rudiger was reluctant to give *Brindabella* an opening. But in the end it was Ellison's boat—and Ellison's life. "Tack the fucking boat!" he ordered.

11:00 P.M.

By the time Brian Willey began his shift in the Canberra war room at 11, chaos reigned. Fifteen blinking EPIRB beacons pleaded for help on his computer screen, but there was no way to tell who was who, or who needed rescue the most. Almost every yacht in distress had lost its mast, and with it its radio aerials, leaving Willey and his dozen co-workers fumbling in the dark, confused and depressed. At nightfall four Australian Navy Sea King and Seahawk helicopters had flown toward the racecourse, but while the navy helicopters had night-auto-hover capabilities, they had no night-vision equipment. Willey was reduced to gathering scattershot and unreliable reports from the helicopters. The crews were so busy battling hurricane-force winds, normal conversation was all but impossible.

At one point Steve Francis, the 56-year-old former air-traffic controller in overall charge of rescue efforts that Sunday night, was in contact with one of the helicopters when he heard the pilot shout, "Look out for that wave!"

Francis thought the helicopter had gone down. Then the pilot came back on for a moment before shouting again, "Look out for that fucking wave!"

A burst of static came through the phone. Again Francis feared the worst. But the pilot came back on again. "Sorry, mate, had a bit of a problem there," he reported. "Trying to stay between the waves and the clouds, you know."

Precious hours were wasted looking for boats that no longer needed rescue. At one point Francis discovered that several yachts on his search list had been sighted, safely at anchor in the harbor at Eden. "They musta run outta beer," he grimly cracked.

WHEN ROB MATTHEWS emerged from belowdecks to take his turn behind the wheel of *Business Post Naiad*, the Tasmanian boat was a wreck. The splintered mast lay roped to the deck. Below, the contents of the refrigerator had spilled out and were sloshing about in eight inches of water along with shattered plates and cups; the stove had broken free of its mounting and was careening about with every wave. Bruce Guy, the boat's owner, flipped on the pumps, but they jammed with debris within minutes and failed. Reluctantly, the crew had activated an EPIRB and, after rigging a new aerial, had radioed in a request for a helicopter evacuation.

As Matthews took the helm, flying spume sandblasted his face. Phil Skeggs, the easygoing locksmith and the boat's least-experienced sailor, stood beside him in the cockpit, shouting out compass readings, as Matthews attempted to ram the boat through waves he could barely see. At one point the moon broke through the clouds, giving Matthews a view of the enormous waves just as they crashed onto the deck. He decided he liked it better in the dark.

Just past 11, after the moon disappeared, leaving them once more wrapped in darkness, Matthews felt the familiar sensation as they began to creep up the face of what seemed like an especially large wave. Then, suddenly, the boat was on its port side and they were airborne once again, falling down the face of the wave. In midair the boat overturned, landing upside down in the trough. Plunged underwater, tangled in a morass of ropes and broken equipment, Matthews held his breath. He tried to remain calm as he waited for the boat to stabilize, as it had before. When it didn't, he attempted to shed his safety harness so he could swim out from beneath the boat. But he couldn't unfasten the hook. Just as he was running out of breath, a wave tossed the boat to one side, allowing a shaft of air into the cockpit, then slammed the boat down on his head yet again.

Coughing and sputtering, Matthews was driven underwater once more. The cockpit walls jackhammered his head and shoulders. Now, convinced that the boat would not right itself, he struggled again to get out of the safety harness. Finally managing to undo it, he kicked free of the boat and surfaced at the stern, where he grabbed a mass of floating ropes, "hanging on like grim death," as he later put it. There was no sign of Skeggs. "Phil! Phil!" he began shouting.

The scene belowdecks was bedlam. Water began gushing into the cabin from the companionway as the six men, trapped upside down, struggled to find their footing on the ceiling. The only light came from headlamps two of the crew had thought to grab, which now, as they lurched about, filled the cabin with a crazy, strobe-like effect. Bruce Guy and Steve Walker, fearful that the boat was sinking, rushed to clear the companionway of debris, then kicked out two boards that blocked their exit to the sea below. In a minute the water level stabilized as the trapped air prevented more seawater from entering, leaving the men up to their waists in water. Guy began trying to muscle one of the black life rafts out the companionway.

"Bruce, wait," Walker said. "We're not taking on any more water. You're going to get another wave shortly. I reckon it'll flip us back over." Just then, the sound of a waterfall, the next giant wave, filled their ears. "We're goin' over!" someone shouted.

The boat flipped once more, sending everyone in the cabin toppling. As the boat righted itself, seawater began cascading over the cockpit into the cabin. Now Walker was certain they were about to sink. As others leapt by him to wade up on deck, Guy suddenly slumped into the water. Walker grabbed him before he went under. He held his friend's head and watched as his eyes rolled back, then shut. Guy, Walker realized, was having a massive heart attack; before he could do anything, Bruce Guy died in his arms. Walker dragged him to a bunk, where he cradled his head and attempted to clear his mouth, but it was too late.

Meanwhile, in the moments before *Business Post Naiad* righted itself, Rob Matthews had clung to the side of the boat, sitting on the broken mast in neck-deep water. As the waves tore at him, he saw he would need to raise himself onto the keel or risk being sucked into the sea. Exhausted, he was just about to set his feet on the submerged mast when the boat began to right itself. To his dismay, the mast beneath him shot upward, flipping him into the air like a flapjack. Matthews landed with a crunch in the cockpit just as the boat finished rolling over. He looked down and saw Phil Skeggs's motionless body, wrapped in a spaghetti of ropes on the floor of the cockpit. As his crewmates hustled up the companionway and administered CPR, Matthews was too exhausted to do anything but watch. Their efforts were in vain. Skeggs, the gentle lock-smith, had drowned.

About 4:00 A.M.

The orange-canopied life raft holding John Stanley and his four friends from *Winston Churchill* began to disintegrate sometime after three that morning. By then everyone aboard was fighting hypothermia and injuries. An outgoing Sydney attorney, John Gibson—"Gibbo" to his mates—had cut two of his fingers down to the bone trying to man-handle a rope during their rushed exit from *Churchill* 12 hours before. Stanley had broken his ankle and torn a net of ligaments in his hip when a wave had tumbled the raft, wildly throwing the five men together. There was no first-aid kit, nor, aside from the biscuit Stanley had stashed in his jacket, any food.

The real problems had arisen after midnight. An unusually large wave—Stanley could often identify the big ones because they sounded like freight trains—had tossed the raft upside down, leaving all five men up to their necks in the water, their feet resting on the submerged canopy, the bottom of the raft inches above their heads. It was impossible to right the raft from inside. Someone would have to swim out through the sub-merged canopy opening, with no lifeline, and try to pull them upright. Jimmy Lawler, the Australian representative for the American Bureau of Shipping, said it wasn't possible. He couldn't get through the opening wearing a life vest, and wasn't willing to shed his vest.

In 20 minutes they began to run out of air. Stanley found himself gasping for breath. To get air, they agreed Lawler would use his knife to cut a four-inch hole in the bottom of the raft. He did so, and for a time they were actually comfortable. But then it happened: another wave flipped the raft upright again. Suddenly the five men found themselves sitting in a life raft with a constantly growing tear in its bottom. The weight of their bodies gradually ripped apart the underpinnings of the raft. In a half-hour they were forced back into the water, this time cling-ing to the insides of their now doughnut-shaped raft. They tried to maintain their spirits, but it was difficult. Other than Gibson, who kept up a steady patter of jokes, the men were too tired to talk much.

In the darkness before dawn no one heard the black wave that final-ly got them. One moment they were inside the raft, shoulder to shoul-der, breathing hard. The next they were airborne, hurtling down the face of the gigantic unseen wave. Stanley was driven deep beneath the raft, but somehow managed to keep his hold on it. Fighting to the surface, he looked all around and saw nothing but blackness. "Is everyone here?" he shouted.

"Yeah!" he heard a sputtering voice answer to one side. It was Gibson, the only one of the five who had worn a safety harness he had clipped to the raft.

Stanley craned his head, looking for the others. His heart sank: about 300 yards back he could see two of the three men. He was never sure whom he missed: Lawler, John Dean, a Sydney attorney, or Mike Bannister. All three men were gone.

"We can't do anything for them," Stanley said. "It's impossible."

"Just hang on," Gibson said. "For ourselves."

Dawn, Monday

As the eastern horizon reddened around 4:30, the scene at the small airport in the resort town of Merimbula resembled something out of China Beach. At first light 17 aircraft were sent searching for *Winston Churchill.* The second priority, curiously, was finding Glyn Charles, who, in the unlikely event he was still alive, would have been in the water more than 12 hours.

Around six, David Dutton, a paramedic aboard one of the SouthCare helicopters flying out of Canberra, spotted a dismasted yacht southeast of Eden. Below him, *Midnight Special,* a 40-foot Queensland boat, was rolling violently. The boat had taken on the solemn air of a floating hospital. The crew, nine longtime friends who sailed out of the Mooloolaba Yacht Club, near the resort city of Brisbane, were older men, most in their 50s, with a variety of occupations and an even wider range of injuries. Ian Griffiths, a lawyer, had a broken leg and crushed cartilage in his back. Neil Dickson, a veteran ocean sailor who at 49 was the youngest crew member, had hit his head against the cabin ceiling during a rollover, which had knocked him momentarily unconscious and left him with a concussion. Peter Carter had crushed vertebrae in his lower back. The others had collected an assortment of cracked ribs and gashed foreheads.

On Sunday the crew had surprised themselves by surfing into Bass Strait in 18th place. Had they not ranked so high, Roger Barnett, the yacht club's commodore, felt, they might have headed back earlier. As it was, *Midnight Special* had plunged south through the mountainous waves until injuries incapacitated much of the crew. Around three P.M. the five men who jointly owned the boat had gathered belowdecks and engaged in a lively debate about whether to forge on. Dickson recalls that in the middle of this discussion, a gigantic wave struck the boat, flinging Griffiths across the cabin, breaking his leg and a large part of the ship's cupboard. That ended the debate. *Sword of Orion*'s three-o'clock report of 75-knot winds ahead of them in Bass Strait silenced any doubters.

A little after three the crew started the engine and began plowing back the 40 miles northwest toward Gabo Island. Conditions worsened as the boat fought heavy seas. Twice *Midnight Special* was slammed on its side, tossing the crew belowdecks, breaking noses and cracking ribs. Then, later that night, a giant wave crashed out of the darkness directly into the cockpit, rolling the three-year-old boat through a 360-degree arc. Windows smashed everywhere, and as water began pouring into the crushed cabin below, large cracks began to appear in the deck. Frantically, Neil Dickson began stuffing sleeping bags into the widening cracks in a vain attempt to maintain the integrity of the hull.

When waves tore the sleeping bags out, the crew resorted to cramming spinnaker sails into the openings. The sails did the trick, but their trailing ropes fouled the boat's propeller, leaving *Midnight Special* dead in the water. The radios were destroyed, and an EPIRB was activated. As red flares from other boats lit the sky all around them, those who could spent the rest of the night bailing.

At dawn the crew spotted a P3C Orion flying overhead; it wagged its wings, buoying their spirits. Not long after, Dutton's chopper arrived, and he motioned for crew members to jump into the waves and begin swimming toward the dangling rescue strop. It was decided that David Leslie should go first. He was their doctor—well, a dermatologist—and could brief the rescuers on their injuries. Leslie plunged into the sea, swam toward Dutton, and slipped his upper body into the strop. Trevor McDonough, a 60-year-old bricklayer, and Bill Butler, a nursery owner, stood on deck and watched as Leslie was slowly lifted up toward the helicopter. The other six crew members stood safely belowdecks, at the bottom of the companionway, swapping smiles. "We're outta here!" someone said joyfully.

No one saw the wave. It hit without warning and, as Dutton and the helicopter crew looked on helplessly, rolled the boat upside down. The first thing Dickson knew, he was on his hands and knees in the pitch-dark cabin with water inching up his thighs. This time Dickson wanted no part of any of his partners' debate; he just wanted out. Without a word he plunged headfirst into the flooded companionway. The exit was blocked by boards and debris, but he found an opening about two feet in diameter and managed to get his shoulders, then his waist through and into the swirling ocean outside. But then, as he fought to get his thighs through the hole, he became stuck. A rope had looped around his mid-section and was holding him tight against the boat. Dickson frantically kicked his legs, trying to get loose.

Trapped beneath the boat, both McDonough and Butler fought to free themselves from entangling ropes; neither was able to do so. In fact, all three men—Dickson, McDonough, and Butler—were as good as dead. And then, with a vicious jerk, the boat swung around and righted itself. After several moments spent gasping for breath Dickson ripped himself free and charged up onto the deck, where he was met by this seriocomic image: Butler standing perfectly upright, mummylike, still trapped in ropes. McDonough lay in the cockpit, seawater streaming from his nose.

As the three men recovered, they were met by a sight that left no one laughing: Dutton's helicopter, low on fuel, was forced to head for land. As the helicopter flew off, Dickson and his crewmates could do nothing but watch, dumbfounded. The boat beneath was sinking slowly by the stern, and every wave threatened to roll it over once more. It took another unnerving half-hour before a second helicopter finally rescued the men on *Midnight Special*.

ALL DOWN THE east coast of New South Wales and out past Gabo Island, the rescues continued in the first hours after dawn. The remaining sailors aboard *Sword of Orion* scrambled aboard a hovering Seahawk, while a medevac out of Canberra winched the seven survivors off *Business Post Naiad*, leaving the bodies of Phil Skeggs and Bruce Guy to be picked up later. *B-52* struggled under its own power into Eden harbor just after lunchtime. In the hour before dawn the yacht's port-side windows had imploded, sending gushers of seawater below; the crew had somehow managed to nail wooden planks over the windows and had spent the rest of the morning bailing with buckets. Tony Mowbray's *Solo Globe Challenge* would be one of the last to reach port, limping into Eden on Wednesday morning.

Late Monday afternoon the lifeboat carrying Richard Winning and three other survivors from *Winston Churchill* was spotted, and everyone was winched aboard a waiting helicopter. Like those aboard *Churchill's*. other raft, Winning's group had capsized twice during the night. Unlike the occupants of the other raft, however, Winning had bravely swum outside and forcibly righted the rubber inflatable, which had then survived the night intact.

9:00 P.M.

Night began to fall with no sign of *Churchill's* second life raft. At the rescue center in Canberra, hope was dwindling that the men would be found. At Merimbula the civilian aircraft—those without any night-rescue capabilities—began landing, one by one. None had seen anything that looked remotely like a life raft. Then, just after nine, a P3C Orion on its way back to Merimbula saw a light flashing in the darkening ocean below. Descending to 500 feet, the pilot spied two men clinging to a shredded orange life raft. It was John Stanley and "Gibbo" Gibson, still alive after 28 hours in the water.

"Gibbo!," Stanley rasped, swinging a handheld strobe. "I think they've seen us!"

Within minutes, during which the sun set, Lieutenant Commander Rick Neville had his navy Seahawk hovering 70 feet above Stanley and Gibson. Petty Officer Shane Pashley winched down a wire into the waves below and, as Neville fought to maintain position in the gusting winds, managed to get a rescue strop around Gibson. As the two men were lifted skyward a terrific gust blew the Seahawk sideways, dumping the pair back into the waves. Neville swung the chopper around once more, and this time the two waterlogged men were successfully winched aboard.

It was too much for Neville. His Radalt auto-hover system was being overtaxed by the winds, and he was unwilling to send Pashley back into the ocean. Stanley, he decided, would have to make it into the rescue strop on his own. As Neville maneuvered the Seahawk back over the raft, Pashley dangled the strop down into the sea, and Stanley somehow grabbed it and hoisted his upper body into it. The winch lifted him into the air, but when he was 20 feet above the waves, Stanley felt a weight around his ankles and realized, to his dismay, that he was still hooked to his life raft, which was sagging in midair below him. Reluctantly he shrugged himself out of the strop and dropped like a stone back into the sea, where he managed to unhook the raft. Once again the strop was dangled to him, and once again he got into it. This time everything worked. After more than a day in the ocean, Stanley and Gibson were on their way home.

8:00 A.M., Tuesday

As *Sayonara* tacked the last mile up the Derwent River toward the Hobart docks, a small launch with a bagpiper aboard swung alongside. It was the most stunning sunrise Ellison had ever seen, splashes of rose and pink and five different hues of blue, and as the pipes played a mournful tune, the enormity of what the fleet had endured hit all 23 men aboard the winning yacht. *Sayonara*'s sideband radio had shorted out, and it hadn't been until late Monday afternoon that the crew learned of the tragedies in their wake. As they reached the dock and piled out to hug their loved ones, Ellison was overwhelmed. "It was an incredible moment of clarity, the beauty and fragility of life, the preciousness of it all; that's when people appreciated what we had been through," he recalls. "Having said that, if I live to be a thousand years old, I'll never do it again. Never."

Amid all-too-predictable recriminations, Hugo van Kretschmar, commodore of the Cruising Yacht Club of Australia, stoutly defended the club's decision to continue the race despite warnings of bad weather. Even as he announced an internal investigation, van Kretschmar pointed out, correctly, that the decision whether to race is traditionally left up to the skipper of each boat. Yachtclub officials, after all, had the same forecasts that every skipper had. As a result, few of the sailors who survived the race were willing to attack the organizers. One exception was Peter Joubert of *Kingurra*, who emerged from several weeks in the hospital sharply critical of race management. "The race organizers weren't properly in touch with what was going on out there—they just didn't know enough." Joubert says. "It's only a yacht race. It's not a race to the death!" Outside Australia, the judgment was just as harsh. "They should have waited; there is ample precedent for waiting," notes Gary Jobson, the ESPN sailing analyst. "But race officials were under a lot of pressure. Live TV, all these people, a major holiday."

Three days after *Sayonara* crossed the finish line more than 5,000 people gathered on Hobart's Constitution Dock for a memorial service for the six men who died in the race. The funerals of Bruce Guy, Phil Skeggs, James Lawler, and Mike Bannister were to follow shortly; the bodies of John Dean and Glyn Charles have never been found. "We will miss you always; we will remember you always; we will learn from the tragic circumstances of your passing," van Kretschmar said as the muted bells of St. David's Cathedral rang out. "May the everlasting voyage you have now embarked on be blessed with calm seas and gentle breezes. May you never have to reef or change a headsail in the night. May your bunk always be warm and dry."

from caldo largo

EARL THOMPSON

JOHNNY HAND, THE randy gringo of Earl Thompson's *Caldo*

Largo (1976), trolls the waters of the Gulf of Mexico looking for

shrimp, women, and freedom in the years of Fidel Castro's struggle for

power. When it looks like a succession of poor runs will end in the loss

of his boat, Hand agrees to smuggle guns into Castro's Cuba. At this

point in the novel, Thompson sends his "noble savage" on a trial fish-

ing expedition that turns into a naughty nautical equivalent of Erica

Jong's "zipless fuck"—a steamy, no-holds-barred erotic encounter

between strangers in the night.

back in the water, the boat looked so clean, bright, new, Eli went and got a camera and we took pictures. She would not look that fine again for a long time.

We drank some cold beer, snapped the pictures, and had a nice time. Chelo was reluctant to loosen up, enjoy herself. Then I gave her one of the flat-top, old-fashioned workingman's caps we all wore—like the golf caps Ben Hogan used to wear. She broke into a smile so wide and white it threatened the sun. She posed on the bow. She waved from the pilothouse door.

She was one of us.

The other captains kidded us a little, but finally, all I had to do was remind them she was Ezequiel Cavazos' daughter and they would sort of understand.

I did not think she would want the job after the first trip. Yet she had worked as well and honestly as any man I had ever known. With her sister in jail for murder, her family needed the money.

THE FIRST NIGHT out it began to blow some. There was some rain. Chelo got seasick. She fought it, then gave way and had to be put in a bunk and given some Dramamine.

We teased her a bit.

By the third day she was all right: rocky, wan, but OK.

She came into the pilothouse looking skinnier than ever. There were dark circles around her black eyes.

"I am sorry. You do not have to pay me for those days," she said. "I am well now. I will be OK."

"Everyone gets sick sometime. I still get a little upset once in a while," I told her.

"I am ashamed."

"Forget it."

"Listen, Chelo," Eli said, "your old man always brought some good weed with him to smoke. Grew it himself. You don't happen to have any of that with you?"

"*Ai*, no. . . . But if you want some, next time I can bring it."

"That would be a beautiful thing for you to do," he assured her. "Wonderful for seasickness."

"¿*Si?*"

"Ah, very much sí!" he said.

"OK. If you want some."

"We should have thought about that before," Eli charged me.

He rolled a joint of what he had on hand and passed it to us. Chelo did not smoke.

"I think I would like to take a bath," she said.

"There's a shower in the head, or you can use the hose on the fantail," I told her.

"The hose is better," Eli said. "We use the hose."

"Then I will make lunch," she said.

When she had gone, Eli said, "She is a nice girl."

"Yow, I like her."

"You think she will be all right?"

"Sure. I think so. I would attend a war with her, if I had to go," I had decided.

"Ah, you are so *romántico*, Johnny."

We heard the hose going on the fantail. We looked at each other. The idea of a slender naked young woman taking a shower back there was a funny feeling.

Did fish pop up out of the sea for a peek? Were we trailing a fishy parade of voyeurs?

Eli and I looked at each other. He grinned and waggled his eyebrows as if to ask which of us was going to wander back there. I grinned back. Neither of us moved. He passed me the joint. I took a smoke and passed it back. We grinned some more. Neither of us was going back there.

"Son of a bitch," he said, grinning.

"Yow."

"We're some kind of a shrimp boat."

"Some kind of crazy."

Soon there was singing in the galley and the smell of food being prepared.

"You sing almost as good as your father!" I called back to her.

She laughed, for she knew her father sang like a sick cat with a sinus condition.

When I went back to the galley, the table was set with red paper napkins by the plates and some yellow flowers in a bowl in the center.

"Where the hell did you get flowers?"

"I brought some. I put them in the refrigerator. Is that OK?"

"Hell, yes."

We put on the automatic pilot so we could all eat together. We laughed and joked. The sun streamed in the windows. The food was good.

"If you head shrimp like you cook, *chica*, we are going to have a good trip," Eli told her, rubbing his belly which was beginning to make him look more like an ex-lineman than a fullback.

"When they hear about this, there is going to be girls on all the boats," Eli vowed.

There were women on other boats. Nearly everyone took his wife and kids with him now and then. A lot of shrimpers started out on their father's boats when they were ten of so. One guy worked his boat with his wife and two daughters. The girls never went to school. They seemed none the worse for that.

If I had a good, intelligent woman and we had a kid, I could see going like that. We could teach him-her as much as, or more than, some half-assed school. I had books. I had seen some of the world. Most of what you learned in school was calculated to please the pushers of some immediate concept, was designed to train you how to work for some other son of a bitch all your life. I didn't think I wanted a kid of mine to do that. Better they should be around people like Chelo's late father, Ezequiel, awhile—crazy? I don't know. I don't think so. The old man was full of wisdom and a way of seeing behind such modern complexities as an insurance policy to essential mysteries that made your damned bones itch, while at the same time imparting a kind of peace, a sense that beyond the bullshit we were alone, or as a species, yet all right. All right.

I did not envy the doctors and scholars, scientists and politicians. Shit, with all their education they couldn't run the world any better than if they had left it alone; they could not run their own lives any better for all they said they understood than Chelo's sister Encanta who had killed her married-deputy lover because he said he would leave his wife and marry her, then, when she got pregnant, gave her five bills or something and told her to go get rid of the kid. I liked her way *better*. It was clean and passionate. I will never forget, the most beautiful young woman I have ever seen standing in her lover's front yard, the pistol in her hand, waiting for the cops to come take her away. No tears in *her* eyes.

What about the wife she widowed?

What about her? She will survive or she won't. She will. She will marry someone else. She will live. How does all the popular psychology make us better? I read. The people who are so hooked on psychology as a way to live better aren't any happier than anyone else. They just have a new, more boring way of talking about things. They take all the surprise and wonder out of things. They always think it terrible that an individual will take a gun and blast the life from some bastard that has done that person a mighty wrong, really crapped on their love, but they will rationalize or ignore that their society makes war for the wrong reasons against the wrong people most of the time. They are willing to profit from businesses that are as crooked as a dog's hind leg and support a government that goes along with it.

Maybe psychology is the intellectual's insurance policy, I thought.

Some things just can't be negotiated, fixed up.

Schools seem to have lost sight of what education is about—lost the wonder of delving into mysteries in the race to get answers. Almost all school was about, as far as I could see, was how to get into a position to skin some other chump for a living, get ahead of someone else. So the kids bored themselves silly or cheated if they cared about passing. What the hell is the point of living like that?

"You look troubled, Captain," Chelo said.

She had come into the pilothouse and had been sitting behind me over against the windows.

"Oh . . . I didn't know you were there. I was just thinking about things."

"What things?"

I told her my theories on education.

"I like your ideas," she said.

After a while she said, "I was afraid of you. I did not know what kind of man you are. My father tells me you have a good character and good spirit. He likes you. But I was a little afraid."

"Yow? Well, he told me the same thing about you. *He* said he was a little afraid of you."

"Are you afraid also?"

"A little."

She smiled.

"Good. We are even."

I looked back at her. You could see her father's bones in her face. She would look strong and beautiful when she was an old woman, or she would look like a witch.

"Come here. I will show you how to steer."

She got between me and the wheel. She smelled nice, of a clean fragrant soap, sunshine, the sea. I showed her what the gauges were about, the throttle, tachometer, explained about the torque curve of an engine. Then, I showed her how to hold a course.

I left her on the wheel and went to sit against the windows to smoke. I studied her. We did not talk. I thought of her back on the fantail taking a shower, washing herself with soap, the suds running off her lithe body under the hose. I thought of Lupe Contreras. I shook the thoughts away and went outside.

Eli and I began to rig for fishing that night.

"The boat is better than new now," he observed.

"She's good. With her bottom all clean and fresh we have picked up a couple of knots. We'll save some fuel."

"There ought to be a way to keep her bottom clean. Someone ought to invent something," he said.

"Maybe they have. Some copper company has built some copper-bottomed trawlers that don't have to be hauled out but once every three years or something like that. I read about it. Very modern boats. Trying them out in the Indian Ocean, I think."

"That's good!"

"Yow. But then you think: when they make such improvements, it makes the boat cost so much no one man can own one. Soon it will be all big companies and everyone will be hired just like in a factory. Will that make our lives any better? Or shrimp cost less to eat?"

"Don't ask me, man."

"Well, maybe a man can still make enough to live OK for a while."

"You ever think what you are going to do when you quit shrimpin?"

"Not really. I don't know. I expect to keep at it until I'm pretty old. Then it doesn't matter much. Get some little place where I can grow most of what I need to eat, watch the sun come up and go down, drive into town to see some good ole boy or another. Just be like everyone else, I guess. I never wanted a lot."

"You have no ambition."

"What the fuck is wrong with *that* ambition?"

"You like your life!" Eli seemed surprised.

I thought about it for a second. "Yow . . . I like my life." It was the first time I had thought about it like that. I liked it—my life.

The try net looked promising. We put over the big trawls to go on the drag.

The sea around the boat was obsidian. I had read that in a book and liked the word. It was like cruising over the surface of an enormous glass sculpture. If you did not know it was water, you would think you might walk on it. Long, low, glassy black swells slid along in a nearly moonless night. The kind of night for good shrimping.

I went into the pilothouse.

I put my arm around Chelo's shoulders and asked, "How do you like it so far?"

"I like it."

Then she turned to look up at me. Her face was close. I shivered involuntarily and let go of her.

"Someone just walked on your grave," she said gently.

"I wonder where it is."

The bag felt very heavy coming up. It looked as if we had found shrimp. A lot of shrimp.

A moonless night is better to fish by. A full moon will sometimes keep the shrimp from coming out of the mud. I wondered at this, for they were so far down, how could moonlight filter through to their beds? But it was a fact.

Chelo was excited as the cable came up streaming water from the weight it held, then the chain to which the doors were fastened. The winch whined. The bag broke the surface.

It was mostly full of an eight- or ten-foot shark twisted in the net, and angry, its big maw full of jagged white teeth slashing at a big hole it had sawed in the cord, its goddamned evil head hanging out of the hole. Shrimp and fish flew in all directions.

"*¡Chinga tu madre! ¡Mira! ¡Mira!*" Eli yelled.

I had already *mira-ed* and was going for my shark gun.

It was an Army surplus twelve-gauge Winchester pump riot gun, loaded with slugs.

The shark was held in the net only by its hind half's being twisted in it. It was thrashing wildly, swinging the net back and forth across the deck. You could see way the hell down its throat. You could see yourself going in there a twenty-pound chunk of you at a time.

I shoved Chelo back against the pilothouse. She stood transfixed and frightened by the monster held aloft by bits of cord which it was fast snapping into string.

I got up close to where it hung just above the deck, took aim on its skull. They allegedly have a brain in there. I pumped two slugs into the shark. The first made it lurch almost free of the net. I put in a third, and it hung limp in the great hole it had torn in our net. That was a nearly new net, too. I was mad then. Before I had been scared. I also did not think the shark was dead. I put in another shot up close, and its right eye popped out.

I reloaded the gun.

"Stay back!" I warned.

"OK."

I yanked the cord, spilling the bag onto the deck.

The fucker twitched and swiveled on its belly and made a snapping lunge at nothing. I did not like seeing its empty eye socket. It lunged back with a swipe of its head and bit into wood of the boat's rail. I pumped two more slugs into it. Chelo was holding her ears at the noise of the gun.

I got a gaff and poked at the shark until I was sure it was really dead. Even then we were careful. They can come alive after goddamn hours sometimes.

"I want to see what is in its belly," Eli cried, coming up with the knife he wore on his belt.

"What are you going to do?" the girl demanded.

"Open it up," Eli said.

He plunged his knife into the white underbelly and sliced the beast open.

"Whew! He stinks," the girl observed.

"It is a girl," Eli explained in Spanish. "See, she has two sexual organs."

"¿Por qué dos?" she wondered.

"Double her pleasure," he said in English. "Who knows? God is unfair." He continued in Spanish: "You would not like to see sharks make love. It is very cruel. The male will get a female by the neck in his teeth and leave her missing a big bite of herself when he is finished."

"The male, he has two organs as well?" she asked in Spanish.

"Sure. I think so. You think he just carries a spare?"

"They are horrible, but they are not ugly."

"You are crazy."

"Look!" He spilled out the contents of the shark's stomach. "Sometimes you can find valuable things inside."

There were some fish in there, a yellow sou'wester fisherman's hat, a piece of a cork life ring, and a 1954 North Carolina license tag.

"Maybe she ate the whole car except for this," Eli told the girl solemnly.

"No?"

"*¡Si!* But maybe just a Volkswagen. She is not so huge a shark. She is not so small either. This is a pretty good hat. You want it?"

"It stinks."

"We will keep the hat. We can wash it."

"You want the liver?" Eli asked me.

"No. Let's get rid of the thing."

It was a sand tiger shark. The Mexicans called them "ragged-tooth," for their teeth were long and less even than other sharks. In Australia, they call this shark gray nurse. They say it is not a man-eater, that it prefers fish. But it is this shark whose young are cannibals in the womb. It births live young, one from each of its wombs. The two it births have eaten all their siblings before they have seen the light of day.

Eli slit open a womb. The shark was pregnant, and one of its intended young bit his hand before he knew what was happening. He shook the tiny prematurely born shark off onto the deck where it leaped around, snapping at anything. Very mad little shark.

Eli showed us the tiny crescent of where the baby had got him in the hand.

Tell *him* the sand tiger is not a man-eater. They may prefer fish, but that does not mean they are religious about it.

He sucked the blood off his wound and stomped the baby to death with his heel.

Chelo cried, "*No!*"

"There are enough sharks in the world," I told her.

We had to haul the mother shark's carcass over the side with the winch.

We watched as other sharks following the boat darted through the darkness and struck their sister in a frenzy that was soon gone from our sight below the surface of the water.

The girl watched passively, interested, noncommittal. I again thought of Rivera's young Indian princess carrying a human leg in a basket as from the market.

We rigged another net and put it over before cleaning up the deck. There were only a few shrimp to head and pack away, some fish for the pot. We hosed down the deck.

There were a couple of shark's teeth in the wood where it had bit the boat. I pried them loose and gave them to Chelo.

"They are beautiful," she said. "I will make a little hole and put one on my chain."

She was a lot like her father.

I examined the torn net. There was one hole over six feet around and another almost as large. It was going to take a lot of mending. A new net cost about four hundred dollars. That was our best net.

THE SHRIMP HAD disappeared. There wasn't enough in the next two hauls to warrant separating them from the trash. Shrimp are like that. Maybe there was going to be a storm, though no weather report spoke of a storm. Maybe something down there was bothering them, though I could see nothing on the fish finder.

"They have just gone, *compadre*," Eli said.

"They burrow into the mud sometimes," I explained to Chelo. "Often it means there is going to be a storm."

I checked the weather frequencies again, both U.S. and Mexican. There were no storm warnings of any kind.

"Still, I think we will run in and lay out the rest of the night in the Boca Jesús María," I told Eli.

"OK."

"How do the shrimp know?" the girl wondered.

"I don't know. Your father says they are very old things. Maybe they feel something in the mud. It is a mystery. I know times when I haven't gone in and gotten pretty wet outnumber the times I have gone in and laid out some rough weather. Before a hurricane they turn apoplectic, get all red and bug-eyed. True."

I showed her the island on the chart of the Mexican coast where we were headed and how to find the course to get us there. She was sleepy but interested.

"It isn't much fun. I warned you," I told her when she could no longer keep from yawning.

"I am sorry. My clock has not gotten used to being up all night and sleeping in the daytime. I will be all right."

"Go back and sleep."

"No. I will work on the torn net."

A FREAK LOCAL storm broke the next morning as we lay snug behind the island in the Boca Jesús María. Winds were sixty, seventy miles an hour. We listened on the radio all day to other boats in trouble. Someone went onto the rocks far from where we were. We heard his May Day for a while, then nothing. It was the boat of a man Eli and I knew. He had a small boat. He shrimped with his twelve-year-old son and another man. Eli crossed himself and prayed for their lives.

We were snug. We had two anchors out and lay sheltered by the steep side of the long, narrow island. There was a pot of Chelo's good *caldo largo* on the stove. It was good to be in there safe with the wind howling over the top of the island, the rain coming almost vertically against our glass. We rocked a bit, but nothing to worry about.

We sat in the cabin mending the torn net, drinking strong black coffee, smoking, talking very little, listening to the rain.

Late in the afternoon a long white schooner made it into us, both masts broken, lines and sails lashed every damned way on her sleek teak decks.

We all went out and took lines so she could anchor and tie up alongside us.

Chelo wore the hat we had taken from the belly of the shark now. Eli had soaked and scrubbed it. She had turned up the cuffs of her foul-weather jacket a couple of times and looked lost inside it, and her father's boots were too big, but she handled the lines pretty damned well for having had no experience. She never stood back. She always pitched right in to try to do her share.

They were rich people, but they were pretty good with that big boat. The skipper was a man in his forties, handsome, tan, with a short black beard. He spoke with a New England accent. We invited him and his party aboard.

He said his name was Matthew. There were two other men and three pretty women and a hired crewman, a blond college boy.

"It's a girl!" one of the women said with surprise when Chelo doffed her slicker and hat and shook out her short black hair.

Chelo gave them soup and some bread.

The skipper sent the blond over, and he came back with some good brandy—the best I had ever tasted.

He told us of their difficulties.

"It just came up so quick. We were carrying a lot of sail. Suddenly the wind went up to about seventy, and there was a wave behind us about fifty feet high."

"I thought we were goners," one of the other men said.

"It broke over us and snapped both sticks."

"You should have heard it down below!" one of the women said. "I thought it was the end of the world."

She was a pretty, studiously thin woman, the kind you see in magazines, or as close to that as she could come. She didn't have an ass at all, like a board, like a man. But her hands were very long and thin with Dragon Lady nails and four diamond rings on her brown fingers.

Matthew's wife was also pretty, but quiet and strong. She looked at you the way he did, as if measuring you inside. She went to help Chelo right away and spoke to her as you would speak to anyone.

The other woman was younger, had dark-red hair; she sat back and looked at you in a different, half-amused, measuring way. She put her tongue in her glass, just touching the brandy with the tip of it and caught me watching her over the rim. She stopped and held her tongue there for a second, then circled the rim of the little glass with it slowly, looking right into my eyes.

I looked at her husband. I looked back, and she opened her eyes wide and cocked her head slightly as if asking a question.

She wore white slacks that fit her as snugly as pants can fit. Looking over her glass she sat with her legs up so I could see the big bulge of her twat framed by the soft bulges of her thighs and bottom. It lay in there like a peach.

I looked at her husband again. He was the handsomest man I have ever seen in person. Tall, over six feet, with a great nose on a strong face, solid chin, wavy dark hair, gray at the temples.

His wife had to be just fooling around. A prickteaser.

His business was tax shelters. What I understood about it amounted to you paying him like five thousand dollars to save yourself fifteen thousand in taxes. Or something like that. It all sounded unreal to me. You paid money, good money, to take a loss.

All the time his wife was looking over the glass and fooling with it with her tongue.

The other man, short and heavy, married to the tall woman, was an attorney. Matthew was also an attorney.

He said they were going down to Yucatán, then on to the Caribbean.

The tall woman was interested in archaeology, had a degree in it, but she did not work at it except as a hobby.

"How's the fishing?" Matthew asked.

I told him about the shark.

The sexy one, whose name was Lee, got interested.

"I think they are gorgeous things!" she said. "They don't take any shit from anybody. So powerful and sleek. They are like jet planes."

"Well, this one ate up most of my best net," I went on. "A pregnant female."

"How can you tell?"

I explained about the peculiarities of the sand tiger shark.

"Two cocks!" she exclaimed.

"Yow."

"Wow! Are they big? You said it was how big a shark?"

"About eight feet or so, I guess. It was a real shark."

"Two? They must be *hung*. I would like to see a couple of big sharks screw," she said.

No one seemed to think what she said was strange.

"Lee is interested in seeing anything screw," the tall woman said.

"There is nothing more basic in the world, more beautiful . . . don't you agree?"

The other woman said nothing.

"Don't you agree, Captain?" she asked me.

"Well, the way sharks I have seen do it, it is pretty basic, but not so beautiful."

I told them about how the male gets his teeth into the female during mating.

"Fucking shark wouldn't be into it five minutes with Lee, right, honey?" the tall woman's husband teased. "If there was anyone losing some skin, it would be the poor shark."

"So I'm a little noisy and like to fuck a lot . . . I'd bite *you* that's for sure, just to see if you were alive."

I looked at Chelo where she sat in corner, sipping her brandy, working at something in her hand with the awl end of her father's old knife.

"This your boat?" Matthew asked.

"More or less. The bank owns the major piece. Eli has a bit, but the papers are in my name."

"You're pretty young, aren't you?"

"There are younger running their own boats."

Lee had gotten up and slipped around the cabin, examined things. She noticed my books in the rack I had made for them.

"Hey! You read these?" she asked.

"Yes."

"Christ, there's a Shakespeare here, Plato's *Republic, Lives!* You go to college?"

"No. Never did. I like to read."

"Hell! I just thought you were a pretty face." She sounded disappointed.

"You are blushing, *compadre*," Eli said.

"Moreover, my dear," the tall woman said, laying her warm, beautiful fingers on my arm lightly, "you have probably just lost the chance for the lay of your long life. Lee is on a noble savage kick at the moment."

"Hey! My people were noble savages," Eli offered.

"Were they?" the tall woman arched.

"I can open a beer bottle with my teeth." He hung in there.

"Really? Is there a lot of call for that?"

"No. It is something I perfected at Texas University."
He showed her his teeth.

"Such nice even teeth too. You must have very strong mandibles."

"Those, too. But I am like the iguana, when I take a bite of you, I don't let go until the sun goes down."

"You hear this, Lee. Maybe this one is the one for you. He bites, too."
She looked Eli over. He sat up straight and threw out his chest and smiled.

"I don't like his number," Lee said, referring to his faded white and orange football jersey. "I never liked football players. I went with one once. He turned out to be queer. He just didn't know it."

"But you convinced him, right, darling?"

"He is probably happier."

Lee's husband kept crossing and recrossing his legs, looking as if he would say something, but then did not.

"What inspired you to read?" the tall woman's husband asked.

"I just always did. You know, you learn to read. Then, I would read a book and it would talk about something I didn't know or mention another book, and I would try to find out what they were talking about or pick up the other book when I ran across it. I live on the boat. I've never had a TV. I don't like TV much. Maybe when they get some good cheap color sets, it will be OK. But I read in color, I can see things better in a book than I can in what there is on TV. There are pictures in the words in books you can't get on TV or in the movies. I just read."

"I think it is wonderful," Matthew's wife said.

I didn't see it as wonderful. I began to feel a bit annoyed that they were making so much over the fact that a man who happened to run a shrimp boat read a couple of books.

Their bottle was gone, and we had all started on our Fundador.

"Well, I envy you," the tall woman's husband said. "I don't have time to read as much as I would like. Too busy making money to keep my kids in their damned schools, paying off a castle of a house we don't need, paying for club memberships to keep us in shape, when a good day's work would do us a lot better. I envy you, Captain." He lifted his glass to me.

"Well, I don't know. I have always wondered what it would be like to be able to just go anywhere you wanted on a great sailing boat like that. I think I could take it for a while," I said.

"A yacht is a hole in the ocean into which you pour money," Lee's husband assured me.

"I know a bit about *that*," I promised him.

"Come over for breakfast in the morning and I'll show you around, if you like," Matthew offered.

"Thanks. I would enjoy seeing what a boat like that is like below."

"You have never been on such a boat?" Lee asked.

"No." I thought. "No, I've never been on anything you would call a yacht."

She had moved close. She laid her hand along my cheek. The palm felt fleshy and warm, moist.

"Come over now and I will give you the grand tour."

"Well, it looks as if it is time for me and my loving wife to call it an evening," her husband said, getting to his feet, finishing his drink. He was not angry, just weary. "Thank you for your hospitality, Captain. That soup is marvelous!" he turned to Chelo.

"Yes!" Matthew's wife exclaimed. "Will you give me the recipe, dear?" she asked Chelo.

"There is no recipe," she said.

"Really? But could you tell me what you put into it?"

"If you like."

"Come on, it's time for all of us to go," Matthew said.

"Perhaps you will tell me tomorrow."

"OK," Chelo said.

"Come on, Lee," her husband said, already at the door.

She bent down and kissed me fully on the lips, opening her mouth a bit, enough to quickly slip me the tip of her tongue. There was an electrical shock through me, then she was gone, waving cheerfully to all.

"Good night! Good night all."

But for a moment she caught my eyes and searched them of their surprise and wonder.

"Don't take it seriously," the tall woman whispered as she brushed past me, again touching my arm reassuringly, "A few days ago it was a country-western singer in a horrible little place in Galveston who had the most atrocious nasal twang." She imitated a snatch of the song the fellow had sung. "Next week it will be a Mexican beach boy or *something*. She likes to flirt a lot."

"Good night," I told her.

When they had gone, Chelo asked, "Why does that woman act like a whore?"

"I don't know," I said.

"Maybe she thinks she is being free, like a man," Chelo said. "She wants to be a whore or a man. That is not being a woman. She has a beautiful husband, much money, she does not have to work or anything. It is stupid."

"Maybe her husband is no good for her for sex," Eli pondered.

"I don't think so. He looks OK to me," Chelo said. "She is screwed up."

We cleaned up the things.

Eli went to sleep in the pilothouse. Chelo climbed into her upper bunk and drew the curtain. I lay down in the lower bunk in my clothes.

The sound of the rain was good to hear on the boat. It came in gusts, rattling against the boat; then it would slacken and gust again. It should have made me sleepy, but I could not sleep.

I could hear the voices of the people on the yacht tied up to us. I heard the tall woman laugh. I heard a murmur in the cabin close to where I lay. I was certain it was Lee and her husband. I heard her laugh briefly, more a short burst, a snort of laughter. Then it was still. I knew they were fucking. I don't know how, I just knew. She cried out once, I was sure of it.

I got up and put on my slicker, turned the collar up, and went out on deck to smoke.

The rain had slackened. You could see the moon breaking through the clouds, which were racing away north. The schooner had a beautiful shape, sweeping back to the low teak doghouse. I looked back up to the bow. When I looked back to the stern of the yacht, someone had come out onto deck. I could see the glow of a cigarette.

I walked back. Our sides were much higher than the yacht's. I was looking down onto the deck. I thought it might be Matthew.

"Rain's stopping," I said. "Be a nice day tomorrow."

"Hi."

It was Lee, barefoot, in a yellow foul-weather jacket much too large for her.

"It's become warm." She put her open palm up to the rain. "Soft."

"Can't sleep?"

"Hunh-unh."

She threw the coat back off her shoulders and arched her body up to the soft rain. She was naked under the coat. She threw back her face and washed her belly and breasts with the rain. She was a very beautiful woman, more so naked than she had been clothed. Rounded and sleek and tan.

I found I had put my hand on my cock, was holding it tight.

She came to the rail and stretched up both her arms. I reached down and felt her bare arms snake up and grip my biceps. I lifted her up and onto my boat. She folded herself into my arms and her wet, open mouth made the rain seem chill again by comparison.

She placed one of my hands on her full, soft breast, and as soon as I touched the nipple, she jerked and ground her pelvis against me and moaned. Her small soft hand clawed at my fly, belt, got my pants open and searched for my cock. When she found it, she said, "Umm. Oh. *I want you.*"

I thought where to lay her down.

She dropped on her knees on the deck and got my jeans down and over my feet. Giving a small cry, she took my cock and popped it into her mouth, sucking and stroking me back to my asshole. It felt as if she were trying to bring my come forth into her mouth. I pried her loose before that and got between her legs on the deck.

She kissed me as if she would tear my tongue out.

"Fuck me! Fuck me! Oh, fuck me!" she breathed into my mouth. "Oh, yes! Fuck me hard! Fuck me hard!"

Her back and ass were banging against the deck. I banged her as if I were trying to hurt her and she asked for more, harder. I was breathing like a long-distance runner when she began to come. She tossed her head back and forth, started to scream the way I had heard her scream earlier. I clamped my right hand over her mouth, fucked her harder yet, let up a bit, then came, too. She bit my palm. Her eyes looked wild as I came and came in her.

Then I collapsed on her. She felt so warm and soft and small beneath me. Her cunt continued to squeeze me until finally it had all but squeezed me from her.

"Kiss me," she asked.

I kissed her.

"That was good," she told me. "You are very good."

"You too."

"I know."

We snuggled up against the pilothouse. It had all but stopped raining. We smoked. She played with my cock. When it began to show sign of life again, she bent her face in my lap and began to suck it once more. When it was erect, she scooted me down onto the deck and got astride me.

"This time, you bust your ass," she said.

She rode my cock for a long time. I felt I could stay hard and not come for a week. She came three times before she decided: "That's enough. God!"

Her thighs and hairs and our bellies were slick with the juices from our fucking. As soon as she was off me, I wanted her again. I rolled her over and got between her legs.

"God, baby, I'm getting sore."

"Now I want to come," I told her.

"Let me suck you off then."

But I wanted to fuck her cunt. I pounded her hard again, not as hard as before, but hard. She whimpered and bit her lower lip, but she fucked back dutifully, and when I came, she gave a little cry and ran the coming out nicely for me though she did not come again.

I still wasn't very soft when I rolled off her. I saw her looking at me. I was a bit curious, too.

She took me in her hand.

"Didn't you come?"

"Yes."

"Christ. You young guys can fuck all night."

"Not all the time. Only when I am inspired."

"Do I inspire you?"

"You must," I said, smiling at my cock.

"What are we going to do with you?" she wondered.

I looked in her eyes, kissed her swollen pale lips, then put my hand flat against the back of her head and applied a bit of pressure until she slowly lowered her face again over my lap and took my cock in her mouth. She sucked lovingly and furiously, cutting looks at my face with her large sexy eyes, jacking the shaft of my cock finally until I came again a tiny bit in her mouth. She sucked and licked me all around after I came.

"You do that better than anyone," I told her.

"Oh, I was famous for it when I was in school. Everyone says I suck cock better than anyone they have ever had. It was how I saved my virginity for my first husband."

"What happened to him?"

"He said I was a nymphomaniac."

"Are you?"

"*No!* Shit, no! I really just like to fuck a lot. I don't *have* to. I just *like* to."

"That's the difference, I guess."

"Damn right."

We smoked, sharing my cigarette.

"What if your old man wakes up and comes looking for you?"

"Scared?"

I thought a moment, grinned. "No."

"What would you do? He carries an automatic."

"I don't know. Maybe get shot. But I'm not scared. Maybe I don't care. I'd just like to fuck my brains out with you." I started to pull her down and kiss her.

She resisted.

"Listen, I'm sore. I came hard four times—five, counting once before I came out. I'm wiped out, baby." She gave me a long, friendly kiss, held my cock and balls in her hand, squeezing. It felt about half erect again. "How long has it been for chrissake since you had a fuck?"

"Over a week," I guessed.

"What about the little girl with you?"

"Chelo? She is just one of us. She doesn't."

"Never?"

"I don't know. I never asked her."

"Why don't you go crawl in with her and give her what's left of this. I'm really tired now . . . OK?"

I was squeezing her tit. I worked my hands between her legs where she was all sticky and warmly liquid inside the swollen lips of her cunt.

"Don't!" she asked and tried to twist away. She wrested herself up with her back against the pilothouse. I guided my cock between her legs which were clamped tight, but as she rose on tiptoe, the head of it slipped into her.

I humped her there while she protested, only about half of me inside. Soon she quit protesting and began to come on. She became wild. She clawed my back with her nails, arched herself to get more of my cock into her, wrapped both legs around my hips and began bucking like mad.

"Fuck me! Fuck me!" she again began to urge into my ear.

I came, but she had not.

"Let me be on top," she insisted.

I lay down on the deck, and she got on top and fed my now half-limp cock into her sopping cunt and ground herself and groaned against me, her cunt grinding against my pelvis until she came again. She fell over me and shuddered in spasms as if she were having some kind of fit.

"Are you all right?" I asked.

She shook her head that she was. But she shuddered several times more before she stopped.

"I've got to get back," she said.

It was about an hour or so before dawn.

I was aware that my knees and elbows were scraped raw in places. She looked bedraggled, her hair stringy and wet. Her eyes looked strange, as if they did not quite focus.

I helped her up. She leaned heavily against me. She came about to my shoulder. I kissed the top of her head.

"I would like to keep going for a week," I told her. "I really like how you are."

"I like you, too," she said softly.

"I wish I could see you again."

"Maybe you will."

"I'd travel a long way to see you again." I thought of all the things we might yet do.

"You like me so much?"

"Hell, yes."

She kissed me long and gently. I held her soft, nice, deep ass in both hands, pressing her against me tightly.

"I think I could go again," I told her.

"No, you can't!" She wrested herself loose.

"Maybe we could meet somewhere soon," I suggested.

"OK. Sure."

We were at the rail of the boat.

"How can I find you?"

"I don't know," she said.

"Tell me where you will be staying. I could get away from the boat for a few days maybe. Could you?"

"I don't know. Why don't you give me your address? I'll get in touch with you when I can." She sounded tired.

"OK. I will write it out and give it to you tomorrow."

"That's fine. Well . . . good night." She put her face up to be kissed.

I lowered her back down onto the yacht. I watched her go the hatch that led below. She stopped halfway down the hatch and waved and blew me a kiss. I blew her a kiss back.

"Very *romántico*," Eli growled from the doorway of the pilothouse.

"You awake?" I said, embarrassed.

"What you think? Think I can sleep when you are fucking yourself silly against my wall? Now you make me so horny I will be miserable the whole trip."

"Sorry, *compadre*."

"That don't make me feel better. You better go to bed. You look bad, man. She will kill a man like you in a week."

"Don't care if I do die, do die, do die," I sang to him.

"That good, hunh?"

"Good!"

"Goddamn!" He went back to bed.

I felt fucked out, almost happy. The scrapes on my elbows and knees burned. Man, I wanted her some more. I wanted her until I could not walk, could not twitch.

I went to sleep wondering if all rich women fucked so much better than anyone else, put so much of themselves into it. I'd sure as hell like to make a survey.

I was awakened by the sounds of the boat next to us untying, getting under way.

I dressed quickly and went out onto deck. Matthew waved to me. The day was clear and bright, already quite hot. I could see steam coming faintly from the yacht's teak decks.

"We are going to run on back to Brownsville. I called a yard there, and they can take us. We can just make it by dark on the engine."

"Good luck," was all I could think to say.

Everyone was out on deck except Lee and the tall woman. Lee came up on deck. She wore a short T-shirt with an anchor on it and very short white shorts that exposed the sweet bulges of her tan cheeks. She had a multicolored silk scarf wound around her hair. She waved, and I waved back.

The yacht was pulling away.

She shrugged her shoulders exaggeratedly, her palms turned helplessly outward at her sides. She made a sad face above her smiling mouth.

I smiled back. She smiled and threw me a big kiss at the full fling of her arm.

Her husband stopped working on deck and looked at her and at me with his hands on his hips.

She turned and went to him, linked her arm in his, and waved to us. He said something, and she reached up on tiptoe and kissed his jaw.

I watched the boat motor out to the inlet and disappear around the headland.

"Maybe you will see her again," Chelo said sneeringly near to me along the rail.

I had the note in my hand I was going to give Lee. It had a few words and my address on it. I felt stupid and crumpled it in my hand and let it fall over the side. It floated on the glassy water where the yacht had been.

"Those people don't care about you," Chelo said. "You should know that. Life is just for them kicks." It sounded like "keeks."

I pinched her little butt. She cursed me in Spanish and gave me a wild shot that I caught on the arm.

She hardly spoke to me or Eli for the next few days.

"She is in love with you," Eli insisted.

"*Chelo?* Don't be stupid." That really pissed me off for some reason.

We worked, but we were not a happy boat for a while.

Nor were we catching any goddamned shrimp.

"The storm has made everything around here no good," Eli said.

"Then we'll run on down to Yucatan if we have to. We need a good catch. I have no money left from paying the bills on the boat. I'd have to borrow to get ice and fuel for the next trip if we don't make some money."

Chelo looked at me as if my fooling around with that rich woman had somehow jinxed us.

dip in the pool

ROALD DAHL

GAMBLING ONBOARD OCEAN liners is a perfect marriage of

nature and artifice, combining the unpredictability of ocean sailing,

especially on the fractious North Atlantic, with the fickleness of fate. In

"Dip in the Pool" (1953) Roald Dahl, who specializes in exposing the

sinister, malevolent, and often macabre interface of adult gentility,

sadistically subjects his pathetic protagonist to the victimization of the

luxury crossing: everything from the banality of seasickness and the

polite obtuseness of fellow passengers, to the fatal allure of betting on

the high seas.

on the morning of the third day, the sea calmed. Even the most delicate passengers—those who had not been around the ship since sailing time—emerged from their cabins and crept on to the sun deck where the deck steward gave them chairs and tucked rugs around their legs and left them lying in rows, their faces upturned to the pale, almost heatless January sun.

It had been moderately rough the first two days, and this sudden calm and the sense of comfort that it brought created a more genial atmosphere over the whole ship. By the time evening came, the passengers, with twelve hours of good weather behind them, were beginning to feel confident, and at eight o'clock that night the main dining-room was filled with people eating and drinking with the assured, complacent air of seasoned sailors.

The meal was not half over when the passengers became aware, by the slight friction between their bodies and the seats of their chairs, that the big ship had actually started rolling again. It was very gentle at first, just a slow, lazy leaning to one side, then to the other, but it was enough to cause a subtle, immediate change of mood over the whole room. A few of the passengers glanced up from their food, hesitating, waiting, almost listening for the next roll, smiling nervously, little secret glimmers of apprehension in their eyes. Some were completely unruffled, some were openly smug, a number of the smug ones making jokes about food and weather in order to torture the few who were beginning to suffer. The movement of the ship then became rapidly more and more violent, and only five or six minutes after the first roll had been noticed, she was swinging heavily from side to side, the passengers bracing themselves in their chairs, leaning against the pull as in a car cornering.

At last the really bad roll came, and Mr. William Botibol, sitting at the purser's table, saw his plate of poached turbot with hollandaise sauce sliding suddenly away from under his fork. There was a flutter of excitement, everybody reaching for plates and wineglasses. Mrs. Renshaw, seated at the purser's right, gave a little scream and clutched that gentleman's arm.

"Going to be a dirty night," the purser said, looking at Mrs. Renshaw.

"I think it's blowing up for a very dirty night." There was just the faintest suggestion of relish in the way he said it.

A steward came hurrying up and sprinkled water on the table cloth between the plates. The excitement subsided. Most of the passengers continued with their meal. A small number, including Mrs. Renshaw, got carefully to their feet and threaded their ways with a kind of concealed haste between the tables and through the doorway.

"Well," the purser said, "there she goes." He glanced around with approval at the remainder of his flock who were sitting quiet, looking complacent, their faces reflecting openly that extraordinary pride that travellers seem to take in being recognized as "good sailors."

When the eating was finished and the coffee had been served, Mr. Botibol, who had been unusually grave and thoughtful since the rolling started, suddenly stood up and carried his cup of coffee around to Mrs. Renshaw's vacant place, next to the purser. He seated himself in her chair, then immediately leaned over and began to whisper urgently in the purser's ear. "Excuse me," he said, "but could you tell me something, please?"

The purser, small and fat and red, bent forward to listen. "What's the trouble, Mr. Botibol?"

"What I want to know is this." The man' s face was anxious and the purser was watching it. "What I want to know is will the captain already have made his estimate on the day's run—you know, for the auction pool? I mean before it began to get rough like this?"

The purser, who had prepared himself to receive a personal confidence, smiled and leaned back in his seat to relax his full belly. "I should say so—yes," he answered. He didn't bother to whisper his reply, although automatically he lowered his voice, as one does when answering a whisper.

"About how long ago do you think he did it?"

"Some time this afternoon. He usually does it in the afternoon."

"About what time?"

"Oh, I don't know. Around four o'clock I should guess."

"Now tell me another thing. How does the captain decide which number it shall be? Does he take a lot of trouble over that?"

The purser looked at the anxious frowning face of Mr. Botibol and he smiled, knowing quite well what the man was driving at. "Well, you see, the captain has a little conference with the navigating officer, and they study the weather and a lot of other things, and then they make their estimate."

Mr. Botibol nodded, pondering this answer for a moment. Then he said, "Do you think the captain knew there was bad weather coming today?"

"I couldn't tell you," the purser replied. He was looking into the small black eyes of the other man, seeing the two single little sparks of excitement dancing in their centers. "I really couldn't tell you, Mr. Botibol. I wouldn't know."

"If this gets any worse it might be worth buying some of the low numbers. What do you think?" The whispering was more urgent, more anxious now.

"Perhaps it will," the purser said. "I doubt whether the old man allowed for a really rough night. It was pretty calm this afternoon when he made his estimate."

The others at the table had become silent and were trying to hear, watching the purser with that intent, half-cocked, listening look that you can see also at the race track when they are trying to overhear a trainer talking about his chance: the slightly open lips, the upstretched eyebrows, the head forward and cocked a little to one side—that desperately straining, half-hypnotized listening look that comes to all of them when they are hearing something straight from the horse's mouth.

"Now suppose you were allowed to buy a number, which one would you choose today?" Mr. Botibol whispered.

"I don't know what the range is yet," the purser patiently answered. "They don't announce the range till the auction starts after dinner. And I'm really not very good at it anyway. I'm only the purser, you know."

At that point Mr. Botibol stood up. "Excuse me, all," he said, and he walked carefully away over the swaying floor between the other tables, and twice he had to catch hold of the back of a chair to steady himself against the ship's roll.

"The sun deck, please," he said to the elevator man.

The wind caught him full in the face as he stepped out on to the open deck. He staggered and grabbed hold of the rail and held on tight with both hands, and he stood there looking out over the darkening sea where the great waves were welling up high and white horses were riding against the wind with plumes of spray behind them as they went.

"Pretty bad out there, wasn't it, sir?" the elevator man said on the way down.

Mr. Botibol was combing his hair back into place with a small red comb. "Do you think we've slackened speed at all on account of the weather?" he asked.

"Oh my word yes, sir. We slackened off considerable since this started. You got to slacken off speed in weather like this or you'll be throwing the passengers all over the ship."

Down in the smoking-room people were already gathering for the
auction. They were grouping themselves politely around the various
tables, the men a little stiff in their dinner jackets, a little pink and over-
shaved and stiff beside their cool white-armed women. Mr. Botibol took
a chair close to the auctioneer's table. He crossed his legs, folded his
arms, and settled himself in his seat with the rather desperate air of a man
who has made a tremendous decision and refuses to be frightened.

The pool, he was telling himself, would probably be around seven
thousand dollars. That was almost exactly what it had been the last two
days with the numbers selling for between three and four hundred
apiece. Being a British ship they did it in pounds, but he liked to do his
thinking in his own currency. Seven thousand dollars was plenty of
money. My goodness, yes! And what he would do he would get them to
pay him in hundred-dollar bills and he would take it ashore in the inside
pocket of his jacket. No problem there. And right away, yes right away,
he would buy a Lincoln convertible. He would pick it up on the way
from the ship and drive it home just for the pleasure of seeing Ethel's
face when she came out the front door and looked at it. Wouldn't that
be something to see Ethel's face when he glided up to the door in a
brand-new pale-green Lincoln convertible! Hello, Ethel, honey, he
would say, speaking very casual. I just thought I'd get you a little present.
I saw it in the window as I went by, so I thought of you and how you
were always wanting one. You like it, honey? he would say. You like the
color? And then he would watch her face.

The auctioneer was standing up behind his table now. "Ladies and
gentlemen!" he shouted. "The captain has estimated the day's run, ending midday tomorrow, at five hundred and fifteen miles. As usual we will
take the ten numbers on either side of it to make up the range. That
makes it five hundred and five to five hundred and twenty-five. And of
course for those who think the true figure will be still farther away,
there'll be 'low field' and 'high field' sold separately as well. Now, we'll
draw the first numbers out of the hat . . . here we are . . . five hundred
and twelve?"

The room became quiet. The people sat still in their chairs, all eyes
watching the auctioneer. There was a certain tension in the air, and as
the bids got higher, the tension grew. This wasn't a game or a joke; you
could be sure of that by the way one man would look across at another

who had raised his bid—smiling perhaps, but only the lips smiling, the eyes bright and absolutely cold.

Number five hundred and twelve was knocked down for one hundred and ten pounds. The next three or four numbers fetched roughly the same amount.

The ship was rolling heavily, and each time she went over, the wooden panelling on the walls creaked as if it were going to split. The passengers held on to the arms of their chairs, concentrating upon the auction. "Low field!" the auctioneer called out. "The next number is low field."

Mr. Botibol sat up very straight and tense. He would wait, he had decided, until the others had finished bidding, then he would jump in and make the last bid. He had figured that there must be at least five hundred dollars in his account at the bank at home, probably nearer six. That was about two hundred pounds—over two hundred. This ticket wouldn't fetch more than that.

"As you all know," the auctioneer was saying, "low field covers every number below the smallest number in the range, in this case every number below five hundred and five. So, if you think this ship is going to cover less than five hundred and five miles in the twenty-four hours ending at noon tomorrow, you better get in and buy this number. So what am I bid?"

It went clear up to one hundred and thirty pounds. Others besides Mr. Botibol seemed to have noticed that the weather was rough. One hundred and forty . . . fifty . . . There it stopped. The auctioneer raised his hammer.

"Going at one hundred and fifty . . . "

"Sixty!" Mr. Botibol called, and every face in the room turned and looked at him.

"Seventy!"

"Eighty!" Mr. Botibol called.

"Ninety!"

"Two hundred!" Mr. Botibol called. He wasn't stopping now—not for anyone.

There was a pause.

"Any advance on two hundred pounds?"

Sit still, he told himself. Sit absolutely still and don't look up. It's unlucky to look up. Hold your breath. No one's going to bid you up so long as you hold your breath.

"Going for two hundred pounds . . . " The auctioneer had a pink bald head and there were little beads of sweat sparkling on top of it. "Going . . . " Mr. Botibol held his breath. "Going . . . Gone!" The man banged the hammer on the table. Mr. Botibol wrote out a cheque and handed it to the auctioneer's assistant, then he settled back in his chair to wait for the finish. He did not want to go to bed before he knew how much there was in the pool.

They added it up after the last number had been sold and it came to twenty-one hundred-odd pounds. That was around six thousand dollars. Ninety per cent to go to winner, ten per cent to seamen's charities. Ninety per cent of six thousand was five thousand four hundred. Well— that was enough. He could buy the Lincoln convertible and there would be something left over, too. With this gratifying thought he went off, happy and excited, to his cabin.

When Mr. Botibol awoke the next morning he lay quite still for several minutes with his eyes shut, listening for the sound of the gale, waiting for the roll of the ship. There was no sound of any gale and the ship was not rolling. He jumped up and peered out of the porthole. The sea—Oh Jesus God—was smooth as glass, the great ship was moving through it fast, obviously making up for time lost during the night. Mr. Botibol turned away and sat slowly down on the edge of his bunk. A fine electricity of fear was beginning to prickle under the skin of his stomach. He hadn't a hope now. One of the higher numbers was certain to win it after this.

"Oh, my God," he said aloud. "What shall I do?"

What, for example, would Ethel say? It was simply not possible to tell her that he had spent almost all of their two years' savings on a ticket in the ship's pool. Nor was it possible to keep the matter a secret. To do that he would have to tell her to stop drawing checks. And what about the monthly installments on the television set and the *Encyclopedia Britannica?* Already he could see the anger and contempt in the woman's eyes, the blue becoming gray and the eyes themselves narrowing as they always did when there was anger in them.

"Oh, my God. What *shall* I do?"

There was no point in pretending that he had the slightest chance now—not unless the goddam ship started to go backwards. They'd have to put her in reverse and go full speed astern and keep right on going if he was to have any chance of winning it now. Well, maybe he should ask the captain to do just that. Offer him ten per cent of the profits. Offer him more if he wanted it. Mr. Botibol started to giggle. Then very suddenly he stopped, his eyes and mouth both opening wide in a kind of shocked surprise. For it was at this moment that the idea came. It hit him hard and quick, and he jumped up from his bed, terribly excited, ran over to the porthole and looked out again. Well, he thought, why not? Why ever not? The sea was calm and he wouldn't have any trouble keeping afloat until they picked him up. He had a vague feeling that someone had done this thing before, but that didn't prevent him from doing it again. The ship would have to stop and lower a boat, and the boat would have to go back maybe half a mile to get him, and then it would have to return to the ship, the whole thing. An hour was about thirty miles. It would knock thirty miles off the day's run. That would do it. "Low field" would be sure to win it then. Just so long as he made certain someone saw him falling over; but that would be simple to arrange. And he'd better wear light clothes, something easy to swim in. Sports clothes, that was it. He would dress as though he were going up to play some deck tennis—just a shirt and a pair of shorts and tennis-shoes. And leave his watch behind. What was the time? Nine-fifteen. The sooner the better, then. Do it now and get it over with. Have to do it soon, because the time limit was midday.

Mr. Botibol was both frightened and excited when he stepped out on the sun deck in his sports clothes. His small body was wide at the hips, tapering upward to extremely narrow sloping shoulders, so that it resembled, in shape at any rate, a bollard. His white skinny legs were covered with black hairs, and he came cautiously out on deck, treading softly in his tennis-shoes. Nervously he looked around him. There was only one other person in sight, an elderly woman with very thick ankles and immense buttocks who was leaning over the rail staring at the sea. She was wearing a coat of Persian lamb and the collar was turned up so Mr. Botibol couldn't see her face.

He stood still, examining her from a distance. Yes, he told himself, she would probably do. She would probably give the alarm just as quickly as anyone else. But wait one minute, take your time, William Botibol, take your time. Remember what you told yourself a few minutes ago in the cabin when you were changing? You remember that?

The thought of leaping off a ship into the ocean a thousand miles from the nearest land had made Mr. Botibol—a cautious man at the best of times—unusually advertent. He was by no means satisfied yet that this woman he saw before him was *absolutely certain* to give the alarm when he made his jump. In his opinion there were two possible reasons why she might fail him. Firstly, she might be deaf and blind. It was not very probable, but on the other hand it *might* be so, and why take a chance?

All he had to do was check it by talking to her for a moment before-hand. Secondly—and this will demonstrate how suspicious the mind of a man can become when it is working through self-preservation and fear—secondly, it had occurred to him that the woman might herself be the owner of one of the high numbers in the pool and as such would have a sound financial reason for not wishing to stop the ship. Mr. Botibol recalled that people had killed their fellows for far less than six thousand dollars. It was happening every day in the newspapers. So why take a chance on that either? Check on it first. Be sure of your facts. Find out about it by a little polite conversation. Then, provided that the woman appeared also to be a pleasant, kindly human being, the thing was a cinch and he could leap overboard with a light heart.

Mr. Botibol advanced casually toward the woman and took up a posi-tion beside her, leaning on the rail.

"Hello," he said pleasantly.

She turned and smiled at him, a surprisingly lovely, almost a beautiful smile, although the face itself was very plain. "Hello," she answered him.

Check, Mr. Botibol told himself, on the first question. She is neither blind nor deaf. "Tell me," he said, coming straight to the point, "what did you think of the auction last night?"

"Auction?" she asked, frowning. "Auction? What auction? . . .

"You know, that silly old thing they have in the lounge after dinner, selling numbers on the ship's daily run. I just wondered what you thought about it."

She shook her head, and again she smiled, a sweet and pleasant smile that had in it perhaps the trace of an apology. "I'm very lazy," she said. "I always go to bed early. I have my dinner in bed. It's so restful to have din-ner in bed."

Mr. Botibol smiled back at her and began to edge away. "Got to go and get my exercise now," he said. "Never miss my exercise in the morn-ing. It was nice seeing you. Very nice seeing you . . . " He retreated about ten paces, and the woman let him go without looking around.

Everything was now in order. The sea was calm, he was lightly dressed for swimming, there were almost certainly no man-eating sharks in this part of the Atlantic, and there was this pleasant kindly old woman to give the alarm. It was a question now only of whether the ship would be delayed long enough to swing the balance in his favor. Almost certainly it would. In any event, he could do a little to help in that direction him-self. He could make a few difficulties about getting hauled up into the lifeboat. Swim around a bit, back away from them surreptitiously as they tried to come up close to fish him out. Every minute, every second gained would help him win. He began to move forward again to the rail, but now a new fear assailed him. Would he get caught in the propeller? He had heard about that happening to persons falling off the sides of big ships. But then, he wasn't going to fall, he was going to jump and that was a very different thing, provided he jumped out far enough he would be sure to clear the propeller.

Mr. Botibol advanced slowly to a position at the rail about twenty yards away from the woman. She wasn't looking at him now. So much the better. He didn't want her watching him as he jumped off. So long as no one was watching he would be able to say afterwards that he had slipped and fallen by accident. He peered over the side of the ship. It was a long, long drop. Come to think of it now, he might easily hurt himself badly if he hit the water flat. Wasn't there someone who once split his stomach open that way, doing a belly flop from a high dive? He must jump straight and land feet first. Go in like a knife. Yes, sir. The water seemed cold and deep and gray and it made him shiver to look at it. But it was now or never. Be a man, William Botibol, be a man. All right then . . . now . . . here goes . . .

He climbed up on to the wide wooden top-rail, stood there poised, balancing for three terrifying seconds, then he leaped—he leaped up and out as far as he could go and at the same time he shouted *"Help!"*

"Help! Help!" he shouted as he fell. Then he hit the water and went under.

When the first shout for help sounded, the woman who was leaning on the rail started up and gave a little jump of surprise. She looked around quickly and saw sailing past her through the air this small man dressed in white shorts and tennis-shoes, spreadeagled and shouting as he went. For a moment she looked as though she weren't quite sure what she ought to do: throw a lifebelt, run away and give the alarm, or simply turn and yell. She drew back a pace from the rail and swung half around facing up to the bridge, and for this brief moment she remained motionless, tense, undecided. Then almost at once she seemed to relax, and she leaned forward far over the rail, staring at the water where it was turbulent in the ship's wake. Soon a tiny round black head appeared in the foam, an arm was raised above it, once, twice, vigorously waving, and a small faraway voice was heard calling something that was difficult to understand. The woman leaned still further over the rail, trying to keep the little bobbing black speck in sight, but soon, so very soon, it was such a long way away that she couldn't even be sure it was there at all.

After a while another woman came out on deck. This one was bony and angular, and she wore horn-rimmed spectacles. She spotted the first woman and walked over to her, treading the deck in the deliberate, military fashion of all spinsters.

"So there you are," she said.

The woman with the fat ankles turned and looked at her, but said nothing.

"I've been searching for you," the bony one continued. "Searching all over."

"It's very odd," the woman with the fat ankles said. "A man dived overboard just now, with his clothes on."

"Nonsense!"

"Oh yes. He said he wanted to get some exercise and he dived in and didn't even bother to take his clothes off."

"You better come down now," the bony woman said. Her mouth had suddenly become firm, her whole face sharp and alert, and she spoke less kindly than before. "And don't you ever go wandering about on deck alone like this again. You know quite well you're meant to wait for me."

"Yes, Maggie," the woman with the fat ankles answered, and again she smiled, a tender, trusting smile, and she took the hand of the other one and allowed herself to be led away across the deck.

"Such a nice man," she said. "He waved to me."

the gentleman
from san francisco

IVAN BUNIN

THE SOLE NOBEL PRIZE laureate among the generation of

modernists who fled the Bolshevik regime, Ivan Alekseyevich Bunin

(1870–1953) wrote some of the most haunting, understated poetry

and prose of Russia's "Silver Age." His sketches of the haute bour-

geoisie detail the fleeting gesture, the subtle inflection that exposes

the essential pathos of a life. In "The Gentleman from San Francisco"

(1916) a luxury cruise, turn-of-the-century style, becomes the vehicle

for a personal apocalypse and an allegory on the vanity of human

ambition in the face of death.

the gentleman from San Francisco—nobody in either Naples or Capri could remember his name—was on his way to the Old World with his wife and daughter, there to spend two whole years devoted entirely to pleasure.

He was firmly convinced that he was entitled to a rest, to pleasure, to a long and comfortable voyage, and to any number of other things. He had his own reasons for being so firmly convinced; first he was a wealthy man, and secondly, he was only beginning to live, although he was already fifty-eight. Until then he had not lived, he had merely existed, not badly at all it must be said, but nevertheless it was nothing but existence, for he had centered all his hopes on the days to come. He had worked without a breathing spell—the Chinese, whom he imported in thousands to work for him, well knew what that meant! And at last he saw that he had achieved a great deal, that he had almost come up to the level of those he had once set up as an example to himself; and then he decided to take a holiday. It was a custom with the class of men to which he belonged to start off with a trip to Europe, India and Egypt when they were ready to enjoy life. He decided to do the same. Naturally, his chief concern was to reward himself for his years of toil; however, he was glad for the sake of his wife and daughter, too. His wife was never known to be particularly impressionable, but then all middle-aged American women are passionate travelers. And as for his daughter, a girl no longer young and rather sickly, the trip was an outright necessity for her. To say nothing of the good it would do her health, what of those happy friendships known to have been made on board ship? You sometimes actually find yourself sitting next to a multimillionaire at dinner or studying frescoes together in the lounge.

The route planned by the gentleman from San Francisco was an extensive one. During the months of December and January he was hoping to bask in the sun of southern Italy, to enjoy the ancient sights, the tarantella, the serenades of the wandering singers, and something that men of his age appreciate with a peculiar poignancy—the love of young Neapolitan girls, even if it isn't entirely disinterested. He proposed to spend Carnival week in Nice and Monte Carlo, where the most select society foregathers at that time, the society which rules and dispenses all the blessings of our civilized world—such as the latest cut of dinner jackets, the stability of thrones, the declaration of wars and the welfare of the hotels—where some of the guests plunge excitedly into automobile and yacht races or into roulette, others into what is customarily known as "light flirtation," and still others into shooting pigeons which, released from their cotes, soar beautifully over the emerald-green lawns, against the background of the forget-me-not sea, and then instantly flop on the ground like little white balls. He wanted to devote the first part of March to Florence and arrive in Rome for Passion Week in order to hear the *Miserere* sung there. His plans included Venice and Paris, bullfighting in Seville, bathing in the British Isles, then Athens, Constantinople, Palestine, Egypt, and even Japan—on the way back of course . . . .And everything began splendidly.

It was the end of November. Icy fogs and slushy snowstorms accompanied them all the way to Gibraltar, but they sailed on quite safely. There were many passengers on board. The famous *Atlantic* was like a huge hotel with so many facilities—an all-night bar, Turkish baths, a newspaper of its own, and life on board ran a scheduled course. They got up early, roused by the horns blaring shrilly in the corridors in that dusky hour of the morning when day was just breaking so slowly and glumly over the gray-green expanse of the sea, rolling heavily in the fog; they put on their flannel pajamas and had coffee, chocolate or cocoa; after that they bathed in marble bathtubs, did their exercises to work up a good appetite and a feeling of fitness, dressed and had their breakfast; until eleven they were supposed to walk briskly up and down the deck, breathing in the cool freshness of the ocean, or to play shuffleboard and other games in order to work up their appetites anew, and at eleven they fortified themselves with sandwiches and beef tea; thus fortified, they read the ship's newspaper with relish and calmly awaited lunch, which was even more nourishing with a greater variety of dishes than breakfast; the next two hours were devoted to rest: deck chairs were then ranged along all the decks, and the passengers lay back in them, wrapped in rugs, gazing at the cloudy sky and the frothy waves through the railing, or falling into a sweet doze; between the hours of four and five, refreshed and cheered, they had strong, fragrant tea and biscuits served to them; at seven, the bugles signaled the approach of the moment that formed the main purpose of this existence, its crowning glory. And, roused by the bugles, the gentleman from San Francisco, rubbing his hands in an access of life and vigor, hurried to his sumptuous cabin *de luxe* to dress for dinner.

At night the *Atlantic* seemed to gape into the darkness with countless blazing eyes, while a great number of servants worked busily in the kitchens, sculleries and wine cellars below. The ocean, moving beyond the walls, was awesome, but no one thought about it, firmly believing it to be in the hands of the Captain, a red-haired man of monstrous size and corpulence, who always looked sleepy and resembled an enormous idol in his black coat with gold-braid bands, and who very seldom emerged from his secret abode to be among the passengers. In the fore-castle the siren kept wailing with infernal gloom or squealing in frantic fury, but not many of the diners heard the siren, for it was drowned by a splendid string orchestra, playing exquisitely and indefatigably in the two-storied marble dining room, which had deep pile carpets on the floor, was festively flooded with lights, thronged with ladies in low-cut evening gowns and gentlemen in tail coats or dinner jackets, with slen-der waiters, deferential *maîtres d'hôtel*, and a wine waiter who actually wore a chain around his neck like a lord mayor. The dinner coat and starched shirt made the gentleman from San Francisco look very much younger than he was. Lean and not tall, ungainly in build but well-knit, polished to a sheen and reasonably gay, he sat in the pearly golden halo of this room with a bottle of amber-colored Johannesburg in front of him, an array of glasses of the finest crystal, and a vase of curly hyacinths. His yellowish face with the neatly trimmed silver mustache had some-thing Mongolian in it, gold fillings gleamed in his teeth, and his strong skull shone like old ivory. His wife, a large, broad and serene woman, wore clothes that were expensive but suitable to her age; while the daughter—tall and slim, with beautiful hair charmingly dressed, her breath sweetened with violet cachous, and with the faintest of little pink pimples, slightly dusted over with powder, around her lips and between her shoulder blades—wore a gown that was elaborate but light and transparent, innocently frank . . . . The dinner went on for over an hour, and after that there was dancing in the ballroom, during which the men—the gentleman from San Francisco among them of course—sprawled in armchairs with their feet up and decided the fate of whole nations on the basis of the latest stock exchange news, smoking them-selves red in the face with Havana cigars and getting drunk on liqueurs in the bar attended by red-coated Negroes with eyeballs that looked like shelled hard-boiled eggs. The ocean roared, heaving black mountains on the other side of the wall, the storm whistled through the sodden, heavy rigging, the ship shuddered and shook as it struggled through the storm and the black mountains, cutting like a plough through their rippling mass which kept swirling into a froth and flinging high its foamy tails. The siren, suffocating in the fog, wailed in mortal agony; the watch up in the crow's-nest froze in the cold, their minds reeling from the unbearable strain on their attention, and the ship's belly below the water line was like the abyss of hell at its most sinister and sultry, its ninth cycle—the belly in which the giant furnaces roared with laughter as, with their blazing maws, they devoured ton after ton of coal, flung down them with a clatter by men drenched in pungent sweat, dirty, half-naked and purple in the glow of the flames. While up here in the bar, legs were flung carelessly over the arms of chairs, brandy and liqueurs were sipped at leisure, clouds of aromatic smoke hung in the air, and in the ballroom all was brilliance, radiating light, warmth and joy; couples whirled in a waltz or swayed in a tango, and the music, insistently and with a sadness that was voluptuous and shameless, sang its plea, always that one plea . . . . Among this brilliant crowd of people there was a certain well-known millionaire, a lanky, clean-shaven man in an old-fashioned dress coat, who resembled a prelate; there was a famous Spanish author, a world-celebrated beauty, and an elegant pair of lovers watched by all with curiosity, who made no secret of their happiness, for he danced with no one but her. And all this was so exquisitely and charmingly performed that no one but the Captain knew that the couple was hired by Lloyds to play at love for a good wage, and had been sailing on the company's ships for a long time.

Everyone was glad of the sun in Gibraltar, it seemed like early spring. A new passenger appeared on board the *Atlantic*, instantly drawing everyone's attention to himself. He was the crown prince of a certain kingdom in Asia, traveling incognito. A small man, perfectly wooden, broad-faced and narrow-eyed, wearing gold-rimmed spectacles, slightly unpleasant because the coarse black hairs of his mustache were stringy like a corpse's, but a nice, simple and unpresumptuous man on the whole. In the Mediterranean there was once again a breath of winter; the sea billowed in high varicolored waves like a peacock's tail, blown by the tramontane which came rushing toward the ship madly and merrily in the brilliant light of a perfectly clear day. And then, on the second day, the sky began to pale, the horizon was wrapped in mist: land was nearing, now there was a glimpse of Ischia and Capri, now if you looked through your binoculars you could see the lumps of sugar strewn at the foot of something dusky blue, Naples. Many of the ladies and gentlemen had already put on their light fur coats; the meek Chinese "boys," who never spoke above a whisper, bowlegged youngsters with pitch-black pigtails hanging down to their heels, with thick maidenly eyelashes, were quietly carrying rugs, canes, suitcases and dressing cases toward the companionway. The daughter of the gentleman from San Francisco stood on deck next to the prince, to whom she had been introduced the night before by a happy chance, and pretended she was following his pointed finger into the distance as he explained something to her hastily and softly. He was so short he looked like a little boy beside the others, seeming quite unprepossessing and odd—his spectacles, derby hat and English overcoat, the horsehair coarseness of his stringy mustache, the thin olive skin stretched tight across his flat face which might have been thinly coated with varnish—but the girl stood listening to him and she was so excited she could not understand a word he was saying; her heart was beating fast, strangely enraptured. Everything, every single thing about him was different from everyone else—his slim hands, his clear skin, beneath which coursed the blood of ancient kings, his very clothes—European and quite plain, but somehow exceptionally neat—held an extraordinary fascination for her. And meanwhile, the gentleman from San Francisco himself, wearing gray spats over his patent-leather shoes, kept glancing at the famous beauty who stood beside him, a tall blonde with a marvelous figure and eyes painted in the latest Parisian fashion, who was talking to a tiny, humpbacked hairless dog which she held on a thin silver chain. And the daughter, feeling vaguely discomfited, tried to take no notice of the father.

He was rather generous when traveling, and therefore he quite believed in the solicitude of all those who fed and waited on him from morning to night forestalling his slightest wish, who safeguarded his peace and kept him immaculate, who summoned porters for him and delivered his trunks to hotels. It had been like this everywhere, it had been so on board ship, it should be so in Naples, too. The city grew larger and nearer; the ship's band, with brass instruments flashing in the sun, was already crowded on deck and suddenly burst into a deafening and triumphant march; the gigantic Captain appeared on the bridge in his dress uniform and, like a merciful heathen god, waved to the passengers with an affable gesture. And, like everyone else, the gentleman from San Francisco fancied that the thundering strains of proud America's march were being played for him alone, and that the Captain was wishing him personally a happy landing. When at last the *Atlantic* entered the harbor and its many-storied mass, with people clustering at the rails tied up to the pier and the chains of the gangplanks clattered—countless hotel porters and their assistants in gold-braided caps, all sorts of commissionaires, whistling urchins and hefty beggars with stacks of colored postcards in their hands, rushed forward offering their services. And he smiled at these beggars as he walked to the car of the hotel where the prince might also be putting up, and calmly spoke through his teeth first in English then in Italian:

"Go away! Via!"

Life in Naples instantly took on a clockwork regularity: in the morning there was breakfast in the gloomy dining room, an overcast sky that held little promise, and a crowd of guides at the lobby doors; then came the first smiles of the warm rosy sun, a view of Vesuvius from the high hanging balcony, the mountain cloaked entirely in the shimmering vapors of dawn, of the pearly silver ripples on the bay and the pale silhouette of Capri on the horizon, of tiny donkeys harnessed in dogcarts, tripping along the muddy quay below, and detachments of toy soldiers marching somewhere to the sounds of vigorous and challenging music. After that came the waiting car and a slow drive through the thronged, narrow gray corridors of streets, between tall, many-windowed houses, visits to the funereally stark and clean museums, lighted evenly and pleasantly but with a snowlike dullness, or to the churches, cold and smelling of wax, where the same thing was repeated over and over again: a stately entrance hung with a heavy leather curtain, and inside a vast emptiness and silence, the soft lights of the seven-branched candelabrum redly flickering in the depths upon the altar draped in lace, a solitary old woman among the dark wooden pews, slippery gravestones underfoot, and on the wall someone's *Descent from the Cross*—invariably famous. At one, there was lunch on the San Martin Hill, where quite a number of the very first-class people gathered toward noon, and where on one occasion the daughter of the gentleman from San Francisco had nearly fainted: she thought she saw the prince sitting in the room, whereas the newspapers said he was in Rome. At five, tea was served at the hotel in the beautiful drawing room which was so warm with its thick carpeting and blazing fires; and after that, dressing for dinner, once again the gong booming sonorously and masterfully through the whole building, once again the string of ladies in low-cut gowns, rustling down the stairs in their silks, reflected in the mirrored walls, once again the doors of the dining room flung open, wide and hospitably, and the red jackets of the musicians on their platform, the black crowd of waiters round the *maître d'hôtel* while he deftly ladled out the creamy pink soup into the plates. The dinners were so rich in food, wine and mineral waters, in sweets and fruit, that by eleven o'clock the maids were required to bring hot-water bottles to all the rooms for the guests to warm their stomachs with.

December, however, was not a very good month that year. When one talked to the porters about the weather they merely raised their shoulders guiltily and muttered that as far as they could remember, there had never been a winter like it, although it wasn't the first year they were obliged to mutter this and blame it on the fact that "something awful was happening all over the world." On the Riviera it stormed and rained as never before, in Athens there was snow, Etna, too, was covered with snow and cast a glow at night; and as for Palermo, the tourists were simply running away from the cold, helter-skelter . . . . The early-morning sun deceived them every day. At noon, the sky invariably turned gray and fine rain began to fall, becoming colder and harder as the day wore on; and then the palm trees at the hotel entrance would shine with a metallic sheen, the town appeared particularly dirty and cramped, the museums too monotonous, the cigar ends, thrown by the fat cabmen whose rubber capes flapped in the wind like wings, unbearably foul, the vigorous cracks of their whips over the heads of their skinny-necked nags too obvious a sham, the boots of the men sweeping the streetcar tracks dreadful, and the women, splashing through the mud, in the rain with their black beads uncovered, disgustingly short-legged; but as for the dampness and the stench of rotting fish coming from the frothing water's edge, the least said about it the better. The gentleman and the lady from San Francisco began to quarrel in the mornings now. Their daughter either had a headache and went about looking wan and pale, or all at once she brightened up, was enthusiastic and keen on everything, and then she was both sweet and beautiful. Beautiful were the tender and complex feelings awakened in her by the homely man with the uncommon blood coursing through his veins, for after all, what awakens a girl's heart—whether it is wealth, fame, or an illustrious name—is not really of great consequence. Everyone assured them that it was quite different in Sorrento and Capri—there it was warmer and sunnier, lemon trees were in bloom, the people more virtuous and the wine better. And so the family from San Francisco decided to proceed to Capri, taking all their trunks along, with the intention of settling down in Sorrento after they had gone all over Capri, had trod the stones where once the palaces of Tiberius stood, visited the fabulous eaves of the Azure Grotto, and listened to the Abruzzian bagpipers who, during the month before Christmas, roamed the island singing praises to the Virgin Mary.

On the day of departure—a very memorable day for the family from San Francisco—even the usual early morning sun was missing. A heavy fog completely hid Vesuvius, hanging in a low gray cloud over the leaden surface of the sea. There was no sight of Capri—as if it had never existed in the world at all. And the small ship making toward it lurched so heavily from side to side that the family from San Francisco had to lie prone on their sofas in the wretched saloon of this poor ship, their feet wrapped in rugs and their eyes closed from nausea. The lady thought she suffered more than the others; nausea gripped her again and again and she believed she was dying, while the maid who came running to her with a basin, and who had for many years been sailing this sea day in, day out, in all weathers, hot or cold, but was indefatigable nevertheless, merely laughed. The daughter was dreadfully pale and she held a slice of lemon between her teeth. The father, who lay on his back dressed in a loose overcoat and a large cap, never unclenched his jaws once during the voyage; his face had grown dark, his mustache seemed whiter, and his head was racked with pain: what with the miserable weather, he had been drinking too heavily and enjoying too many "living tableaux" in certain haunts during the last nights on shore. And meanwhile the rain lashed at the rattling portholes, water dribbled down on to the sofas, the wind tore through the masts with a howl, and now and again came together with the onslaught of the swell to lay the little ship on its side, and then something could be heard rolling and rumbling below. It was a little quieter at the stops in Castellammare and Sorrento, but even there the swell was dreadful and the shores with all their precipices, gardens, pineries, pink and white hotels and dusky curly green hills, flew up and down as though on swings. Boats kept knocking against the side of the ship, the third-class passengers were shouting heatedly, somewhere a child was choking with screams as if it had been crushed, a damp wind blew in at the door with never a moment's pause, from a boat tossing on the waves, flaunting a flag of the Royal Hotel came the sound of a boy's shrill lisping voice shouting incessantly as he tried to entice the passengers with his "*Kgoyal! Hôtel Kgoyal!*" And the gentleman from San Francisco, feeling very old—which was what he should have felt—now thought with boredom and anger of all these "Royals," "Splendids" and "Excelsiors," and of those greedy, garlic-stinking little wretches called Italians. Once, during a stop, be opened his eyes and, sitting up on the sofa, saw a pile of such miserable little stone hovels, moldy through and through, stuck one on top of the other at the foot of a sheer rock close to the water's edge beside some boats, heaps of rags, empty tins and brown fishing nets, that a feeling of despair seized him as he remembered that this was the real Italy which he had come to enjoy . . . . At last, when it was already dusk, the black mass of the island, shot through with the little red lights at its foot, began to bear down on them; the wind abated, becoming warmer and more fragrant, and golden snakes, gliding away from the lampposts on the quay, came floating on the subdued waves which gleamed like black oil. Then, suddenly, the anchor began to rumble and with a clatter of chains flopped into the water with a splash, the furious cries of boatmen, vying with one another, came from all sides; and instantly one felt one's spirits lifting, the cabin lights shone more brightly, one wanted to eat, drink, smoke and move about. Ten minutes later the family from San Francisco boarded a roomy barge; in a quarter of an hour they disembarked on the quay, and then they were sitting in a bright little car and whirring up a sheer mountainside past vine poles, crumbling stone walls and wet, gnarled orange trees protected here and there with matting, their bright-colored fruit and thick shiny leaves flashing past the open windows of the car and gliding downhill. In Italy the earth smells sweetly after rain, and every one of the islands has its own peculiar smell.

The Island of Capri was damp and dark that night. But now it came to life for a moment and put on lights here and there. A crowd of those whose duty it was to give the gentleman from San Francisco a fitting welcome, were already waiting at the top of the hill on the funicular platform. There were other arrivals, too, but they deserved no attention—a few Russians who had settled down in Capri, absent-minded and untidy men wearing spectacles and beards, the collars of their threadbare overcoats turned up; and a party of long-legged, round-skulled young Germans in Tyrolese suits with canvas rucksacks slung on their shoulders, who were in need of no services from anyone and felt at home wherever they happened to be and were not at all generous with their money. As for the gentleman from San Francisco, who calmly shunned both the Russians and the Germans, he was instantly marked down. He and his ladies were hurriedly helped out of the car; men started running ahead of him to show him the way; he was again surrounded by urchins and those stalwart Capri peasant women who carry on their heads the suitcases and trunks of decent tourists. Their wooden sandals clattered down the small square which was like an opera set with its globe of light swinging above in the damp breeze, and its crowd of urchins breaking into birdlike whistling and turning somersaults. And the gentleman from San Francisco strode in their midst as though he were making a stage entrance, through a kind of medieval archway formed by the houses, merging together overhead, beyond which lay the noisy little street, climbing up toward the brilliantly lighted hotel entrance, with a tuft of palm leaves showing above the flat roofs on the left and a black sky studded with blue stars above and ahead. And once again it seemed that it was in honor of the guests from San Francisco that this damp little stone town on the rocky island in the Mediterranean had come to life, that it was they who had made the owner of the hotel so happy and hospitable, that for them the Chinese gong was waiting to boom all through the building, summoning everyone to dinner the minute they entered the lobby.

The owner, who welcomed them with a polite and courtly bow, an exceedingly elegant young man, gave the gentleman from San Francisco a momentary start, for when he saw him he suddenly remembered that among all the other muddled dreams which had thronged his sleep the previous night he had seen the replica of this gentleman, wearing the same roundly cutaway morning coat, his hair plastered down to the same mirrorlike gloss. Amazed, he all but stopped in his tracks. But since his soul had been cleansed of any so-called mystical feelings years ago, to the last mustard seed, his amazement instantly faded away; he jokingly mentioned this strange coincidence between dream and reality to his wife and daughter as they walked down the hotel corridor. His daughter, however, looked up at him in alarm when she heard it; her heart suddenly cringed with a feeling of sadness, of frightening loneliness on this strange, dark island . . . .

A person of exalted rank—Rais XVII—who had been visiting Capri, had just left. And the guests from San Francisco were allotted the suite he had occupied. They had the prettiest and smartest maid appointed to them, a Belgian girl whose waist was drawn hard and thin by her corset, and whose starched cap perched on her head like a small toothed crown. They were given the most imposing of valets, a black-haired fiery-eyed Sicilian, and the nimblest of "boots," a small, plump man called Luigi, who had held many such jobs in his time. And a minute later, the gentleman from San Francisco heard a light knock on his door, followed by the appearance of the French *maître d'hôtel* coming in to inquire if the new guests would be dining, and to inform them, should their answer be in the affirmative (of which, however, there was no doubt), that there was lobster, roast beef, asparagus, pheasants, and so on, on the menu. The gentleman from San Francisco still felt the floor rising and falling under him—that's how seasick the rotten little Italian ship had made him—but he calmly went and rather clumsily closed the window which had burst open at the *maître d'hôtel's* entrance, and through which came the smells of a kitchen far away and wet flowers in the garden below. He replied with unhurried precision that they would be dining, that their table was to be placed well back in the room, a good distance away from the doors, that they would be drinking a local wine, and every word he uttered was echoed by the *maître d'hôtel* in tones of the most varied pitch, all of which, however, had but one meaning: that the rightness of the gentleman's wishes could not be doubted, and that everything would be carried out to the letter. Finally he inclined his head and asked tactfully:

"Will that be all, sir?"

And, hearing a thoughtful "y-yes" in reply, he volunteered the information that after dinner that night a tarantella would be danced in the lounge by Carmella and Giuseppe, well-known all over Italy and to all the "tourist world."

"I've seen her on postcards," said the gentleman from San Francisco in a voice that expressed nothing. "And that Giuseppe fellow—is he her husband?"

"Her cousin, sir," the *maître d'hôtel* replied.

And after a moment of hesitation, thinking of something but saying nothing, the gentleman from San Francisco dismissed the man with a nod.

After that he started dressing for dinner with as much care as if he were preparing for his wedding. He switched on all the lights, flooding all the mirrors in the room with brilliance, glitter and the reflection of furniture and open trunks. He began to shave and to wash, ringing the bell incessantly, while other impatient rings, coming from the rooms of his wife and daughter, clashed with his and assailed the corridor with peals. And Luigi, in his red apron, distorting his face with a grimace of horror which reduced the maids, who were running past with jugs of water, to tears of laughter, bounded along to answer the gentleman's bell with the lightness inherent in so many fat men. Rapping on the door with his knuckles, he asked with feigned humility, exaggerated to inanity:

"*Ha sonato, signore?*"

And from the other side of the door came a drawling, rasping and pointedly polite voice:

"Yes, come in. . . . "

What did the gentleman from San Francisco feel, what did he think about on that night that was to be so momentous for him? Like anyone else who had just had a rough crossing, be wanted nothing but his dinner and dreamed with relish of his first spoonful of soup, his first sip of wine; he was actually somewhat flurried as he performed his customary ritual of dressing for dinner, so he had no time for thought or feeling.

When he had shaved and washed and neatly fitted his false teeth back into place, he stood before the looking glass and wielding a pair of silver brushes vigorously put the strands of sparse pearly white hair into place on his dark yellow skull. Then he pulled his cream-colored underwear on his aged but still strong body, its waistline thickened from overeating, put his black silk socks and pumps on his lean flat feet; then bending his knees he adjusted the silk braces that held up his black trousers, tucked in his snow-white shirt with its bulging starched front, fixed a pair of shining links into his cuffs, and began the struggle to force the collar stud into the stiff collar. He still felt the floor was heaving, the tips of his fingers hurt dreadfully, the stud pinched the sagging skin under his Adam's apple, but he was adamant and at last he got the better of the job. His eyes shining from exertion, his face livid because the tight collar was strangling him, he sank down exhausted on the stool in front of the dressing table and faced his full-size reflection which was repeated in all the other mirrors in the room.

"Oh, it's dreadful!" he muttered, dropping his strong bald head, without trying to understand, without thinking what it was he found so dreadful. Then, from habit, he keenly inspected his short fingers with their gout-hardened joints, his large almond-shaped, almond-colored fingernails, and repeated with conviction, "It's dreadful . . . "

But just then the dinner gong boomed for the second time, sonorously as in a heathen temple. And, getting up hurriedly, the gentleman from San Francisco tightened his collar still more with a tie, drew in his stomach with a waistcoat, put on his coat, straightened his cuffs, and looked himself over in the glass once more. "That Cannella girl, olive-skinned with artifice in her eyes, like a mulatto, in her flowery orange dress, must be an exceptionally good dancer," he mused. And briskly walking out of the room, he followed the carpeted corridor to his wife's room next door and asked in a loud voice if they would be ready soon.

"In five minutes!" his daughter's voice, lilting and already gay, called back.

"Fine," said the gentleman from San Francisco.

And with leisurely steps he started down the corridors and red-carpeted stairs in quest of the reading room. The servants he met flattened themselves against the wall when they saw him, while he strode by, apparently unaware of them. There was an old lady, who was late for dinner, hurrying along the corridor in front of him as quickly as she could—an old lady with milky-white hair and a back that was already stooped, but who wore, despite this, a low-cut gown of pale-gray silk. Her gait was funny, like an old hen's, and he had no difficulty in catching up with her and leaving her behind. At the glass doors leading into the dining room, where everybody was already seated and had begun to eat, he stopped in front of a table loaded with boxes of cigars and Egyptian cigarettes and, choosing a large Manila, he threw three lire down on the table. As he passed through the winter garden he glanced casually out of the open window. A gentle breeze wafted from the darkness, he fancied he saw the top of the old palm tree spreading its gigantic-looking branches from star to star, he heard the steady wash of the sea in the distance. In the quiet, cosy reading room, unlighted but for the lamps shining over the tables, was an old gray-haired German who stood reading some rustling newspapers, a man who looked like Ibsen, with crazy, bewildered eyes behind round silver-rimmed spectacles. Eyeing him coldly up and down, the gentleman from San Francisco settled himself in a deep leather armchair in a corner, beside a green-shaded lamp, put on his pince-nez and, twitching his head because the collar was choking him, he disappeared entirely behind his newspaper. He quickly ran through some of the headlines, read a few lines about the never-ending war in the Balkans, turned the page over with a customary gesture—and suddenly the lines blazed up before him with a glassy brilliance, his neck strained forward, his eyes bulged, and the pince-nez slipped down his nose. He jerked forward, he tried to take a breath—and gave a bestial wheeze. His lower jaw sagged open, gold fillings gleamed in his mouth, his head fell back on his shoulder and lolled helplessly, the hard front of his shirt jutted out, and his whole body began to slip down to the floor, while he kept struggling with someone and kicking up the carpet with his heels.

If it had not been for the presence of the German in the reading room, they would have managed to hush up this horrible occurrence quickly and neatly, instantly whisking away the gentleman from San Francisco by his head and his feet down the back alloys, as far away as possible, and never a soul from among the hotel guests would have known what he had been up to. But the German rushed screaming out of the reading room, raised a commotion in the dining room, and roused the whole place. Many of the guests jumped up from their dinner, overturning chairs, many went pale and ran to the reading room, crying, "What's happened, what's it all about?" in different languages, and no one gave them an answer. No one could make out what had happened because to this day people find death the most amazing thing in the world, and they flatly refuse to believe in it. The hotel-owner dashed from one guest to the other in an effort to hold back the rout and to calm them with hurried assurances that it was

nothing, a mere trifle, a little fainting fit that had seized a certain gentleman from San Francisco. But no one was listening to him, for many had
seen the waiters and valets tearing off the gentleman's tie, waistcoat and
crumpled dinner jacket, and even, for some unknown reason, dragging the
pumps off his black, silk-clad flat feet. But be was still writhing. He
doggedly struggled with death, he refused to give in to the thing that had
borne down on him so unexpectedly and rudely. He jerked his head from
side to side, be wheezed as though his throat had been cut, he rolled his
eyes drunkenly. When they had hastily carried him in and laid him on the
bed of room No. 43—the smallest, poorest, dampest and coldest room at
the end of the ground floor corridor—his daughter came running in with
her hair streaming, her dressing gown gaping open to reveal the bare
bosom lifted high by her corsets, and after that came his wife, big and
heavy, quite dressed for dinner, her mouth round with horror. But by that
time he had even stopped jerking his head.

Within a quarter of an hour everything more or less settled down to
normal at the hotel. But the night was irreparably ruined. Some of the
guests came back into the dining room and finished their dinner, but in
silence and with injured expressions, while the owner went from table
to table, shrugging in helpless and seemly annoyance, feeling that he was
blamelessly guilty, assuring everyone that he understood perfectly "how
unpleasant it all was" and promising to do "everything in his power" to
remove this unpleasantness. But the tarantella had to be canceled, nevertheless. Extra lights were put out, most of the guests left for the beer hall,
and everything grew so quiet that you could hear the clock ticking in
the lobby which was deserted except for the parrot who muttered
woodenly, fussing in its cage before settling down to sleep and finally
doing so with one claw flung ridiculously over the top perch. The gentleman from San Francisco lay on a cheap iron bed, covered with coarse
woolen blankets, in the dim light of a single bulb close to the ceiling. A
rubber ice bag hung down on his cold, wet forehead. His livid and
already dead face was cooling gradually, the hoarse rattle, breaking
through his open mouth with its glitter of gold, was growing weaker. It
was no longer the gentleman from San Francisco who was wheezing—
he was no more—it was someone else. His wife, his daughter, the doctor and the servants stood and looked at him. Suddenly, the thing they
had been waiting for, the thing they dreaded, happened—the wheezing
ceased. And slowly, very slowly, before the eyes of all of them, a pallor
spread over the face of the deceased, his features grew finer and lighter,
with a beauty that would have befitted him long ago.

The owner came in. "*Già è morto*," the doctor told him in a whisper. The owner shrugged, his face impassive. The lady came up to him with tears trickling down her cheeks, and timidly suggested that the deceased should now be taken up to his room.

"*Mais non, madame*," the owner objected hastily and politely but with no gallantry whatsoever now, and he spoke to her in French and not in English, for he had no further interest at all in those trifles which the visitors from San Francisco might now leave behind in his cashbox. "It's quite impossible, madame," he said and added, in explanation, that he valued the suite most highly and that if he agreed to her request, the whole of Capri would come to know of it and tourists would refuse to stay in the rooms.

The daughter, who had been looking strangely at him all this time, dropped into a chair and, smothering her mouth with her handkerchief, burst into sobs. The mother's tears dried instantly and her face flushed red. She raised her voice, she became insistent, stating her demands in her own language and still unable to believe that all respect for them had been irrevocably lost. The owner rebuked her in politely dignified tones: if madame disapproved of the hotel rules, he dared not hold her there; and he declared firmly that the body was to be removed by morning, that the police had been notified and a representative was due immediately to carry out the necessary formalities. Was it possible to get a coffin, even if it was only a plain ready-made one on Capri, madame asked? No, he was sorry, it was quite impossible and the time was too short to have one made. Some other way would have to be found. His English soda water, for instance, was shipped out to him in large, long packing cases . . . the partitions from one of the cases could be taken out . . . .

The hotel was plunged in sleep. They opened the window in room No. 43—which faced a corner of the garden where a sickly banana tree grew in the shadow of the tall stone wall with broken glass stuck on top. They switched off the light, left the room and locked the door. The dead man remained in the darkness. Blue stars gazed down upon him from the sky. A cricket in the wall began to chirp its melancholy, carefree song.

Two maids were sitting on the window sill in the dimly lit corridor, darning. Luigi came in with a pile of clothes in his arms and shoes on his feet.

"*Pronto?*" (Ready?), he asked anxiously in a loud whisper, rolling his eyes at the frightening door at the end of the corridor. And, waving his free hand lightly in that direction, he hissed loudly, "*Partenza!*" which is the usual shout in Italy when a train steams out of a station, and the maids clung closely together, choking down their soundless laughter.

And then he ran up to the door with soft leaps, rapped upon the panel lightly and with his head inclined asked in an under-tone, in a most deferential manner:

"*Ha sonato, signore?*"

Now, constricting his throat, jutting his lower jaw forward, in a voice that was rasping, sad and drawling, he spoke the answer, as if it was coming from the other side of the door:

"Yes, come in."

At daybreak, when the sky grew light beyond the window of room No. 43 and the damp breeze rustled in the ragged leaves of the banana tree, when the blue sky of morning awakened and spread its cloak over the Island of Capri, and the pure, clear-cut top of Monte Soliaro turned golden in the reflection of the sun, rising beyond the distant blue mountains of Italy, when the road menders started out on their way to work, repairing the island's paths for tourists to tread, then a long soda-water packing case was brought to room No. 43. Shortly afterward it became very heavy and pressed painfully against the knees of the junior porter who was taking it in a one-horse cab at a brisk pace along the white highroad that wound down the mountain-side. The driver, a flabby man with bloodshot eyes, in a shabby old coat, short in the sleeves, and down-at-heel boots, had a hangover, for he had been playing dice all night long at the inn. He kept whipping his sturdy young horse, which was decked out in the Sicilian fashion with briskly jingling, clamoring bells of different shapes on the bridle, adorned with red wool pompons, and on the tips of the high copper ridge of the pommel, and with a quivering, yard-long feather sticking up from its trimmed forelock. The cabman was silent, crushed by his own dissoluteness and his vices, and the fact that the night before he had lost all those coppers with which his pockets had been crammed. But the morning was crisp and with air as fresh as this, the nearness of the sea and the blue skies above, a head is soon cleared of its drunken haze, and lightheartedness is quickly recovered; and then the cabman also found consolation in the unexpected fee he had earned from some gentleman from San Francisco, who was rolling his dead head about in the packing case behind his back. The small ship, lying like a beetle on the bright and delicate blue that filled the Bay of Naples so generously, was already sounding the last hoots and these were eagerly echoed over the whole of the island whose every bend, every mountain ridge and every stone was so clearly visible, as if there were no atmosphere at all. At the quay the cab was overtaken by the car in which the senior porter was bringing the mother and daughter, both of them pale, with eyes sunken from tears and a sleepless night. And ten minutes later, the little ship was again chugging away in a swish of water to Sorrento and Castellammare, taking the family from San Francisco away from Capri forever. And once again peace and quiet was restored to the island.

On that island, two thousand years ago, there lived a man who got hopelessly entangled in his foul and cruel deeds, who for some reason rose to power over millions of people and who, losing his head from the senselessness of this power and from his fear that someone might thrust a knife into his back, committed atrocities beyond all measure. And mankind remembered him forever, and those who with combined effort are now ruling the world with as little reason and, on the whole, with as much cruelty as he did, come here from all over the world to take a look at the remains of the stone house on one of the sheerest sides of the island, where he used to live. That beautiful morning, all those who had arrived in Capri for this particular reason were still asleep in their hotels, although a string of little mouse-gray donkeys with crimson saddles were already being led up to the hotel entrances, for the Americans and Germans—men and women, young and old—to clamber on to when they got out of bed and had stuffed themselves with food, to be followed at a ran along the rocky paths, all the way to the very top of Monte Tiberio, by old Capri beggarwomen with staffs in their gnarled hands. The travelers slept in peace, comforted by the thought that the dead man from San Francisco, who had been planning to go with them but had instead just frightened them with a reminder of death, had already been shipped to Naples. And the island was still wrapped in silence, the shops were still shut. The fish and vegetable market in the small square was the only place open to business, and there was no one there but the common people. Among them idling his time away as usual, stood the tall boatman Lorenzo, a carefree old rake so unusually handsome that be was known all over Italy, where he had often sat for painters. He had brought along a couple of lobsters he had caught in the night and he had already sold them for next to nothing, and now they were rustling in the apron of the cook from the same hotel where the family from San Francisco had spent the night. Lorenzo was now free to stand there till evening if he so wished, glancing about him with a regal air and cutting a figure with his tatters, his clay pipe and his red flannel beret, worn over one ear. Two Abruzzian mountaineers came down the steep Monte Soliaro from Anacapri, down the ancient Phoenician path, with steps hewn out of the rock. One of them had a bagpipe under his leather cloak—a large goatskin bag with two pipes—while the other carried something that looked like a wooden flute. They were coming downhill, and the whole country lay below, joyous, beautiful and fulgent: the rocky bumps of the island, almost all of which lay at their feet, the fabulous azure in which it floated, the vapors of morning rising from the sea toward the east, shimmering in the blinding sun which was already hot as it rose higher and higher in the sky, the dimly blue mass of Italy with its mountains near and far still vague in the morning haze, the beauty of which man has no words to express. Halfway down the mountain they slowed their pace. There, above the path, in a niche in the rocky wall of Monte Soliaro, stood the Mother of God, bathed in sunlight, warmth and brilliance, clad in snow-white plaster robes, wearing the crown of a queen, rustily golden from the rains, meek and merciful, with eyes raised heavenward to the eternal and blissful abode of her thrice blessed Son. They bared their heads and raised their flutes to their lips—and praises poured forth, naïve and humbly joyous, to the sun, to the morning, and to her, the Immaculate Intercessor for all the suffering in this wicked and beautiful world, and to the One who had been born of her womb in a cave at Bethlehem, in the poor shepherds' shelter, in the far land of Judea.

And in the meantime, the body of the old man from San Francisco was returning home to its grave on the shores of the New World. After suffering much humiliation, much carelessness at the hands of men, traveling from one harbor warehouse to another for about a week, it found itself at last on board the same famous ship which had only such a short while ago brought it to the Old World in so stately a manner. But now they were hiding him from the living—they lowered him in his tarred coffin into the blackness of the hold. And once again the ship sailed off on its long voyage. That night it passed the Island of Capri and its lights, slowly vanishing in the dark sea, seemed sad to those who were watching it from the island. But there, on board, in halls flooded with light and gleaming with marble, a great ball was being held that night, true to custom.

A ball was held on the second and the third night out too—once again a furious storm was raging over the ocean, making it drone like a dirge and roll in mountains that were somber and black like a funeral pall, edged with a silvery fringe. To the Devil watching from the rock of Gibraltar, the stony gateway between the two worlds, the countless, blazing eyes of the ship were hardly visible behind the curtain of snow, as the ship sailed away into the night and the storm. The Devil was as vast as a rock, but the ship was even vaster than he was, many-tiered and many-funneled, created by the arrogance of a New Man with an old heart. The storm tore at its rigging and its wide-mouthed funnels, white with snow, but it was firm, stalwart, majestic and—frightening. On the very top deck, lonely amid the whirling snow, rose the cozy, dimly lighted apartments, where the corpulent Master, so like a heathen god, presiding over the whole ship, slept lightly and fitfully. He heard the deep howls and the furious squeals of the siren choking in the storm, but he sought reassurance in the proximity of something in the next room that was, in reality, the thing he could understand least of all: that large cabin, armor-clad it seemed, which every now and again was filled with a mysterious roar, a flickering and a dry sputtering of blue lights, which flared up and burst around the pale-faced radio operator with a half circle of metal round his head. At the very bottom, in the underwater depths of the *Atlantic* where the twenty-ton steel bulks of the boilers and other machinery shone dimly, hissed out steam and dripped boiling oil and water, in that kitchen where the motion of the ship was being cooked over infernal fires heated from below, power was churning, power frightening in its concentration, transmitted to the very keel, to the endlessly long vault, into the rounded and dimly lighted tunnel, where a colossal shaft rotated slowly in its oily bed with an inexorability that was crushing to a man's soul, as if it were a live monster stretched out in the muzzlelike tunnel. But the middle part of the *Atlantic*, its dining rooms and ballrooms, radiated light and joy; they hummed with the voices of a well-dressed crowd, sang with string orchestras and emanated the fragrance of flowers. And again there was the slender and graceful couple of hired lovers, swaying sinuously or clinging together convulsively, among the crowd, amid the brilliance of lights, silks, diamonds and women's naked shoulders: the pretty girl with downcast eyes that were depraved and modest, with innocence in her coiffure, and the tall young man with black hair that seemed glued down, his face pale with powder, dressed in a narrow long-tailed dress coat and graceful patent-leather pumps, a beautiful man who looked like a huge leech. And no one knew that it had long been nothing but drudgery for this couple to writhe in their sham bliss to the strains of the lewdly sad music, nor did anyone know that a coffin stood on the floor of the dark hold, far, far below them, close to the gloomy, sultry depths of the ship fighting against the darkness, the ocean and the storm . . . .

Vasilyevskoye, October, 1915

a maritime people

JAMES REID PARKER

IN THE COURSE of his eclectic career as *The New Yorker's* radio-restaurant-fashion reviewer, English teacher, and humorist, James Reid Parker developed a wicked eye for the hilarious incongruity between self-image and reality. Academics, attorneys, and wives suffered the same devastating scrutiny in his anecdotes. Here, Parker turns his attention to the allegedly innate nautical savvy of a British couple, unflappable victims of their own clichés.

the brilliant sunlight not only intensified the blue of the bay but dramatically heightened the autumn coloring of the scrub growth on the many small islands we see from the southeast windows of our house on the New England coast. Never before had the foliage of the low-bush blueberries seemed such a flamboyant red. For nearly a week, the days had been wonderfully warm, although the nights had been more than crisp enough to remind us that fall was nearly at an end. I asked my wife and our two English house guests, the Kynastons, to excuse me, and got up from the breakfast table and went outdoors to make sure of the wind direction and to do some amateur forecasting.

"It's almost certain to stay sunny throughout the day, and probably tomorrow, too," I said when I returned. "There's a moderate westerly breeze. It may freshen a bit later on, but the barometer is still at 'Fair.' "

"Very gratifying," Professor Kynaston said, in his thin mandarin voice.

"What would you like to see today?" I asked him.

He considered the matter at some length, and with his customary gravity, before replying. "I believe we exhausted the conifers yesterday, and most of the other acid-loving trees," he said. "However, I'm not entirely sure that my notes on the hollies are complete. Did I understand you to say at dinner last night that we had seen *all* your indigenous hollies?"

I should explain that Professor Kynaston had been making a comparative study of our trees and those that grow along the coastal areas of western Scotland, prior to making a report to some sort of royal commission for the improvement of barren land over there. As for me, I am a local tree warden, and my wife and I were entertaining the Kynastons because a higher authority had asked us to. Our guests were in their middle fifties or thereabouts, and exceedingly sedate. This was the third day of their stay with us, and they were to depart the next morning. No real intimacy had developed between us, inasmuch as my wife and I respected the fact that the Kynastons simply weren't the kind of people who could thaw, or even make a pretense of thawing, on short acquaintance.

"Yes," I said. "At least, we've seen all the hollies that can be described as being useful for any practical purpose. As I said yesterday, most New England tree wardens and foresters consider hollies quite hopeless for windbreaks and that kind of thing, except perhaps for the *Ilex glabra*."

"Oh, I agree," he broke in quickly. "And as far as *Ilex glabra* is concerned, I must say I'm fascinated to see how well it does for you. When you say that we have seen all the 'useful' hollies, I assume you mean there is one, or perhaps more, that we have *not* seen."

I admitted that this was the case. The previous summer, I said, I had found seven specimens of a dwarf variety on one of the more remote islands in the bay.

"A true dwarf?" Professor Kynaston asked. "Are you sure they weren't merely examples of an ordinary variety that had been wind-pruned?"

"Oh, no," I said. "They're true dwarfs, all right. They're not exactly common in this part of the country, but you do run across them sometimes."

"I should like very much to see dwarf hollies growing in such an exposed location. Couldn't we secure a boat of some sort and treat ourselves to a pleasant outing? I need hardly say that I'd be glad to pay all the necessary expenses. After all, I *am* permitted to make field trips, and, for that matter, we might turn it into a combined field trip and picnic for the four of us. You'd enjoy that, wouldn't you, Sybella?"

Mrs. Kynaston assented with a stately nod. A day on the water, she said, would be extremely pleasant. "Are you fond of punting?" she asked me, and I had to explain that in New England we have very few streams with the requisite shallow bottom and slow current.

"Salt-water sailing is what we go in for mostly in these parts," I told her. "In fact, I was about to say that it wouldn't be any problem at all for us to get hold of a boat to take us out to Tern Island, where I found the dwarf hollies. I have an eighteen-foot sloop. The Nonpareil was built for racing, so she isn't the last word in comfort, but I think I can promise you she'd run us out to Tern and back without any trouble."

"Splendid!" the Professor said. "And I assure you we shan't complain if your cushions and back rests aren't precisely designed for sybarites. A day on the water will be a treat in itself."

There are no back rests on the Nonpareil, and while I suppose the hard, canvas-covered mats on the locker seats are technically "cushions," I myself never ventured to apply so voluptuous a term to them.

"We have friends who live near Henley," Mrs. Kynaston remarked. "When we go to them for Whitsun, as we always do, we so enjoy watching the holiday pleasure craft on the Thames. Literally a *multitude* of boats going up and down the river!"

I couldn't quite see the connection. With a certain nervousness, I began to wonder whether the Kynastons really understood what sort of day they were in for. Already several small incidents had suggested to me that Professor Kynaston, although wonderfully informed about trees, was perhaps a trifle vague about matters *not* pertaining to trees. As for Mrs. Kynaston, I still hadn't been able to form a clear idea of what she was really like.

My wife, who loves to sail, said with regret that she wouldn't be able to go with us, because she had a one-thirty appointment at her hairdresser's. "Which is just as well, for your sake," she remarked to Mrs. Kynaston. "Four's a crowd on the Nonpareil. I'd better hurry out to the kitchen and start fixing you a picnic lunch. My husband will probably want to make an early start if he's taking you as far as Tern."

Professor and Mrs. Kynaston begged her not to supply them with anything more elaborate than a single sandwich apiece and perhaps a piece of fruit. After English austerity, they said, they simply couldn't seem to accustom themselves to our "largish American luncheons."

Apologetically, I told my wife that she had better put in at least two sandwiches for me and a thermos of hot soup. "I'll go down to the wharf and start bailing out," I told her. "Will you dig up some sweaters and denims for the Kynastons? And see if you can fit them out with old sneakers from that pile in the cupboard under the front stairs." Turning to Professor Kynaston, I explained that shoes with leather soles are more of a drawback than an asset on board a sloop. "If we sail in about half an hour, we can make Tern Island by eleven-thirty or twelve, see the hollies and have our lunch, and be home by four-thirty or five or thereabouts," I said. "Tern is the southernmost island of a group that's strung out like a necklace. Getting there takes time and involves a good deal of tacking, as a rule."

THE KYNASTONS TURNED up at the wharf while I was still bailing, and to my amazement I saw that they were dressed as if for a garden party. The Professor was wearing white flannels, and Mrs. Kynaston had changed into a somewhat fluttery blue silk crêpe, quite stylish shoes, and a fussily elaborate hat. Each of them had a rolled waterproof tucked under an arm, and the Professor was carrying a picnic basket. Mrs. Kynaston was also equipped with a furled umbrella, which I somehow couldn't quite visualize her putting to any really practical use on board the Nonpareil.

"Didn't my wife say *anything* to you about clothes?" I asked, aghast at beholding their attire.

"Oh, yes!" they assured me, and the Professor said amiably, "She was solicitude itself, but we rather thought we'd be a bit more comfortable in some of our own things. We knew you wouldn't mind."

"I'm afraid I didn't do too good a job of explaining what our day would probably be like," I said, aware that I had failed to dispel their Henley-inspired notions about boating. "If the wind freshens, as it's almost certain to do, the return trip will be downright rough!"

Seemingly undismayed, the Professor remarked to his wife, "Apparently our outing will be more in the nature of a day at Cowes."

The prospect clearly gratified Mrs. Kynaston, who said, "*We* shan't mind if it's a bit chippy-choppy. In fact, I rather hope it *will* be."

"It may be considerably more than that," I said.

"Neither William nor I will be seasick," Mrs. Kynaston said with dignity as her husband and I helped her step down into the Nonpareil. "We enjoyed the Queen Elizabeth immensely, coming over."

"You must remember that we are a maritime people," Professor Kynaston reminded me, not altogether jocosely.

I said I hadn't been thinking so much of seasickness as of their getting drenched. "The only extra clothes I've got stowed away here are a couple of old sweatshirts, and at best they'll be dampish, I'm afraid," I said.

"You must stop worrying about us," Professor Kynaston said evenly as he and his wife established themselves on a narrow locker seat. "After all, we have our macks." They were sitting bolt upright and studying the rigging with interest.

Surrendering to the British, as so many others before me have done, I went to work raising the mainsail. Then I cast off, and presently raised the foresail. One of the things that had brought about the present complication, I decided, was the phenomenally warm Indian-summer weather we were having. Like a good English June, it had, as a matter of routine, connoted white flannels and garden-party hats to the Kynastons, in connection with genteel outdoor pleasures. As I steered the sloop out into the gently ruffled bay, I made a point of chatting informatively about Indian summer. Also, I explained about jibing, the theory of the centerboard, and the functions of the various sheets.

"Boating seems to be rather more work than I had supposed," Mrs. Kynaston said, raising her eyebrows. "I must adjust some of my preconceptions."

"I confess I had no idea the pastime was so complicated," the Professor agreed.

We were sailing through a channel, a sort of marine avenue defined by red buoys and black "nuns," and we were gaining speed.

"But delightful," Mrs. Kynaston added. She took a deep breath of the delicious air, and exhaled it with an expression not unlike that worn by the men in cigar ads. "It really is, you know, William."

"As soon as we pass the last nun, I'm going to jibe," I said. We sailed on for a bit, and then I called out, "Ready? Ready to jibe?"

"Oh, quite," Professor Kynaston said.

"Such amusing words," Mrs. Kynaston remarked to her husband. "The 'nuns' are the floating black canisters, I believe Mr. Parker said, but I forget his exact definition of 'jibe.' "

"*Duck!*" I shouted.

The boom swung around and by a miracle Mrs. Kynaston escaped a concussion. Missing her scalp by perhaps an inch, the boom swept her hat off her head with the precision of a football player executing a neat kickoff.

"Oh, God!" I groaned. "Are you hurt?"

"Not at all," she said with great calm. "Merely dishevelled, I should imagine."

"I'm terribly sorry. And your hat is gone forever, I'm afraid."

"It never was a great success at the University, actually," she said. "And my husband always felt there were rather too many grapes around the brim."

IN OPEN WATER, the Nonpareil suddenly began to demonstrate her special talent for skimming the surface like an uninhibited gull.

"I say, Sybella!" the Professor exclaimed, suddenly lapsing into the phraseology of an excited schoolboy. "Isn't this ripping!"

Unexpectedly, we cut through a medium-large wave instead of winging our way over it. All of us received a thorough drenching, and Mrs. Kynaston in her once-fluttery blue crêpe looked much the most waterlogged.

I said wretchedly that this was what I had been expecting. To my astonishment, Mrs. Kynaston abandoned all her reserve and cried, "Glorious! Oh, William, isn't this superb?" The Professor agreed with her fervently. "And now that we're wet all over, there won't be any point in our putting on our macks," she added, as if she had a real hatred of mackintoshes.

"You'd better let me dig out those old sweatshirts," I said, but the Kynastons scorned the suggestion. The Professor said, "Your—er—Indian sun will soon dry us nicely," and it did, but only briefly. We had many more deluges of spray before the day was over.

As we skirted Mackerel Island, at about eleven o'clock, and as the low nubbin of land known as Tern Island became visible, Mrs. Kynaston announced that she was ravenous. She had crawled onto the gunwales about an hour before, and was lying sprawled on her stomach, with one arm prudently hugging the mast in case of a sudden lurch. Her iron-gray hair had come loose and was flying, pennant-fashion, in the wind. Clearly, she was taking a sensuous delight in the warm sunlight, as I was doing myself. I could hardly believe that we were within a day or so of November, so delectable was this bonus weather we were having.

"Why not go ahead and have your lunch?" I said. "You needn't wait until we reach Tern. I'm sorry you asked my wife to make only one sandwich apiece for you." I fished out the lunch basket and inspected its contents. "She took you at your word, I'm afraid, but she put in two for me and some hot soup."

"When I came down to breakfast this morning, I was a reasonable facsimile of a civilized man, but I now find that I have sloughed off civilization completely," Professor Kynaston declared cheerfully. "I shall probably slit your throat and cast your body overboard, merely for two additional sandwiches and a spot of hot soup."

"There are some odds and ends in the cabin, as a rule," I said. "Can you eat things cold, out of cans?"

"I could eat a rat *saignant,*" Professor Kynaston said with decision.

"If you'll take the tiller, I'll go and have a look," I said. Professor Kynaston took over, and I crawled into the tiny cabin and searched for provisions. I found a can of chili con carne, a can of condensed vegetable soup, and a can of hamburgers in brown gravy. There was a small Sterno outfit but no fuel. Hearing an ominous slapping sound, I poked my head out of the cabin and said to the Professor, "You're luffing. Pay out enough to fill your sails again."

"You're making the sails flap too much, William," Mrs. Kynaston bellowed, in a quarter-deck voice. "Loosen the what-you-may-call-it and recapture the wind!"

Professor Kynaston obeyed these combined orders after some momentary fumbling, and the Nonpareil again flew over the water. I emerged carrying the three tins and a can opener. Already the Kynastons had done away with the small snacks my wife had fixed for them, and were doing their best not to let their glances wander toward my own rations. "Here are some oddments," I said, displaying the canned food. "If you'd like my sandwiches and soup, I wouldn't in the least mind eating one of these. Or if you think you'd like to try stuff out of a can, you're welcome to anything in this assortment."

"Why don't we share *everything?*" Mrs. Kynaston cried with the utmost enthusiasm. I found a rusted fork and spoon in the cabin, and Mrs. Kynaston, who had already applied the can opener to the tin of hamburgers, called to me exultantly, "We won't need utensils for these. They're little *rissoles*, apparently, and we can pick them up with our fingers."

I shared my sandwiches and hot soup with the Kynastons, and we all scooped out forkfuls and spoonfuls of the cold canned food.

"Magnificent!" said Professor Kynaston, wolfing cold chili.

"Sheer heaven!" said Mrs. Kynaston, devouring condensed vegetable soup.

"The flavor!" said Professor Kynaston, licking his fingers after plucking from the third tin a hamburger coated with congealed grease and eating the stuff with relish, "I don't know when I've ever tasted anything so delicious."

When Mrs. Kynaston had polished off a trifle more than her share of the condensed soup, she asked wistfully how we proposed to allot "the fourth little *rissole*." It hardly seemed worth while to divide it, she said carelessly. And so of course we handed it over to her. "Really quite in a class with Simpson's or Scott's," she said with admiration. "What a superb lunch you've given us! I could do with a serviette, as my handkerchief is in an extremely bedraggled state, but who cares? Could anything matter less?" She wiped her mouth with the back of her hand.

As WE NEARED Tern Island, I said, "Pull the centerboard up, please," to Professor Kynaston, and began to do some quick work with the sheets. Very shortly, I heard a light crunching sound. "Up centerboard!" I shouted. It was too late. We hadn't quite gone aground, but the centerboard had eased into the shallow, sandy bottom just enough to serve as an anchor for us. We were perhaps seventy feet from Tern itself. "If you and I jump out and push her off carefully, we can raise the centerboard and then edge ourselves closer to shore," I said to Professor Kynaston. "If we don't, the tide will soon go out enough to ground us. I hate to ask you to help, because of your white flannels, but I'm afraid you've already got them wet many times over, and as far as shrinking is concerned, not much more damage could possibly be done."

The Professor said reasonably, and in a most unmandarinlike voice, "Why don't I take them off? Because I most certainly propose to do my share of the pushing." He began to unbutton his trousers. "With your permission, Sybella," he said over his shoulder, in a perfunctory aside.

She waved graciously but did not speak, being engaged in trying to drain the teaspoonful or so of liquid that still remained in the thermos, which she had tilted to her lips in the manner of a Hogarth drunkard.

The Professor leaped over the side in his shorts, and he and I succeeded in clearing the Nonpareil's centerboard. We then worked the sloop nearer to the shore. "I completely forgot to tell you at breakfast that you'd probably have to take off your shoes and stockings and wade ashore," I said to Mrs. Kynaston. "It wouldn't be necessary if the tide were higher, but, as it happens, it's going out. The water is freezing cold, but the sun is so hot you'd dry off right away on shore if you want to risk it."

In no time, Mrs. Kynaston bare-legged, was wading ashore, her teeth chattering. I said earnestly that I hoped she wouldn't catch pneumonia. She seemed much amused. "I happen to be English," she said.

We spent only a few minutes on Tern, just long enough to "do" the hollies and to satisfy Professor Kynaston that they were true dwarfs and not wind-pruned specimens of a larger type. Then we shoved off and retraced our course of the morning. The Professor's seamanship showed a steady improvement, and Mrs. Kynaston, too, became remarkably proficient. In fact, the two of them took on the handling of the foresail entirely. In appearance, they were by this time as raffishly unkempt as a couple of pirates out of an Errol Flynn epic. Even before midafternoon, my guests were hungry again, but I could find nothing for them except a few broken pilot biscuits. For these crumbs they were touchingly grateful.

WHEN WE ARRIVED at the house, the Kynastons told my wife enthusiastically and with nautical camaraderie that they were going upstairs for a few minutes and that when they came down, she would find them ready for a tea of mammoth proportions. "Give us enough for at least eight people," Mrs. Kynaston called down, with bluff geniality, from the stair landing. "It won't be too much!"

Obviously amazed at the sea change that apparently had come over our guests, my wife hurried out to the kitchen to prepare tea, while I went to put on some clean, dry clothing, although nothing at all special. The Kynastons, on the other hand, lost no time in getting into soberly conservative outfits of the utmost correctness. They came downstairs looking much as they had looked at breakfast, except that their complexions were ruddier. I couldn't help noticing that they were wearing not only dignified clothes but a dignified manner as well.

"Now tell me about your day," my wife said, sitting down to preside at the tea table.

"It was most enjoyable," Mrs. Kynaston said sedately.

"Most," the Professor concurred with dignity, and in the mandarin voice. "I was so pleased to be able to broaden my acquaintance with your hollies. The dwarfs were well worth seeing."

"So green and glossy," murmured Mrs. Kynaston. "I should like to have one of the same sort—potted, you know—for my morning room at home."

For several moments, I listened to the seemly crunching of buttered toast and wondered whether the whole day could have been something I had imagined. Then I remembered Mrs. Kynaston, knee-deep in icy water, saying to me with calm amusement, "I happen to be English," and I felt entirely reassured.

from the seabourn
spirit to istanbul

PAUL THEROUX

THE GENESIS ACCOUNT of Noah and the ark has spawned a

prolific line of nautical yarns that include such allegorical satires as

Sebastian Brant's *Das Narrenschiff* (1494), Mark Twain's *The*

Innocents Abroad (1869), and Katherine Anne Porter's *A Ship of Fools*

(1962). In "The Seabourn Spirit to Istanbul" (1995), novelist and trav-

el writer Paul Theroux weds reportage to allegory as he takes an acer-

bic look at the antics of the financially, chronologically, and temporally

over-endowed passengers of a super-luxurious, sybaritic cruise ship.

On our third day at sea we were all given a printed directory, a little four-page brochure, as elegant as a gourmet menu, of the passengers' full names, and where they lived. I kept it, read it carefully, used it as a bookmark, and as it became rubbed and foxed with use I scribbled notes—question marks, quotations, warnings to myself—beside some of the names.

From Richmond Virginia, then, came Mr. William Cabell Garbee, Jr., and Mrs. Kent Darling Garbee, and from Southold, New York, the Joe Cornacchias, whose horse "Go for Gin" had just won the Kentucky Derby; from East Rockaway, the Manny Kleins, to whom on the quay at Giardini Naxos, near Taormina, I gave instructions in the use of an Italian public telephone. Mr. Pierre Des Marais II and Ms. Ghislaine LeFrancois had come from Ile Des Soeurs, Quebec; Ambassador Bienvenido A. Tan, Jr., and Mrs. Emma Tan, from Manila, Republic of the Philippines—the ambassador, retired, now did "charitable work," in a public manner; and the Uffners, the Tribunos and the McAllisters from New York; all these joined the *Seabourn Spirit* that day on the quay at Nice.

The Mousers were from Boca Raton, and smoked heavily and invented fabulous new destinations with their malaprops, such as their cruise "to Rio J. DeNiro" and "Shiva, Fuji." And from Honolulu there were the Bernsteins: Mark, who had once been obliged to destroy on behalf of a client twenty-two million Philippine pesos (one million U.S. dollars), a five-hour job on his office shredder; and his wife, Leah, who represented the popular Hawaiian singer Israel Kamakawiw'o'ole, whose current weight was over seven hundred pounds. Mrs. Sappho Drakos Petrowlski from Simsbury, Connecticut (but formerly a dealer in fresh flowers in the Florida Keys), was traveling as a companion to Mrs. Mary P. Fuller, ninety-one years old, of Bloomfield, Connecticut, widow of brush tycoon Alfred Fuller, who sold brushes door-to-door and then founded the Fuller Brush Company.

There was Harry Jipping, a developer, from Reno, Nevada, who said, "Malta—is that an island, or a country? Isn't it part of Italy? You mean it's got its own money and all that?" and "That black stuff—what's it called? Right, caviar—that Cornacchia guy's always chomping on it."

Harry was traveling with his wife, Laverne, a Frisbie from Grand Junction. The Joneses from New York, the Smiths from Toronto, the Greens from Wooton Wauwen, England, Mrs. Doris Brown from Lauderdale, Florida, the Burton Sperbers from Malibu. And Jack Greenwald from Montreal, who wore a blazer with solid gold buttons, and his regimental tie of the Household Cavalry, and who addressed the waiters in French, usually to describe his personal recipes which he insisted on their delivering to the head chef, Jörg, and seldom spoke to another passenger on board except to say, "Can you tell me what a drongo is?" or "I'm down to two desserts." Mr. Greenwald's wife was the former actress Miss Constance Brown.

The Zivots from Calgary, the Alfred Nijkerks from Antwerp, Belgium, the Sonny Prices from Sylvania, Ohio, and the Rev. Deacon Albert J. Schwind from Beach Haven, New Jersey, Señor and Señora Pablo Brockmann from Mexico City, Mr. Ed and Mrs. Merrilee Turley from Tiburon, California. Mrs. Blanche Lasher from Los Angeles was on her twelfth cruise; so were the Ambushes and the Hardnetts.

And Mrs. Betty Levy of London and the Algarve was on her thirtieth cruise and had been up the Amazon. "I love your books, I've read every one of them," Mrs. Levy said to me. "Are you writing one about this cruise?"

"No, unless anything interesting happens," I said, so confused by her directness that I realized that I was telling her the truth.

The Fritzes, the Norton Freedmans, the Louie Padulas—all these people, and more, boarded the *Seabourn Spirit* that day in Nice.

THE SUMMER HAD passed. It was low season again. I needed an antidote to Albania and the shock I had gotten in Greek Corfu, an island leaping with chattering tourists that reminded me of the rock apes on the slopes of Gibraltar. I had gone home and tended my garden, and then in late September I went to Nice. I joined this cruise. I had never been on a cruise before, or seen people like this.

Many were limping, one had an aluminum walker, Mrs. Fuller was in a wheelchair, some of the wealthiest looked starved, a few were thunderously huge, morbidly obese. Like many moneyed Americans who travel they had a characteristic gait, a way of walking that was slow and assured. They sized up Greek ruins or colorful natives like heads of state reviewing a platoon of foreign soldiers, with a stately and skeptical squint, absolutely unhurried. That, and an entirely unembarrassed way of laughing in public that was like a goose honking ten tables away.

"You've got to be a mountain climber to get up these stairs!"

"Why don't they turn the air conditioner on?"

"Who's that supposed to be?"

It was the color portrait on B Deck of the Norwegian King and Queen—two of Scandinavia's bicycle-riding monarchs, King Harald V and Queen Sonia. The ship was Norwegian, registered in Oslo.

Some were rather infirm or very elderly or simply not spry, with a scattering of middle-aged people and only one child (Miss Olivia Cockburn, ten, of Washington, D.C., traveling with her grandparents). The majority were "seniors," as they called themselves, who had the money or time to embark on such a cruise. Hard of hearing, the passengers mostly shouted. Their eyesight was poor. Eavesdropping was a cinch for me, so was note-taking.

"This is our eighth cruise—"

"Did you do the Amazon—?"

"Vietnam was very unique—"

Most of them, on this luxury cruise through the Mediterranean, were sailing from Nice to Istanbul. Some were going on to Haifa. Betty Levy was headed into the Indian Ocean with the ship. The cost for this, excluding airfare, was one thousand dollars a day, per person.

I was a guest of the shipping company. There was no disgrace in that. It often happens that a writer is offered free hospitality, in a hotel or on a ship. Few newspapers or magazines actually pay a penny for the trips their writers make, and so travel journalism is the simple art of being slurpingly grateful. It posed no moral problem for me, but because my writing made me seem as though I was continually biting the hand that had fed me, my ironizing was nailed as "grumpy" and I was seldom invited back a second time. That was fine with me. In travel, as in many other experiences in life, once is usually enough. . . .

THE *SEABOURN SPIRIT* was a moderate-sized ship of ten thousand tons. Its 180 passengers were accommodated not in cabins—the word was not used—but in two-room suites: double beds, bathtubs, a liquor cabinet, a television set, and not a porthole but a picture window through which you could see the Mediterranean. On various decks, there were a swimming pool, several Jacuzzis, an exercise room, a sauna room; a large marina unfolded from the stern, complete with two speedboats.

Tipping was forbidden on the *Seabourn Spirit*. You could eat whenever you liked, alone or with a group of people. You could host a dinner party at short notice and they would prepare a table for twelve. You could call room service and say, "Caviar for six and two bottles of champagne," and it was there in your suite in ten minutes.

I had always thought you worked and saved to put your kids through college. I had now discovered that there were Americans who worked and saved to take vacation cruises on ships such as the *Seabourn Spirit*. A fourteen-day cruise for two in 1994 was about equal to what it cost the average student in the United States to attend a good private university for one academic year: that is, about $28,000. . . .

THE WHITE SHIP growled south bathed in full sunshine on the glittering sea, following the low shore of Italy that was never more than a long narrow stripe at the horizon, like the edge of a desert, a streak of glowing dust.

Our progress was following one of the oldest routes in the Mediterranean. "Coasting was the rule" in the Mediterranean Fernand Braudel wrote in *The Structures of Everyday Life*. It was rare for any ship to risk the open sea, even as late as the seventeenth century, because the fear of the unknown was so great. "The courage required for such an unwonted feat has been forgotten." Mediterranean sailors usually went from one port to the next, along the coast, and it was a brave sailor of the high seas who ventured out of the sight of land, from Mallorca to Sicily, or Rhodes to Alexandria. "The procession of coasting vessels steered by the line of the shore, to which they were constantly drawn, as if by a magnet."

But our ship steered parallel to the coast for the pleasure of seeing it, and hovering, as a reminder of where we were.

The clear day of unobstructed sun became a blazing late afternoon, the western sky and sea alight, and at last in a reddening amphitheater of light, a buttery sunset.

AN INVITATION HAD been clipped to my door: Did I wish to join the First Officer and his guests for dinner?

There were ten people, and the subject at my end of the table was what we did for a living.

Millie Hardnett said that her husband had made his fortune in specialty foods—canned fruit, jars of peaches in wine, exotic syrups—and after selling his business to a food conglomerate they now spent their time cruising.

Twisting his dinner roll apart, Max Hardnett asked me, "Someone told me you were a writer, Paul. Have you published anything under your own name?"

"My husband sold his company to Sara Lee," the woman to my left said.

This was Mary Fuller, whose husband had founded Fuller Brush. And another fact: Sara Lee was a real person, a middle-aged woman whose father had named the cheesecake, the company, and everything else after her. She had a last name, but no one could remember it.

Her companion, Sappho, said to me, "Alfred wrote a book, too. You say you're a writer? You should read it."

A Foot in the Door, by Alfred Fuller, described (according to his widow) how he had grown tired of being a poor farmer in Nova Scotia and took a hint from his brother, who worked for a brush company, and decided to sell brushes door-to-door. What's that? You mean I don't have the brush you require? Well, describe it to me and I will supply it to you. Alfred was open to customers' suggestions and created brushes to fill their needs. Bottle brushes, wide brooms, whisks and dust mops. This was pioneering salesmanship and soon Alfred had teams of men out there, ringing doorbells and hustling for commissions.

"It was a real Horatio Alger story," she said.

"What do you think about that?" Sappho asked me.

"I met Arthur Murray once in Honolulu," I said. Why was I telling her this? He was another famous name on a business. "I even know someone who danced with him. Arthur Murray taught her to dance in a hurry."

"Alfred thought up the idea of direct selling," Mary Fuller said. "It's not popular now because of crime."

She was ninety-one and kept to her wheelchair but she was not at all frail, and she had a good appetite. At times, surveying the table, she looked like a sea lion, monumental and slow in the way she turned her head. She kept her good health, she said, by visiting mineral baths in places like Budapest and Baden-Baden. She mumbled but she was lucid. She spent each summer in Yarmouth, Nova Scotia.

"How did you meet Alfred?" I asked.

"He courted me in New York," she said. "He was very determined. When he wanted something he got it. That's why he was so successful in business, too. My mother called him 'The Steam Roller.' "

She went on a cruise every year, she said. This simple assertion brought forth a torrent of cruise memories from the rest of the table.

"This is our sixth cruise in three years—"

"We were up the Amazon—"

"So were we. I wanted to go into the jungle in a canoe, but instead we shopped in Manaus—"

"I went to Antarctica. In the summer of course. Penguins—"

"We cruised China. That was special—"

"Down the Yangtze—"

"Vietnam on the *Princess*—"

IN THE MORNING we were anchored off Sorrento, high steep cliffs and pretty palms and dark junipers, the carved porches and stucco walls of hotels and villas. At the Hotel Vittoria Excelsior it was possible to see the suite where Caruso had stayed. Across the bay was Mount Vesuvius, Naples in its shadow, smothered in a cloud of dust.

This was a different Italy from the one I had seen in the winter. I had been traveling second-class on trains, among working people and students; in my Italy of cheap hotels and pizzas I often lingered to watch people arguing, or goosing each other, or making obscure gestures. I seldom saw a ruin or a museum. But this *Seabourn* Italy was the Grand Tour of the Italy of colorful boatmen and expensive taxis and day trips. It was the coast of castles and villas, but there was no need to go ashore: you could sit under the awnings and simply admire Italy, its glorious seaside. Just look at it, and then doze and let the ship sail you to a new coast. After all, the Mediterranean shore was much prettier viewed at a distance. . .

THE MODERN VERSION of Pompeii is probably the nearby town of Positano, a small harbor shared unequally by the idle rich and the landladies and the fishermen. If Positano were to be buried in volcanic ash today, future generations would understand as much about our wealth and our pleasures and the prosaic businesses such as bread-making and ironmongery as Pompeii taught us. They might not find a brothel, but they would find luxury hotels, the San Pietro and Le Sirenuse. The Roman author and admiral Pliny the Elder died in the Pompeii disaster; a Positano disaster could gobble up the film director Franco Zeffirelli, who lives in a villa there. It was perhaps this coast's reputation for wickedness that induced Tennessee Williams to make his decadent Sebastian Venable in *Suddenly Last Summer* begin to go to pieces in Amalfi, before he was finally eaten by cannibalistic boys in an other Mediterranean resort, the mythical Cabeza del Lobo.

The *Seabourn* was not leaving until late, and so I paid a Sorrentino driver eighty dollars to take me to Positano. This was my expansive *Seabourn* mood: I would never have paid that money when I was jogging along on trains and ferries.

Along the Amalfi drive, winding around the cliffs and slopes of this steep coast—much too steep for there to be a beach anywhere near here—I told the driver my fantasy of Positano being buried in ash. The driver's name was Nello, and he was animated by the idea.

"It could happen," Nello said, and began to reminisce about the last eruption.

It was in 1944, he was twelve. "My madda say, 'Hashes!'"

Nello insisted on speaking English. He claimed he wanted practice. But that was another thing about travel in a luxurious way: the more money you had, the more regal your progress, the greater the effort local people made to ingratiate themselves and speak English. I had not known that money helped you off the linguistic hook.

"Vesuvio wassa making noise and zmoke. The hashes wassa flying. Not leetle hashes but ayvie, like theese," and he weighed his hands to show me how heavy they were. "We has hambrella. Bat. The weend blows hashes on de roof and—piff—it barns.

" 'Clean de roofs!' my madda say."

"It sounds terrible," I said.

"It wassa dark for two day. No san. Hashes!"

And it was certain to erupt any minute, Nello said. The volcano was long overdue.

We got to Positano. Isn't it lovely? Nello said. Yes, it was, a steep fun-nel-shaped town tumbled down a mountainside into a tiny port. What could be more picturesque? But it was a hard place to get to—the nar-row winding road. It was expensive. It was the sort of place, like Pompeii, that you took a picture of and showed your friends and said, "We went to Positano." And they said, "Isn't it darling? Those gorgeous colors." It was the Mediterranean as a museum: you went up and down, gaping at certain scenes. But really I had learned more about Italy in the crum-bling village of Aliano or the seedy backstreets of Rimini.

On the way back to Sorrento and the ship Nello said he was too tired to speak English, and so, in Italian, we talked about the war.

"The Germans had food when they occupied Naples," he said. "We didn't have anything to eat. They threw bread away—they didn't give any to us. And we were hungry!"

"What happened after Liberation?"

"The Allies gave us food, of course. They handed out these little boxes with food in them. Delicious."

"So the war was all about food, right?"

"You're making a joke!"

But I was thinking that this precise situation was happening across the Adriatic: the Serbians had food, the Bosnians had none; the war was being fought as viciously as ever.

WE SAILED FROM SORRENTO after dark, and sometime in the night we passed through the Straits of Messina. This time I did not think of Scylla and Charybdis. I was absorbed in my meal and probably being a buffoon, saying, "Yes, Marco, just a touch more of the Merlot with my carpaccio." The ship was silent and still in the morning. I pressed the button on my automatic window shade and it lifted to show me the coast of Sicily. Craning my neck, I could see Etna, and on the heights of the cliffs on the nearby shore the bright villas and flowers of Taormina.

It was so beautiful from the deck of this ship anchored in the bay that it seemed a different town from the one I had trudged around some months ago. I had been a traveler then, looking for D. H. Lawrence's house. This time I was a tourist. I bought some ceramic pots, then I walked to the quay and showed Manny Klein how to use the public telephone.

"You're an old pro," he said.

Later, in the lounge, the *Seabourn Spirit* passengers said they were a bit disappointed in Sicily. But it wasn't really that. It was a growing love for the ship which eventually took the form of a general reluctance to leave it, to look at any ruins, to eat ashore, or even go for a walk on the pier when the *Seabourn Spirit* was in a port. The ship had become home—or more than home, a luxury residence, a movable feast.

"MAY I SUGGEST the Two Salmon Terrine with caviar and tomato, followed by Essence of Pigeon with Pistachio Dumplings?" the waiter, Karl, asked. "And perhaps the Game Hen with Raisin Sauce to follow?"

Karl, of Italian, German and Ethiopian ancestry, was the spit and image of the Russian poet Alexander Pushkin, one of whose grandmothers was a black Abyssinian.

"As I mentioned the other day, I try not to eat anything with a face," I said. "Which is why I had the asparagus and truffles last night, and the stir-fried vegetables."

"Yes, sir."

"Nor anything with legs."

"Yes, sir."

"Nor anything with a mother."

"No fish, then."

"Fish is a sort of vegetable," I said. "Not always, but this Gravlax with mustard sauce, and the Angler Fish with Lobster Hollandaise might fall into that category."

"Soup, sir?"

I looked at the menu again.

"I'll try the sun-dried blueberry and champagne soup."

For dessert I had a banana sundae with roasted banana ice cream, caramel and chocolate sauce. The man at the next table, gold buttons flashing, had just finished a plate of Flamed Bananas Madagascar and was about to work his way through a raspberry soufflé with raspberry sauce.

After dinner I went on deck and strolled in the mild air for a while. The night was so clear that from the rail I could see the lights of Sicily slipping by; the places I had labored through on the coastal trains were now merely a glowworm of winding coast, Catania, Siracusa and, farther down, at the last of Sicily, the twinkling Gulf of Noto. . . .

THAT NIGHT, AS the *Seabourn Spirit* crossed the Ionian Sea at twelve knots, I dawdled over my note-taking and went to the dining room late. On this ship, everyone had a right to eat alone, but the maitre d' said that if I wished he would seat me with some other people—providing they did not object.

That was how I met the Greenwalds, who were from Montreal. Constance was demure, Jack more expansive—the previous night I had seen him polish off two desserts.

"What did you think of Malta?" I asked.

"If you wanted to buy a brass door-knocker," he said, "I guess you'd come to Malta. There are thousands of them for sale there, right? Apart from the door-knockers, it wasn't much."

"Did you buy one?"

He was a bit taken aback by my question, but finally admitted yes, he had bought a brass door-knocker. "I thought it was an eagle. But it's not. I don't know what it is."

"Isn't that a regimental tie you're wearing?" I asked.

"Yes, it is," he said, and fingered it. "The Royal Household Cavalry."

"They let Canadians join?"

"We are members of Her Majesty's Commonwealth," he said. "Though as you probably know, there's a secessionist movement in Quebec."

"What sort of work do you do?"

He semaphored with his eyebrows in disgust and said, "Scaffolding."

"Really?"

He smiled at me and said, "See, that's a conversation stopper."

"Mohawks in New York City are capable of climbing to the top of the highest scaffolds," I said, to prove it was not a conversation stopper.

"I'm not in scaffolding, I was just saying that," he said. "'What do you do?' is the first question Americans ask. But it's meaningless. 'I'm Smith. I'm in steel manufacturing.'"

He was a big bluff man, and his habit of wearing a blazer or a peaked cap gave him a nautical air, as though he might be the captain of the *Seabourn* if not the owner of the shipping line. He seldom raised his voice, and he took his time when he spoke, and so it was sometimes hard to tell when he had finished speaking.

The waiter was at his elbow, hovering with a tureen of soup.

"Oh, good," Jack Greenwald said. "Now I'm going to show you the correct way of serving this."

After we began eating the conversation turned to the cruise. Most people on the cruise talked about other cruises they had taken, other itineraries and shipping lines and ports of call. They never mentioned the cost. They said they took ships because they hated packing and unpacking when they traveled, and a ship was the answer to this. It was undemanding, the simplest sort of travel imaginable, and this sunny itinerary was like a rest-cure. The ship plowed along in sunshine at twelve knots through a glassy sea by day, and the nights were filled with food and wine. Between the meals, the coffee, the tea, the drinks, in the serene silences of shipboard, young men appeared with pitchers of ice water or fruit punch, and cold towels. And there was always someone to ask whether everything was all right, and was there anything they could do for you.

"I was on a Saga ship, cruising to Bali," Jack Greenwald said. "Forty-one passengers and a hundred and eighty crew members. "Can you imagine the number of times I was asked, 'Is everything all right?' "

Over dessert—again Jack was having two, and being very careful not to spill any on his regimental tie—and perhaps because I had not asked, he volunteered that he had been the producer of a number of plays and revues. The names he mentioned meant nothing to me. *Up Tempo* was one. It rang no bells. *The Long, the Short and the Tall?* Nope. Titles of plays or musicals, because they were usually reworded clichés, sounded familiar but inspired no memories.

"*Suddenly This Summer?*"

"Rings a bell."

"Parody of Tennessee Williams," Jack said. "Did very well."

"Before my time, I think."

"I sometimes have problems with writers," he said. "There was one that made problems. I had to pay him two-fifty a night for one joke he had written. Just one line."

"What was the line?"

"Someone in the cast says, 'Will the real Toulouse-Lautrec please stand up?' "

"That's not very funny," I said.

"No. And the writer complained that he was not being paid on time. His lawyer sent me a big long lawyer letter. I said to myself, 'Hell with it,' and took the line out. Writers."

"That's what I do for a living."

"Know the story about the writer?" he said. "Writer makes it big in Hollywood and wants to impress his mother. So he invites her out to visit him. She takes the train and he goes to the station with flowers, but he doesn't see her anywhere. Finally he goes to the police station to see whether they know anything, and he spots her there. 'Ma, why didn't you have me paged at the station?' She says, 'I forgot your name.' "

"That's not funny either," I said, but I was laughing.

"It's odd, isn't it, Brownie?" he said to his wife. "We've broken our rule. We've actually had dinner with another passenger."

"I hope that wasn't too painful for you," Constance said to me.

"Tomorrow I'll tell you how I made some lucky investments in the Arctic," Jack said. "Frobisher Bay. Making a deal with some Eskimos while they ate a raw seal on the floor. I'm not joking."

AFTER A MAN has made a large amount of money he usually becomes a bad listener. Jack Greenwald was not a man in that mold, he was not in a hurry, and he was a tease, but with an air of mystery. "I happen to be something of an authority on Persian carpets," he would say. Or it might be Kashmiri sapphires, or gold alloys, or oil embargoes. If I challenged him I was usually proven wrong.

These deals in the Canadian Arctic, this talk of "my carver," "my goldsmith," and the billiard room he was planning to build, with a blue felt on the billiard table, made him seem like the strange tycoon Harry Oakes, whom he somewhat resembled physically; but there was an impish side to him too, a love of wearing Mephisto sneakers with his dinner jacket, and a compulsion to buy hats, and wear them, and a tendency to interrupt a boring story with a joke.

"Hear the one about the eighty-year-old with the young wife?" Jack said, when the subject of Galaxídhion, our next port, was raised in the smoking room, where he had just set a Cuban cigar aflame. "His friend says, 'Isn't that bad for the heart?' The old man says, 'If she dies, she dies.' "

I HAD FLED from Corfu after arriving on the boat from Albania. I had tried and failed to get to Ulysses' home island of Ithaca. But there was only one ferry a week. The *Seabourn* passed south of it in the night and I felt I had returned to roughly where I had left off and was continuing my Mediterranean progress. I had felt a deep aversion to Corfu which even in the low season was a tourist island. The whole of Greece seemed to me a cut-price theme park of broken marble, a place where you were harangued in a high-minded way about Ancient Greek culture while some swarthy little person picked your pocket. That, and unlimited Turkophobia.

We had sailed south of the large island of Cephalonia, and passed Missolonghi, where Lord Byron had died, into the Gulf of Corinth, anchoring off the small Greek village of Galaxidhion, on a bay just below Delphi. Indeed, beneath the glittering slopes of Mount Parnassus. Tenders took us ashore, where we were greeted by the guides.

"My name is Clea. The driver's name is Panayotis. His name means 'The Most Holy.' He has been named after the Blessed Virgin."

The driver smiled at us and puffed his cigarette and waved.

"Apollo came here," Clea said.

Near this bauxite mine? Great red piles of earth containing bauxite, used to make aluminum, had been quarried from depths of Itea under Delphi to await transshipment to Russia, which has a monopoly on Greek bauxite. In return, Russia swaps natural gas with Greece. Such a simple arrangement: we give you red dirt, you give us gas. Apollo came here?

"He strangled the python to prove his strength as a god," Clea went on, and without missing a beat, "The yacht *Christina* came here as well, after Aristotle Onassis married Jackie Kennedy, for their honeymoon cruise."

Through an olive grove that covered a great green plain with thousands of olive trees, not looking at all well after a three-month drought, we climbed the cliff to Delphi, the center of the world. The navel itself, a little stone toadstool *omphalos*, is there on the slope for all to see.

"I must say several things to you about how to act," Clea began.

There followed some nannyish instructions about showing decorum near the artifacts. This seemed very odd piety. It was also a recent fetish. After almost two thousand years of neglect, during which Greek temples and ruins had been pissed on and ransacked—the ones that had not been hauled away (indeed, rescued for posterity) by people like Lord Elgin had been used to make the walls of peasant huts—places like Delphi were discovered by intrepid Germans and Frenchmen and dug up.

Delphi had not been operational since the time of Christ. In the reign of Claudius (A.D. 51), "the site was impoverished and half-deserted," Michael Grant writes in his *Guide to the Ancient World*, "and Nero was said to have carried 500 statues away." Delphi was officially shut down and cleared by the Emperor Theodosius (379–95), who was an active campaigner for Christianity. It is no wonder that what remains of Delphi are some stumpy columns and the vague foundations of the temples—

hardly anything in fact except a stony hillside and a guide's Hellenistic sales pitch. Anyone inspired to visit Delphi on the basis of Henry Miller's manic and stuttering flapdoodle in *The Colossus of Maroussi* would be in for a disappointment.

The Greeks had not taken very much interest in their past until Europeans became enthusiastic discoverers and diggers of their ruins. And why should they have cared? The Greeks were not Greek, but rather the illiterate descendants of Slavs and Albanian fishermen, who spoke a debased Greek dialect and had little interest in the broken columns and temples except as places to graze their sheep. The true phil-hellenists were the English—of whom Byron was the epitome—and the French, who were passionate to link themselves with the Greek ideal. This rampant and irrational phili-Hellenism, which amounted almost to a religion, was also a reaction to the confident dominance of the Ottoman Turks, who were widely regarded as savages and heathens. The Turks had brought their whole culture, their language, the Muslim religion, and their distinctive cuisine not only here but throughout the Middle East and into Europe, as far as Budapest. The contradiction persists, even today: Greek food is actually Turkish food, and many words we think of as distinctively Greek, are in reality Turkish—*kebab, doner, kofta, meze, taramasalata, dolma, yogurt, moussaka,* and so forth; all Turkish.

Signs at the entrance to Delphi said, *Show proper respect* and *It is forbidden to sing or make loud noises* and *Do not pose in front of ancient stones.*

I saw a pair of rambunctious Greek youths being reprimanded by an officious little man, for flinging their arms out and posing for pictures. The man twitched a stick at them and sent them away.

Why was this? It was just what you would expect to happen if you put a pack of ignoramuses in charge of a jumble of marble artifacts they had no way of comprehending. They would in their impressionable stupidity begin to venerate the mute stones and make up a lot of silly rules. This *Show proper respect* business and *No posing* was an absurd and desperate transfer of the orthodoxies of the Greeks' tenacious Christianity, as they applied the severe prohibitions of their church to the ruins. Understanding little of the meaning of the stones, they could only see them in terms of their present religious belief; and so they imposed a sort of sanctity on the ruins. This ludicrous solemnity was universal in Greece. Women whose shorts were too tight and men wearing bathing suits were not allowed to enter the stadium above Delphi, where the ancients had run races stark ballocky naked. In some Greek places photography of ruins was banned as sacrilegious.

In spite of this irrationality, the place was magical, because of its natural setting, the valley below Delphi, the edge of a steep slope, the pines,
the shimmering hills of brilliant rock, the glimpse of Mount Parnassus.
Delphi was magnificent for the view it commanded, for the way it
looked outward on the world. The site had also been chosen for the
smoking crack in the earth that it straddled, that made the Oracle, a
crone balancing on her tripod, choke and gasp and deliver riddles.

" 'What kind of child will I give birth to?' someone would ask the
Oracle," Clea said. "And the Oracle was clever. She would say, 'Boy not
girl,' and that could mean boy or girl, because of the inflection."

"I don't get it," someone said. "If the Oracle could see the future, why
did she bother to speak in riddles?"

"To make the people wonder."

"But if she really was an Oracle, huh, why didn't she just tell the
truth?"

"It was the way that oracles spoke in those days," Clea said feebly.

"Doesn't that mean she really didn't know the answer?"

"No."

"Doesn't that mean she was just making the whole thing up?"

This made Clea cross. But the scholar Michael Grant describes how
the prophecies were conservative and adaptable to circumstances, and he
writes of the Oracle, "Some have . . . preferred to ascribe the entire phenomenon to clever stage management, aided by an effective information
system."

Clea took us to the museum, where one magnificent statue, a life-
sized bronze of a charioteer, was worth the entire climb up the hill. As
for the rest I had some good historical sound bites for my growing collection.

—*The Oracle sat on this special kettle and said her prophecies.*

—*Pericles had very big ears, which is why he is always shown wearing a helmet.*

On the way back to the ship, while the guide was telling the story of
Oedipus—how he got his name, and killed his father, and married his
mother, while frowning and somewhat shocked *Seabourn* passengers listened—I began to talk to the Cornacchias, Joe and Eileen, who told me
about their recent win at the Kentucky Derby. It was the second time a
horse of theirs had been triumphant—"Strike the Gold" had won in
1991, and "Go for Gin" this year.

"What's your secret?" I asked.

"I have a very good trainer who knows horses. He feels their muscles.
I also have a geneticist, who checks them out. It's a science, you know."

The Cornacchias lived on the north shore of Long Island, some miles east of Gatsby country. Eileen was an admiring and pleasant person and Joe an unassuming man, who did not boast. He was also very big. "I tell the horses, 'If you don't win, I'm going to ride you.' "

"What was the purse this year?"

"I won eight-point-one million bucks. Broke even."

"Where's the profit, then?"

" 'Go for Gin' is starting to make money as a stud."

Back on the ship, we resumed our voyage, and as the sun set behind Corinth we slid through the narrow Corinth Canal, with just a few feet to spare on either side. Jack Greenwald stood on deck in his blazer, smoking a thick Monte Cristo, waving to the Corinthians on shore. . . .

"THE SEA," WROTE Kazantzakis, rhapsodizing in *Zorba the Greek*, "autumn mildness, islands bathed in light, fine rain spreading a diaphanous veil over the immortal nakedness of Greece." Happy is the man, I thought, who, before dying has the good fortune to sail the Aegean Sea.

"Many are the joys of this world—women, fruit, ideas. But to cleave that sea in the gentle autumnal season, murmuring the name of each islet, is to my mind the joy most apt to transport the heart of man into paradise. Nowhere else can one pass so easily and serenely from reality into dream. The frontiers dwindle, and from the masts of the most ancient ships spring branches and fruits. It is as if here in Greece necessity is the mother of miracles."

Dreamy, sentimental, passionate Kazantzakis, of the purple prose and the purple nose! His Greece, especially his native Crete, is mostly gone now and the paradox is that (if I may borrow an empurpled leaf from one of the master's own books) it seems that Kazantzakis's Oedipal feeling for his motherland produced the inevitable Greek tragedy. Tourists came in droves to verify Kazantzakis's sensuous praise of the Greek sluttishness, and rumbunctiousness, and goodheartedness, the cheap food and the sunshine.

The early visitors were not disappointed, but in the end Greece—so fragile, so infertile, so ill-prepared for another invasion—became blighted with, among nightmares of tourism, thousands of Zorba Discos, Zorba Tavernas, Zorba Cafes and the *Zorba the Greek* bouzouki music from the movie soundtrack played much too loudly in so many souvenir shops. All the curious, the fake icons, the glass beads, the t-shirts and carvings and plates (Souvenir of Mycenae); and regiments of marching Germans, resolutely looking for fun. Greece had needed a few metaphors. Kazantzakis provided the highbrow, or at least literary, metaphors; movies and television provided the rest.

The *Seabourn* lay at anchor at the Greek port of Ágios Nikólaos ("Ag Nik" to its habitués). There were many Zorba businesses here, and the sign *As seen on the BBC* was displayed at various parts of town, for this place, specifically the nearby leper island of Spinalonga, was the setting for a popular and long-running series entitled "Who Pays the Ferryman."

"You didn't see it?" a German said to me at a cafe in town. He was incredulous, and he mocked my ignorance. I was not offended. Since I spent many days mocking other people's ignorance, this was fine with me. "When this show was on television in Germany, the streets were empty. Everyone was at home watching it. Me, too. That's why I came here."

The port and the town and everything visible had been given over to tourists; there was not a shop nor any sign of human activity, nor any structure, that was not in some way related to the business of tourism. All the signs were repeated in four languages, German taking precedence.

Writing about tourists—whether it is a harangue or an epitaph—is just pissing against the wind. There is a certain fun to be had from snapping the odd picture, or cherishing the random observation. But I had vowed at the beginning of my trip to avoid tourists and, whenever possible, not to notice them. Haven't we read all that elsewhere? I went ashore, bumped into the Greenwalds (Jack: "I've just been offered a genuine Greek icon for fifty dollars. Think I should buy it?"), walked around a little, and finding the crowds of milling tourists much too dense, I rented a motorcycle and left Ágios Nikólaos at sixty kilometers an hour. I rode east, down the coast, then southward over the mountains to the opposite side of Crete, to the town of Ierápetra. This place looked very much like Ágios Nikólaos which I had fled from: curio shops, tavernas, postcard shops, unreliablelooking restaurants, *Rooms for Rent! Bikes for Hire!*

There were plenty of Zorba enterprises here, too. And bullying restaurateurs and their touts brayed at passersby at Ierápetra.

"Meester—you come! You eat here! *Sprechen Sie Deutsch?* Best food in Griss! Where you go? Not some other place—you eat here!"

Every five feet there was an insistent tout, hustling people off the pavement and seating them, before any competitor could snag them. There was probably a more unpleasant figure one could be assaulted by than an unshaven Greek howling commands at me in ungrammatical German, but if so I could not think of one at the moment. They were seriously browbeating the perambulating tourists—just the mood to

whet your appetite; and when the people kept walking they were insult-
ed and abused by the touts they had passed.

All that and a foul beach, but the muddiest beach at Ierápetra was
called Waikiki, a misnomer that was merely a harmless desecration compared to the violence of calling a boardinghouse outside town The Ritz.

Elsewhere in Ierápetra the eighteenth-century mosque in a quaint
part of town had been wrecked and partly rebuilt. The minaret was still
standing. The Arabic calligraphy remained. But the interior was defiled,
having been turned into a tiny auditorium. Chairs had been set up, facing music stands, and the bass drum was propped against the wall.

Was this worse than the Turks in Istanbul revamping the Byzantine
magnificence of Santa Sophia's and making it a mosque, along with any
number of Christian churches? Probably not. But there were still
Christians functioning in Turkey and there were no Muslims in Greece.
Apart from the tourists and some retirees, there were no foreigners in
Greece. There were Arabs in Spain, Albanians and Africans in Italy,
Moroccans in Sardinia, Algerians in France; but there were no immi-
grants of any kind in Greece. The Albanians that came had been sent
back. Whether it was Greece's feeble economy that kept everyone except
Albanians (whose economy was abysmal) from wishing to settle there, or
Greek intolerance, was something I did not know. Perhaps it was both—
or neither, since the Greeks were themselves migrants, leaving in great
numbers for America and Australia.

Was Crete the ancient homeland of the Jews? Tacitus thought so. His
theory was inspired by the name of Crete's highest mountain, in the central part of the island: "At the time when Saturn was driven from his
throne by the violence of Jupiter, they abandoned their habitation and
gained a settlement at the extremity of Libya. In support of this tradition, the etymology of the name is adduced as a proof. Mt. Ida, well
known to fame, stands on the isle of Crete: the inhabitants are called
Ideans; and the word by a barbarous corruption was changed afterwards
to that of Judeans." . . .

AFTER WARM PURPLE Cauliflower with Olives in White Truffle
Vinaigrette, Chilled Plum Bisque, and Marinated Breast of Guinea Fowl
with Juniper Gravy—or did I salve my conscience with the Vegetable
Gratin?—I bumped into Mrs. Betty Levy and asked why she had been
missing at dinner.

"I'm feeling a bit precious today," Mrs. Levy said. "I had some consom-
mé in my suite. I don't want to get anything. They've all got something."

Now, well into our second week of this Mediterranean cruise on this glittering ship, we had learned a little about history (toilets were called Vespasians in ancient Rome, Pericles had enormous ears, Athenians ate porridge for breakfast), and found out a lot about each other. In many ways it was like being an old-time resident of an exclusive hotel. Passengers knew each other, and their families, and their ailments, and were confident and hearty.

"How's that lovely wife of yours, Buddy?"

"Say, is your mother any better?"

"Lovely day. How's the leg?"

The only stress was occasioned by the visits ashore—not that it was unpleasant being reverentially led through the ground plans of ancient sites, and down the forking paths of incomprehensible ruins, many of them no larger than a man's hand ("Try to imagine that in its day, this structure was actually larger than the Parthenon"). It was rather that every daily disembarkation for a tour was like a rehearsal for the final disembarkation, the day when we would leave the comfort of the *Seabourn*, and that was too awful to contemplate.

This ship was now more than home—it had become the apotheosis of the Mediterranean, a magnificent vantage point in the sea which allowed us to view the great harbors and mountains and cliffs and forts in luxury. At sundown we were always back on board, away from the uncertainty and the stinks of the port cities, and the predatory souvenir-sellers. We were on our floating villa which, in its way, contained the best of the Mediterranean. We drank the wines of the Midi and the Mezzogiorno, our dishes were better than anything we saw in the harborside restaurants, and rather than risk the detritus of the beaches, we had our own marina on the stern. Even with his billions, Aristotle Onassis had felt there was no greater joy on earth than cruising these sunny islands, and his honeymoon trip with his new wife, Jacqueline, was the very journey we were embarked on, sailing—it must be said—in our vastly superior ship.

From Crete, we sailed through the islands called the Sporadhes, living up to their name as sporadic—isolated and scattered—and onward past the Greek island of Kos, to the coast to Turkey, the port of Bodrum, with its crusader castle and its crumbling city wall and its market, which contained both treasures and tourist junk.

It was immediately apparent, even in the swift one-day passage from Greece to Turkey, that we were in a different country. I compared them, because as old enemies they were constantly comparing each other.

Turkey was both more ramshackle and more real. Travelers tended to avoid Turkey, which was not a member of the European Community (thanks in part to Greece's opposition), so Turkey had not depended on tourists for its income and had had to become self-sufficient, with the steel industry and the manufacturing that Greece lacked. Turks were calmer, more polite, less passionate, somewhat dour—even lugubrious; less in awe of tourists, and so they were more hospitable and helpful. Greeks were antagonistic toward each other, which made them hard for foreigners to rub along with; Turks, more formal, had rules of engagement, and also seemed to like each other better. Turkey had a bigger hinterland and shared a border with seven countries, yet Turks were less paranoid and certainly less xenophobic, less vocal, less blaming, perhaps more fatalistic.

We had crossed from Europe to Asia. Turkey is the superficially westernized edge of the Orient, Greece is the degraded fringe of Europe, basically a peasant society, fortunate in its ruins and (with most of the Mediterranean) its selective memory. But it was wrong to compare Greece with Turkey, since their geography and their size were so different. Greece's landscape was more similar to Albania, and if Greece was a successful version of Albania, Turkey was a happier version of Iran—perhaps the only moderate Muslim country in the world.

After the assault by touts at Greek ports it was restful to walk down the quay in Bodrum and not have Turks flying at us. That restraint was an Asiatic virtue. Turks also had Asian contempt, and were famously cruel, both knowing they were so and believing that most people in the world were just the same. If you abused Turkish hospitality (as I did frequently) and asked Turks whether they tortured their prisoners, they spat and said, "Everyone tortures their prisoners!"

It was raining in Bodrum. Half the *Seabourn* passengers did not bother to go ashore. But even in the rain the harbor looked alive, an effect perhaps of being full of beautiful wooden sailboats in port for a regatta. The crusader castle was intact, except for the occasional mark of an infidel's aggression. There were pious Latin inscriptions over the battlements and gateways ("No victory is possible without your help, O Lord"), a nice reminder that Christianity had kept its faith robust with its own *jihads*—holy wars that had lasted for centuries.

Walking past a carpet shop—an unmistakable sign that we were in Asia—I saw Jack Greenwald being harangued by the carpet dealer.

"This is not a carpet! This is a piece of art!" he cried. "I am selling art!"

Jack beckoned me in, introduced me to the dealer, Mr. Arcyet, as "my millionaire friend," and soon carpets were being unrolled and were flopping one on another. It was another Greenwald tease to abandon me to the hysteria of a Turkish carpet dealer who believed he had an American tycoon captive in his shop, on a rainy day in Bodrum.

His hysteria was short-lived, interrupted by a more dramatic event. Outside the shop, a huge Turkish woman had collapsed on the street, and she lay in the rain, her skirt hiked up, while a Turkish man slapped her face in a violent attempt to revive her, and other Turks sauntered by to stare. Soon there was a crowd of murmuring Turks, watching the supine woman, and when a taxi came to take her away, it required four of them to haul her into the backseat.

That unscheduled event was the only drama in Bodrum that day. It was too rainy to go anywhere. The phones would not work without a Turkish phone card, and there were no cards for sale anywhere in the town ("You come back next week"). I looked at the old mausoleum and the new casino and the suburbs of bungalows and condominiums of the sort that were being retailed elsewhere in the Mediterranean as holiday homes for Europeans in less congenial climates. The prices of this Turkish real estate ranged from $30,000 to $60,000—cheaper than, but just as hideous as, the ones in Spain, Malta and Greece.

Resolute about staying ashore, I had a Turkish lunch of eggplant, fava beans, stuffed peppers and a gooey dessert, and afterwards, back on the ship, realized that the people who had stayed on board had had a better lunch, a drier time of it, and still enjoyed the thrill of seeing the castle and the sailboats and the shapely Turkish mountains.

At dinner, the *Seabourn* was sailing north to Lesbos, and Jack Greenwald was in unusually high spirits in anticipation of dessert—one of his own recipes, *Fraises au poivre*, Strawberries with Black Pepper. Greenwald's high spirits took the form of teasing, and as we were at a larger than usual table, he was able to range over it, poking fun. To the Panamanian, he said: "Noriega was a very patriotic man, above all, don't you think?" To a woman wrinkling her nose: "That is how Eskimos say no. They say yes by lifting their eyebrows—here, do you think you can manage that, too?" To a rationalist at the head of the table: "Of course I believe in ghosts, and our prime minister, Mackenzie King, believed in ghosts, too."

This chatter was no more absurd than that of the other passengers.

"—Harry and I were at the Barbara Sinatra benefit for abused children," a woman was saying. "Tom Arnold was one of the speakers. He talked about the man who had abused him—"

"—figured, if you're in Turkey you've got to get a Turkish carpet. I measured the spot in the house and I've got the measurements with me. We're looking for something floral—my wife loves flowers. We don't want anything geometric—"

"—a couple of icons. They swore they were genuine—"

"—stayed for a whole week in the Sea Shells—they're islands in the Indian Ocean."

"—next time up the Amazon."

"—get to Rio J. DeNiro, during Carnaval."

At last, the waiter rolled a trolley toward Jack Greenwald with several bowls, and the strawberries, and in bottles and saucers various other ingredients for his dessert. Jack supervised and narrated the preparation.

"Nine plump fresh strawberries—good," he said. "Now, take that pepper mill and grind twelve twists of pepper," and he counted as the black pepper fell upon the crimson strawberries. "Take a tablespoon of Pernod and macerate them, yes, like that. And a tablespoon of Cointreau. Macerate. Lift them, let it reach all the berries. Now a tablespoon of Armagnac. Macerate, macerate."

"Yes?" The waiter showed Jack the bowl of slick speckled berries.

"A few pinches of sugar and three-quarters of a tablespoon of fresh créme," Jack said. "Mix carefully, just coat them with the créme. You notice how I pronounce that word 'clem'—that's because I'm from Montreal."

There was a bit more business with the *Fraises au poivre*. The plates were wrong. No, not soup bowls—but flat plates were needed for the serving, and the sauce had to be dripped just so.

"What do you think?" he asked, after I had sampled some.

It was hard to describe the taste, which was both a slow sweet burn, and peppery and syrupy and alcoholic and fruity; and I did not want to tell him that no taste could compete with the pleasure of watching this dessert being concocted by him and the deferential waiter.

To add to my pleasure, Jack immediately ordered a helping of Cherries Jubilee, another Greenwald variation, flambéed, with ice cream, and tucking in, he said, "Doesn't this go down nicely after the strawberries?"

Afterwards, he said that he had joined the cruise—he was going on to Haifa after Istanbul—in order to lose forty pounds, "but I'm having my doubts.". . .

MOST OF THE PASSENGERS were getting off the ship in Istanbul. A few were going on to Haifa. Mrs. Betty Levy was threatening to stay aboard for another month or more. Her dream, she told me, was to be at sea for weeks—no ports, no tours.

This impending sense of departure gave our progress up the Dardanelles the following morning a gloomy air of abandonment, and the funereal pall was not lightened by the knowledge that we were passing Gallipoli, and the two hundred thousand graves of fallen soldiers. The Dardanelles is like a canal, no more than a mile wide in some places, linking the eastern basin of the Mediterranean to the Sea of Marmara, where another canal—the Bosporus—divides Istanbul, and so on, to the Black Sea.

The Dardanelles is also the Hellespont of Leander, who swam back and forth to be with Hero; and of Lord Byron, in homage and in imitation. I had thought of swimming it myself—a mile was swimmable—but it looked uninviting in late October, with four- to five-foot breaking waves, and a heavy chop, with a cold wind blowing from Thrace on the north side.

"Freeze the vodka," Jack Greenwald was saying to the waiter in French, preparing him for the caviar course at tonight's dinner. "Wrap the bottle in a wet towel, put an apple in it for taste and keep it so cold it gets syrupy. Do you follow me?"

The bloody battlefield of Gallipoli was now the little Turkish village of Gelibolu, mainly fisherfolk, and where Xerxes and Alexander had marched their armies across on pontoon bridges, where Jason had sailed with his Argonauts in search of the Golden Fleece, there were rusty freighters, and more villages, and a town, Canakkale—some mosques and minarets visible, along with the factories and the clusters of houses. But it was wrong to expect anything dramatic. It was an old sea, of myths and half-truths and sound bites of history; its periods of prosperity and peace had been interrupted by even longer periods of disruption and pillaging. It was the center of many civilizations, but there had always been barbarians at the gates—and inside the gates.

Yet so little was left of the Mediterranean past that it was possible to travel the sea, from port to port, and never be reminded of the ancients. Even the recent brutality of Gallipoli was buried on the featureless shore—just another cemetery. There were so many graves on the shores of this sea.

Fog rolled in, dusk fell, blurred lights shone from the shore, some indicating the crests of hills. And then in this mist, a nocturne of misty light, there emerged and remained printed on the night a vision from the past, of a skyline that was purely minarets and towers, and mosque domes and bridges and obelisks, like a promise made in Byzantium that was being honored in the present. We had crossed the Golden Horn.

Closer to the European shore, which is the site of the old city, their features were more distinct, first the squarer lines of the Topkapi Palace, then Agya Irene, and the fifteen-hundred-year-old Agya Sophia, every brick intact; and behind its minarets, the six minarets of the Blue Mosque, and on the crest of the hill Nur Osmanye—the Light of God—the thick Byzantine fire tower, Yeni Mosque beneath it, at the end of the Galata Bridge, and beyond the vast almost unearthly masterpiece of Sinan, the Sülleyman Mosque, pale and glittering even in this shifting fog.

Ferries were crossing the Bosporus, passing the *Seabourn*, hooting, their lights illuminating the sea and giving the scraps of hanging fog the shimmering and golden texture of an antique veil, a little tattered and brittle, perhaps, but still usable for conveying mystery.

Just before I left the *Seabourn Spirit*, Jack Greenwald took me aside and gave me a gaily wrapped present. Inside was a Turkish lapel pin and his Household Cavalry tie.

"Wear them both," he said. "The pin will be useful here in Turkey. The tie is helpful everywhere."

"I'll feel like an imposter wearing this tie."

"Don't be silly."

"And isn't it an insult to your regiment?"

"Not at all," he said. "My regiment wasn't half as impressive as that one.

"Jack, do you mean you weren't a member of the Household Cavalry?"

"Oh, no, I was in another regiment—you wouldn't be impressed by that one," he said. "I only wear ties from fancy regiments. I get good results too. I'm always being saluted when I'm in London."

the voyage out

JOHN ROLFE GARDINER

WITH ITS inaccessible hold, unseen crew, and arcane navigational

procedures, an ocean-faring ship is, under the best of circumstances,

a complicated and mysterious place. But in wartime, when the dan-

gers of rough weather are compounded by the threat of submarine

and air assault, the ocean liner is truly the last resort of the desperate.

Shuttling between continents and years, and alternating deftly

between correspondence and journal entries, John Rolfe Gardiner tells

about a British schoolboy's passage to safety.

tony hoskins, at twelve, was an intellectual child, wary of sensation. Not a prodigy exactly, but at the head of his form at Cacketts School. He could declaim on several tales from Chaucer, and on the paths of the planets, even on the curious journeys of human sperm and ovum, although he hadn't a clue about finding a girlfriend or about what might be asked of him in pleasing one.

On this day he was saying all the wrong things. First to his father: "Daddy, at least I'll be sailing on a British ship, under a British flag."

"Actually not," he was told. "It's an American vessel. You'll be all right."

This was before the German began to aim his torpedoes at Yanks, before his subs began to hunt in wolfpacks.

"Not to worry," his father went on. "You'll be in convoy."

Why a convoy if no need to worry? His father, in Royal Army lieutenant's uniform, bare of medals, could not answer.

Hoping to put his religion in order before embarkation, Tony looked to his mother. "Tell me again, what's the Trinity?" he said unexpectedly just before the ship pulled out.

"Tiresome boy," she said. "Three in one and one in three. If you don't understand that, you shan't have a chocolate."

Again he was confused; his mother's simplistic formulation seemed at odds with her piety. Hardly off the gangplank, his legs rubbery with fear, he didn't want candy, only assurance that this huge and blunt-prowed merchant ship with a woman's name, the Ellen Reilly, riding high in the water, would come to safe port across the Atlantic and that his new school would be tolerable.

He saw other parents retreating, crying into handkerchiefs, stumbling off the boat and along the dock, giving their boys up to the sea and a new world. The drawn lips of his father and mother began to quaver as they turned away. And enemies appeared beside him, his second-form mates Booth and Jeffries, full of questions:

"Do the lifeboats have engines?"

"Is it daytime in Canada?"

"Will we take a secret course to avoid submarines?"

The same boys who despised him in the classroom, who had called him "twit" and "wonkie" for his privileged conversations with the masters, were hovering around him. Why should he nurse their fears?

And here came Rasson-Pier, who was older, a fifth former who had once caned Tony for impudence. Rasson-Pier told them all to shut up. He said the lot of them should be ashamed for leaving their country in wartime. And if it were up to him he'd be in uniform, not in retreat.

"Hoskins, you're in my cabin," he announced. "See that the beds are made taut."

Rasson-Pier, tall, well muscled, and lording it over the others from Cacketts, with gray eyes under blond bangs, and sufficient beard to be permitted a razor in his kit.

Riding down the channel from Folkstone, Tony tried to use his father's advice: "Think of the ship as the floating island of a country still at peace." Over on their left was France, which he knew to be alive with Germans; on the right, his own island, which, after dark, would be under attack again from the air.

Only three weeks earlier, Tony's headmaster, strolling across his playing fields at night, had been killed by a bomb far off its city target. A miraculous and devastating event, a direct hit on school morale. In the ensuing rearrangements of the school year, Tony and six other boys, and Mr. Pardue, history master of the stunned academy, had been booked on this empty supply ship—refugees for resettlement in a Canadian boarding school.

The Ellen Reilly came clear of the coast and swung to the west. There was no convoy, only open sea. Tony took the blank journal his father had given him that morning (with the advice of writing five hundred words a day at bedtime) and threw it over the side.

"You mustn't be angry," Pardue admonished. "It will only be fourteen days." But Tony gestured at the zigzag wake of the ship, the pattern of fear they were leaving on the sea behind them.

"Never mind," Pardue told him, "you'll be at their organ in two weeks. Maybe some of your Chopin, eh?"

"Maybe some of his Chopin, eh?" The other boys played with the line, but anxiety cracked their voices.

IN THE BOYS' new school, an oddity of brick and stone nestled in farm fields to the west of Toronto, they came to be known as "Me Boys from Cacketts," or "The Boys from Cacketts Minus One," after the tragedy at sea, while their teacher shepherd became "Pastor Pardue" among his new colleagues, who found him to be a total loss as an instructor, and a fount of useless homily: "There are no ifs in history."

They were set apart as a curious subculture among the relatively coarse population of Canadian boys—a little band with a higher order of fealty to the King, and led in intellect by the youngest, the pale scholar Tony. He was allowed into the school chapel each afternoon to practice at the organ, while the others were led off to a field to fight over a leather ball or flail away with cricket bats. Tony had come with two copies of his medical excuse, proof of his asthma—one to be filed in the school infirmary, and the other for his pocket. Thus reprieved from athletic torment, he was free to demonstrate his case that the body's only sensible purpose is to carry around the brain.

ON OCTOBER 28,1941, Lieutenant Gerald Hoskins dashed off a note, from his office in the London Cage, to his son, Tony, at the Charter Bridge School:

Dearest Tony,

Horrible, horrible. We had the awful news before your letter arrived. There are not enough tears in the world to answer for the loss of a child. And such a well-favored boy by all reports. You must be numb. Our only response to such an untimely death can be surpassing love for those who survive. Try to think of our love for you.

You say the Trinity was revealed to you on the crossing. Very well, but remember you are stuck to the planet by gravity, and from an Oriental perspective you may be upsidedown, worshipping the devil. But no more—the Colonel is calling.

P.S. No, we don't keep animals here. Nor are there Nazis in dank cells. "London Cage" is simply the informal name given to this interrogation center. From time to time I will write you from my office here, where I won't have your mother looking over my shoulder. The address here must remain unknown to you. Your letters should be posted home.

A second letter from the Lieutenant to his son, dated November 15, 1941:

Dearest Tony,

Nothing from you this month. Our assumption must be that you have settled in and found a schedule suited to your special needs. We

have a report from Dean Hastie, who tells us your academic proficiency
is "not balanced by contribution to community."

While offering the excuse of your harrowing journey, he cites you
for sarcastic remarks about the Canadian students, for shirking work in
the school garden, and resisting dress regulations.

Though your mother and I agree that shorts are not suited to the
climate, the answer is to bundle heavily on top. Wear the sweater, scarf,
and cap as prescribed in the school manual. You know that long trousers
come in the third form, just as they do at Cacketts.

You may have heard on the wireless that we are managing quite well
in the air. When I am not translating or writing interrogation reports,
they have me reading prisoners' mail. There, I've told you a little secret,
and you must keep it to yourself.

A sympathy committee has been got up here. We take turns visiting
the Rasson-Piers. When you have a moment you will write them whatever you can muster of David's last days.

Perhaps something you found heroic in him, or you could express
your wonder at his potential. As the last to see him you are a target of
their curiosity. They have questions beyond the police type, which they
are too discreet or griefbound to ask. It will be your job, now or later,
to anticipate and console.

It's too awful to think he might have been showing off acrobatically
so close to the side. Showing off for whom? one asks, since no one saw
him go overboard. So dreadful for all of you, wondering if he were hiding somewhere or actually lost at sea.

We hope the investigation has ended and we pray for your happiness.
Or, I should say, your mother prays and I beg of fate. Have you been
faithful to your journal? It will be a revelation to you in time to come.

After the blank journal had gone over the side, Mr. Pardue had gone
to his cabin to fetch a substitute, another bound notebook with marbled
cover.

"Your father told me how much this means to him," he said to Tony.
"I've put some starter lines in for you." He pointed to the first page:

> For every trouble under the sun,
> There be a remedy or there be none.
> If there be one, try and find it,
> If there be none, never mind it.

"You take it from there," he said, smiling.

Before they left the channel someone had puked. And now the boys' stomachs felt the rise, fall, and side shift of the Atlantic's heavy quartering waters. The first officer promised only more discomfort. "That's right—we're empty," he announced on the boat deck. "And the higher she rides, the further she rolls."

He had come from the bridge to lay down ship's rules for the Cacketts boys. At mealtime they would go to the mess deck, officers' side. The rest of the day they would remain in their cabins doing schoolwork. For exercise, they could walk the main deck, but only with Mr. Pardue's supervision. The bridge and hold of the ship were off-limits. The boys must stay out of the crew's cabins and out of the galley, or risk losing a hand to the steward's cleaver.

The officer had no sooner turned back when Rasson-Pier performed the first of his handstands on the ship's railing. Upside-down, he had winked at Tony as the ship rocked in a rising swell.

"See that, Hoskins?" The older boy's hand was on Tony's shoulder as they went to their cabin. "You can count on me, you see. I'll be watching out for you. You have nothing to fear from the chaps in Canada."

DEAN HASTIE AT the Charter Bridge School to the parents of Tony Hoskins in Brasted, Kent, November 30, 1942:

We normally write to parents of the boys from Cacketts at the end of each term. However, the head and I felt it would be wrong to delay in reporting that Tony is in a fair way to surpassing school records for third-form boys in Mathematics, Latin, and History of the Empire. He might achieve similar distinction in Composition if he could be kept to assigned topics.

We should recommend your son for immediate advancement to fourth form if his social and emotional maturity were up to the same marks. As you know, at Charter Bridge we strive to develop the fully rounded boy. We had expected that in his second year here Tony would have put new-boy diffidence behind him and joined with a will in some extracurricular pursuit.

Perhaps Tony has mentioned the motto cut in stone over our chapel door. "Remember Now Thy Creator in the Days of Thy Youth." We take the charge seriously, so you must not misunderstand when I say the religious conversion your son experienced on his journey here is troubling in its intensity. Our chaplain cannot shake him from his testimony that the Trinity was revealed to him on the ocean as three glowing balls. We see no joy in his faith.

I must tell you that the transfer has not been a complete success. The boys from Cacketts tend to remain a clique, though they sometimes quarrel among themselves. Your son does not seem to be a member, even of this separate band. We sense a residual grieving here for the loss of their young idol, and a weight of unfinished business. One boy has suggested that Tony's original account of the events at sea may not be reliable. And now, more than a year after the fact, our Mr. Pardue comes forward to say that your son may have kept a journal which might clear him of all suspicion. We wouldn't think of invading his privacy without warrant. Perhaps you would advise him to open relevant pages to our scrutiny.

A brighter note. Our musical instructor is leaving Charter Bridge this month, and we are asking Tony to fill in as chapel organist for Sunday service and Wednesday vespers. It's our little scheme to get him more involved.

On the journal's first page Pardue's verse has been scribbled over and splashed with ink:

Sept. 23, 1941. Aboard the Ellen Reilly: The ship is black, red, and rusty. Sailed 1420 Greenwich. R.-P.'s stunt behind Pardue's back takes everyone's breath. Supper: mashed potatoes, bright-yellow gravy of uncommon viscosity, and salty fish, white and cooked to a mush like the potatoes. One serving of greens a day; we missed them by coming aboard too late for lunch.

Tonight Jeffries came into our cabin crying. He wanted to know why I was put with R.-P. R.-P. said wouldn't the Germans love to see him like that. Jeffries left sniveling. R.-P. asked me down from my upper to play cards on his bunk. Twenty-one. No money, playing for favors, he said. I lost terribly, what do I owe him? R.-P. has torch with extra dry cells. He will allow me to use it to keep my notes. Says he's at sea in Latin. Quite so! And I, a second former, might help.

Booth came in shaking with fear. The idiot thinks he heard a torpedo propeller passing under us. No one can sleep.

A year after the crossing, the notebook was more useful to Tony as a chronology of odd particulars than as a thorough going journal—a skeleton on which his memory hung the dangerous flesh, the things he would never have written down. For example, the way Rasson-Pier's tone had changed after lights-out from cold command to simpering—as if he were taking the part of a woman in a play.

With the notion of water rushing in to drown him in his sleep, Tony had sneaked out of his cabin in the middle of the first night and wandered through dim-lit passages, down metal stairways, into empty cargo compartments. Somewhere close to the throbbing center of the ship he heard a horse whinny and a lion roar. Alarmed by what he took to be his own inventions, he became confused in retreat, and spent an unconscionable time finding his cabin again.

FROM LIEUTENANT GERALD HOSKINS at the London Cage to Tony Hoskins at the Charter Bridge School, April 13, 1943:

> Yes, we support your refusal to show any part of the journal. Violation of your private thoughts is tantamount to rape of the spirit.
>
> There is mischief here, too. I'm sorry to say we are no longer speaking with the Rasson-Piers since they find more comfort in the gossip of the Jeffrieses, passed along by their son Arthur. A poisonous little chap, I'd guess, but you would know better than I.
>
> Yes, traits in an individual can be correlated with national origin, the pieties of Mr. Pardue to the contrary notwithstanding. It's quite possible that the impulsive and vainglorious side of David Rasson-Pier was passed along by the father's French parents. As to the question of cultural distinction, consider the opening lines of two letters which crossed my desk this week, the first from a German: "Dear Mother, The most awful thing has happened. We have been captured by the English and are being held in Oran, waiting transfer to a prison camp in America."
>
> The second from an Italian: "Dear Mama, The most wonderful thing has happened. We have been captured by the English and will soon be on our way to the United States."
>
> Don't mistake me, I'm not advocating one attitude over the other. But if your Pardue doubts the relevance of my example, I suggest he visit the prison camp in Bowmanville. I'm told the Germans there are goose-stepped by their officers to the mess hall, where Italians happily prepare the food and banter about the women waiting for them in the town.
>
> No, we do not hold it against the Dean for denying you further use of the chapel organ. Really! A two-octave glissando at the end of "God Save the King" while the school waited for amen! Did you expect to get away with that?

Guard your journal.

September 25, 1941, aboard the Ellen Reilly:
This whole ship trembles with the thump of its engines. Diesels, I'm told. Above this constant drumming is the daylong rattle of electric paint chippers as the crew works at their endless chore of scraping and painting. They'll go from bow to stern, then start all over again.

No one actually studied today. In spite of the din, fell asleep over my books. R.-P. woke me before Pardue came in. Anyone caught napping during study time gets twenty-four-hour cabin confinement. I've been made tutor of second and third formers. Pardue says those not prone to seasickness must minister to those who are. He is. So is Jeffries. I am not.

Booth apologized for rudeness. As R.-P. has taken my part, others are shifting colors, too, seeking my favor. At present, most of them are unable to function. While they moan in their bunks, I explore.

Dolphins weaving under the prow. Watched them for most of an hour before slipping below again. One of the crew stopped me. Only wanted to talk. This was Sam, an able-bodied seaman, who is missing two fingers, and limps. Asked did I know there were unfortunates below. Heard animals again in lower cargo compartments. Couldn't find them.

Night walk. The deck was dark but for moonlight. No outside lights permitted. Passageways only faintly lit. Memorized numbers on doors and did not get lost. No one believes I saw a black-haired girl in bathing costume. She was rattling a cup of coins and chanting something sad, as if practicing to be a beggar. Someone called from another compartment, *"Raklo! Raklo!"* and she stood still as a stone. If R.-P. doesn't believe any of this, why does he keep asking how old the girl was and what she looked like? Very young. Her skin a mottled ochre.

Someone filched my breakfast orange. R.-P. boxed Booth's ear. Doesn't matter who did it, he says, just doesn't want it happening again.

Tony had put aside pen and notebook when Rasson-Pier offered his soft invitation.
"Do you want to come down to my bunk?" All the courage and bluster vanishing again.
"No."
"For a little visit?"
"No."
"You're to be kind to those who aren't feeling well."
He didn't believe the older boy was sick, only dodging the books for another day, with the sympathy of Pardue.

"No."

FROM DEAN HASTIE at the Charter Bridge School to the parents of
Tony Hoskins in Brasted, Kent, May 21, 1943:

Looking toward vacation, we are suggesting that Tony not remain in
dormitory with Mr. Pardue and the other boys from Cacketts. We
would not want a repeat of last summer's incident. With your permission, Tony will spend the interim at the Croyston farm, which provides
the school with milk and eggs.

A picture of the family is enclosed. In truth, I think the Croystons
would welcome an appropriately innocent companion for their shy
daughter, Margaret, and your son seems well suited for the job. Though
the family won't provide intellectual stimulation, they keep a whole-
some life, devout yet not without humor.

Tony will be expected to help with farm chores, perhaps just the
thing for the continuing melancholy. A break from the high academic
standard to which he holds himself, and from his difficult religion. May
I quote him? "The faith at Charter Bridge is to true faith as water is to
wine." Perhaps the justification for his little musical joke on the school.

We have not discounted homesickness—the long, unnatural separation from the two of you. Too, the Rasson-Pier case will not go away.
As I explained months ago, the initial investigation produced little but
tears and mystery. Should we discourage the family from persisting? So
many loose ends. From their distance can they be sure the appropriate
questions were asked? Our Cacketts boys have kept the stew at a boil.

You ask again for the facts free of the children's fantasy. The ship's log
reported the child missing on October 1, 1941. Captain Andrew Shad
made inquiries and established that David had been given to reckless
displays of daring. He concluded one of these must have been the boy's
final act.

The Ellen Reilly made its first port, Halifax, on October 7. Our boys
disembarked and were detained there two days for questioning, first by
the R.C.M.P., later by a visiting magistrate from London. Before the
investigation was completed and the Captain's finding upheld, the ship
had already taken on grain and tinned food, and sailed the night of
October 8 for Baltimore. There the loading of war supplies was completed. With the same officers and crew the boat turned back for
England on October 14.

We now believe there was another element on board the Ellen

Reilly between England and North America, a group kept apart from legitimate ship's company but sighted several times if we are to believe the Jeffries boy and your own child. A band of Polish performers? Gypsies? Lithuanian Jews? How they came to be on the ship and where they disembarked are as open to speculation as their nationality.

We had, too, the crass report of a seaman named Sam, put off the boat in Halifax for the theft of a pair of shoes. He was a rough sort who befriended several of our boys and entertained them with bawdy talk in his quarters, which they knew were off-limits.

This Sam testified to having seen passengers in the hold. He fouled his account with details of a dark young lady, little more than a child by his word, offering her favors to several of the crew. If people didn't believe him, he said, they could ask our boys what she'd do.

As to the mysterious travellers, whether Captain Shad gave them passage as a humanitarian gesture or for his own profit is unclear. Their arrival was not recorded by Canadian immigration. Shad, who survives as a master in the merchant marine (the Ellen Reilly went down in January, off the Azores), does not deny that such a group could have been stowaways during his command.

We are told that the docks in Halifax are too closely patrolled for any such band to have disembarked without papers. They may never have come ashore in North America unless they were spirited off the ship in Baltimore. The United States was not yet at war, and security was doubtless lax. This seems a remote possibility but so does their very existence on board. Given the curious tatterdemalion migrations and urgencies of wartime, their passage is not beyond belief. Perhaps sympathy, reinforced by coin, eased the path into America.

Again we ask you to urge your child to come forward with his journal, if it exists, and any relevant information that might soothe the family. We have again advised the Rasson-Piers against a crossing.

Though we find Tony a difficult boy, the faculty is interested by him, and, if I may say so, fond of him. We would see nothing unnatural in an infatuation he may have had for David Rasson-Pier. These things are common as hiccups among schoolboys, and are left behind as naturally as they arrive.

Our comptroller reminds me that we have not received your share of reparations for the water damage in Tony's room last August. We appreciate your faith in Tony's innocent part. However, a clear culprit was not found, and all the boys from Cacketts must share the cost of repair.

September 26, 1941, aboard the Ellen Reilly:

Ocean calm but Sam says we're headed into "weather to pump the boys' stomachs again." Complimented me for my sea legs. Told him R.-P. is faking it to avoid the books. If he were sick, how could he use the ship's rail for a gymnast's horse? He spins his legs right around over the side. Jeffries, Phillips, and Booth have all seen him do it. Gives me the willies. Booth said he wouldn't care if R.-P. lost his balance.

Found another route to the forward cargo bay. Hid in a crate and watched the show. Bales of hay set out in a circle. There appears to be a family circus travelling with us. Preparing its act for America? A small black bear was brought in, muzzled and growling softly. Is this the noise I took for a lion's roar? Can bears survive on ship's rations? There is also a miniature pony that whinnies like a full-grown horse.

I suppose the man must throw knives every day or get out of practice. Tonight the girl was pitiable, with her chin fallen to her chest, and her arms stretched wide, like Christ on the cross, and surrounded by the steel blades delivered in rapid order. By her father? Her brother?

A woman unleashed the bear and placed it on the seat of a small bicycle. Maybe upset by the motion of the ship, it could not keep the pedals going and tumbled over.

R.-P. says I must pay my gambling debt. I'm sure he cheated me.

Tony had recorded nothing of what happened the next day, or the following night when, after lights-out, Rasson-Pier had climbed into the upper bunk with him, whispering urgently, "The others needn't know." He wrote nothing of his haunted sleep, of this famous athlete poking around behind him with his stupidly swollen thing.

From Captain Gerald Hoskins at the London Cage to Tony Hoskins at the Charter Bridge School, September 20, 1943:

Dearest Tony,

Your mother and I would transfer you to another school in an instant if it were reasonably within our power. Our distance, our ignorance of alternatives, and the dean's reluctance to recommend "some inferior academy" all work against us. It is an outrage that your notebook was stolen. We have demanded an apology from Hastie. He seems to us a great blandifier. Believe me, you have nothing to fear from him but his dangerous good will.

It is out of the question for you to return to England now. The Americans have only just begun to appreciate the logic of convoys. In

the meantime their coastal waters have become a continent-long fire-
works display, with U-boats sinking tankers and supply ships at will.
Hardly a time to play "Red Rover, Red Rover, Let Tony Come Over."

There is nothing to be ashamed of in your account of the crossing
save the occasional grammatical lapse, though eyebrows are raised at the
mention of gambling. The hounds have what they've bayed for, a dry
bone. Now let them bury it.

The Dean says you worked admirably for the Croystons and amazed
their church youth fellowship with the force of your testimony. I know
your mother's letters are full of admiration for your spiritual awakening.
She warns me not to disrupt your faith with petty sophistry. Still, I can't
approve a dogma which condemns to perdition all those beyond its
pale. This is *entre nous.*

It's no special boast to tell you I've been promoted to Captain. All
officers here at the Cage have taken one step up. So, nothing heroic,
though I am credited with devising a new purgative for the tight-lipped
Germans. I stamp their papers N.R. (*Nach Russland*, to Russia) and their
mouths run a torrent.

FROM DEAN HASTIE at the Charter Bridge School to the parents of
Tony Hoskins in Brasted, Kent, January 24, 1944:

Again the school offers its full apology to you and your son. That
Tony's journal should have been taken from his room is altogether
unacceptable. That pages were copied and distributed is despicable.

We don't know who stole the notebook. It appeared in the office of
our school paper, the *Charter Sentinel*, where the editor, one of our
senior boys, cut a stencil of certain pages and ran them off on the
mimeograph machine. This misguided chap, who comes to us from
Detroit with a warped notion of press freedom, has been relieved of all
journalistic duty.

I now believe it was a mistake to badger Tony for his record of the
voyage. The notes have only raised the anxiety of the Rasson-Piers, who
insist they could not be the work of a twelve-year-old. In their new
anguish they suspect the cruel mischief of an adult—a post-dated fabri-
cation supporting the police report of a foolhardy, self-inflicted death.

The family's theory was reinforced by your son's admission that the
notebook was not the original, lost at sea, but a substitute provided by
Mr. Pardue. Thus, he too is a subject of suspicion. The evidence of a
missing page, the ragged edge in the journal, where a sheet was torn

from it, adds to our confusion. The more so, since this was apparently part of the entry for October 2, 1941, the day after David's disappearance was first recorded.

We have assured the family that the original notes are in Tony's skilled hand, and that your son is capable of the vocabulary and sentiment, even the occasional poetic flourish. We couldn't swear to the dating of the entries, but have no reason to doubt their honesty. The headmaster and I were disturbed by references to gambling, punishable at Charter Bridge by immediate expulsion. However, we accept Tony's word that nothing of value was to be exchanged, only favors.

That the mysterious travellers below-decks are transformed into a Gypsy circus seems a wild leap of imagination. Our school physician advises me that the mind under stress (all the Cacketts boys have acknowledged their numbing terror of submarines) may take refuge in illusion.

A copy of the mimeographed notes is now in the hands of the police, who have asked to speak with Tony once more. Be assured that the school's attorney will again be on hand to prevent investigative bullying. If Tony chooses to tell them he remembers nothing, that will suffice. We pray for a return to academic tranquillity.

September 28, 1941, aboard the Ellen Reilly:
The rattle of the paint chippers stopped for a merciful hour this morning. Pardue took advantage of the relative quiet, calling a meeting in his cabin to rally spirits. He never rose from his bunk. The air was horrid.

Our workbooks will be collected tomorrow, though there is not a word or cipher in most of them. Took Pardue some tea this morning and was caught out by Phillips watching from the door of his room. Phillips says it will all come out when we reach Canada, all the broken rules. And there will be whippings. Told him there is no corporal punishment at Charter Bridge. He seemed much relieved. He asked what R.-P. talks about and does he do stunts in the cabin.

Pardue whined pitifully for me to take his tray away. The smell of toast and margarine was making him ill again. Jeffries tried to trip me at his doorway. Called me "suck-bottom."

I can tolerate the pitch and roll of the ship. Also, the further one descends through the lower decks, the less one notices the roll. Sam says the people below are stealing food. The galley is missing a dozen tins of beef. Bear provender? Captain Shad is furious and says we've been roving through his ship against orders. I'm the one. I suppose the others would rather die in their cabins.

I have seen a periscope like a black needle in the waves behind us.

October 1, 1941, aboard the Ellen Reilly:
R.-P. did not return to the cabin last night. A search for him began this morning. Certain we won't find him.
There followed a line obliterated, washed over with ink. How many times had he been asked, "If you wrote 'certain,' were you not certain?" And "Why did you cross this out?" Why should he tell them, "I did not cry with the rest"?

On the evening of September 29, Rasson-Pier followed Tony down through the maze of passages to the performance chamber, complaining repeatedly of the grease stains the metal stairways were leaving on his trousers.
"Periscope? Girl in a bathing costume? What next, Hoskins?"
"Why didn't Pardue put Phillips with you?" Tony asked him. "Someone more your age."
"I asked for you," he said. "Thought it might give you a boost."
The hero of the Cacketts playing fields had asked for *him*? Anxious about displeasing Rasson-Pier again, he prayed the girl would be there.
She was sitting on a bale, with her back to them. A long black dress appliquéd with red and orange rings gave the effect of contouring her ample young figure in tight-fitting bracelets.
"Run along," Rasson-Pier ordered. "I'll speak to her alone."
"She doesn't speak English," Tony said. "I could try a little French for you."
Why had he wanted to be helpful? He was only pushed aside.
The girl turned and stared at them without modesty. Before Rasson-Pier could sit beside her, she had risen, taken his arm, and was leading him away through the hatch at the far end of the compartment. Perhaps a fortune-teller, Tony thought, leading him to a private place to read his palm.

FROM DEAN HASTIE at the Charter Bridge School to the parents of Tony Hoskins, Brasted, Kent, January 26, 1944:

I dare to presume a friendship has developed between us in our pursuit of your son's welfare. This letter following close on the heels of the last is prompted by a surprising turn in the Rasson-Pier case. There is now a theory the boy may be alive.
We are told by the police that there was a family row before the

voyage, a shouting match in which David called his parents such names as "Pale cowards" and "funny little people." He threatened never to come back if they packed him off to Canada. This was followed by one of his acrobatic demonstrations, a walk on his hands down a stone stairway in front of their home in Kent. Certainly a thoughtless display in front of his troubled parents.

The imaginations of the Rasson-Piers must be racing along with the flow of news and rumor from the families of our Cacketts contingent. I'm told that "Gypsy circus" is oxymoronic, that, while Gypsy children are often sent out to beg, the families never perform or work for money, unless it be in telling the future.

The Rasson-Piers now cling to the frail chance that a rebellious David might have been drawn to, or charmed away by, this band that must have intended to land in America. That they may have seen profit in his gymnastic virtuosity. But who is to say they were Gypsies? Haven't they also been called Lithuanian Jews and Polish performers?

I turn again to Tony's situation. Why do the other children continue to torment him? If the authorities don't trust his written account, how will they credit his oral testimony?

Your child has taken refuge in his faith. All worthy counsel, he avers, comes from the three-person God, though we know he looks daily to his letter box for guidance from you. Your son has lost weight. We try to see that he eats well.

From Captain Gerald Hoskins at the London Cage to Tony Hoskins at the Charter Bridge School, February 15, 1944:

Dearest Tony,

We're proud of you. Stick to your guns, and ask yourself this: Why would they have you impeach yourself? What good could come of it? Can the lost boy be brought back? If you find yourself in a compromising box, don't jump out in public. If there is something to say that can cause only humiliation take it to this higher being of yours, all three of him if necessary. I am dead serious. Take proper nourishment, and hold on. You will cross this way in victory the moment the Atlantic is secure.

Early on September 30th. Rasson-Pier had come back to the cabin quite exhausted.

"They don't wash, you know," he said. He sighed and fell asleep. Tony covered for him through the morning, calling "Studying, please" when the others knocked for their morning chats.

At noon, Rasson-Pier was awake and irritable.

"Who doesn't wash?" Tony asked him.

But the older boy was looking into the future. "If you say anything of what's happened in this cabin, I'll report your funny business when I caned you at Cacketts."

"What business?"

"The way you enjoyed it. Even more without trousers."

"I never. Whatever do you mean?"

"Yes, well, who will they believe?" He fell back on his bunk. "Perhaps I'll tell them anyway," he said.

He slept again for several hours, woke, and asked, 'What if she's given me the disease?"

"What disease?"

"You sap. The one that takes your brain."

"I believe there's a cure for that."

The older boy nodded slowly.

"Don't look for me tonight" was the last Tony heard him say.

If the girl's odor displeased him, if he thought her infected, why had he gone to see her again? Goatish, Tony had heard his mother say, but would not a goat demand exclusively a mate of opposite gender?

The October 1st journal entry had concluded: The ship went a drunken path through the glowing sea when the sky was torn into three ragged black sheets by lightning.

TONY HAD STAYED out on the open deck that evening in order to avoid his roommate. Standing at the stem, he watched the serpentine course of the ship recorded in the roiled wake. With the first bolt of lightning, he swung around and saw a figure far up the deck balanced upside down and turning with his hands on the rail, his legs, at that instant, over the side. And someone was standing there, close to him, perhaps the girl. All went black and a moment later they were all brilliantly lit by a second bolt. The spinning body was disconnected from the rail, floating out into the night.

So obvious of Rasson-Pier. Showing off for the girl. Performance was the only language they had in common. Tony made his way forward in the dark, but the two of them had vanished. No time to applaud the trick; the next act of his floating circus had already begun. A spectral ball was gliding down the stay that ran from antenna mast to the bow. It split into two glowing spheres, and then there were three of them, evenly spaced, moving back and forth along the taut metal line. He watched for several minutes until they merged into one again and disappeared.

October 2, 1941, aboard the Ellen Reilly:
Is he pestering the dolphins? Sawn into rude portions by sharks? Have I seen the spirit of God in triplicate?

The next page had been torn from the notebook.

From Tony Hoskins at the Croyston farm to his parents in Brasted, Kent, August 23, 1944:

The summer has flown. I am two inches taller. Six feet! The second haying is finished. I was allowed to work the rake, an old-fashioned thing once pulled by a horse, this season by an ancient tractor, petrol being available. For two weeks, I've been sitting on the metal seat of the rake and lifting its tines at each windrow with a hand lever. As a result my right arm is appreciably muscled, and I must do something to bring the left into balance.

Yesterday a man came to replace some rotten boards in the north end of the haymow. I was asked my estimate of the barn's height at the point of the gable. I could tell them quite precisely, I said, by measuring the shadow of the barn and that of a pole of known length, then applying simple geometry. By the time I gave my answer, Mr. Croyston had made a calculation of his own and the carpenter was on his way to the lumberyard. My figure was off by half a foot, Mr. Croyston's correct to the inch. So my fancy education is a thing of some amusement here, though Margaret is keen to share my books and ideas.

Last Thursday I was asked to escort her to a "young people's" in the village. It's not the social gathering it sounds. There is some flirtation, but only so much as is possible when you are seated in church pews under the eyes of a preacher.

Between hymns, each boy and girl is expected to rise, in turn, and share a faith-affirming experience. I think I blushed awfully when the minister's eyes fell on me, but I was able to stand and tell again of the three balls of fire over the deck of the Ellen Reilly. By the end of my story the pastor's eyes were brimful, and I was embarrassed for him. Margaret, seated to my right, took my hand when I sat down again.

From Captain Hoskins at the London Cage to Tony Hoskins at the Charter Bridge School, September 10, 1944:

A note to tell you that civilians are crossing again! Given proper escort, it appears to be safe. I've made inquiries, and will find a berth for you the moment space is available on a secure ship. You've been so long there under brutish circumstances. It would be cruel of us to leave you longer than is prudent for your safety. We know that there is still talk of your journal's missing page. I fear the gossips will never give it up.

From Tony Hoskins at the Charter Bridge School to his parents in Brasted, Kent, October 5, 1944:

Please do not book passage for me. I'm content and intend to finish here.

Fair questions have been raised, and there is something I want to clear up about the voyage out. When I saw David Rasson-Pier spinning above the ship's rail, I thought he'd learned a new trick. It never occurred to me he was out of control. Not until it was far too late to give an alarm.

The following day I returned to the same place on the deck. Looking down, I saw a row of three lifeboats suspended over the side. One could speculate about David's having possibly fallen onto the canopy covering one of these and climbing back onto the deck below. But the chance is so minuscule. Believe me, he perished at sea. It's too late to raise another slim hope that can only give anguish.

If you must know, the page torn from the journal held my thoughts on the family below decks. Particularly the girl, and Rasson-Pier's use of her. I did not invent the girl. Think of her under a rain of knives, and try to imagine throwing knives at me for a living.

The Dean is quite mistaken about Gypsies. They frequently take itinerant work, and are known for their rapport with animals, notably as trainers of circus acts. And when I went down in the ship, I heard "*Raklo Raklo!*" called out like a crow's warning. It's the Gypsy word for a non-Gypsy boy. I doubt I will see her again, or know what befell her, but we were all Gypsies on that voyage, I now believe, and I would cry "*Raklo!*" now to those who did not make the crossing. Our chaplain says the war has blown seed, good and bad, to all points of the compass, and it remains to be seen what will germinate. High hopes for me. But what of the rootless Gypsies? I like to think of the girl and her family moving across America, performing, escaping from one camp to the next.

I'm confident her troupe survives. Almost as certain as I am that David Rasson-Pier is dead. The passage of time has not weakened my resolve not to write to his family. You will have to guess at my reasons.

About my "hard faith," as Hastie calls it. You shouldn't think I ever believed the fireballs over the ship's deck were the actual embodiment of the Trinity. I took them, rather, as a phenomenal sign of Mother's faith. No more periscopes after that. They helped me complete the crossing without going mad. And why should that sign be erased now, by some scientific explanation? Really, for men who profess faith, some of my instructors are quite hopelessly literal.

For all that, I like the teachers here quite as well as the masters at Cacketts. The Atlantic may, as you say, be secured for Allied shipping. Nevertheless, I don't wish to return to England before graduation from Charter Bridge.

From Dean Hastie at the Charter Bridge School to the parents of Tony Hoskins in Brasted, Kent, November 20, 1944:

We shall never hope to understand this war's random terror, why we are spared here in our snug academy while refugees from all walks are driven pillar to post. I do believe we can now take hope in these few boys from Cacketts who were washed up on our shores. I am their Dean, yet I sense that they are children no more. The heat of war has fired them, and they shine with a new hardness and brilliance. Especially your son.

You would not recognize Tony. His second summer on the Croyston farm did wonders. He is quite filled out in athletic proportion, and happy as we have never seen him. It will please you to hear, too, that your son has found common ground with students and masters alike, and can be seen on occasion roughhousing and joking with his mates from Cacketts.

Something has cleared the air. There is less ostentation in his religious assertion. I don't think the other boys ever believed he was guilty of any complicity in the Rasson-Pier tragedy. Rather, they resented his claim to a private audience with God on the voyage out. Without boasting, we give our faculty credit here, in particular our Department of Physical Science. Mr. Theonel believes his lecture on electricity was responsible. As he says, "Knowledge must rush in where dispelled superstition leaves a vacuum." Tony now concedes that the three balls of light he saw on the ship's antenna must have been static electricity, the phenomenon called "St Elmo's fire."

We think it gave him comfort to learn from our History instructor that early mariners also believed they witnessed holy bodies in the rigging of their ships—the *corpus sancti*, or corposants, as they called them. Tony will be returning to you with a new maturity. Once more, he has our permission to practice his music on the chapel organ. Eventually, I'm sure, he'll be trusted to play for our services again.

The third anniversary of David Rasson-Pier's disappearance will not have escaped your notice. It was observed here by a special prayer at evening vespers, and a reading of this note from the family: "We believe our son perished at sea by his own dangerous devices. To those children who survive, we offer our blessing. Your useful lives must be our monument to David's memory." The school is much relieved by their sad but sensible resignation.

The Charter Bridge students filing in to the final chapel service of the year were surprised to see Tony Hoskins seated at the organ. Excited, they squirmed and whispered in their pews, as if assured of a sacrilege to spice the imminent summer rebellion.

They were disappointed to hear scarcely a hint of the expected irreverence. Buttercup's theme floated over "Faith of Our Fathers," so cleverly hidden in tempo and contrapuntal disguise that no one but the new music instructor was wise to it. From the choir he winked approval at his richly gifted student.

the great wave

MARY LAVIN

THE SEA HAS a way of teaching you to see – not just by making

the eye dance across the surface of things, jigging, sweeping, swoop-

ing, taking measure in ways the landlocked eye can't even conceive.

It's trickier: teasing you to look at what's bobbing at the edge of your

vision, at what lies beyond: deep inside, locked in memory or destiny.

Mary Lavin's "The Great Wave" (1959) begins with a gaze from the

sea that swells into a Joycean epiphany.

the Bishop was sitting in the stern of the boat. He was in his robes, with his black overcoat thrown across his shoulders, and over his arm he carried his vestments, turned inside out to protect them from the salt spray. The reason he was already robed was that the distance from the Irish mainland across to the island was only a few miles, and it spared the island priest the embarrassment of a long delay in his small damp sacristy. Then, the islanders received a visit from their bishop only every four years, on the occasion of the confirmation ceremony, and to have His Grace arrive thus in his robes was only their due—a proper prolongation of episcopal pomp. In his alb and amice, he would easily be picked out by the small knot of islanders who would gather on the pier the moment the boat was sighted on the tops of the waves. The Bishop had a reason of his own, too, as it happened, but he was hardly aware of it anywhere but in his heart.

He wrapped his white skirts tighter around him, and looked to see that the cope and chasuble were well doubled over, so that the colored silks would not be exposed when the currach got away from the lee of the land and the waves broke on the sides. The cope, above all, must not be tarnished. That was why he stubbornly carried it across his own arm—the beautiful cope that came all the way from Stansstad, in Switzerland, and was so overworked with gilt thread that it shone like cloth of gold. The orphreys, depicting the birth and childhood of Christ, displayed the most elaborate work that His Grace had ever seen come from the *Paramentenwerkstatte*, and yet he had long been familiar with the work of the sisters there, in St. Klara. Ever since he attained the bishopric, he had commissioned vestments and altar cloths from them, for use throughout the diocese. And he had once, at their instigation, broken a journey to Rome to visit them. When he was there, he had asked those brilliant women to explain to him the marvel, not of their skill but of his discernment of it, telling them of his birth and early life as a simple island boy, on this island toward which he was now faced.

"Mind out!" he said sharply as one of the men from the mainland, who was pushing them off with the end of an oar, threw the oar into the boat, scattering the air with drops of water from its glossy blade. "Could nothing be done about this?" he asked, seeing water under the bottom boards of the boat. It rippled up and down with a little tide of its own, in time with the tide outside, which was already carrying them swiftly out into the bay. "Tch, tch, tch," said the Bishop, for some of the water had saturated the hem of the alb, and he set about tucking it under him on the seat. "Tch, tch," he repeated, but no one was unduly bothered by his ejaculations. His eyes were soft and mild, and didn't they know him? They knew that in his complicated episcopal life he had to contend with a lot, and it was common knowledge that he hated to hear his old house-keeper thumping her flatiron late at night when she ought to be in bed.

"You'd want to keep that yoke there from getting wet, though, Your Grace," said one of the men, indicating the crosier, which had fallen on the boards. For all that they mightn't heed his little old-womanish ways, they had a proper sense of what was fitting for an episcopal appearance.

"I could hold the crosier, perhaps," said Father Kane, the Bishop's sec-retary, who was farther up the boat. "I still think it would be more suitable for the children to be brought over to you on the mainland than for you to be traipsing over here like this, and in those foreign vestments at that!"

He is thinking of the price that was paid for them, thought the Bishop, and not of their beauty or their workmanship. And yet, he reflected, Father Kane was supposed to be a highly cultivated man, who would not have had to depend on the seminary to put the only bit of gloss on him he'd ever get—like me, he thought. He looked down at his beautiful vestments again. A marvel it was, no less.

"It isn't as if they'll appreciate them over there," said Father Kane with sudden venom, nodding toward the island, which was a vague green mass on the horizon.

"Ah, you can never say that for certain," said the Bishop mildly, even indifferently. "Take me," he said. "How did I come to appreciate such things?"

He saw the answer in the secretary's hard eyes—that it was parish funds that paid for the knowledge, and diocesan funds for putting it into practice. And maybe he's right, the Bishop thought, smiling to himself. Who knows anything at all about how we're shaped, or where we're led, or how, in the end, we are ever brought to our rightful haven?

"How long more till we get there?" he asked, because the island was no longer a vague green mass. Its familiar shapes were coming into focus: the great high promontory throwing its purple shade over the shallow fields by the shore, with their sparse white cottages; the pierhead that ran straight out into the water, a cheap piece of cementwork constantly needing repairs; and, higher up, on a ledge of the promontory itself, the plain cement church, with its spire alone standing out against the sky, bleak as a crane's neck and head.

To think the full height of the promontory was four times the height of that steeple! The Bishop gave a great shudder.

One of the rowers was talking to him. "Sure, Your Grace ought to know all about this bay. Ah, but I suppose you forget them days altogether now."

"Not quite, not quite," said the Bishop quickly. He slipped his hand inside his robe to rub his stomach, which had begun to roll after only a few minutes of the swell.

WHEN HE WAS a little lad, over there on the island, he used to think he'd run away someday and join the crew of one of the French fishing trawlers that were always moving backward and forward on the rim of the sky. He used to go to a quiet place in the shade of the Point, and, settling into a crevice in the rocks, out of reach of the wind, he'd spend the day long staring at the horizon—now in the direction of Liverpool, now in the direction of the Norwegian fiords.

Yet although he knew the trawlers went from one great port to another, he did not really associate them with the sea. He never thought of them as at the mercy of it, in the way he thought of the little hide-covered currachs that had made his mother a widow and that were bounced about by every wave. The trawlers seemed out of reach of the waves, away out on the black rim of the horizon.

He had in those days a penny notebook in which he put down the day and hour a trawler passed, waiting precisely to mark it down until it passed level with the pier. He put down other facts about it that he deduced from the small outline discernible at that distance, keeping what his imagination allowed him to believe was a full and exhaustive report. He had to sneak out of the cottage, off to his cranny in the rocks, for his mother didn't hold with his hobby.

"Ah, Jimeen, son, aren't you all I've got! Why wouldn't I fret about you?" she'd say when he chafed under her care for him.

That was the worst of being an only child, and the child of a sea widow into the bargain. She was in sore dread of his even looking out to sea, it seemed. And as for going out in a currach! Hadn't she warned every currach crew on the island against taking him out?

"Your mammy would be against me, son," they'd say when he pleaded with them, one after another on the shore, and they getting ready to shove their boats down the shingle and float them out on the tide.

How will I ever get out to the trawlers if I'm not let out in the currachs, he used to think. That was when he was a little fellow, of course. When he got a bit older, he stopped pestering them and didn't go down near the shore at all when they were pulling out. They'd got sharp with him by then.

"We can't take any babbies out with us. A storm might come up. What would a babby like you do then?"

He couldn't blame them for their attitude; by this time he knew they could often have found a use for him out in the boats when there was a heavy catch.

"You'll never make a man of him hiding him in your petticoats," they'd say to his mother when they'd see him with her in the shop. There was a special edge on the remark—men were scarce, as was easily seen in the shop on a Saturday night, when the black frieze jackets of the men made only small patches in the big knots of women, with their flaming-red petticoats.

His mother had a ready answer for them. "And why are they scarce?" she'd cry.

"Ah, don't be bitter, Mary."

"Well, leave me alone, then. Won't he be time enough taking his life in his hands when there's more to be got for a netful of ling than there is this year!"

For the shop was always full of dried ling. When you thought to lean on the counter, it was on a board of ling you leaned, and when you went to sit down on a box or a barrel, it was on top of a bit of dried ling you'd be sitting. And right by the door the greyhound bitch belonging to the shop was always dragging at a bit of ling that hung down from a hook on the wall, and was chewing at it, not furtively but to the unconcern of all, growling when it was tough, and attacking it with her back teeth, her head to one side, as she'd chew an old rind of hoof parings in the forge.

"There'll be a good price for the first mackerel," said poor Maurya Keely, their near neighbor, whose husband was ailing, and whose son, Seoineen, was away in a seminary on the mainland studying to be a priest. "The seed herring will be coming in any day now. You'll have to let Jimeen out on that day if it looks to be a good catch," she said, turning to his mother. "We're having our currach tarred today, so's to be ready."

Everyone had sympathy with Maurya, knowing her man was nearly done, and that she was in great dread he wouldn't be fit to go out and get their share of the new season's catch, and she counting on the money to pay for Seoineen's last year in the seminary. Seoineen wasn't only her pride but the pride of the whole island as well, for, with the scarcity of menfolk, the island hadn't given a priest to the diocese in a decade.

"And how is Seoineen? And when is he coming home at all?" another woman asked as they crowded around Maurya. "He'll soon be facing into the straight," they said, meaning his ordination, and thinking how when Seoineen was a young fellow he used to be the wildest lad on the island, always winning the ass race on the shore, the first to flash into sight around the point coming up the straight, keeping the lead easily to finish at the pierhead.

"He'll be home for a last leave before the end," said his mother, and everyone understood the apprehension she tried to keep out of her voice; it steals into the heart of every priest's mother, thinking of the staying power a man needs to reach that end. "I'm expecting him the week after next," she said suddenly, as her joy in the thought of having him in the home again took place over everything else.

"Ah, let's hope the mackerel will be in before then!" said the women. Seoineen would have to call at every single cottage on the island, and every single cottage would want to have plenty of lemonade and shop biscuits, too, to put down before him.

Jimeen listened with interest and pleased anticipation. Seoineen always took him along on the calls, and he got a share in all that was set down for the seminarian.

But that very evening Seoineen stepped onto the pier. There was an epidemic in the college, and the students who were in their last year were let go home a whole week before their time. Maurya was not down at the pier, but all that were there walked up to the house with him, expecting her to show great joy at the sight of him. But Maurya began to bewail having no feast.

Seoineen laughed. "Sure, it's not for what I get to eat that I come home, Mother!" he cried. "If there's anything astray with the life I've chosen, it's not shortage of grub! And anyway, we won't have long to wait." He went to the door and glanced up at the sky. "The seed will be swimming inward tomorrow on the first tide!" he said.

"Oh, God forbid!" said Maurya. "We don't want it that soon, either, son, for our currach was only tarred this day!" And her face was torn with two worries now, instead of one.

Jimeen had seen the twinkle in Seoineen's eye, and thought he was only letting on, for how would he have any such knowledge at all, and he away at schools and colleges the best part of his life?

The seed was in on the first tide, though, the next day. It was taken all over the island to be a kind of prophecy.

"Oh, they have curious ways of knowing things that you'd never expect them to know," said Jimeen's own mother.

"Ah, he was only letting on, Mother," said Jimeen, but he got a knock of her elbow over the ear.

"It's time you had more respect for him, son," she said as he ran out the door for the shore.

Already most of the island boats were pulling hard out into the bay, and the others were being pushed out as fast as they could be dragged down the shingle. But the Keely boat was still lying upended in the dune grass under the promontory, and the tar gleamed on it wetly. The women were clustered around Maurya, giving her consolation.

"Ah, sure, maybe it's God's will," she said. "Wasn't himself doubled up with pain in the early hours, and it's in a heavy sleep he is this minute—I wouldn't wake him up, whether or no! He didn't get much sleep last night. Him and Seoineen stayed late, talking by the fire. Seoineen was explaining to him all about the ordination—the fasting they have to do beforehand, and the holy oils and chrism, and the laying on of hands. It beat all to hear him! He didn't get much sleep himself, either, but he's young and able, thank God. I'll have to be going back now, to call him for Mass."

"You'll find you won't need to call Seoineen," said one of the women. "Hasn't him and the like of him got God's voice in their hearts all day, and they ever and always listening to it? He'll wake of himself, you'll see. He'll need no calling!"

And sure enough, as they were speaking, who came running down the shingle but Seoineen. "My father's not gone without me, is he?" he cried, not seeing their own boat or any sign of it on the shore, and a cloud came over his face. He began to scan the bay, which was blackened with boats by this time.

"He's not, then!" said Maurya. "He's above in his bed still, but leave him be, Seoineen." She nodded her head back toward the shade of the promontory. "He tarred the boat yesterday, not knowing the seed'ud be in so soon, and it would scald the heart out of him to be here and not able to take it out. But as I was saying to these good people, it's maybe God's will the way it's happened, because he's not fit to go out this day!"

"That's true for you, Mother," said Seoineen quietly. "The poor man is nearly beat, I'm fearing." The next minute, he threw back his head and looked around the shore. "Maybe I'd get an oar in one of the other boats. There's surely a scarcity of men, like always."

"Is it you?" cried his mother, because it mortally offended her notion of the dignity due him that he'd be seen with his coat off, maybe—in his shirtsleeves maybe, red in the face, maybe, along with that, and, God forbid, sweat maybe breaking out of him!

"To hear you, Mother, anyone would think I was a priest already. I wish you could get a look into the seminary, and you'd see there's a big difference made there between the two sides of the fence!" He gave a sudden laugh, but it fell away as sudden when he saw that all the boats had pulled out from the shore and he was alone with the women on the sand.

Then his face hardened. "Tell me, Mother!" he cried. "Is it the boat or my father that's the unfittest? For if it's only the boat, then I'll make it fit! It would be going against God's plenitude to stay idle with the sea teeming like that—look at it!"

Even from where they stood, when the waves wheeled inward they could see the silver seed herring glisten, and when the slow wheels broke on the shore, they left behind a spate of seed sticking to everything, even to people's shoes.

"And for that matter, wasn't Christ Himself a fisherman! Come, Mother, tell me the truth! Is the tar still wet or is it not?"

Maurya looked at him. She was no match for arguing with him in matters of theology, but she knew all about tarring a currach. "Wasn't it only done yesterday, son!" she said. "How could it be dry today?"

"We'll soon know that," said Seoineen, and he ran over to the currach. They saw him lay the palm of his hand flat on the upturned bottom of the boat, and then they heard him give a shout of exultation.

"It's not dry, surely!" exclaimed one of the women, and you could tell by the faces of all that they were remembering the way he prophesied about the catch. Had the tar dried at the touch of his hands, maybe?

Seoineen was dragging the currach down the shingle. "Why not?" he cried. "Wasn't it a fine dry night? I remember going to the door after talking with my father into the small hours, and the sky was a mass of stars, and there was a fine sharp wind blowing that you'd be in dread it would dry up the sea itself! Stand back there, Mother!" he cried, for her face was beseeching something of him, and he didn't want to be looking at it. But without looking he knew what it was trying to say. "Isn't it toward my ordination the money is going?" he cried. "Isn't that argument enough for you?"

He had the boat nearly down to the water's edge. "No, keep back, young Jimeen," he said as the boy tried to help him. "I'm able to manage it on my own. Let you get the nets and put them in, if you want something to do, and then let you be ready to skip into it before I push out, because I'll need someone to help haul in the nets."

"Is it Jimeen?" said one of the women, and she laughed, and then all the women laughed. "Sure, he's more precious again nor you!" they said. But they turned to his mother all the same. "If you're ever going to let him go out at all, this is your one chance, surely?" they said. "Isn't it like it was into the hands of God Himself you were putting him, woman?"

"Will you let me, Ma?" It was the biggest moment of his life. He couldn't look at her, for fear of a refusal.

"Come on, didn't you hear her saying yes—what are you waiting for?" cried Seoineen, giving him a push, and the next minute he was in the currach, and Seoineen had given it a great shove, running out into the water in his fine shoes and all. He vaulted in across the keel. "I'm destroyed already at the very start!" he cried, laughing down at his feet and trouser legs. "I'll take them off," he cried, kicking the shoes off him, and pulling off his socks, till he was in his bare white feet. "Give me the oars!" he cried, but as he gripped them, he laughed again, and loosed his fingers for a minute, and, one after the other, he rubbed his hands on a bit of sacking on the seat beside him. The bleached oars were marked with the track of his hands, palm and fingers, in pitch-black tar.

"The tar was wet!"

"And what of it?" cried Seoineen. "Isn't it easy to give it another lick of a brush?" But he wasn't looking at Jimeen; his eyes were glancing along the tops of the waves to see if they were pulling near the other currachs.

The other currachs were far out in the bay already, for the sea was running strong. Yet, for all that, there was a strange, still look about the water. Jimeen sat quiet, exulting in his luck. The waves did not slap against the sides of the currach, as he'd have thought they would do, and they didn't even break into spray where the oars split their surface. Instead, they seemed to go lolloping under the currach and up again on the far side, till it might have been on great glass rollers they were slipping along.

"God! Isn't it good to be out on the water!" cried Seoineen, and he stood up in the currach, nearly toppling them over in his exuberance, drawing in deep breaths, and his eyes taking big draughts of the coastline, which was getting farther and farther away. "Ah, this is the life! This is the real life!" he cried, but they had to look to the oars and look to the nets then, and for a while they couldn't look up at the sea or sky.

When Jimeen looked up at last, the shore was only a narrow line of green.

"There's a bit of a change, I think," said Seoineen, and it was true. The waves were no longer round; they had small sharp peaks on them now, like the rocks near the Point that would rip the bottom out of a boat with one tip, the way the tip of a knife would slit the belly of a fish. For all their appearance, though, when they hit against the flank of the boat, it was only the waves themselves that broke and patterned the water with splotches of spray.

It was while Jimeen was looking down at these white splotches that he saw the fish. "Oh, look, Seoineen, look!" he cried, because never had he seen the like.

They were not swimming free, or separate, but a great mass of them together, till you'd think it was at the floor of the sea you were looking, only it was nearer and shallower.

There must have been a million fish—a million million, Jimeen reckoned wildly—and they were pressed as close as the pebbles on the shore. And they might well have been motionless and only seeming to move, like on a windy day you'd think the grass on the top of the promontory was running free like the waves, with the way it rippled and ran along a little with each breeze.

"Holy God, such a sight!" cried Seoineen. "Look at them!"

But Jimeen was puzzled. "How will we get them into the net?" he asked, because it seemed that there was no place for the net to slip down between them but that it must lie on top of that solid mass of fish, as on a floor.

"The nets: begod, I nearly forgot what we came out here for!" cried Seoineen, and they became aware then of activity in the other boats, which had drawn near without their knowing. He yelled at Jimeen. "Catch hold of the net there, you lazy good-for-nothing! What did I bring you with me for if it wasn't to put you to some use!" and he caught at a length of the brown mesh in the bottom of the boat, and began to haul it up with one hand, and with the other to feed it out over the side.

Jimeen, too, began to pull and haul; so that for a few minutes there was only a sound of the net swishing, and every now and then a bit of a curse, under his breath, from Seoineen, as one of the cork floats caught in the tholepins.

At first, it shocked Jimeen to hear Seoineen curse, but he reflected that he wasn't ordained yet, and that even if he were, it must be a hard thing for a man to go against his nature.

"Come on, get it over the side, damn you!" cried Seoineen, as Jimeen had slowed up, thinking about the cursing. "It isn't one netful but thirty could be filled this day! Sure, you could fill the boat in fistfuls!" he cried, leaning over and delving into the water with his bare hand. With a shout, he brought up two fish, held one against the other in the one grip, so they were as rigid as if they were dead. "They're overlaying each other a foot deep!" he cried. When he opened his fist and freed them, they writhed apart to either side of his hand in two bright arcs, and fell into the bottom of the boat. But next moment they flashed over the side of the currach.

"Ah, begorra, you'll get less elbow-room down there than up here, my boys!" cried Seoineen, and he roared laughing as he and Jimeen leaned over the side and saw that, sure enough, the two mackerel were floundering for a place in the glut of fishes.

But a shout from one of the other currachs made them look up. It was the same story all over the bay. The currachs were tossing tipsily in the water with the antics of the crews, who were standing up and shouting and feeding the nets ravenously over the sides. In some of the boats that had put out early, they were still more ravenously hauling them up, strained and swollen with the biggest catch they had ever held.

There was not time for Seoineen or Jimeen to look long at them, for the keel of their own currach began to dip into the water.

"Look out! Pull it up! Catch a better grip than that, damn you! Do you want to be pulled into the sea? Pull, damn you, pull!" Every other word that broke from Seoineen's throat was a curse, or what you'd call a curse if you heard it from another man, or in another place, but in this place, from this man, hearing them issue wild and free from Seoineen's throat, Jimeen understood that they were like psalms. They rang out over the sea in a kind of praise to God for all his plenitude.

"Up! Pull hard—up, now, up!" he cried, and he was pulling at his end like a madman.

Jimeen pulled, too, till he thought his heart would crack, and the big white belly of the loaded net came in sight over the water. He gave a groan, though, when he saw it. "Is it dead they are?" he cried, for there was no stir at all in the great white mass they had hauled up in the net. "Is it dead they are?" he cried again.

"Ah, why would they be dead? It's suffocating they are, even below in the water, with the welter of them is in it!" cried Seoineen.

He dragged the net over the side, where it emptied and spilled itself onto the bottom of the boat. They came alive then, all right! Flipping and floundering, and some of them flashing back into the sea. But it was only a few on the top that got away; the rest were kept down by the very weight and mass. Seoineen straightened, and swiped a hand across his face to clear it of the sweat that was pouring out of him. "Ah, sure, what harm if an odd one leps for it!" he cried. "We'll deaden them under another netful! Throw out your end!"

As Jimeen rose up to his full height to throw the net out wide, there was a sudden terrible sound in the sky over him, and the next minute a bolt of thunder went volleying overhead, and in the same instant, it seemed, the sky was knifed from end to end with a lightning flash.

Were they blinded by the flash? Or had it suddenly gone as black as night over the whole sea? "Oh, God's Cross!" cried Seoineen. "What is coming? Why didn't someone give us a shout? Where are the others? Can you see them? Hoy, there! Martin! Seumas? Can you hear?"

For they could see nothing. It was as if they were alone in the whole world. Then, suddenly, they made out Martin's currach near to them— so near that, but for Seoineen flinging himself forward and grabbing the oars, the two currachs would have knocked together. Yet no sooner had they been saved from knocking together than they were sundered so far they could hardly hear Martin when he called out to them.

"What's happening, in Christ's name?" bawled Seoineen. He had to put up his hands to trumpet his voice, for the waves were now so steep and high that even one was enough to blot out the sight of Martin. Angry white spume showed on the crests.

"It's maybe the end of the world," said Jimeen, terror-stricken.

"Shut up and let me hear Martin!" said Seoineen, for Martin was bawling at them again.

"Let go the nets!" Martin was bawling. "Let go the nets, or they'll drag you out of the boat!"

Under them they could feel the big pull of the net, which had filled up again in an instant with its dead weight of suffocating fish.

"Did you hear? He's telling us to let it go!" Jimeen cried, and he tried to free his fingers from the brown mesh that had closed tight upon them with the weight. "I can't let her go," he cried, looking to Seoineen, but he shrank back from the strange wild look in Seoineen's eyes.

"Take care would you do anything of the kind!" Seoineen cried.

"It's cutting off my fingers!"

Seoineen glared at him. "A pity about them!" he cried, but when he looked over and saw them swelling and reddening, he cursed. "Here— wait till I take it from you!" he cried, and he started to free his own right hand, but first he laced the laden fingers of his left hand into the mesh above the right, and even then the blood spurted out in the air when he finally dragged it free of the mesh.

Seoineen shoved his bleeding fingers into his mouth and sucked them; then he reached out and caught the net below where Jimeen was gripping it. As the weight slackened, the pain of the scarring strings lessened, but next minute the pull below got stronger and the pain tore into Jimeen's flesh again.

"Let go now, if you like; I have a bit of a hold of it, anyway. The weight of it is off you," said Seoineen.

Jimeen tried to drag free. "I can't!" he screamed. "The strings are cutting into my bones!"

From far over the waves the voice of Martin came to them again, faint, unreal, like the voice you'd hear in a shell if you held it to your ear. "Cut free! Cut free!" it cried. "Before you're destroyed altogether."

"Have they cut free themselves? That's what I'd like to know!" cried Seoineen.

"Oh, do as he says, Seoineen! Do as he says!" screamed Jimeen. A bit of ragged net, and another and another, rushed past on the water that was now almost level with the rowlocks, and he knew that they had indeed all done what Martin said. "For the love of God, Seoineen!" he cried.

Seoineen hesitated still for a moment. Then, finally, he made up his mind, and, reaching along the seat, he felt for the knife that was kept there for slashing dogfish. "Here goes!" he cried, and with one cut of the knife he freed Jimeen's hands, the two together at the same time, but, letting the knife drop into the water, he reached out wildly to catch the cut ends of the net before they could shed any of their precious freight. "What a fool I'd be," he gasped, "to let go. They think because of the collar I haven't a man's strength about me any more. Then I'll show them. I'll not let go this net, not if it pulls me down to Hell." And he gave another wild laugh. "And you along with me!" he cried. For a moment, the whole sea seemed littered with tattered threads of net. "Is that the way?" he cried. "They've all let go. I'll show them one man will not be so easy beat! Can you hear me?" he cried, because it was hard to hear him with the noise of the wind and the waves.

"Oh, cut free, Seoineen!" Jimeen implored, although he remembered the knife was gone now to the bottom of the sea, and he knew that the terrible swollen fingers were beyond help in the mangling ropes of the net.

Seoineen seemed unaware. "I'll show them all!" he cried. "We'll be the only boat'll bring back a catch this night, and the sea seething with fish." He gave a laugh. "Sure, that was the only thing spoiling my pleasure in the plenty—thinking that when the boats got back, the whole island would be fuller of fish, than the sea itself! Sure it wouldn't be worth a farthing a barrel! Oh, but I'll have the laugh on them now, with their hollow boats, and their nets cut to flitters! I'll show them a man is a man no matter what vows he takes, or what way he's called to deny his manhood! Where are they, anyway? Can you—see them—at all?" he cried. He had begun to gasp worse than the fish in the bottom of the boat. "Damn you—don't sit there—like that! Stand up—there—and—tell me—can you—see—them!"

Jimeen raised his eyes from Seoineen's hands caught in the meshes of the net. All he saw was a great wall, a great green wall of water. No currachs anywhere. It was as if the whole sea had been stood up on its edge, like a plate on a dresser. Down that wall of water there slid a multitude of dead fish.

Then down the same terrible wall, sliding like the dead fish, came an oar—a solitary oar. And a moment afterward, inside the glass wall, imprisoned as if under a glass dome, he saw—oh God!—a face looking out at him, staring at him through a foot of clear green water. It was the face of Martin. For a minute the eyes of the dead man stared into his eyes. With a scream, Jimeen threw himself against Seoineen and clung to him tight as iron.

How many years ago was that? The Bishop opened his eyes. They were so near the shore of the island that he could pick out the people by name who stood on the pierhead. His stomach had stopped rolling. It was mostly psychological, that feeling of nausea. But he knew it would come back in an instant if he looked left from the shore, left and up, where, over the little cement pier and over the crane-bill steeple of the church, the promontory that they called the Point rose black with its own shadow.

For it was on that promontory—four times the height of the steeple—they had found themselves, he and Seoineen, in the terrible dawn that came after the nightmare of the Wave, lying in a litter of dead fish, with the netful of fish sunk like an anchor into the green grass.

When he came to himself and felt the slippy bellies of the fish all about him, he thought he was still in the boat, lying in the bottom among the mackerel, and when he opened his eyes and saw what he thought was the darkness of the night over his head, he imagined it was still the darkness of the storm and he closed them again in terror. Just before he closed them, though, he thought he saw a star, and he ventured to open them again, and then he saw that the dark sky over him was a sky of hide stretched taut over timber laths, and the star was a glint of light coming through a split in the bottom of the currach. The currach was on top of him, not he in the bottom of it.

Then why was he not falling down and down and down through the green waters? His hands rushed out to feel around him, groping through the fishes, and the most miraculous thing he thought to grasp was a fistful of sand; the most miraculous thing he thought to have to believe was that they had been cast up safe upon the shore.

What his hands came on, though, was not sand but grass, and not the coarse dune grass that grew back from the shore to the foot of the Point. It was soft sweet little grass, like the grass he saw once when Seoineen and he had climbed up the face of the Point, and stood up there, in the sun, looking down at all below—the sea and the pier, and the shore and the fields, and the thatch of their own houses, and, on a level with them, the gray spire of the chapel itself.

He opened his eyes wide at last, and he pushed the currach over, and when he saw, out from him a bit, the black-gray tip of that same chapel spire, he knew where he was. He threw the fish to left and right and struggled to get to his feet.

It was a miracle! And it must have been granted because Seoineen was in the boat. He remembered how Seoineen prophesied the seed would be on the tide, and in his mind he pictured their currach being lifted up in the air and flown, like a bird, to this grassy point.

But where was Seoineen?

"Oh, Seoineen! Seoineen!" he cried when he saw him standing on the edge of the Point, looking downward, as the two of them had looked that day, on all below. "Oh, Seoineen, was it a miracle?" he cried, and he didn't wait for an answer, but he began to shout and jump in the air.

"Quit, will you!" said Seoineen, and for a minute he thought the anger he heard must be modesty on Seoineen's part, it being through him the miracle was granted, and then he thought it might be the pain in his hands, because he had his two hands pressed under his armpits.

Suddenly he remembered the face of Martin he had seen under the wall of water, and his eyes flew out over the sea, which was as flat and even now as the field of grass under their feet. Was Martin's currach lost? And what of the others?

He craned over the edge of the promontory to see what currachs were back in their places, turned upside down and leaning a little to one side, under the wall that divided the sand from the dune, so you could crawl under them if you were caught in a sudden shower.

There were no currachs under the wall; none at all.

There were no currachs on the sea.

Once, when he was still wearing a red petticoat, like a girsha, there had been a terrible storm, and half a score of currachs were lost. He remembered the night, with all the women on the island down on the shore, storm lamps swinging in their hands, and they calling out over the noise of the waves. The next day they had still been there, only kneeling on the pier, praying and keening.

"Why aren't they praying and keening?" he cried, for he knew at last that the other currachs—all but theirs—were lost.

"God help them," said Seoineen. "At least they were spared that." And he nodded to where, stuck in the latticed shutters on the side of the steeple, there were bits of seaweed and—yes—a bit of the brown mesh of a net.

"God help you," he said then. "How can your child's mind take in what a grown man's mind can hardly hold? We're all alone—the two of us—on the whole island. All that was spared by that wall of water."

"All that was on the sea, you mean?" he cried.

"And on the land, too," said Seoineen.

"Not my mother?" he whimpered.

"Yes, and my poor mother," said Seoineen. "My poor mother that tried to stop us from going out with the rest."

It was a grief too great to grasp, and still, still, even in the face of it, Jimeen's mind was enslaved to the thought of their miraculous salvation. "Was it a miracle, Seoineen?" he whispered. "Was it a miracle we were spared?"

But Seoineen suddenly closed his eyes and pushed his crossed arms deeper under his armpits. The grimace of pain he made—the first he had shown—was, even without his words, a rebuke to Jimeen's exultation. Then he opened his eyes again.

"It was my greed that was the cause of it," he said, and there was such a sorrow in his face that Jimeen, only then, began to cry. "It has cost me my two living hands," said Seoineen, and the anguish of his eyes was in his voice as well.

"But it saved your life, Seoineen!" he cried, wanting to comfort him.

Never did he forget the face Seoineen turned to him. "For what?" he asked.

There was such despair in his voice that Jimeen knew it wasn't a question but an answer, and for a few minutes he was silent. Then he said, "You saved my life, too, Seoineen."

Seoineen turned dully and looked at him. "For what?" he said.

But as he uttered them, those same words took on a change, and a change came over his face, too, and when he repeated them, the change was violent. "For what?" he demanded. "For what?"

Just then, on the flat sea below, Jimeen saw the boats coming across from the mainland—not currachs such as they had on the island but boats of wood, made inland in Athlone and brought down to the shore on lorries.

"Look at the boats!" he called out. Four, five, six—any amount of them—they came rowing for the island.

Less than an hour later, Seoineen was on his way to the hospital on the mainland, where he was to spend many months before he saw the island again. Jimeen was taken across a few hours later, but when he went it was to be for good. He was going to an aunt, far in from the sea, of whom he had never heard tell till that day.

NOR WAS HE to see Seoineen again, in all the years that followed. On the three occasions when he had come over to the island for the day of confirmation, he had not seen him. He had made inquiries, but all he could ever get out of people was that Seoineen was a bit odd. "And why wouldn't he be?" they added.

But although he never came down to the pier like the rest of the islanders to greet the Bishop, it was said he used to slip into the church after it had filled up, thinking he was unnoticed. And afterward, although he never came down to the pier to see the boat off, the islanders told how he never went back into his little house until the boat was gone clear across to the other side of the bay. From some part of the island, it was certain he'd be the last to take leave of the sight.

It had been the same on each visit the Bishop made, and it would be the same on this one. When he would be leaving the island, there would be solicitous entreaties for him to put on his overcoat. Certainly he was always colder going back in the late day. But he'd never give in to do more than throw it over his shoulders, from which it would soon slip down onto the seat behind him.

"You'd do right to put it on, like they told you," said his secretary, buttoning up his own thick coat.

But there was no use trying to make him do a thing he was set against. He was a man had deep reasons for the least of his actions.

afternoon of the sassanoa

JASON BROWN

THE HARDEST LESSON you learn at sea is that you are undone

not by what you fail to see, but what you refuse to see. A deadly seri-

ous business even when undertaken for fun, sailing tolerates no

games, and brooks no broken promises. Jason Brown's tense and

moving tale of filial piety is set Down East, in the traditional nautical

culture of Maine, where generations thrived despite treacherous tides,

currents, and winds, but only by dint of religiously heeding the lessons

of survivors, and listening to the unerring voice of intuition.

jacob's father had business in the city that afternoon and the next morning. "Go with him," Jacob's mother said. "You two can spend the night, and you can sign up for pre-season soccer tomorrow morning. It will save me having to give you a ride down."

Jacob agreed to go, even though it would take him away from the island and would involve a trip across to the mainland in the skiff and a seemingly endless hour's drive on the highway. Not bothering to grab a change of clothes, he jumped off the back porch and followed his father down to the island dock.

The fetch between Heron Island and the mainland darkened as Jacob's father, in the stern, thumbed tobacco into his pipe. After a few attempts he gave up trying to light the pipe in the wind, and as if this failure tumbled him toward another, he pushed away from the dock and started to row. Jacob was in the oarsman's seat, and his father, rowing this way, had difficulty keeping the leathers from popping out of the locks. The bags under his father's eyes looked even heavier than usual, and a thin line of blood traced across his freshly shaved neck. His shoulders bunched as he reached forward, his round face growing red and puffy after only a few strokes.

"You take it." His father pushed the oar handles toward Jacob. Even though it was not far to the dock on the mainland, they would blow downwind, toward Robinhood Cove, unless Jacob pulled as hard as he could. As a way of not looking at his father's face, he gazed through the Townsend Gut, the narrowest point between the island and the main, where the water funneled in and the wind whipped between the columns of tall pines, kicking up rows of chop.

"It's the best day for sailing we've had yet," his father said. Jacob shot a glance at the *Sassanoa*, riding high on her white hull above the water. Her nose pointed into the wind, and she jumped up like a thorough-bred against her mooring tether.

"Let's go for a short sail, just once across the bay, and then I'll still have time to get to town."

"I thought you had to be there by four. We might not even make it if we start now."

"By five, five-thirty. I just have to meet a guy so he can sign some papers and then have someone take them over to the courthouse before it closes."

Jacob didn't say anything. He had already said enough to his mother about not wanting to go to town. He wanted to play soccer, but he hated anything that took him away from the island. Also, he and his father would be alone for the night, and then Jacob would have to hang around the house on Woodmont Street the next day, waiting for his father to finish work so they could drive back to the island.

He wondered if it was a good idea for his father to leave so little time to get his client to sign the papers, and he knew that when his father rushed, he always drove too fast, and sometimes got a ticket in the speed trap where Route One met the main highway. That would put him in a foul mood for the whole week. Jacob didn't want to say anything about not sailing, didn't want to screw up his chances of taking the boat out alone the next year, while his father was at work, when he could sail by himself down the Maine coast to Five Islands. The tourists there, eating lobsters and clams, would look at him as though he had stepped into their lives from a past century. The year before, his father had said he could take the boat out when he was twelve, the same age at which Jacob's grandfather had let his father go out alone, but this year his father had changed the age to thirteen. Jacob wasn't sure he would ever be old enough at this rate.

"We'll just go across the bay and back," his father said, and nodded in the direction of the *Sassanoa*. Jacob pushed harder on the port oar and swung them around. The day was indeed good for sailing. The pines swayed; the breeze was southerly but cool. Jacob started to row for the island dock. His father's hand shot forward and wrapped around the starboard oar, shoving it into Jacob's chest so hard that it knocked the breath out of him.

"What about the boat bag?" Jacob asked.

"We're just going across the bay once."

His father looked away, apparently realizing that he had accidentally been too rough. Jacob wasn't going to argue about the boat bag. Even his grandfather had gone without it on short sails—just to spite the yacht-club guys and their overprecautions, he would say. Jacob's father opened his briefcase for the cell phone, unfolded the mouthpiece, and pushed POWER, bringing the clear buttons to life with yellow light. He dialed and held the phone to his head, reaching out with the other hand to grab the *Sassanoa*. Frustrated, he handed the phone to Jacob.

"When your mother picks up, tell her we're just going across the bay and back before we head into town."

Jacob took the phone. His father rested his briefcase on the deck of the *Sassanoa*, balanced himself precariously on the seat of the skiff, and pulled himself up. Both Jacob and his mother hated having cell phones on the island, where they came to escape such things, and his mother was already upset about his father's rushing to the city three days into his late-August vacation for an emergency meeting.

"You don't have your windbreaker," his mother said, after Jacob told her what they were doing.

"It's warm out."

"Tell her we're not going to be out long."

Jacob's mother heard her husband. "So call me from town tonight," she said. Jacob didn't know what to say. He said good-bye, his mother said good-bye, and he put the phone in the briefcase.

JACOB COULDN'T REMEMBER a time when they had not come to the island in the summer. Now that his grandmother was too old to stay on the island, Jacob came with just his mother and father. Jacob often helped his mother to scrub clothes against the washboard behind the cottage, using water they caught from the sky and stored in a large tank. Jacob's grandfather had been the pilot of Portland Harbor and his grandparents had lived on the island year-round, without insulation and many other things the cabin still didn't have—things that Jacob wished their house in Portland didn't have either. Sometimes in the fall, after returning to Portland, Jacob refused to use the phone, lights, or running water, as a way of pretending he was still on the island.

As if they were trying to escape, or as if the rush that Jacob expected on the highway had already begun, his father tugged frantically at the sail ties, pulling out the boom crutch and tossing it carelessly under the foredeck, whereas Jacob had been taught to lash it forward to keep it from banging around once they were under way.

Things were done in a certain way on the island, not only because they had been done that way for sixty years but also because it was the right way. Jacob had learned everything about the island from his grandfather. Now that his grandfather was gone, Jacob sometimes wondered if his father was forgetting things. The previous fall Jacob had had to remind him to spread wood chips beneath the *Sassanoa* in the boathouse, to absorb moisture through the winter. The fifty-year-old oak planks, cut from trees on the island, would get dry rot in one season without the wood chips, and he worried that his father did not think of it.

"Just tie the skiff up now," his father yelled. They had always tied the skiff to the stern until the *Sassanoa* was ready to sail. Otherwise the two boats would rub. Jacob moored the skiff to the buoy, as he had been told, and of course his father had not raised the main by then, so he had to sit on the deck and separate the two boats with his legs. His father tugged on the halyard, but it was stuck.

"Damn," his father grumbled. "Jacob, help me for a second." Jacob was reluctant to let the two boats rub, but his father was frustrated, so Jacob pushed the skiff off as far from the sailboat's hull as he could and rushed back to hold the halyard while his father jiggled the runner free. The sail rose easily then, snapping at the air, and Jacob hurried to the bow to find the rail of the skiff rubbing against the *Sassanoa*'s white hull. He swore to himself, pushed the skiff away, and leaned over to see what damage had been done. He saw a scratch three inches long. It hadn't penetrated to the wood, but the skiff had gouged out several layers of white paint and left a green smudge. It would allow moisture closer to the wood. He should fix the scratch right away, as his grandfather had taught him to do, though the only way to really take a scratch out was to haul the *Sassanoa* and repaint the entire hull. Jacob was trying not to think about it, but he knew they shouldn't sail now. Not with a scratch in the hull.

"Cast off," his father yelled. The sail was up, but the tiller was still lashed. Jacob untied the bow line but did not let go of the mooring buoy until his father had freed the tiller. Then they drifted back with the wind until the sail scooped the air and leaned them to port. It was a perfect breeze. With the jib up they would move along nicely. The *Sassanoa* never moved very fast. She was nineteen feet on the waterline, but otherwise very much like a Herreshof Bullseye, with a full keel and a wide beam; Jacob's grandfather had designed her to transport his family and their supplies to and from shore.

Jacob raised the jib and tied down the sheet. His father held the tiller and the mainsheet, so Jacob had nothing to do except watch the skiff at the mooring become smaller as they tacked back and forth in the narrow space between the island and the mainland. As they came through the gut and faced the bay, the sails braced against the wind coming in off the ocean. His father loosened the main, leaned back, and eyed the telltales. The telltales had been his father's addition, after his grandfather's death, and Jacob knew they weren't right. He never looked at them when he sailed, but felt the boat's movement under him to find the wind. If the breeze was stiff but he felt no tension on the tiller and little heel, he was off the wind. His grandfather had taught him to rely as little as possible on sight. Eyes were no good in fog or darkness.

"I bet we can make Knubble Head in one tack," his father said. Jacob tried to gauge how the wind and tide would take them over the three quarters of a nautical mile. The wind was shifting around to the southwest, so they could head farther out, but Jacob wondered how long they'd need to get back. If the wind stayed southerly, or even if it moved completely westerly, they would have no problem ploughing straight across the bay. Jacob looked around for the Coast Guard, but the bay was empty except for a few lobster boats and a trawler. They had often sailed across the bay without the boat bag—the *Sassanoa* could handle any kind of rough weather that might come up unexpectedly. But the Coast Guard had fined them twice for not having life jackets; his father had tried to argue himself out of the ticket each time.

Jacob looked back at the granite face of Heron Island, jutting south like the prow of a ship. His mother was working beside the house on the island, taking laundry in off the line. Inside the cabin Jacob's dead grandfather stared down with cold eyes at the dining-room table from a framed photo on the wall. Jacob assumed that the circumstances of his time had made him hard. Jacob remembered when he had rowed over to the island with his grandfather in the winter to cut down a Christmas tree; steam had risen from the water in white patches like ghosts and blown with the wind across the bay. The scene had seemed medieval; the cracked brown knuckles of his grandfather's hands moved toward him and away, rowing. Jacob had removed his glove and dipped his hand in the water, which felt warm, like a bath, compared with the air.

Even now, Jacob thought, the year could have been 1878 on the island— nothing about the kerosene lamps or cast-iron pots suggested that people elsewhere had ever seen electricity, and in the weeks they spent on the island each summer, Jacob forgot the appliances of their house in Portland, where his father rose and dressed in a suit each morning before driving off to a twelve-story glass building. From his office Jacob's father could see the bridge and the bay where his own father had guided ships, and the ocean beyond, where his grandfather had fished the Grand Banks.

"Haul in the jib," his father snapped, and Jacob obeyed, even though he knew the jib would not come in any farther without spilling air and losing some of what his father wanted, which was to point higher so that they could reach Knubble in one tack. His father pulled in the mainsheet, running the line down around the cleat. The *Sassanoa* heeled over in response. Rollers from a storm that had never reached shore pitched them up. Jacob did not worry. He and his grandfather had been out in fifty-knot winds. The ribs and planks creaked, but nothing gave, not even the old hand-sewn sails. But the boat was weaker now, since his grandfather's death.

AS THEY APPROACHED the Knubble lighthouse, Jacob saw tourists standing on the rocks raise binoculars to examine them. The *Sassanoa* was an unusual sight, with its mahogany brightwork on deck, its white hull and blood-red sails, the spars themselves varnished spruce, cut from a forest on the mainland less than a mile from the island. Jacob saw a boy about his age borrow binoculars from his father and look out, and Jacob envied the boy for seeing the boat, though he would rather be where he was, sailing her. She sailed very nicely, not fast like the new fiberglass boats built with long fin keels and flat bottoms. Those were good for speed, but not for rollers and sudden winds. Jacob would take the *Sassanoa* in any bad weather over one of those ugly boats. The *Sassanoa* rolled over the swells and did not slap spray back into the cockpit. A powerful, curling swell could punch a hole in the side of a fiberglass hull, but the *Sassanoa*, with its thick oak planks, absorbed each blow like a prizefighter sizing up his opponent's strength.

"Let's sail over to Mauldin," his father said. "From there it'll be a straight shot back in."

Jacob looked down at his watch. "I don't know if you'll have time to make it into town if we don't head back now."

"It won't make much difference," his father said, looking up at the sail. "We can't miss a wind like this."

"I don't think we'll have enough time," Jacob said again, staring at the floorboards.

Instead of getting angry, as Jacob expected, his father smiled, looking up at the sail. "A wind like this will take us anywhere." Jacob looked at his father and saw his crooked yellow teeth and bumpy nose, the swell of fat girdling his jaw. For the first time, he saw his father as he imagined a woman might see him, in the clear, unforgiving sunlight.

Jacob glanced up toward the southwestern sky, at a line of thick dark clouds moving toward them with the freshening wind. Already his father had to ease off on the mainsheet to accommodate the extra force. Thunderheads. "Head for shore when you see those," his grandfather had said.

After a long tack they came up on the high granite side of Mauldin Island. Some people in a house above sat on their porch looking in the direction of the thunderheads, probably discussing whether they should secure the shutters. The weather was unpredictable, even when one could see it coming, but finally Jacob mentioned it.

"What about those thunderheads?"

"Those are thunderheads," his father said matter-of-factly. No smile this time. Suddenly, as a small cloud shaded the sun, his father looked down into the green water at the small ripples curling into the windward side of the hull. He seemed to be concentrating on a difficult decision.

The bow of the *Sassanoa* ploughed through the water toward the rocks. The shallows dropped off immediately, but they were closing fast, fifteen yards, twelve, and still his father looked over the windward side. Jacob determined not to say anything and found himself almost hoping the boat would crash into the granite. He shook his head at the thought. Five yards away his father casually swung the tiller across and brought them about. Jacob unhitched the jib and cleated it on the port side. He readied himself to let the sail out for heading downwind, but his father kept them headed out of the bay, straight for New Wagon Harbor.

"I thought we were going to head in," Jacob said, trying not to sound anxious.

"I thought we would head out and sail through the 'trickiest bit of sailing in the East,' " his father said, quoting Jacob's grandfather. His father gave a quick nod in the direction they were heading, and Jacob saw the corner of his mouth rise as he leaned down to pull in the main-sheet.

"What about your client and signing those papers?"

"Fuck it. Just fuck it."

Jacob waited for him to say more, but his father studied the luff in the canvas where the main joined the mast. "Winds like this don't come around every day." He narrowed his eyes, pulling in on the sheet and carefully adjusting the tiller. Jacob had never seen him look so determined. "We can make New Wagon Harbor in one tack."

Jacob wondered about his father's work—if people would be left waiting in town and if they would be angry. Over the past months Jacob had heard conversations between his parents about his father's practice, and Jacob was not sure that everything was going well.

NEW WAGON HARBOR, on the southern tip of a peninsula, was formed by three small, burly islands nestled close to shore. They sailed within ten yards of the mainland on the port side, trying to edge into the harbor without tacking again. Jacob could see the pale, sharp rocks below the tidal line, and the red keel that edged up toward the surface as they heeled over.

"How much room we got?" his father asked.

"You got it," Jacob answered.

"One tack."

They were inside the harbor, the mainland and dock to their left, the three islands to their right, and Jacob felt relieved. As if a hand had released its pressure on the mast, they tilted upright as the wind diminished behind the islands.

That wasn't the trickiest bit of sailing either. Now they were going to sail between the northern and eastern islands, where unmarked rocks spiked up from the bottom. Jacob thought the tide was too low, which was the only thing that had made his grandfather describe this reef as tricky. They simply needed to know where the rocks were and to go at the right tide.

"Our momentum will carry us until we can catch the wind again," his father said. "And I'll steer us around the rocks."

Jacob nodded, though he was doubtful. They couldn't see the rocks beneath the surface, but his father had sailed this many times before, with his own father and alone. Jacob didn't know how shallow it would be. The rollers crashed into the windward side of the islands, but the water in the harbor was calm.

"Pull the jib in," his father said. Some wind would come around and they would heel, so they would draw less. That would help.

Jacob uncleated the jib and recleated it, but the maneuver was pointless—the jib had been lashed too tight to begin with.

"Good." His father pulled in on the mainsheet, preparing for the wind. The tide was moving out, lowering every minute now. Several families were eating lunch on the pier outside the Lobster Shack. They stopped cracking their lobsters for a moment to stare at the red sails of the *Sassanoa*, gliding by from sheer momentum on the flat water. One of the youngest children leaped up when she saw the sails and raced toward the end of the pier. Her mother ran after, yelling the girl's name. The girl could have run off the end of the pier. She stopped at the last minute, though, and pointed at the red sails.

Jacob could see, twelve, ten yards ahead, a line of blue water marking the wind. As they drew closer, the wind receded and the shallow rocks appeared, yellow and white beneath the surface. Jacob watched the blue patch of wind on the water draw back like a snake into its hole and vanish. Now they were drifting straight onto the rocks, with no wind coming between the islands to make them heel. His father knew and had only a few seconds to decide what they would do. He could gradually steer them to port, but without any wind there was no point in throwing the tiller over. They would still drift forward. Before either could act or speak, Jacob saw just behind his father's head a patch of dark-blue water, a stiff gust, advancing from the north. Jacob barely had time to release the jib, though he realized later that it was the wrong thing to do. The wind caught inside the loose jib and lurched them straight forward at no heel. His father dropped his jaw and put his hands out to the side, as if some enormous creature had lifted him off the ground and were preparing to swallow him whole. Jacob waited for the sound of the rocks, but halfway through the passage none had come, and he thought maybe they would make it all the way through. Then came a thud that seemed distant, lurching the *Sassanoa*'s bow down and her stern into the air. The wind caught the trimmed mainsail and pulled them sideways off the rock. When they were broadside to the wind and going over, Jacob finally unleashed the mainsail and let the boom fly. The wind spilled out; they were off the rock. His father leaned over the side of the boat to check for damage.

"No harm done," he said, and grabbed the tiller. There had been only a thud, Jacob thought. His father steered them toward the channel. Jacob trimmed the jib, and they sped along with the wind and rocks behind them. The collision seemed never to have happened, and Jacob knew they would not talk about it—as if it were a secret they would have to keep from his dead grandfather.

OUTSIDE THE HARBOR the wind blew twice as strong, and the swells rose high into the air. The hull planed. Jacob sat on the rail and adjusted the jib sheet, while his father sat on the transom so that he could see over the bow. When they rose to the top of a swell, they could see out to sea as if from the top of a mountain. The bow sliced up one side of a wave and the stern coasted down the other side, just as his grandfather had designed them to do, and Jacob was immensely proud in that moment, thinking of his grandfather's mind and hands creating such an efficient and worthy craft. More than that: the *Sassanoa* was a work of art, perfectly balanced between the wind and the ocean, that at her mooring in the morning sat as calm as a sleeping dove.

Jacob looked back at his father, who grinned like a child, his open mouth and bright wide eyes pointed up at the blood-red sail as if the very idea of the wind's moving a boat over water at such a speed were a discovery he had just made for the world.

As they coasted down a swell, Jacob leaned over and placed his hand on the side of the hull. He did not think of turning around even as they passed Damirscove Island. He could see in through the windows of the old Coast Guard station there; at a certain height he could see in one window and out another. Europeans had settled on the treeless island, he knew, before Plymouth or Jamestown. They had fished there, and lived in cold shacks. Several hundred years later the Coast Guard had come, and now it was gone too, and the island was empty except for the terns, gulls, herons, and snowy egrets that swarmed over the grass.

After Damirscove there were no other landmarks for gauging distance over water, and Jacob did not look back except to check his father's eyes darting from the sails to the ocean in perfect concentration. Jacob didn't care how far they sailed, as long as his father continued to smile.

Jacob looked up at the sail and noticed how the pressure of the wind moved from one side to the other as his father shifted the lines and the tiller. Some of the wind spilled out the side of the sail, swirled around to the other side, and caused a luff. With a slight adjustment they were back on track. Then Jacob noticed that the rear stay was frayed. Three or four of the metal threads that twisted around each other had snapped, which left two or three at the most to hold all the weight of the sail and the wind. Any number of bad things would happen, Jacob thought, if the rear stay broke. The mast would snap immediately, and might drag the boat over in this strong a wind. The weight of the keel would probably keep them upright. Even so, without the sail they had only a paddle. No motor. Jacob promised himself he would check all the rigging the next day.

"Dad, look." Jacob pointed up at the stay, and as he pointed, he knew he was also pointing a finger at his father for not keeping the boat up to his grandfather's standards. His father glanced up and saw the fray but did not seem concerned.

"It'll hold."

The wind vanished, not immediately, as often happened, but gradually, to Jacob's relief, until his father didn't need to concentrate so hard on their heading. Jacob could tell that his father's mind was on some other worry, probably something to do with work.

"We should head in," Jacob said. He hadn't even looked back for some time. He wanted his father to be the first one.

His father did look, and raised his eyebrows, not in shock but in surprise, so Jacob looked back too. They were a good distance from shore. The wind usually switched in the evening, after a lull. This was that lull. They would just have to wait for the switch. With any luck it would be a south or a west wind. In any case, the water around the *Sassanoa*, for as far as they could see in all directions, was smooth and dull gray-green.

JACOB NEVER NOTICED the cold when the sails were full, when they were moving, but now, in the stillness, he rubbed the goosebumps on his arms.

His father pulled the collar of his sports coat up around his neck and looked down. "Damn!" he yelled, and yanked his briefcase off the floor. He brushed the water off the leather surface. "I don't think any water got inside." At first Jacob thought he was talking about the *Sassanoa*.

The sails were swaying now, like curtains, in the dim light. The horizon had just turned orange. The night was going to be clear, though fog might roll in from offshore. For the first time, Jacob noticed that his sneakers were soaked. That's why he was so cold. Under way, he seemed to lose all sensation, but now he could see that his feet rested in water that hadn't been there while the boat was heeling. Their bow had dipped, riding the swells, but Jacob hadn't seen any water coming over.

His father let go of the tiller and the mainsheet. With no wind they couldn't control the *Sassanoa*'s direction. Jacob looked at the back of his father's hands, resting on top of the briefcase. With the dried sea salt on the tanned skin, Jacob thought his father looked like a man who had been out to sea a very long time, though the briefcase and sports jacket suggested that he was on the way to his office. Jacob understood that the *Sassanoa* was leaking through the bilge, probably where the keel was bolted to the hull. When they had thudded against the rock in New Wagon Harbor, they must have loosened the joint.

"I think we're taking on," Jacob said.

"I know," his father said, not looking up. "I'm thinking."

Jacob was silent. He decided he had better think too. As a matter of pride, his grandfather had never kept a motor on board. The hand-pump bailer was on the island, with the life jackets and flares, in the boat bag. His father went under the foredeck and rummaged around. He came out a moment later holding the anchor, a twenty-pound aluminum hook attached to a length of chain and rope. The water had risen two inches above the floorboards and was still rising. Jacob wondered how far they were from shore—maybe a mile, maybe more. More. A lobster boat motored by on its way home a little to the west, but neither Jacob nor his father thought to wave. The boatman would not have seen them anyway.

His father held a paddle in one hand and the anchor in the other. Suddenly he stood up on the deck and waved the paddle in the direction of the lobster boat. "Hey! Hey!" They could see the man in yellow waders behind the wheel, looking forward, not back.

Jacob had never in his life seen his father or grandfather call for help while on the water. His heart pounded, and he was no longer cold or tired. He had been thinking about his mother's shepherd's pie, but now he saw what he should have seen before.

"What are we going to do?"

His father sat down. "We'll be fine. Let's see what the problem is down there." He lifted the floor hatch and stared down through the water to the bottom of the bilge. The compartment narrowed to a V, where Jacob could see the keel bolts protruding. His father removed his jacket, folded it carefully on top of his briefcase, and reached his hand down into the bilge.

"I can feel the water flowing in around one of the bolts. I think." He lifted his arm out. All the rollers had vanished now, and the water was flat for as far as they could see. His father removed his shirt. Jacob was startled by the white skin and curly black hairs. He recognized the future shape of his own body, but had trouble imagining himself covered with so much hair. His father ripped the shirt on a cleat, tore it into strips, and leaned back into the bilge. The water was so deep now that he had to crane his neck to keep his face from going underwater. He gave up trying and plunged both his arms and his head under the water. Jacob watched numbly as his father's back muscles bulged and strained against the skin. He popped out a moment later, dripping and gulping for air.

"I wrapped the cloth around the bolt. Hand me the anchor and I'll pound it down. That should wedge the cloth in and stop the leak."

Jacob handed the anchor to his father, who went back underwater. Jacob heard the thud of the metal anchor against the top of the bolt, and occasionally the sound of his father missing and hitting the wooden spine. His father came up for air and went back down. Finally he rested, and set the anchor down. "That should do it."

Jacob nodded. His father was shivering violently. "Put on your jacket, Dad."

"Yeah." After wrapping himself in the jacket for a moment and rubbing his arms, his father looked intently at Jacob. "We shouldn't have tried the trickiest bit."

"We'll fix it when we get back. We should probably replace those bolts anyway."

"You're right about that. Those bolts must be twenty-five years old. This is an old boat, you know. Let's get this water out of here. You start, will you? You'll have to use what's left of my shirt to sop it up, and I'll start paddling."

Jacob picked up the shirt and soaked it in the water, but quickly realized that his father was not thinking right. Instead of using the shirt, he took off his sneakers and started to scoop out the water. "The tide's going out," he said.

"I know."

They were moving farther away from shore.

His father paddled as Jacob scooped up water and dumped it over the side. His father kept looking down at him, and Jacob guessed what he was thinking. He wanted to somehow hide it from his father, he didn't want his father to get angry at himself, but Jacob couldn't help it—the water was still rising.

His father sat down and stared back into the bilge. His feet were wet and he was shivering again. Jacob looked down too, but in the darkness he couldn't see the bottom. His father removed his jacket again and thrust himself beneath the water. He stayed down so long that Jacob almost touched the white skin of his father's back to make sure he was all right. Then his father burst out and stumbled back across the boat, landing against the tiller. "Damn. It's not the bolt. There's a crack in one of the lower planks. One of the ribs must have pushed out when we hit and split the plank or something. I don't know. I can't patch it from inside."

His father's eyes widened when he saw his briefcase sitting on one of the seats. He lunged across the boat and fumbled with the latches.

"Let me," Jacob said, rising and standing next to his father, but his father pushed him away.

"I got it." The two latches clicked up and the briefcase popped open. His father grabbed the phone with his numb hands. He had to cradle it in one palm and aim with the index finger of the other hand at the POWER button. Jacob could see his father's teeth gleaming in the moonlight, but he turned his attention to the phone and waited for the yellow lights to appear on the panel. Nothing happened. His father pushed again, and again.

"The battery's dead. Didn't you turn the power off?" His father looked at the phone in total disbelief, and then at Jacob, who, to avoid his father's eyes, also looked at the phone. He tried to remember if he had pushed the POWER button after talking to his mother. His father let out an awful noise, half growl, half scream, and threw the phone toward shore. Jacob heard it plop like a small stone. His father picked up his briefcase, too, swung it against the deck of the boat with a crack, and then hurled it out as well. White papers fluttered through the air like a flock of panicked terns before drifting slowly to the water and vanishing. The open briefcase tipped sideways and sank from view.

His father watched the place where it had been. Jacob watched his father and thought that they could have used the briefcase to bail. Maybe they could have stayed ahead of the leak until morning, when someone would see them for sure. "Maybe someone will see us out here tonight," he said.

His father looked up at the rigging, his shoulder blades pinching together. "Not with red canvas. We'll have to patch the crack from the outside. Hand me my shirt there, and the anchor."

Jacob rested them on the deck as his father removed his shoes and slacks, groaning when his body slid into the cold water. The white arm came up and grasped the shirt and anchor. Then he put the anchor back on the deck.

"You'll have to dangle the anchor over the side for me while I use the edge of it to stuff the rag into the crack." His father's voice was shaky, and his teeth chattered.

Jacob leaned over the side and watched his father descend into the dark water.

"Give me a little more slack," his father said after coming up for air. Then he went back down again, and Jacob heard faint taps on the hull. His father came back up. "It's a long, narrow crack," he said. "It must bend inward, but we can't get to it from the inside without ripping up the floor. Even then I think it's out of reach from the inside."

Jacob didn't want to say anything. His father went down again, tapped, and came up. This time he let out a long moan before sucking in air and going back down. Tapping turned to banging. Jacob could see the outline of the silver anchor swinging through the water below. His father was swinging as hard as he could through the water at the crack. Jacob had an idea which plank it was. The last thud was muffled. He looked down to see his father pulling back on the anchor.

"No!" Jacob said, but it was too late. His father jimmied the anchor out and then came up for air. Jacob hauled the anchor aboard and stuck his arm down into the bilge. He could not reach the plank his father had been hitting, but he could feel the flow of water rushing in where the anchor had made a gash.

"I'm too cold," his father said.

Jacob turned and wrapped his hands around one of his father's arms and pulled. His father kicked and lunged up, eventually getting his stomach over the gunwale and grabbing the edge of the seat. Jacob put his arms around his father's waist, feeling the hair on his father's back press against his face, and tugged. The flesh was cold to his lips and hands, and Jacob was afraid to let go, even when his father was safely on the seat.

His father drew away, rose to his feet, and found the anchor. He dropped it, and then clamped it between his hands and swung it over his head like an ax. The anchor bounced off the deck and fell to the floor. His father grabbed it out of the water and lifted it over his head again.

"No, no!" Jacob reached for his father, who was using the last of his full strength to swing the anchor against the deck. This time the anchor bounced into the ocean. They both watched as the chain and fifty feet of rope snaked out of the boat, snapped in the air, and disappeared. Jacob felt embarrassed for having cried out.

His father sat down on the seat. The water rose almost to his knees. Jacob shook, but his father was beyond that stage. His eyes drooped.

"We'll have to swim." His father barely mumbled, he was so groggy with cold.

Jacob nodded, but he knew that was impossible. The tide had taken them farther out. Even in late August the water was cold, and they wouldn't have much time before hypothermia set in. Jacob was an excellent swimmer. He swam for a team at school, but that was in eighty-degree water at an indoor pool. The distance to shore would take him an hour and a half. A long string of lights followed the shoreline of New Wagon Harbor and seemed close enough to touch.

"You swim for shore and get help."

Jacob couldn't see his father's lips moving. "No."

"Don't argue. Take the paddle and swim as well as you can. Don't let go of it. Go now."

Jacob stood on the gunwale with the paddle in his hand, looking down into the water. The deck was less than a foot off the surface now. He eased himself in, gripping the paddle in his hand.

"I'll be right back," Jacob yelled, but he heard no response. He could see the silhouette of his father's head and thought about checking on him, but decided he had better keep going, focusing on the brightest light on shore, probably someone's dock, and kicking with all his force.

He felt strong at first, but then he grew stiff, his legs moving in slow motion. He looked behind him. The outline of the sails seemed lower in the water. He turned and kicked harder, afraid to lose sight of the dock but also thinking that maybe the wind would still come up. Soon he could barely move his legs, and the water felt warmer as he turned onto his back to rest. His thoughts slowed. Tomorrow, he thought, they would tow the *Sassanoa* to Heron Island and patch the hole. But the dark triangle set against the stars sank into the blue-black horizon, and there was no sign of the pale shoulders and arms of the man who had promised him summer afternoons when he would finally sail alone.

from my ship is so small

ANN DAVISON

SAILING THE ATLANTIC from Plymouth, England, to Antigua,

in the West Indies, in 1952, Ann Davison became the first woman ever

to cross an ocean alone. Her feat was all the more remarkable for

being undertaken in a boat of exceptionally small size—a mere twen-

ty-three feet in length and seven and one half feet in width—hard on

the heels of an earlier attempt that had ended in shipwreck and her

husband's death. By turns lyrical and philosophical, Davison's sus-

penseful account explores the physical and psychological challenges

of solo sailing, neatly steering clear of the braggadocio and nauti-

calese typical of male accounts. The three segments that follow

encapsulate the first leg of her journey toward self-reliance and self-

discovery on the *Felicity Ann*.

"two eggs!" said Grace, looking at my plate. "Look, they've given you *two* eggs—what have you done to deserve that?"

Rationing was still in force in England, and two eggs were not a normal issue for a hotel breakfast.

"It is not what she has done," said Pete sententiously. "It is what she hopes to do. You could get another egg by simply telling them you are going to sail the Atlantic. They might believe you—they are obviously a trusting lot . . . ."

He looked down at his own one-egg plate and then at the camera on the chair beside him as if he had half a mind to take a picture.

"No you don't," I warned. Professional photographers are indefatigable. To anyone else two eggs on a plate simply means a good breakfast—with perhaps a little influence in rationing times—but to a cameraman they can suggest anything from a new light on human relations to atomic warfare. Pete worked for *Life* Magazine and I was his current assignment, so he had been haunting me for days, appearing at the most incredible times in the most unlikely places, recording my every move. A very unnerving procedure for anyone unused to being a human angle.

Last evening my ship had been put out at moorings for the first time, and I had spent the night aboard, hoping at last to escape his unrelenting surveillance. But such was his devotion to duty he rowed out from the shore at dawn to portray what a woman looks like after her first night afloat, or, as the press boys would say, "on the dawn of her great adventure." Great adventure perhaps: dawn it certainly was, and for me a somewhat testy period at the best of times . . . .

Now I was embarking on what was likely to be the last honest, old-fashioned English breakfast I would enjoy for a long time. In comfort at any rate. Possibly the last . . . . The thought edged to the forefront of my mind . . . I considered it academically; a possibility for someone else. What would a last breakfast be like? Two eggs? The condemned man ate a hearty . . . No. That was a midnight thought, not a morning one.

"A special breakfast," I said aloud. "Not for publication."

THE LITTLE HOTEL DINING-ROOM was crowded. Mostly on my account, I reflected with surprise. Newspaper reporters, radio and television interviewers and operators, photographers, wellwishers and sensation-seekers mingled with the sprinkling of habitués, all eating their one eggs and waiting for me to make the final move. Extraordinary, I thought. Make one step aside from the conventional and the spotlight is on you. You are isolated and observed like a goldfish in a bowl. I looked out through the dining-room window across the waterfront to where the River Tamar flowed past with the serenity of the unwitting. Or the uncaring. The ferryboat from Plymouth was just nosing into the pier in front of the hotel. A ferry I had grown to know pretty well during the past few weeks, and the last time I had crossed on it, two days . . . a lifetime . . . ago, had been at night, and I had looked up at the mast silhouetted against the dark blue sky, imagining it was my boat on the dark water with *my* mast swaying across the stars. But now my imagination broke down. I could not see any further ahead than the next few hours.

"If you have finished hogging all those eggs," said Grace, "I'll give you a hand to finish packing."

Pete said, "You don't pack a ship, you stow it," and picked up his camera.

As we made to pay the bill the manageress came forward, smiling. "There'll be no charge for your breakfast, Mrs. Davison," she said, and added, with an unexpectedly emotional clasping of her hands, "Oh, I do wish you the very best of luck, but I know . . . I feel sure . . . you'll make it. You'll be all right." She felt in her pocket and then held out a little bottle with a ship in it. "Will you take this along with you for luck?"

I have always wanted a ship in a bottle. And at that moment I could have wished it was the only sort of ship I ever had wanted.

"Two eggs, no charge, ships in bottles," said Grace. "There must be more in this than I thought . . . . Too late to join in as cabin boy?"

Pete said he was going down to the quay to get "some crowd shots," and the reporters rose purposefully from their tables.

"Mrs. Davison, is it true you are making your first call at Madeira?"

"Mrs. Davison, how long will it take you to cross the Atlantic?"

"Mrs. Davison, where do you intend to land in America?"

"Why are you going alone, Mrs. Davison?"

"Aren't you going to take a cat or something?"

"Why are you going, Mrs. Davison?"

Mrs. Davison replied with a bland assurance as though she knew the answers. I listened to my voice as if it was someone else speaking, and wondered what the reaction would be if I said I didn't know why I was going, couldn't sail a boat, was terrified of the sea, and that it would be nothing short of a miracle if I made Madeira, America, or anywhere out of Plymouth Sound. But though it pays to tell the truth, it rarely pays to tell the whole truth, so I just went on giving the stock answers as convincingly as I could.

"Ann," Grace interrupted, "you'll never be ready . . . .Come on."

"Stop chivvying," I said sharply, addressing not Grace but the inexorable Fates, appealing to the gods to stop their mills for a moment. Just a moment. I would feel braver then. Brave enough to set out on the venture I had dreamed of and worked on for so long, to sail across the Atlantic single-handed. But the gods were deaf, the mills went on grinding, and the moment of departure drew nearer minute by minute. You dream a dream and then you are stuck with it.

Grace said, not as indignantly as she might, "I am not chivvying, but do come on."

WE WENT OUT of the hotel and across to the shipyard near by. The shipyard that had been home for me during the past three months whilst the ship was being fitted out, but which was now assuming the transient uncertainty of a railway-station. It was nearing high water, and the ship, my innocent accomplice, had been brought in from her moorings to alongside the stone jetty, where a multitude of people in holiday mood were milling about waiting for the spectacle I was to provide. We did not go to the ship, though, but went first to the store in a loft at the far end of the yard, to see if anything had been overlooked in the loading. This had been done the night before last by flashlight, and we had worked like beavers, for the gear—provisions and spares—when piled up on the jetty looked bigger than the ship they were going into, and even Pete lent a hand between pictures. Assured that nothing had been forgotten, we went then to the office to clear up last-minute details and ring through for a weather report. A final check on conditions—as if at that point there was likely to be any startling change—after which I retired to a quiet corner to study the chart and lay off a course. It was an Admiralty Chart, the eastern portion of the Atlantic Ocean, of a scale that usually reduces a long voyage to reasonable proportions; only nothing seemed reasonable just then. As if a record was being played over, I could hear my voice telling the reporters, "I intend to sail sou'west from here clear out into the Atlantic, and then run down for Madeira." Just like that. Good grief, Madeira was a thousand miles away. I fiddled with the dividers and parallel rule, and stared at the chart as if I had never seen anything like it before.

I read the weather report again, but it might have been in Chinese for all it conveyed. I had been doing simple dead reckoning for years, having once earned my living as a flying pilot, but now my mind was blank. I doodled a few stylized ships on a stylized sea on the edge of the chart, pulled my wits together and, without thinking, laid off a course, noted some figures, rose and went to the ship. She looked smart and defiant and workmanlike, and moved me with her beauty, as she had done ever since I had first set eyes on her; but she meant no more to me then than an instrument with which I hoped to accomplish the task I had so incredibly chosen.

The shipyard was owned, managed, and worked in by the Mashford Brothers, all six of whom appeared to be on board, making last-minute additions, alterations, and modifications, lashing down and making fast on deck those items for which there was no stowage space below, and doing what were then to me incomprehensibly seamanlike things to rope.

"All for You," one of the brothers sang gaily. I smiled wanly and went below. There, with his coat off and sleeves rolled up, was Sid Mashford, designer of the ship and managing director of the firm, busily engaged in fixing a loud-speaker to a locker bulkhead. He looked round as I entered the cabin and said, "Nearly ready," in a conciliatory tone, as if I was raring to go.

I sat on the settee bunk, and wondered how many times this particular pattern had occurred in my life. It was always the same. I would work blindly and wholeheartedly toward a certain point, and when it came I would go numb. And feel sick. I felt sick now. I said so to Sid.

"Keep calm. Keep calm," he said, sweat running off his brow as he savaged the screwdriver. "You'll be all right. Just keep calm."

You don't look too calm yourself, I thought, and you're not going . . . . The responsibility, I suppose. You designed the ship and built her and fitted her out. But I'm going to sail her, and if anything goes wrong it will be my fault. And why should anything go right? All that ocean . . . And I don't know anything about sailing . . . Well, hardly anything. Sid knows that, but he never discouraged me . . . . In fact, no one has discouraged me since the beginning of this idea . . . ."Go on, Ann. You'll make it," is what they've said all along. Which is what I wanted them to say, isn't it? So what am I griping about? Because I am frightened. Face it, you fool, frightened silly. Oh, God, why must I always have to prove something?

The sudden cessation of activity aboard interrupted my reverie. The ship was ready. The moment had come.

I went ashore to say goodbye. People pressed round. People who yesterday had been my friends; people I knew and loved, whose lives and hopes and ambitions I had shared. Now they were strangers from another world. Or I was. They spoke, and it was as if I could not hear or understand what they were saying. I spoke without knowing what I said. Without looking I was aware of Pete running round in a photographic frenzy. Without listening I was aware of Grace at my elbow, reminding and anxious. Friends who had travelled far for the occasion were giving last-minute gifts and messages; but it was as if I had already gone, for between us was a barrier, invisible and impenetrable. Abruptly I turned away and climbed down on to the boat again.

Bill Mashford, another member of the firm, said, "I'll give you a hand getting under way—the launch can pick me up in the Sound."

So we started the engine and put up the sails and cast off, and ran up river a little way to sort things out. At least, Bill did most of the sorting, which was just as well, as left to myself, being as I was under an emotional anesthetic, anything might have happened, and the onlookers provided with more of a spectacle than they bargained for. As we motored back, people in the shipyard waved. They were waving out of the hotel windows, and all along the waterfront. The ferryboat crossed ahead of us blowing her hooter, and the passengers aboard raised a small forest of arms. Mechanically I waved back. The yard launch rushed after us filled with my friends, all laughing and gay. It was as if the life I had forsaken was reaching out after me. In Plymouth Sound the launch came alongside, and Bill transferred himself aboard it.

The sun had a halo round it, and a small and fitful breeze was blowing. Sid Mashford leant over the side and called out, "Ann! Take in your jibsheet!" Jibsheet? . . . Jibsheet? . . . Ah, the staysail was flogging. I hadn't noticed. Also in the Sound was the aircraft carrier H.M.S. *Eagle*, with a vast crew aboard waving encouragement. So I was told two years later, but at the time I never saw her. If I could miss the *Eagle* I could hardly be expected to notice a little thing like a flapping staysail.

I took a pull on the sheet and belayed it with extraordinary care, and relaxed as if the day's work was done. Then suddenly bethought me of a telegram, promised but not sent. This oversight slipped into the void of my consciousness and swelled to enormous proportions. Whatever else, that telegram must go. I scribbled a note on a piece of paper and roared up to the launch in the manner of one bringing the news from Ghent, thrust the message into someone's outstretched hand, and if the launch hadn't shied away, would have torn off our topsides in the process, for it never occurred to me to slow down.

The launch kept nervously out of reach after that, and as we neared the open sea two sailboats joined the fleet. Graceful and white-winged and under full control, their burgees were dipped in elegant salute. I felt I ought to reply, but decided against it as being too difficult, so flapped an ineffectual hand and wished they would all go home and leave me to face what had to be faced. They represented the last thin thread holding me to a life that was past, and I wanted to be alone to face my future, stretching there before me, from horizon to horizon, the broad, sparkling, illimitable Atlantic, enigmatic and promising nothing. At last the boats turned away from seaward, back as it were to yesterday, whilst I kept straight on, for tomorrow.

The tenuous thread was broken and I was on my own.

AT HALF-PAST three that afternoon, Eddystone lay abeam, close to starboard. The wind had died away, and the lighthouse, like a huge admonitory finger, pointed to heaven from a glass-calm sea. Eddystone was my departure point, and I looked at it with a lingering fascination as it slowly fell astern, the last signpost on the long, long road to Madeira.

The sky was clear overhead, but there was a thickish haze which gave a curious mirage quality to the sea that exactly matched my mood. The dark blue sails hung limp as the little ship motored through the limpid mirror of the sea, and time crept forward as the sun swung slowly across the sky to melt red in the mist on the western horizon. All color faded as the day died; then night, darkly enveloping, spread a mantle of solitude over the sea. An immeasurable solitude that reached up from the bottom of the ocean and stretched out beyond the stars, that penetrated every particle of water and permeated the very structure of the ship, that muffled the sound of the engine, that was life and death and everywhere and nothing.

With night came the wind. It whispered first, then sang in the rigging, and kicked up little waves that grew bigger and rougher as the wind gained confidence. And it blew from the sou'west, which was awkward as that was the way I wanted to go. The little ship, grossly overladen, bucked and pitched in the head sea, and seemed to me, in my colossal ignorance, to be horribly insecure. Overly cautious, I reefed the mainsail and changed the staysail for the storm jib, a ridiculous piece of canvas for the wind that was blowing then; but there were all the long night hours ahead, and as this was the first time I had ever sailed a boat on my own I was not taking any chances.

Then I sat in the cockpit, steering south and thinking of my friends, at home now, safe at home, warm and dry, with roofs over their heads and the good earth solid and steady under their feet. They were on land, where there were forests and fields and flowers and roads leading with comparative certainty to a specific destination. Where the warm yellow light through windows would stab the country darkness and the glow from a whole town lighten the night sky. Where there were people, wise, sensible people who stayed at home and never let their dreams run away with them.

But land was invisible, and the sea was dark and desolate. There was not a ship in sight. My only companions were the stars and the wind and the waves, remote and impersonal. The ship heeled and water slapped her bow, lapped over the lee rail and ran searchingly aft. It was cold and the chill struck through the defenses of my duffle-coat.

Cold and lonely and frightened, I wondered why I had let a dream run away with me. Why, for heaven's sake, why?

THE ACTUAL REALIZATION of a dream is neither better nor worse than imagined. It is entirely different. Before setting out, I thought I had no illusions about the voyage or sailing alone. I expected to be lonely. I expected to be frightened. What I did not expect was the positive panic of emotion that swamped me at the outset of the voyage. I was so lonely that whenever a ship appeared I could not take my eyes off her until she vanished. Once I turned and followed a trawler for nearly an hour, although she was apparently bound for Iceland, because I could not bear the friendless vista of an empty sea. Loneliness does not come from the physical state of being on one's own so much as from fear, the same old fear that stems from ignorance; and having thrust myself out into the unknown with only myself to rely on, I had reverted at once to the primitive. A child with a bogey round every corner. I was not only afraid of the wind and the sea. I was afraid of the ship. I was afraid of reefing the sails, or putting them up or changing them in any way. I was afraid of stopping the engine, and having stopped it, afraid of starting it again.

The numbness with which I set out wore off very slowly, and the first few days passed in a frightened haze upon which the entries in my log book throw very little light. These entries were mostly recordings of times, a sort of notch-cutting to mark the passing of hours. It is inconceivable that I did not eat for five days, but there is no mention of my having done so, and I cannot recall a single meal, not even a cup of coffee. Fortunately I was not seasick, but I had guarded against *that* contingency by repeated doses of drammamine, a very effective protection against seasickness, the only snag being that it is inclined to make one drowsy. Neither do I remember actually going to sleep during those first few days, though I must have done so. I do remember feeling so tired that my only ambition was to fold up and sleep for a week.

The second night out is identifiable in my memory because of the fog. Nothing particularly horrific occurred, except that a steamer loomed up astern and scared me even more witless, quite unnecessarily, as she sheered off to starboard and disappeared into the murk, wailing like a lost soul. The rest of the night was spent in clammy discomfort in the cockpit, expecting to be run down any moment.

THE COURSE I was trying to steer was sou'westerly but this was hampered by a head wind, so I made in general southerly directions, plotting estimated positions by dead reckoning, on the chart. I made several attempts to take sights with the sextant, and found it a very different proposition in real life, infinitely more difficult than taking a sight from the high cliffs of Devon with the Commander standing by with a stop watch. The high cliffs of Devon stay put in their nice firm underpinnings, but the deck of a lively little vessel offers a poor support for an inexperienced sight-taker. I concluded it was an impossible undertaking and unreasonable of anyone to think otherwise.

On the fourth day out the log read 230 miles. By then it seemed I had spent a lifetime at sea, and there was another 700 miles to go to Madeira. How embarrassing it would be if Madeira failed to turn up at the appointed time. There was, so far as I could see, very little reason why it should. And what would one do then? Turn right? Or left? Or keep straight on? Or accost a passing vessel. "Have you seen Madeira lately?"

Then, as if a kindly Fate interposed to keep me from getting too discouraged, the following night granted a few hours of sheer magic. One of those rare glorious experiences that lift you right out of the commonplace (though God knows there is little of the commonplace about being at sea single-handed) on to Olympian heights of delight. The wind had backed right round to the northeast, and *Felicity Ann* was flying before it, her boom way out and lifting, tugging at the mainsheet as if she was alive and impatient of restraint. Her mainsail, taut and straining, was silhouetted against the night sky. And the night sky was a black velvet backcloth for countless glittering stars. Wavelets tumbled in a foam

of phosphorescence spelling a thousand bright jewels on the sea. A
comet spanned the heavens leaving a broad white wake on the water. All
the loneliness and the fears were forgotten, dissolved into nothing by an
ecstacy of being so pure, so complete, that nothing else mattered or
existed. There was no past, no future, only the participation of a brilliant
present. An exquisite distillation of the meaning of life.

Then the kind Fate went off duty. Before dawn it was blowing all hell
and I was staring in horror at the mounting waves. I reefed the main and,
when that was not enough, took it in altogether and changed the staysail for the storm jib. The dawn was scowling and bleak, overhung with
a canopy of low cloud. Later, the wind eased a little but left a heavy cross
sea for the ship to wallow in. I was in no mood for another bout with
the sails, so started the engine and plugged on towards the never-never
land of Madeira.

Then the ship began to behave strangely. So much was obvious even to
me. She seemed sluggish, rising to the seas with an effort, quite unlike her
usual buoyancy, and she rolled with slow deliberation as if waterlogged. I
slid back the hatch and looked into the cabin. She was waterlogged. The
cabin was awash, with water way up over the floor-boards and slopping
from side to side, leaving an oily ridemark on the woodwork. Both bilge
pumps were jammed solid when I tried to use them. Anyone else would
have pulled up the floor-boards, baled the ship out, cleared the pumps,
found out why the water was coming in, and taken steps to stop it. I did
none of these things. They never occurred to me. I was too stupid with
fatigue, too tense and too tired from an excess of experience to think con-
structively. I was confused, and wanted to stop and take stock of the situation. I wanted to be still and free from the incessant motion, I wanted,
most desperately, to sleep. The ship was half full of water which I was
unable to get out by the obvious methods, therefore I must find somewhere where I could start thinking again under normal conditions. I
looked at the chart and decided to make for Brest, the nearest port, about
70 or 80 miles away if my reckoning was correct.

Later on in the morning the clouds lifted and broke apart, the sun
shone and my outlook improved enormously until the color of the
water changed to light green. This was disturbing, as it was different and
therefore probably dangerous. Everything was suspect at that stage of my
seagoing, which no amount of reassurance from the charts and reckoning could allay.

I passed two fishing boats, very gay and colorful and French, neither
of them fishing, but lying to, rolling heavily, evidently waiting for the

tide or weather. The fishermen, as colorful as their boats, leant over the side and watched our progress with interest. Some of them waved and I waved back, much heartened by the sight of real live people. Then it occurred to me it would be sensible to ask for a position check, so I turned back to the nearest ship, a bright blue, broad-beamed trawler called *Fends les Vagues*, which seemed a pretty appropriate choice under the circumstances. I motored round and round her trying to convey in basic French and Indian sign language what I wanted. "Où est Brest?" I shouted, that being the nearest I could get to expressing my needs. Fishermen crowded to the bulwarks, looking eager, interested, and absolutely blank. I expressed these needs several times on both sides of the fishing boat, up wind and down wind, but succeeded only in throwing the entire crew into a fever of excitement as they threshed from side to side across the deck trying to keep me in sight. I motored round to the stem of the vessel and read the port of registry. Douarnenez. All right then: "Où est Douarnenez?" I tried, with no better result, and regretted, not for the first, nor by any means the last, time in my life, having started something that was proving difficult to continue and impossible to stop. And I would have gone on my way, but a handsome young man wearing a dashing cap and chewing on a cigarette end and looking as if he had stepped straight out of a French movie, authoritatively waved me alongside, a maneuver I accomplished with a masterly and quite unexpected precision. Several agile men then leapt down on to *FA* and held her off with a dramatic show of strength and dexterity. "Venez abord, Madame," invited the handsome young skipper courteously, and completely fascinated by the turn of events, I climbed up on the trawler, a fairly athletic feat, and appreciated as such by the onlookers, as the two ships were rolling wildly and inharmoniously.

"Et maintenant," said the skipper politely. "Qu'est-ce que vous desirez, Madame?"

I pointed to *FA*, to the chart I had had the forethought to bring with me, made a sweeping gesture in the general direction of where Brest ought to be, said "Brest" in a loud clear voice, and hoped it conveyed the general idea. The fishermen crowded round the chart, gazing intently at it as if looking for X marks the spot. "Douarnenez," said one of them suddenly, pointing it out triumphantly as if he had found the key to the problem; and the rest nodded wisely. But the skipper tapped me on the shoulder, said something I freely translated into "Radio," pointed to the wheelhouse, and beckoned. I followed him into the wheelhouse, down a companionway, and into the main cabin. This compartment, a large piratical-looking affair, managed to give the effect of guttering candles in spite of electric light. There were tiers of berths all round the sides, built-in like the old "but-and-bens" of Highland cottages, a few wooden kegs at strategic points, and if there had been a roll of parchment on the chart table I would have accepted it unquestioningly; but it was a D.F. chart, and the delicious atmosphere of Treasure Island was thrown off center somewhat by the incongruous intrusion of a huge radio, which jutted out into the cabin and occupied most of the forward bulkhead.

The skipper went to this functional-looking machine, handed me a pair of headphones, put on a pair himself, switched on the ship-to-shore apparatus and called up Brest. I could not follow all the moves in the game, but caught the general gist. The shore operator and the skipper held an animated discussion to which I listened with admiration, wondering how they managed to communicate without seeing one another, French conversation being so visual. Then the skipper turned to me, indicating it was question time and to go ahead. I took fright at once, "Mais, je ne parle pas Français," as if he didn't know. And the next thing, there was Land's End at the other end of the phone. Small world. Feeling the situation was getting away from me, I tried to explain.

"I only want to check my position. The, er, ship, my ship . . . yacht *Felicity Ann* out of Plymouth . . . is making a bit of water and the pumps are jammed. I am going into Brest to fix things . . . just an idea, you know, to get a position check, but my, huh, French isn't up to it." Nor my English either.

"You are on board the trawler now?" The operator at Land's End sounded puzzled. "Are they giving you a tow in?"

"Oh, no," I said, very British and liable to give a light laugh any moment. "It is nothing serious . . . all I want is a position check . . . ."

"That I can't give you," said he briskly. "Ask the skipper . . . he'll tell you. Good luck."

Well now, I thought, that had been the idea. Still . . . "Thanks," I said, "I will."

There was an outbreak of Gallic garrulity on the air and the skipper signed off, looking pleased with himself at having given a demonstration of the modern mysteries of science. He leant over the chart table with the expression of a magician about to produce a truly enormous rabbit out of the hat, but the trick was interrupted by a great commotion breaking out on deck. Amidst the general confusion, anguished cries of "le petit bateau" were recognizable. The skipper's expression changed to one of alarm and he flew up the companionway. I flew after.

Felicity Ann had broken away and was careering off under bare poles with three fishermen aboard. They stood on deck looking helpless and rather woebegone at having been abducted. This escape produced more activity aboard the trawler than a tiger at large in a cattle market. Gesticulating men rushed to and fro, leaping up and down companion-ways, running into one another, and skipping over fishing gear. Ropes were thrown, orders shouted, bells rung, machinery started, and with a roar of mighty engines the trawler got under way. Cheer-leaders yelled encouragement to the men on *FA*, to me, to one another, and to every-one in earshot. With the maximum of fury and the minimum of effort *FA* was waylaid, captured, and tied up alongside.

The three men immediately climbed back on to the trawler, much relieved for themselves, but very concerned for me, having discovered the water in the cabin. "Trop de l'eau," they cried in great agitation. "Oh, trop," I agreed. And a passionate discussion took place among the men. Finally the skipper detached himself from the committee meeting to inform me of the findings. Catching about one word in ten, I under-stood him to say that fishing being what it was, and *FA* being in the state she was, why didn't I let them tow her into Douarnenez? Frankly, it seemed a very good idea. I had never been to Douarnenez, I had never been aboard a French trawler before, and surely one of the reasons for coming to sea was the assimilation of new experiences, so why not? Then I thought of what tows mean in the marine world, and said the only word I knew in the language to cover the situation: "Combien?" which the skipper brushed aside as an insult to chivalry, and action was taken to put *FA* in tow.

She got away again, by herself this time, and I was really worried for a moment, but once again, amidst fearful tumult, she was caught, and finally lashed up short under the stem so that she had no option but to follow the trawler's every move. When assured that "le petit bateau" was safe and under control, the men went through a convincing demonstra-tion of eating in mime, and we all trooped below.

There did not appear to be a regular cook in the crew; they all fixed their own meals, producing from personal lockers knives, forks, plates, mugs, long loaves of bread, and bottles of wine, then vanished one by one into the galley to reappear with an omelette, fried fish, or whatev-er. They vied with one another to fix a meal for me. Everyone con-tributed something, brooking no refusal, and as it was a large crew I hogged the biggest meal since the two-egg breakfast in Plymouth. The conversation flowed as easily as the wine, so that we gathered all sorts of interesting and doubtless entirely erroneous information about one another, and in no time flat what remained of the afternoon and evening was gone. Then the skipper put his hands together, tested the side of his face on them and closed his eyes, the rest of the crew following suit to make the meaning quite clear. They pointed to the bunk by the radio and said, "Pour vous, Madame." It was the skipper's. What sailor could offer more?

I rolled into the bunk and pulled the blanket up round my ears, revelling in the indescribable bliss of the prospect of a whole night's sleep.

"Bonne nuit, dormez bien," called the men. The lights went out. All was quiet but for the muffled throb of the engine, a giant heart beating in the night, and the secret sounds of a ship moving through the water. The barely perceptible motion, a smooth lifting and rolling, was soothing, soporific: I faded out of consciousness, inexpressibly content, Lovely, lovely people . . . blessed . . . blessed sleep . . .

THE WIGHT THAT first said "Pride goeth before a fall" must have tried to reef down in a strong northerly. The winds waited until we got nicely out to sea and some forty miles on our way to Gibraltar and then, just on nightfall, said, "There she is!" and came tearing along full of vigor and rumbustiousness, at which my new-found confidence retired to let old man Caution take over again, and I turned up into wind to shorten sail. *FA* at once went into her demented see-saw act, and I crawled forward to change jibs feeling uncommonly like an apprentice lion-tamer about to attempt the subjugation of a singularly angry lion, for, heavens, how that sail can hate. It throbs with a rage that shakes the ship and lashes out with canvas, sheets, and shackles, making a terrible noise, the embodiment of unbridled ferocity, whilst its wet and windy supporters on the sidelines scream derision and hurl great dollops of spray.

By the time I had taken in the staysail and hanked on the storm jib I was soaked, battered, and worn out.

Reefing the mainsail does not present any problems with roller reefing providing it is tackled in the proper manner but make one false move on a ship and the resultant hurrah's nest is horrible to behold. And worse to rectify.

I didn't get the sister-hooks on the topping-lift—a tackle that takes the weight of the boom when you lower the sail—properly hooked on to the shackle on the cob collar at the end of the boom, so that the collar jammed and revolved with the boom instead of allowing the boom to revolve inside it, and in no time flat the mainsheet was wound round the boom, round the mainsail, and for reasons best known to itself, round the boom gallows as well. The tangle up had the Laocoon making daisy chains by comparison. I was forrard of course, winding the reefing gear, paying out the main halyard, easing the mainsail down, and holding on, a simple operation, calling for only four hands. When I saw what was happening, I rushed aft, forgetting to belay the main halyard, which promptly flew out to sea and then wrapped itself round the upper cross-trees. So then I scrambled back and forth, scrabbling at the lash-up in a frenzy, swearing all I knew and a lot I didn't and achieving absolutely nothing at all, until FA lost patience and gave me one easy lesson in how to keep your head by nearly removing mine. She swung a classic hay-maker with her boom and dropped me neatly into the cockpit.

After a while I got up and sat on the seat. FA had returned to her see-saw routine, rocking up and down, spitting spray and grumbling: "Why the stampede? There's all the time in the world. If only you thought what you were going to do before you did it, you would save yourself so much trouble."

Maybe she did not say it. Maybe the crack on my head just made me think she did. But I learnt something all the same.

WE RAN ALL night under reefed main and storm jib, but by seven o'clock the following morning the north winds were blowing in earnest and I had to take the mainsail in altogether and run under storm jib only. The seas were high, gray, and impressive. They came up under the ship and lifted her until all the world was spread about beneath, then they rushed on and left her to sink back into a canyon of tall, toppling waters. Stray bits of advice from quay men came percolating back from fitting out days: "Never let her run too fast, she's too fine aft." Never let her run too fast. What is too fast? A big sea curled over and broke on the quarter deck. That was enough for me. I can take a hint. Out went the sea-anchor. It was amazing the difference it made. FA might have been set in concrete. The anchor warp thrummed with strain. Then I dropped the jib and FA, who had been riding by the stern, came round and lay broadside on to the seas. I did not like this, but did not know what to do about it then, so went below and left FA to look after herself. She knew so much better than I.

The cabin was wonderfully reassuring. It was hard to believe there was so much unpleasantness going on outside, except for the noise. The scream of the wind, the roar of the sea, the hiss of a big wave, the thrrrrrup of spray on deck, occasionally a crash when she took it green. Then the cabin would go dark, and I would look up from my book and see water solid through the portholes as though looking into an aquarium, and I would turn several pages without a notion of what I was reading.

It was quite a wind. Within the next twenty-four hours no less than four steamers hove to and hooted at us, all set for a big rescue operation. I used to slide back the hatch and wave with a false nonchalance, and dive below before too much sea got into the ship. I hated to see them go, but was inestimably comforted by their concern.

We lost the sea-anchor; it fridged through its own fastenings at the end of the warp. I reckoned we made a sou'westerly drift of about 24 miles in that blow, which eased to the merest breath after a couple of days and worked its way through east to south, leaving a lumpy and confused sea to contend with. I started the engine, because it is aggravating to hang about to no purpose, and so found the clutch was suffering from a surfeit of sea water and had frozen in gear, which made starting rather hard work. The southerly wind freshened and a shark swam round the ship which was somehow rather dispiriting, and I was very tired. Then we had a day of flat calm to recover in, but this was immediately followed by a northerly wind that blew with even greater ferocity than before.

We lay to a warp for two days. During the nights I had to keep constant watch for ships, as none of the oil lamps would stay alight in those conditions and there was not a hope of our being seen. A small ship does not even show up on the radar screen. It was frankly terrifying, but a high pitch of fear cannot be sustained for long—it turns to a state of apathetic resignation. All the same I wore myself out worrying. I worried about the gear; whether there was anything I could or should do; if there was a ship bearing down . . . they were very close by the time you could see them in those seas . . . and the more I fretted the wearier I got, and the wearier I got the more I worried.

The windage of the mast and the rigging was enough in that wind to lay the ship over, and she had a curious way of jiggling, rocking herself very quickly, until she was hit by a big sea, then she would remain perfectly still for a moment as if shocked—you can't do this to me—then she would pull herself together and start rocking again. When this happened the primus gimbals, swinging clear out of the galley over the floor of the cabin, would groan ooooh . . . ooh in the most pathetic and appropriate manner. They should have been oiled and made groanproof, but were so amusing in a rather unfunny situation that I left them alone to state the case for me vicariously, and then it wasn't necessary. A monster sea caught the ship and threw her on her beam ends. One never quite knows what happens on these occasions. The sound of the wave breaking was like an explosion, and it felt as if *FA* was trying to do a barrel roll. Everything on the starboard side of the cabin broke loose and crashed over to port. Cups, plates, books, charts, navigation instruments, pepper, salt, soap detergents hurtled through the air. The entire galley, primus stove, gimbals and all, came out by the roots. Kettles, bowls, and pans tumbled about in frantic confusion. Something hit the compass and smashed it. Water poured through the sliding hatch as if it was wide open. As soon as *FA* came up for air I looked out to see if anything was left on deck. The cockpit was filled to the coamings and the whole ship was dripping as if she had just been fished up from the bottom of the sea, but otherwise everything was as it should be, nothing had parted or been carried away, or gone ping. I helped the self-drainers drain the cockpit by baling with a bucket, and then worked like a maniac in the cabin trying to restore order, as if doing so could prevent another big sea getting us.

Actually it did moderate after that, and about midday the clouds broke apart and bright sunshine shone down upon the water. A heartening feature; disaster never seems quite so imminent when the sun shines.

The following day we pottered along uncomfortably in a high sea that did not have enough wind to support it. I reckoned we were off Cape St Vincent by evening, and was surprisingly rewarded by the flash of its light at nightfall. We had been ten days at sea, and had covered most of the distance from Vigo at a fast drift. The wind freshened during the night again, and there were so many ships about I fidgeted and could not sleep and started the next day's work limp and nervous. We rounded the Cape and altered course for the Straits of Gibraltar, navigating by the hand-bearing compass as the other was out of commission. The sea was lumpy and confused and our progress was slow.

I hove to at six o'clock, worn out and discouraged by the small advance made for the energy expended. A steamer hove to near by and looked at us questioningly, but I waved reassuringly as usual, and she went on her way to leave us to get through another restless and uncomfortable night. It blew with gale force, and although the seas were nothing like as high as before, they were short and fast with plenty of weight in them, which made them harder to take than the bigger seas. I barely had the strength to get under way the following day, one of peculiar emptiness. The sky was hard and absolutely cloudless. There were no birds and no ships to be seen. Land was out of sight. The sea did not sparkle, it was dull and angry and leaden for all the clarity of atmosphere. I looked in the water, but even the fish seemed to be hibernating. One little cloud would have been welcome. Lonely, weary, and acutely depressed, I cast about in the lockers for something to eat, not having done so for a couple of days. Cold food in bad weather is singularly unappetizing, but since the stove had gone out of action there had been no alternative. I found a tin of plum cake which I had forgotten, one slice of which held the magic of recuperation, and I was heartened enough to experiment with a self-steering device I thought I had invented. I had not, and was compelled to continue steering. The wind was nearly west by now, on the port quarter, and at nine-thirty P.M. I hove to and turned in, oblivious and uncaring of ships, seas, or anything else, and passed out cold until eleven o'clock the next day, when I woke refreshed and slightly guilty, to find gorgeous motoring weather with only the merest suggestion of air from the west. The respite did not last long, however, the weather turned squally, then the wind went into the east and blew half a gale, and so it went on, day after day, and it seemed as though I had never known and never would know anything but a life of dismal, damp endurance.

One night we were nearly run down. The seas were fierce, and we were lying to without any canvas, when suddenly a steamer appeared on the crest of a wave, a triangle of lights, port, starboard, and masthead, coming straight for us. No time to get sail up, no time to prime the engine. I swung the starting handle with strength borrowed from fear, and the engine started. We climbed out of the way as the big freighter slid by to disappear as quickly as she came, hidden by the seas.

After that there was no more sleep.

The following night the loom of a light appeared on the horizon sky ahead, and I took it to be the one I was expecting to see on the Spanish coast at the entrance to the Straits of Gibraltar. It was not possible to time the light and check it, as most of the time it was obscured by waves. None the less, I altered course to go through the Straits and plugged on all through the night, only to find we were plugging our way smack on to the African coast somewhere down by Larache in the morning. I could have kicked myself. The light had been Cape Spartel. For a moment I was almost of a mind to carry on to Casablanca, but having said I was going to Gibraltar, to Gibraltar I was going if it took the rest of my life.

We thumped north along the African coast under motor and a sweltering sun. There was no wind at all and the sea was smooth and oily;

there was a thick pink haze, and I sat at the tiller, sweating and burning, acutely discomforted by the violent change of conditions. The clutch was slipping badly, so it was eight P.M. by the time we reached Cape Spartel, and I was dizzy with fatigue, having been at the helm without sleep or respite for forty-eight hours; and there had been little enough sleep or respite before then either. Life now simply resolved itself into one of imperative urges, and the most imperative urge of all was sleep. I wanted oblivion with every fibre of my being. And here we were right at the entrance to the Straits, where ships were crowding through like sheep at a gate. One might as well pull up in the middle of Broadway for a quiet nap.

Extreme fatigue does strange things. As in a dream I became aware of two other people aboard, and as in a dream it seemed perfectly natural that they should be there. One of them sat on the coachroof and the other came aft holding on to the boom quiescent in its gallows. "O.K.," he said. "You kip down. We'll keep watch." Obediently I went below and slept till morning.

Stretching and yawning and still weary, I climbed into the cockpit in the light of day. "Thank you," I said. "That was good . . . " but they had gone. Never had the cockpit looked so empty.

A small gray freighter was hanging solicitously in the offing, officers on the bridge training their binoculars on *Felicity Ann*. I was too tired even to wave.

There was a nice westerly breeze blowing, the sort of wind that makes a person say, if he likes that sort of thing, "Let's go sailing today."

"Well, don't just sit there." *FA* was rolling impatiently. "Why don't we get some sail on and use this breeze. First decent one since we left home.... Jeez—what I got for a skipper—or maybe you think Gibraltar will come out to you?"

I dragged the sails up by their back hair, tottered back to the cockpit, turned down wind and ran for the Straits. *FA* lifted her boom and gave a little tug on the mainsheet: " 's better."

WITHIN A COUPLE of hours we were romping along the Straits and I was sitting at the tiller with my feet hitched up on the coamings, singing as if I hadn't a care in the world. For there was Africa, with great big blue-gray African mountains on one side, and there was Spain with green not so big mountains on the other, and there, yes, there was Gibraltar ahead, not looking the least as I had always imagined, much longer and greener. Achievement, for recuperative purposes, has the wonder drugs beat a mile. A colossal Italian liner overtook us, passing close on the starboard side, playing pom titty pom pom, pom POM on her hooter in a very unorthodox and friendly manner, whilst deckloads of laughing passengers leant over the side and waved, so that I waved back in extravagant good humour.

The strong and constant current flowing eastward out of the Atlantic into the Mediterranean gave us such a boost we were through the Straits and entering Gibraltar Bay in five hours, and there I took in the sails and log line, put up the ensign and Q flag, and started the motor; but the clutch was slipping so badly that we bucked the outgoing stream in the Bay for an unconscionably profitless time.

I ENTERED THE Harbor finally with a certain uneasiness, for some-where in the back of my mind was the notion that you didn't just wander into a Naval Base like this—there are formalities—and sure enough a little police boat came out of a dock at the double and fussed toward us, watchdog in every strake. The clutch was only engaging in fits and starts, but as attack is the best form of defense, I wasn't taking any chances, and pushed the lever into neutral so that we swung and drifted helplessly.

As soon as they were within *my* throwing distance, I shouted,

"Good, just the men I am looking for," and threw them a line before they could say "Now, what's all this 'ere," which I fully expected, as they were dressed in blue uniform like London policemen, except for an official plainly the Health Officer. He stood authoritatively in the cockpit and spread his arms as if he expected the police to rush *FA* and said, "No one aboard until I've cleared this vessel."

Drifting about in the middle of the harbor he examined my papers so carefully that I began to think perhaps I was a schizophrenic and a smuggler in my other life. Then suddenly he pushed them away and took off his hat and official manner and smiled and said, "We've been waiting for you. But," he sighed, "I wish we had met ashore." Then he asked for a photograph and I was so flabbergasted I gave him one. Then I convinced the police that the clutch was completely and utterly inoperable (I was not going to be turned out of that harbor for the Admiral himself—and I had extracted the information that you had to get formal permission for entry) and they towed us into the Cormorant Camber, a quiet, secluded dock, where there were already a number of presumably legitimate yachts lazing alongside.

After the police boat had gone I puttered about tidying the decks in a warm aura of delight, thinking Gibraltar, this is *Gibraltar*, the second port we've set out to find and found; Gibraltar, over a thousand miles from England.

All the fears, all the weariness and misery of the past nineteen days were forgotten. They might never have been. The late sun still shimmered on the quay walls, the water was calm as if water could never be anything else. High above towered the Rock. There were sounds of traffic, of people; somewhere a dog barked. It was as if I had never been hungry, weary, frightened, or desperate for sleep, had never crouched in the cabin pretending to read whilst great gray waves ravaged the ship. This was Gibraltar and what was past had gone.

A large, imposing gentleman in immaculate white uniform and large white knees halted smartly on the quay by *FA*.

"A little trouble, eh?"

"Oh, no," I said deprecatingly, "not really."

"Most irregular," he said severely. "All yachts are required to anchor *outside* the harbor and request entry if they wish to come in."

Oh-oh, wrong tactics. "Actually," I said, "the clutch won't engage at all. She can't move under her own power, but," hesitantly, "I daresay the police boat could tow us out again."

"Most irregular," he repeated, frowning. "Well, since you're here, suppose you had better stay till you get your engine fixed."

He gave me a look that made it quite clear that if I had any notions of taking the Rock single-handed I could shelve them once and for all. Then he looked over *FA* searchingly, taking in the detail from stem to stem and keel to truck.

"From England?"

"Yes," I said.

"Alone?"

"Yes, "I said.

"Good trip?"

"Yes," I said. I very nearly said "*Rather.*"

"Good show, "he said and briskly walked away.

from the big sea

LANGSTON HUGHES

THE BIG SEA: *An Autobiography* (1940) tells of a young man's

impatience with book learning, the doctrine of Manifest Destiny, and

the racial claustrophobia of America in the 1920s. Hughes' journey of

self-discovery is full of high spirits, an urgent physicality, and a driving

lust for stories and words. Touching lightly on the deeper agenda of his

odyssey—the return to Africa of the once native son—Hughes begins

his autobiography not with his physical birth, but with the rupture and

emancipation marked by his first sea voyage.

melodramatic maybe, it seems to me now. But then it was like throwing a million bricks out of my heart when I threw the books into the water. I leaned over the rail of the S.S. *Malone* and threw the books as far as I could out into the sea—all the books I had had at Columbia, and all the books I had lately bought to read.

The books went down into the moving water in the dark off Sandy Hook. Then I straightened up, turned my face to the wind, and took a deep breath. I was a seaman going to sea for the first time—a seaman on a big merchant ship. And I felt that nothing would ever happen to me again that I didn't want to happen. I felt grown, a man, inside and out. Twenty-one.

I was twenty-one.

Four bells sounded. As I stood there, whiffs of salt spray blew in my face. The afterdeck was deserted. The big hatches were covered with canvas. The booms were all tied up to the masts, and the winches silent. It was dark. The old freighter, smelling of crude oil and garbage, engines pounding, rolled through the pitch-black night. I looked down on deck and noticed that one of my books had fallen into the scupper. The last book. I picked it up and threw it far over the rail into the water below, that was too black to see. The wind caught the book and ruffled its pages quickly, then let it fall into the rolling darkness. I think it was a book by H. L. Mencken.

You see, books had been happening to me. Now the books were cast off back there somewhere in the churn of spray and night behind the propeller. I was glad they were gone.

I went up on the poop and looked over the railing toward New York. But New York was gone, too. There were no longer any lights to be seen. The wind smelt good. I was sleepy, so I went down a pair of narrow steps that ended just in front of our cabin—the mess boys' cabin.

Inside the hot cabin, George lay stark naked in a lower bunk, talking and laughing and gaily waving his various appendages around. Above him in the upper bunk, two chocolate-colored Puerto Rican feet stuck out from one end of a snow-white sheet, and a dark Puerto Rican head from the other. It was clear that Ramon in the upper bunk didn't understand more than every tenth word of George's Kentucky vernacular, but he kept on laughing every time George laughed—and that was often.

George was talking about women, of course. He said he didn't care if his Harlem landlady pawned all his clothes, the old witch! When he got back from Africa, he would get some more. He might even pay her the month's back rent he owed her, too. Maybe. Or else here he waved one of his appendages around—she could have what he had in his hand.

Puerto Rico, who understood all the bad words in every language, laughed loudly. We all laughed. You couldn't help it. George was so good-natured and comical you couldn't keep from laughing with him— or at him. He always made everybody laugh—even when the food ran out on the return trip and everybody was hungry and mad.

Then it was ten o'clock, on a June night, on the S.S. *Malone*, and we were going to Africa. At ten o'clock that morning I had never heard of the S.S. *Malone*, or George, or Ramon, or anybody else in its crew of forty-two men. Nor any of the six passengers. But now, here were the three of us laughing very loudly, going to Africa.

I had got my job at a New York shipping office. Ramon got his job at another shipping office. But George just simply walked on board about supper time. A Filipino pantry boy got mad and quit at the last moment. Naturally, the steward didn't want to sail short-handed. He saw George hanging around the entrance to the pier, watching the steve-dores finish loading. The Filipino steward said: "Hey, colored boy! You, there! You want a job?" And George said: "Yes," so he walked on board, with nothing but a shirt and a pair of overalls to his back, and sailed.

Now, he lay there in his bunk, laughing about his landlady. He said she intended to put him out if he didn't find a job. And now that he had found a job, he wouldn't be able to tell her for six months. He wondered if she knew Africa was six months away from Harlem.

"*Largo viaje*," said Ramon.

George commented in pig-Latin—which was the only "foreign" language he knew.

I might as well tell you now what George and Ramon were like.

Everybody knew all about George long before we reached the coast of Africa. But nobody ever knew much about Ramon.

George was from Kentucky. He had worked around race horses. And he spoke of several white gentlemen out of his past as "Colonel." We were all about the same age, George, Ramon, and I.

After Kentucky, George had worked in a scrap-iron yard in St. Louis. But he said the work wasn't good for his back, so he quit. He went and got a job in a restaurant near the station in Springfield, Illinois, washing dishes. A female impersonator came through with a show and took George with him as his valet. George said he got tired of being maid to the female impersonator, so as soon as he got a new suit of clothes, he quit in Pittsburgh. He found a good job in a bowling alley, but had a fight with a man who hit him with one of the balls because he set the pins up wrong. George claimed he won the fight. But he lit out for South Street in Philadelphia to avoid arrest. And after that, Harlem.

George had a thousand tales to tell about every town he'd ever been in. And several versions of each tale. No doubt, some of the stories were true—and some of them not true at all, but they sounded true. Sometimes George said he had relatives down South. Then, again, he said he didn't have anybody in the whole world. Both versions concerning his relatives were probably correct. If he did have relatives they didn't matter—lying there as he was now, laughing and talking in his narrow bunk on a hot night, going to Africa.

But Ramon of the upper bunk didn't talk much, in English or Spanish. He simply did his work in the morning. Then he got in bed and slept all the afternoon till time to set up the sailors' mess hall for supper. After supper, he got in bed and laughed at George until George went to sleep.

Ramon told us once that his mother was a seamstress in Ponce. Ernesto, the Puerto Rican sailor aboard, said "seamstress" was just another name for something else. Anyhow, Ramon was decent enough as a cabin mate, and practically always asleep. He didn't gamble. I saw him drunk only once. He seldom drew any money, and when he did he spent it on sweets—seldom on a woman. The only thing that came out of his mouth in six months that I remember is that he said he didn't care much for women, anyway. He preferred silk stockings—so halfway down the African coast, he bought a pair of silk stockings and slept with them under his pillow.

George, however, was always saying things the like of which you never heard before or since, making up fabulous jokes, playing pranks, and getting in on all the card games or fights aboard. George and I became pretty good pals. He could tap dance a little, shuffle a lot, and knew plenty of blues. He said he could play a guitar, but no one on the *Malone* possessed a guitar, so we never knew.

I had the petty officers' mess to take care of and their staterooms to make up. There was nothing hard about a mess boy's work. You got up at six in the morning, with the mid-Atlantic calm as a sunpool, served breakfast, made up the rooms, served luncheon, had all the afternoon off, served dinner, and that was all. The rest of the time you could lie on deck in the sun, play cards with the sailors, or sleep. When your clothes were dirty, you washed them in a bucket of soapsuds and lye. The lye made the washing easy because it took all of the dirt out quick.

When we got to Africa we took on a full African crew to supplement the regular crew who weren't supposed to be able to stand the sun. Then I had an African boy to do my washing, my cleaning, and almost all my work—as did everybody on board. The Africans stood both work and sun without difficulty, it seems.

Going over, it was a nice trip, warm, calm, the sea blue-green by day, gold-green at sunset. And at night phosphorescent stars in the water where the prow cut a rift of sparkling foam.

The S.S. *Malone* had been built during the war. It was a big, creaking, old freight boat, two or three years in the African trade now. It had cabins for a half dozen passengers. This trip the passengers were all Nordic missionaries—but one. That one was a colored tailor, a Garveyite who had long worshipped Africa from afar, and who had a theory of civilization all his own. He thought that if he could just teach the Africans to wear proper clothes, coats and pants, they would be brought forward a long way toward the standards of our world. To that end, he carried with him on his journey numberless bolts of cloth, shears, and tailoring tools, and a trunk full of smart patterns. The missionaries carried Bibles and hymnbooks. The Captain carried invoices and papers having to do with trade. We sailors carried nothing but ourselves.

At Horta, our only port of call in the Azores, we anchored at sea some distance from the rocky shore. Everybody went ashore in rowboats or motor launches. Some of the boys made straight for women, some for the wine shops. It depended on your temperament which you sought first. Nobody had much money, because the Captain didn't permit a draw. I had an American dollar, so George and I bought a big bottle of cognac, walked up a hill to the top of the town, and drank it. The sun was setting. The sea and the palm trees and the roofs of Horta were aglow. On the way down the hill in the amber dusk, George smashed the cognac bottle against the wall of a blue house and said: "I wants to holler."

"George, don't holler right here on the main street," I cautioned.

George said: "This town's too small to holler in, but I got to holler, anyhow." And he let out a tremendous "Yee-hoo-oo-o!" that sent children rushing to their mothers' arms and women scurrying into doorways. But a sleepy-looking cop, leaning against a wall with a lantern, must have been used to the ways of sailors, because he paid George no mind. In fact, he didn't even stir as we went on to the center of the village, where there were lots of people and lights.

We came across the bo'sun and some sailors in a bar, emptying their pockets, trying to get enough together to pay for a round of drinks that Slim—who didn't have a penny—had ordered for all. I had four cents to contribute. Chips had a quarter. But, all told, it didn't make enough to pay for the drinks, so the bartender said they should give him the rest when the S.S. *Malone* came back to Horta in five months. So everybody agreed they would settle then. Whereupon, the bartender set up another round of drinks for nothing.

The *Malone's* whistle began to blow. The bo'sun said: "Come on, you bloody so-and-so's, the Old Man's calling you!" We went down to the wharf. Some other boys were there. An Irish kid from Brooklyn and his cousin had two girls on their arms, and the wireless man, Sparks, was in the middle between the two girls. Sparks said they were the best two girls in town and that he always traded with them. The Irish kid said his was the best girl he ever had.

His cousin said: "Aw, nuts! You never had one before!" (The Irish kid was just out of high school and this was his first trip to sea. He looked like a choirboy, except that he couldn't sing.) We waited for the launch that we had paid to take us back. Finally it came. At seven bells we went on toward Africa, the engines chugging soft and serene.

The next day was Sunday and the missionaries wanted everybody to come to prayers in the saloon, but nobody went except the Captain and the Chief Mate. The bo'sun said he'd go if the missionaries had any communion wine, but the missionaries didn't have any, so he didn't go.

When we got to Teneriffe, in the Canary Islands, it was midafternoon and very bright. The Canaries looked like fairy islands, all sharp peaks of red rock and bright sandy beaches and little green fields dropped like patchwork between the beaches and the rocks, with the sea making a blue-white fringe around.

The Captain let us draw money—so Las Palmas seemed a gay city indeed. Ashore, three or four of us, including Ernesto and a Norwegian boy named Sven, had supper at a place with very bright lights, where they served huge platters of delicious mixed fish with big bottles of cool, white wine. Then we all went to a white villa by the sea, called *El Palacio de Amor* and stayed all night. In the morning very early, when the sun was just coming up, we drove back to the wharf in an open carriage. We kept thinking about the girls, who were Spanish, and very young and pretty. And Sven said he would like to take one of them with him.

But all those days I was waiting anxiously to see Africa. And finally, when I saw the dust-green hills in the sunlight, something took hold of me inside. My Africa, Motherland of the Negro peoples! And me a Negro! Africa! The real thing, to be touched and seen, not merely read about in a book.

That first morning when we sighted the coast, I kept leaving my work to lean over the rail and look at Africa, dim and far away, off on the horizon in a haze of light, then gradually nearer and nearer, until you could see the color of the foliage on the trees.

We put in at the port of Dakar. There were lots of Frenchmen, and tall black Senegalese soldiers in red fezes, and Mohammedans in robes, so that at first you couldn't tell if the Mohammedans were men or women.

The next day we moved on. And farther down the coast it was more like the Africa I had dreamed about—wild and lovely, the people dark and beautiful, the palm trees tall, the sun bright, and the rivers deep. The great Africa of my dreams!

But there was one thing that hurt me a lot when I talked with the people. The Africans looked at me and would not believe I was a Negro.

from to the lighthouse

VIRGINIA WOOLF

TO THE LIGHTHOUSE (1927), Virginia Woolf's fifth novel, tells

the story of the Ramsays, a family who summer with friends on the

Scottish coast immediately before and after the Great War. This selec-

tion is taken from the last part of the book, where Mr. Ramsay, a 71-

year-old widowed philosopher, sets off with his two surviving children

on an excursion which Mrs. Ramsay had planned a decade earlier, but

which bad weather, the outbreak of World War I, her death, and the

death of two of their four children, had deferred. The original is told

through the alternating perspectives of the Ramsays and Miss Lily

Briscoe, a family friend, who watches them from land. We have

retained only the Ramsay plot line, which explores, in Woolf's sublime

stream of consciousness technique, the inextricable tangle of emo-

tions that bind children to parents.

the sails flapped over their heads. The water chuckled and slapped the sides of the boat, which drowsed motionless in the sun. Now and then the sails rippled with a little breeze in them, but the ripple ran over them and ceased. The boat made no motion at all. Mr. Ramsay sat in the middle of the boat. He would be impatient in a moment, James thought, and Cam thought, looking at her father, who sat in the middle of the boat between them (James steered, Cam sat alone in the bow) with his legs tightly curled. He hated hanging about. Sure enough, after fidgeting a second or two, he said something sharp to Macalister's boy, who got out his oars and began to row. But their father, they knew, would never be content until they were flying along. He would keep looking for a breeze, fidgeting, saying things under his breath, which Macalister and Macalister's boy would overhear, and they would both be made horribly uncomfortable. He had made them come. He had forced them to come. In their anger they hoped that the breeze would never rise, that he might be thwarted in every possible way, since he had forced them to come against their wills.

All the way down to the beach they had lagged behind together, though he bade them "Walk up, walk up," without speaking. Their heads were bent down, their heads were pressed down by some remorseless gale. Speak to him they could not. They must come; they must follow. They must walk behind him carrying brown paper parcels. But they vowed, in silence, as they walked, to stand by each other and carry out the great compact—to resist tyranny to the death. So there they would sit, one at one end of the boat, one at the other, in silence. They would say nothing, only look at him now and then where he sat with his legs twisted, frowning and fidgeting, and pishing and pshawing and muttering things to himself, and waiting impatiently for a breeze. And they hoped it would be calm. They hoped he would be thwarted. They hoped the whole expedition would fail, and they would have to put back, with their parcels, to the beach.

But now, when Macalister's boy had rowed a little way out, the sails slowly swung round, the boat quickened itself, flattened itself, and shot off. Instantly, as if some great strain had been relieved, Mr. Ramsay uncurled his legs, took out his tobacco pouch, handed it with a little grunt to Macalister, and felt, they knew for all they suffered, perfectly content. Now they would sail on for hours like this, and Mr. Ramsay would ask old Macalister a question—about the great storm last winter probably—and old Macalister would answer it, and they would puff their pipes together, and Macalister would take a tarry rope in his fingers, tying or untying some knot, and the boy would fish, and never say a word to any one. James would be forced to keep his eye all the time on the sail. For if he forgot, then the sail puckered and shivered, and the boat slackened, and Mr. Ramsay would say sharply, "Look out! Look out!" and old Macalister would turn slowly on his seat. So they heard Mr. Ramsay asking some question about the great storm at Christmas. "She comes driving round the point," old Macalister said, describing the great storm last Christmas, when ten ships had been driven into the bay for shelter, and he had seen "one there, one there, one there" (he pointed slowly round the bay. Mr. Ramsay followed him, turning his head). He had seen four men clinging to the mast. Then she was gone. "And at last we shoved her off," he went on (but in their anger and their silence they only caught a word here and there, sitting at opposite ends of the boat, united by their compact to fight tyranny to the death). At last they had shoved her off, they had launched the lifeboat, and they had got her out past the point—Macalister told the story; and though they only caught a word here and there, they were conscious all the time of their father— how he leant forward, how he brought his voice into tune with Macalister's voice; how, puffing at his pipe, and looking there and there where Macalister pointed, he relished the thought of the storm and the dark night and the fishermen striving there. He liked that men should labour and sweat on the windy beach at night; pitting muscle and brain against the waves and the wind; he liked men to work like that, and women to keep house, and sit beside sleeping children indoors, while men were drowned, out there in a storm. So James could tell, so Cam could tell (they looked at him, they looked at each other), from his toss and his vigilance and the ring in his voice, and the little tinge of Scottish accent which came into his voice, making him seem like a peasant him- self, as he questioned Macalister about the eleven ships that had been driven into the bay in a storm. Three had sunk.

He looked proudly where Macalister pointed; and Cam thought, feel- ing proud of him without knowing quite why, had he been there he would have launched the lifeboat, he would have reached the wreck, Cam thought. He was so brave, he was so adventurous, Cam thought.

But she remembered. There was the compact; to resist tyranny to the death. Their grievance weighed them down. They had been forced; they had been bidden. He had borne them down once more with his gloom and his authority, making them do his bidding, on this fine morning, come, because he wished it, carrying these parcels, to the Lighthouse; take part in these rites he went through for his own pleasure in memory of dead people, which they hated, so that they lagged after him, and all the pleasure of the day was spoilt.

Yes, the breeze was freshening. The boat was leaning, the water was sliced sharply and fell away in green cascades, in bubbles, in cataracts. Cam looked down into the foam, into the sea with all its treasure in it, and its speed hypnotised her, and the tie between her and James sagged a little. It slackened a little. She began to think, How fast it goes. Where are we going? and the movement hypnotised her, while James, with his eye fixed on the sail and on the horizon, steered grimly. But he began to think as he steered that he might escape; he might be quit of it all. They might land somewhere; and be free then. Both of them, looking at each other for a moment, had a sense of escape and exaltation, what with the speed and the change. But the breeze bred in Mr. Ramsay too the same excitement, and, as old Macalister turned to fling his line overboard, he cried aloud.

"We perished," and then again, "each alone." And then with his usual spasm of repentance or shyness, pulled himself up, and waved his hand toward the shore.

"See the little house," he said pointing, wishing Cam to look. She raised herself reluctantly and looked. But which was it? She could no longer make out, there on the hillside, which was their house. All looked distant and peaceful and strange. The shore seemed refined, far-away, unreal. Already the little distance they had sailed had put them far from it and given it the changed look, the composed look, of something receding in which one has no longer any part. Which was their house? She could not see it.

"But I beneath a rougher sea," Mr. Ramsay murmured. He had found the house and so seeing it, he had also seen himself there; he had seen himself walking on the terrace, alone. He was walking up and down between the urns; and he seemed to himself very old and bowed. Sitting in the boat, he bowed, he crouched himself, acting instantly his part— the part of a desolate man, widowed, bereft; and so called up before him in hosts people sympathising with him; staged for himself as he sat in the boat, a little drama; which required of him decrepitude and exhaustion and sorrow (he raised his hands and looked at the thinness of them, to confirm his dream) and then there was given him in abundance women's sympathy, and he imagined how they would soothe him and sympathise with him, and so getting in his dream some reflection of the exquisite pleasure women's sympathy was to him, he sighed and said gently and mournfully,

> But I beneath a rougher sea
> Was whelmed in deeper gulfs than he,

so that the mournful words were heard quite clearly by them all. Cam half started on her seat. It shocked her—it outraged her. The movement roused her father; and he shuddered, and broke off, exclaiming: "Look! Look!" so urgently that James also turned his head to look over his shoulder at the island. They all looked. They looked at the island.

But Cam could see nothing. She was thinking how all those paths and the lawn, thick and knotted with the lives they had lived there, were gone: were rubbed out; were past; were unreal, and now this was real; the boat and the sail with its patch; Macalister with his earrings; the noise of the waves—all this was real. Thinking this, she was murmuring to herself, "We perished, each alone," for her father's words broke and broke again in her mind, when her father, seeing her gazing so vaguely, began to tease her. Didn't she know the points of the compass? he asked. Didn't she know the North from the South? Did she really think they lived right out there? And he pointed again, and showed her where their house was, there, by those trees. He wished she would try to be more accurate, he said: "Tell me—which is East, which is West?" he said, half laughing at her, half scolding her, for he could not understand the state of mind of any one, not absolutely imbecile, who did not know the points of the compass. Yet she did not know. And seeing her gazing, with her vague, now rather frightened, eyes fixed where no house was Mr. Ramsay forgot his dream; how he walked up and down between the urns on the terrace; how the arms were stretched out to him. He thought, women are always like that; the vagueness of their minds is hopeless; it was a thing he had never been able to understand; but so it was. It had been so with her—his wife. They could not keep anything clearly fixed in their minds. But he had been wrong to be angry with her; moreover, did he not rather like this vagueness in women? It was part of their extraordinary charm. I will make her smile at me, he thought. She looks frightened. She was so silent. He clutched his fingers, and determined that his voice and his face and all the quick expressive gestures which had been at his command making people pity him and praise him all these years should subdue themselves. He would make her smile at him. He would find some simple easy thing to say to her. But what? For, wrapped up in his work as he was, he forgot the sort of thing one said. There was a puppy. They had a puppy. Who was looking after the puppy today? he asked. Yes, thought James pitilessly, seeing his sister's head against the sail, now she will give way. I shall be left to fight the tyrant alone. The compact would be left to him to carry out. Cam would never resist tyranny to the death, he thought grimly, watching her face, sad, sulky, yielding. And as sometimes happens when a cloud falls on a green hillside and gravity descends and there among all the surrounding hills is gloom and sorrow, and it seems as if the hills themselves must ponder the fate of the clouded, the darkened, either in pity, or maliciously rejoicing in her dismay: so Cam now felt herself overcast, as she sat there among calm, resolute people and wondered how to answer her father about the puppy; how to resist his entreaty—forgive me, care for me; while James the lawgiver, with the tablets of eternal wisdom laid open on his knee (his hand on the tiller had become symbolical to her), said, Resist him. Fight him. He said so rightly; justly. For they must fight tyranny to the death, she thought. Of all human qualities she reverenced justice most. Her brother was most god-like, her father most suppliant. And to which did she yield, she thought, sitting between them, gazing at the shore whose points were all unknown to her, and thinking how the lawn and the terrace and the house were smoothed away now and peace dwelt there.

"Jasper," she said sullenly. He'd look after the puppy.

And what was she going to call him? her father persisted. He had had a dog when he was a little boy, called Frisk. She'll give way, James thought, as he watched a look come upon her face, a look he remembered. They look down, he thought, at their knitting or something. Then suddenly they look up. There was a flash of blue, he remembered, and then somebody sitting with him laughed, surrendered, and he was very angry. It must have been his mother, he thought, sitting on a low chair, with his father standing over her. He began to search among the infinite series of impressions which time had laid down, leaf upon leaf, fold upon fold softly, incessantly upon his brain; among scents, sounds; voices, harsh, hollow, sweet; and lights passing, and brooms tapping, and the wash and hush of the sea, how a man had marched up and down and stopped dead, upright, over them. Meanwhile, he noticed, Cam dabbled her fingers in the water, and stared at the shore and said nothing. No, she won't give way, he thought; she's different, he thought. Well, if Cam would not answer him, he would not bother her, Mr. Ramsay decided, feeling in his pocket for a book. But she would answer him; she wished, passionately, to move some obstacle that lay upon her tongue and to say, Oh, yes, Frisk. She wanted even to say, Was that the dog that found its way over the moor alone? But try as she might, she could think of nothing to say like that, fierce and loyal to the compact, yet passing on to her father, unsuspected by James, a private token of the love she felt for him. For she thought, dabbling her hand (and now Macalister's boy had caught a mackerel, and it lay kicking on the floor, with blood on its gills) for she thought, looking at James who kept his eyes dispassionately on the sail, or glanced now and then for a second at the horizon, you're not exposed to it, to this pressure and division of feeling, this extraordinary temptation. Her father was feeling in his pockets; in another second, he would have found his book. For no one attracted her more; his hands were beautiful, and his feet, and his voice, and his words, and his haste, and his temper, and his oddity, and his passion, and his saying, straight out before every one, we perish, each alone, and his remoteness. (He had opened his book.) But what remained intolerable, she thought, sitting upright, and watching Macalister's boy tug the hook out of the gills of another fish, was that crass blindness and tyranny of his which had poisoned her childhood and raised bitter storms, so that even now she woke in the night trembling with rage and remembered some command of his; some insolence: "Do this," "Do that," his dominance: his "Submit to me."

So she said nothing, but looked doggedly and sadly at the shore, wrapped in its mantle of peace; as if the people there had fallen asleep, she thought; were free like smoke, were free to come and go like ghosts. They have no suffering there, she thought.

YES, THAT IS their boat, Lily Briscoe decided, standing on the edge of the lawn. It was the boat with grayish-brown sails, which she saw now flatten itself upon the water and shoot off across the bay. There he sits, she thought, and the children are quite silent still. And she could not reach him either. The sympathy she had not given him weighed her down. It made it difficult for her to paint.

She had always found him difficult. She never had been able to praise him to his face, she remembered. And that reduced their relationship to something neutral, without that element of sex in it which made his manner to Minta so gallant, almost gay. He would pick a flower for her, lend her his books. But could he believe that Minta read them? She dragged them about the garden, sticking in leaves to mark the place.

"D'you remember, Mr. Carmichael?" she was inclined to ask, looking at the old man. But he had pulled his hat half over his forehead; he was asleep, or he was dreaming, or he was lying there catching words, she supposed.

"D'you remember?" she felt inclined to ask him as she passed him, thinking again of Mrs. Ramsay on the beach; the cask bobbing up and down; and the pages flying. Why, after all these years had that survived, ringed round, lit up, visible to the last detail, with all before it blank and all after it blank, for miles and miles?

"Is it a boat? Is it a cork?" she would say, Lily repeated, turning back, reluctantly again, to her canvas. Heaven be praised for it, the problem of space remained she thought, taking up her brush again. It glared at her. The whole mass of the picture was poised upon that weight. Beautiful and bright it should be on the surface, feathery and evanescent, one colour melting into another like the colours on a butterfly's wing; but beneath the fabric must be clamped together with bolts of iron. It was to be a thing you could ruffle with your breath; and a thing you could not dislodge with a team of horses. And she began to lay on a red, a grey, and she began to model her way into the hollow there. At the same time, she seemed to be sitting beside Mrs. Ramsay on the beach.

"Is it a boat? Is it a cask?" Mrs. Ramsay said. And she began hunting round for her spectacles. And she sat, having found them, silent, looking out to sea. And Lily, painting steadily, felt as if a door had opened, and one went in and stood gazing silently about in a high cathedral-like place, very dark, very solemn. Shouts came from a world far away. Steamers vanished in stalks of smoke on the horizon. Charles threw stones and sent them skipping.

Mrs. Ramsay sat silent. She was glad, Lily thought, to rest in silence, uncommunicative; to rest in the extreme obscurity of human relationships. Who knows what we are, what we feel? Who knows even at the moment of intimacy, This is knowledge? Aren't things spoilt then, Mrs. Ramsay may have asked (it seemed to have happened so often, this silence by her side of tears at first) which, without disturbing the firmness of her lips, made the air thick, rolled down her cheeks. She had perfect control, of herself—Oh, yes!—in every other way. Was she crying then for Mrs. Ramsay, without being aware of any unhappiness? She addressed old Mr. Carmichael again. What was it then? What did it mean? Could things thrust their hands up and grip one; could the blade cut; the fist grasp? Was there no safety? No learning by heart of the ways of the world? No guide, no shelter, but all was miracle, and leaping from the pinnacle of a tower into the air? Could it be, even for elderly people, that this was life?—startling, unexpected, unknown? For one moment she felt that if they both got up, here, now on the lawn, and demanded an explanation, why was it so short, why was it so inexplicable, said it with violence, as two fully equipped human beings from whom nothing should be hid might speak, then, beauty would roll itself up; the space would fill; those empty flourishes would form into shape; if they shouted loud enough Mrs. Ramsay would return. "Mrs. Ramsay!" she said aloud, "Mrs. Ramsay!" The tears ran down her face.

[Macalister's boy took one of the fish and cut a square out of its side to bait his hook with. The mutilated body (it was alive still) was thrown back into the sea.]

"MRS. RAMSAY!" LILY cried, "Mrs. Ramsay!" But nothing happened. The pain increased. That anguish could reduce one to such a pitch of imbecility, she thought! Anyhow the old man had not heard her. He remained benignant, calm—if one chose to think it, sublime. Heaven be praised, no one had heard her cry that ignominious cry, stop pain, stop! She had not obviously taken leave of her senses. No one had seen her step off her strip of board into the waters of annihilation. She remained a skimpy old maid, holding a paint-brush.

And now slowly the pain of the want, and the bitter anger (to be called back, just as she thought she would never feel sorrow for Mrs. Ramsay again. Had she missed her among the coffee cups at breakfast? not in the least) lessened; and of their anguish left, as antidote, a relief that was balm in itself, and also, but more mysteriously, a sense of some one there, of Mrs. Ramsay, relieved for a moment of the weight that the world had put on her, staying lightly by her side and then (for this was Mrs. Ramsay in all her beauty) raising to her forehead a wreath of white flowers with which she went. Lily squeezed her tubes again. She attacked that problem of the hedge. It was strange how clearly she saw her, stepping with her usual quickness across fields among whose folds, purplish and soft, among whose flowers, hyacinths or lilies, she vanished. It was some trick of the painter's eye. For days after she had heard of her death she had seen her thus, putting her wreath to her forehead and going unquestioningly with her companion, a shade across the fields. The sight, the phrase, had its power to console. Wherever she happened to be, painting, here, in the country or in London, the vision would come to her, and her eyes, half closing, sought something to base her vision on. She looked down the railway carriage, the omnibus; took a line from shoulder or cheek; looked at the windows opposite; at Piccadilly, lamp-strung in the evening. All had been part of the fields of death. But always something—it might be a face, a voice, a paper boy crying *Standard, News*—thrust through, snubbed her, waked her, required and got in the end an effort of attention, so that the vision must be perpetually remade. Now again, moved as she was by some instinctive need of distance and blue, she looked at the bay beneath her, making hillocks of the blue bars of the waves, and stony fields of the purpler spaces, again she was roused as usual by something incongruous. There was a brown spot in the middle of the bay. It was a boat. Yes, she realised that after a second. But whose boat? Mr. Ramsay's boat, she replied. Mr. Ramsay; the man who had marched past her, with his hand raised, aloof, at the head of a procession, in his beautiful boots, asking her for sympathy, which she had refused. The boat was now half-way across the bay.

So fine was the morning except for a streak of wind here and there that the sea and sky looked all one fabric, as if sails were stuck high up in the sky, or the clouds had dropped down into the sea. A steamer far out at sea had drawn in the air a great scroll of smoke which stayed there curving and circling decoratively, as if the air were a fine gauze which held things and kept them softly in its mesh, only gently swaying them this way and that. And as happens sometimes when the weather is very fine, the cliffs looked as if they were conscious of the ships, and the ships looked as if they were conscious of the cliffs, as if they signalled to each other some message of their own. For sometimes quite close to the shore, the Lighthouse looked this morning in the haze an enormous distance away.

"Where are they now?" Lily thought, looking out to sea. Where was he, that very old man who had gone past her silently, holding a brown paper parcel under his arm? The boat was in the middle of the bay.

THEY DON'T FEEL a thing there, Cam thought, looking at the shore, which, rising and falling, became steadily more distant and more peaceful. Her hand cut a trail in the sea, as her mind made the green swirls and streaks into patterns and, numbed and shrouded, wandered in imagination in that underworld of waters where the pearls stuck in clusters to white sprays, where in the green light a change came over one's entire mind and one's body shone half transparent enveloped in a green cloak.

Then the eddy slackened round her hand. The rush of the water ceased; the world became full of little creaking and squeaking sounds. One heard the waves breaking and flapping against the side of the boat as if they were anchored in harbour. Everything became very close to one. For the sail, upon which James had his eyes fixed until it had become to him like a person whom he knew, sagged entirely; there they came to a stop, flapping about waiting for a breeze, in the hot sun, miles from shore, miles from the Lighthouse. Everything in the whole world seemed to stand still. The Lighthouse became immovable, and the line of the distant shore became fixed. The sun grew hotter and everybody seemed to come very close together and to feel each other's presence, which they had almost forgotten. Macalister's fishing line went plumb down into the sea. But Mr. Ramsay went on reading with his legs curled under him.

He was reading a little shiny book with covers mottled like a plover's egg. Now and again, as they hung about in that horrid calm, he turned a page. And James felt that each page was turned with a peculiar gesture aimed at him: now assertively, now commandingly; now with the intention of making people pity him; and all the time, as his father read and turned one after another of those little pages, James kept dreading the moment when he would look up and speak sharply to him about something or other. Why were they lagging about here? he would demand, or something quite unreasonable like that. And if he does, James thought, then I shall take a knife and strike him to the heart.

He had always kept this old symbol of taking a knife and striking his father to the heart. Only now, as he grew older, and sat staring at his father in an impotent rage, it was not him, that old man reading, whom he wanted to kill, but it was the thing that descended on him—without his knowing it perhaps: that fierce sudden black-winged harpy, with its talons and its beak all cold and hard, that struck and struck at you (he could feel the beak on his bare legs, where it had struck when he was a child) and then made off, and there he was again, an old man, very sad, reading his book. That he would kill, that he would strike to the heart. Whatever he did—(and he might do anything, he felt, looking at the Lighthouse and the distant shore) whether he was in a business, in a bank, a barrister, a man at the head of some enterprise, that he would fight, that he would track down and stamp out—tyranny, despotism, he called it—making people do what they did not want to do, cutting off their right to speak. How could any of them say, But I won't, when he said, Come to the Lighthouse. Do this. Fetch me that. The black wings spread, and the hard beak tore. And then next moment, there he sat reading his book; and he might look up—one never knew—quite reasonably. He might talk to the Macalisters. He might be pressing a sovereign into some frozen old woman's hand in the street, James thought, and he might be shouting out at some fisherman's sports; he might be waving his arms in the air with excitement. Or he might sit at the head of the table dead silent from one end of dinner to the other. Yes, thought James, while the boat slapped and dawdled there in the hot sun; there was a waste of snow and rock very lonely and austere; and there he had come to feel, quite often lately, when his father said something or did something which surprised the others, there were two pairs of footprints only; his own and his father's. They alone knew each other. What then was this terror, this hatred? Turning back among the many leaves which the past had folded in him, peering into the heart of that forest where light and shade so chequer each other that all shape is distorted, and one blunders, now with the sun in one's eyes, now with a dark shadow, he sought an image to cool and detach and round off his feeling in a concrete shape. Suppose then that as a child sitting helpless in a perambulator, or on some one's knee, he had seen a waggon crush ignorantly and innocently, some one's foot? Suppose he had seen the foot first, in the grass, smooth, and whole; then the wheel; and the same foot, purple, crushed. But the wheel was innocent. So now, when his father came striding down the passage knocking them up early in the morning to go to the Lighthouse down it came over his foot, over Cam's foot, over anybody's foot. One sat and watched it.

But whose foot was he thinking of, and in what garden did all this happen? For one had settings for these scenes; trees that grew there; flowers; a certain light; a few figures. Everything tended to set itself in a garden where there was none of this gloom. None of this throwing of hands about; people spoke in an ordinary tone of voice. They went in and out all day long. There was an old woman gossiping in the kitchen; and the blinds were sucked in and out by the breeze; all was blowing, all was growing; and over all those plates and bowls and tall brandishing red and yellow flowers a very thin yellow veil would be drawn, like a vine leaf, at night. Things became stiller and darker at night. But the leaf-like veil was so fine, that lights lifted it, voices crinkled it; he could see through it a figure stooping, hear, coming close, going away, some dress rustling, some chain tinkling.

It was in this world that the wheel went over the person's foot.

Something, he remembered, stayed and darkened over him; would not move; something flourished up in the air, something arid and sharp descended even there, like a blade, a scimitar, smiting through the leaves and flowers even of that happy world and making it shrivel and fall.

"It will rain," he remembered his father saying. "You won't be able to go to the Lighthouse."

The Lighthouse was then a silvery, misty-looking tower with a yellow eye, that opened suddenly, and softly in the evening. Now—

James looked at the Lighthouse. He could see the white-washed rocks; the tower, stark and straight; he could see that it was barred with black and white; he could see windows in it; he could even see washing spread on the rocks to dry. So that was the Lighthouse, was it?

No, the other was also the Lighthouse. For nothing was simply one thing. The other Lighthouse was true too. It was sometimes hardly to be seen across the bay. In the evening one looked up and saw the eye opening and shutting and the light seemed to reach them in that airy sunny garden where they sat.

But he pulled himself up. Whenever he said "they" or "a person," and then began hearing the rustle of some one coming, the tinkle of some one going, he became extremely sensitive to the presence of whoever might be in the room. It was his father now. The strain was acute. For in one moment if there was no breeze, his father would slap the covers of his book together, and say: "What's happening now? What are we dawdling about here for, eh?" as, once before he had brought his blade down among them on the terrace and she had gone stiff all over, and if there had been an axe handy, a knife, or anything with a sharp point he would have seized it and struck his father through the heart. She had gone stiff all over, and then, her arm slackening, so that he felt she listened to him no longer, she had risen somehow and gone away and left him there, impotent, ridiculous, sitting on the floor grasping a pair of scissors.

Not a breath of wind blew. The water chuckled and gurgled in the bottom of the boat where three or four mackerel beat their tails up and down in a pool of water not deep enough to cover them. At any moment Mr. Ramsay (he scarcely dared look at him) might rouse himself, shut his book, and say something sharp; but for the moment he was reading, so that James stealthily, as if he were stealing downstairs on bare feet, afraid of waking a watchdog by a creaking board, went on thinking what was she like, where did she go that day? He began following her from room to room and at last they came to a room where in a blue light, as if the reflection came from many china dishes, she talked to somebody; he listened to her talking. She talked to a servant, saying simply whatever came into her head. She alone spoke the truth; to her alone could he speak it. That was the source of her everlasting attraction for him, perhaps; she was a person to whom one could say what came into one's head. But all the time he thought of her, he was conscious of his father following his thought, surveying it, making it shiver and falter. At last he ceased to think.

There he sat with his hand on the tiller in the sun, staring at the Lighthouse, powerless to move, powerless to flick off these grains of misery which settled on his mind one after another. A rope seemed to bind him there, and his father had knotted it and he could only escape by taking a knife and plunging it. . . . But at that moment the sail swung slowly round, filled slowly out, the boat seemed to shake herself, and then to move off half conscious in her sleep, and then she woke and shot through the waves. The relief was extraordinary. They all seemed to fall away from each other again and to be at their ease and the fishing-lines slanted taut across the side of the boat. But his father did not rouse himself. He only raised his right hand mysteriously high in the air, and let it fall upon his knee again as if he were conducting some secret symphony.

(The sea without a stain on it, thought Lily Briscoe, still standing and looking out over the bay. The sea stretched like silk across the bay. Distance had an extraordinary power; they had been swallowed up in it, she felt, they were gone for ever, they had become part of the nature of things. It was so calm; it was so quiet. The steamer itself had vanished, but the great scroll of smoke still hung in the air and drooped like a flag mournfully in valediction.)

IT WAS LIKE that then, the island, thought Cam, once more drawing her fingers through the waves. She had never seen it from out at sea before. It lay like that on the sea, did it, with a dent in the middle and two sharp crags, and the sea swept in there, and spread away for miles and miles on either side of the island. It was very small; shaped something like a leaf stood on end. So we took a little boat, she thought, beginning to tell herself a story of adventure about escaping from a sinking ship. But with the sea streaming through her fingers, a spray of seaweed vanishing behind them, she did not want to tell herself seriously a story; it was the sense of adventure and escape that she wanted, for she was thinking, as the boat sailed on, how her father's anger about the points of the compass, James's obstinacy about the compact, and her own anguish, all had slipped, all had passed, all had streamed away. What then came next? Where were they going? From her hand, ice cold, held deep in the sea, there spurted up a fountain of joy at the change, at the escape, at the adventure (that she should be alive, that she should be there). And the drops falling from this sudden and unthinking fountain of joy fell here and there on the dark, the slumbrous shapes in her mind; shapes of a world not realised but turning in their darkness, catching here and there, a spark of light; Greece, Rome, Constantinople. Small as it was, and shaped something like a leaf stood on its end with the gold-sprinkled waters flowing in and about it, it had, she supposed, a place in the universe—even that little island? The old gentlemen in the study she thought could have told her. Sometimes she strayed in from the garden purposely to catch them at it. There they were (it might be Mr. Carmichael or Mr. Bankes who was sitting with her father) sitting opposite each other in their low arm-chairs. They were crackling in front of them the pages of *The Times*, when she came in from the garden, all in a muddle, about something some one had said about Christ, or hearing that a mammoth had been dug up in a London street, or wondering what Napoleon was like. Then they took all this with their clean hands (they wore grey-coloured clothes; they smelt of heather) and they brushed the scraps together, turning the paper, crossing their knees, and said something now and then very brief. Just to please herself she would take a book from the shelf and stand there, watching her father write, so equally, so neatly from one side of the page to another, with a little cough now and then, or something said briefly to the other old gentleman opposite. And she thought, standing there with her book open, one could let whatever one thought expand here like a leaf in water; and if it did well here, among the old gentlemen smoking and *The Times* crackling then it was right. And watching her father as he wrote in his study, she thought (now sitting in the boat) he was not vain, nor a tyrant and did not wish to make you pity him. Indeed, if he saw she was there, reading a book, he would ask her, as gently as any one could, Was there nothing he could give her?

   Lest this should be wrong, she looked at him reading the little book with the shiny cover mottled like a plover's egg. No; it was right. Look at him now, she wanted to say aloud to James. (But James had his eye on the sail.) He is a sarcastic brute, James would say. He brings the talk

round to himself and his books, James would say. He is intolerably ego-
tistical. Worst of all, he is a tyrant. But look! she said, looking at him.
Look at him now. She looked at him reading the little book with his
legs curled; the little book whose yellowish pages she knew, without
knowing what was written on them. It was small; it was closely printed; on the fly-leaf, she knew, he had written that he had spent fifteen
francs on dinner; the wine had been so much; he had given so much to
the waiter; all was added up neatly at the bottom of the page. But what
might be written in the book which had rounded its edges off in his
pocket, she did not know. What he thought they none of them knew.
But he was absorbed in it, so that when he looked up, as he did now
for an instant, it was not to see anything; it was to pin down some
thought more exactly. That done, his mind flew back again and he
plunged into his reading. He read, she thought, as if he were guiding
something, or wheedling a large flock of sheep, or pushing his way up
and up a single narrow path; and sometimes he went fast and straight,
and broke his way through the bramble, and sometimes it seemed a
branch struck at him, a bramble blinded him, but he was not going to
let himself be beaten by that; on he went, tossing over page after page.
And she went on telling herself a story about escaping from a sinking
ship, for she was safe, while he sat there; safe, as she felt herself when she
crept in from the garden, and took a book down, and the old gentleman, lowering the paper suddenly, said something very brief over the
top of it about the character of Napoleon.

She gazed back over the sea, at the island. But the leaf was losing its
sharpness. It was very small; it was very distant. The sea was more important now than the shore. Waves were all round them, tossing and sinking, with a log wallowing down one wave; a gull riding on another.
About here, she thought, dabbling her fingers in the water, a ship had
sunk, and she murmured, dreamily half asleep, how we perished, each
alone.

MR. RAMSAY HAD almost done reading. One hand hovered over the
page as if to be in readiness to turn it the very instant he had finished it.
He sat there bareheaded with the wind blowing his hair about, extraor-
dinarily exposed to everything. He looked very old. He looked, James
thought, getting his head now against the Lighthouse, now against the
waste of waters running away into the open, like some old stone lying
on the sand; he looked as if he had become physically what was always

at the back of both of their minds—that loneliness which was for both of them the truth about things.

He was reading very quickly, as if he were eager to get to the end. Indeed they were very close to the Lighthouse now. There it loomed up, stark and straight, glaring white and black, and one could see the waves breaking in white splinters like smashed glass upon the rocks. One could see lines and creases in the rocks. One could see the windows clearly; a dab of white on one of them, and a little tuft of green on the rock. A man had come out and looked at them through a glass and gone in again. So it was like that, James thought, the Lighthouse one had seen across the bay all these years; it was a stark tower on a bare rock. It satisfied him. It confirmed some obscure feeling of his about his own character. The old ladies, he thought, thinking of the garden at home, went dragging their chairs about on the lawn. Old Mrs. Beckwith, for example, was always saying how nice it was and how sweet it was and how they ought to be so proud and they ought to be so happy, but as a matter of fact, James thought, looking at the Lighthouse stood there on its rock, it's like that. He looked at his father reading fiercely with his legs curled tight. They shared that knowledge. "We are driving before a gale—we must sink," he began saying to himself, half aloud, exactly as his father said it.

Nobody seemed to have spoken for an age. Cam was tired of looking at the sea. Little bits of black cork had floated past; the fish were dead in the bottom of the boat. Still her father read, and James looked at him and she looked at him, and they vowed that they would fight tyranny to the death, and he went on reading quite unconscious of what they thought. It was thus that he escaped, she thought. Yes, with his great forehead and his great nose, holding his little mottled book firmly in front of him, he escaped. You might try to lay hands on him, but then like a bird, he spread his wings, he floated off to settle out of your reach somewhere far away on some desolate stump. She gazed at the immense expanse of the sea. The island had grown so small that it scarcely looked like a leaf any longer. It looked like the top of a rock which some wave bigger than the rest would cover. Yet in its frailty were all those paths, those terraces, those bedrooms—all those innumerable things. But as, just before sleep, things simplify themselves so that only one of all the myriad details has power to assert itself, so, she felt, looking drowsily at the island, all those paths and terraces and bedrooms were fading and disappearing, and nothing was left but a pale blue censer swinging rhythmically this way and that across her mind. It was a hanging garden; it was a valley, full of birds, and flowers, and antelopes. . . . She was falling asleep.

"Come now," said Mr. Ramsay, suddenly shutting his book.

Come where? To what extraordinary adventure? She woke with a start. To land somewhere, to climb somewhere? Where was he leading them? For after his immense silence the words startled them. But it was absurd. He was hungry, he said. It was time for lunch. Besides, look, he said, "There's the Lighthouse. We're almost there."

"He's doing very well," said Macalister, praising James. "He's keeping her very steady."

But his father never praised him, James thought grimly.

Mr. Ramsay opened the parcel and shared out the sandwiches among them. Now he was happy, eating bread and cheese with these fishermen. He would have liked to live in a cottage and lounge about in the harbour spitting with the other old men, James thought, watching him slice his cheese into thin yellow sheets with his penknife.

This is right, this is it, Cam kept feeling, as she peeled her hard-boiled egg. Now she felt as she did in the study when the old men were reading *The Times*. Now I can go on thinking whatever I like, and I shan't fall over a precipice or be drowned, for there he is, keeping his eye on me, she thought.

At the same time they were sailing so fast along by the rocks that it was very exciting—it seemed as if they were doing two things at once; they were eating their lunch here in the sun and they were also making for safety in a great storm after a shipwreck. Would the water last? Would the provisions last? she asked herself, telling herself a story but knowing at the same time what was the truth.

They would soon be out of it, Mr. Ramsay was saying to old Macalister; but their children would see some strange things. Macalister said he was seventy-five last March; Mr. Ramsay was seventy-one. Macalister said he had never seen a doctor; he had never lost a tooth. And that's the way I'd like my children to live—Cam was sure that her father was thinking that, for he stopped her throwing a sandwich into the sea and told her, as if he were thinking of the fishermen and how they lived, that if she did not want it she should put it back in the parcel. She should not waste it. He said it so wisely, as if he knew so well all the things that happened in the world that she put it back at once, and then he gave her, from his own parcel, a gingerbread nut, as if he were a great Spanish gentleman, she thought, handing a flower to a lady at a window (so courteous his manner was). He was shabby, and simple, eating bread and cheese;

and yet he was leading them on a great expedition where, for all she knew, they would be drowned.

"That was where she sunk," said Macalister's boy suddenly.

THREE MEN WERE drowned where we are now, the old man said. He had seen them clinging to the mast himself. And Mr. Ramsay taking a look at the spot was about, James and Cam were afraid, to burst out:

But I beneath a rougher sea,

and if he did, they could not bear it; they would shriek aloud; they could not endure another explosion of the passion that boiled in him; but to their surprise all he said was "Ah" as if he thought to himself, But why make a fuss about that? Naturally men are drowned in a storm, but it is a perfectly straightforward affair, and the depths of the sea (he sprinkled the crumbs from his sandwich paper over them) are only water after all. Then having lighted his pipe he took out his watch. He looked at it attentively; he made, perhaps, some mathematical calculation. At last he said, triumphantly:

"Well done!" James had steered them like a born sailor.

There! Cam thought, addressing herself silently to James. You've got it at last. For she knew that this was what James had been wanting, and she knew that now he had got it he was so pleased that he would not look at her or at his father or at any one. There he sat with his hand on the tiller sitting bolt upright, looking rather sulky and frowning slightly. He was so pleased that he was not going to let anybody share a grain of his pleasure. His father had praised him. They must think that he was perfectly indifferent. But you've got it now, Cam thought.

They had tacked, and they were sailing swiftly, buoyantly on long rocking waves which handed them on from one to another with an extraordinary lilt and exhilaration beside the reef. On the left a row of rocks showed brown through the water which thinned and became greener and on one, a higher rock, a wave incessantly broke and spurted a little column of drops which fell down in a shower. One could hear the slap of the water and the patter of falling drops and a kind of hushing and hissing sound from the waves rolling and gambolling and slapping the rocks as if they were wild creatures who were perfectly free and tossed and tumbled and sported like this for ever.

Now they could see two men on the Lighthouse, watching them and making ready to meet them.

Mr. Ramsay buttoned his coat, and turned up his trousers. He took the large, badly packed, brown paper parcel which Nancy had got ready and sat with it on his knee. Thus in complete readiness to land he sat looking back at the island. With his long-sighted eyes perhaps he could see the dwindled leaf-like shape standing on end on a plate of gold quite clearly. What could he see? Cam wondered. It was all a blur to her. What was he thinking now? she wondered. What was it he sought, so fixedly, so intently, so silently? They watched him, both of them, sitting bareheaded with his parcel on his knee staring and staring at the frail blue shape which seemed like the vapour of something that had burnt itself away. What do you want? they both wanted to ask. They both wanted to say, Ask us anything and we will give it you. But he did not ask them anything. He sat and looked at the island and he might be thinking, We perished, each alone, or he might be thinking, I have reached it. I have found it; but he said nothing.

Then he put on his hat.

"Bring those parcels," he said, nodding his head at the things Nancy had done up for them to take to the Lighthouse. "The parcels for the Lighthouse men," he said. He rose and stood in the bow of the boat, very straight and tall, for all the world, James thought, as if he were saying, "There is no God," and Cam thought, as if he were leaping into space, and they both rose to follow him as he sprang, lightly like a young man, holding his parcel, on to the rock.

passage to fudaraku

INOUE YASUSHI

IN THIS ODDLY exhilarating narrative of a Buddhist abbot's

progress to sanctity, Japanese poet and novelist Inoue Yasushi

(1907–1991) puts an ironic spin on a recurrent theme of his work: the

use of discipline to cover malaise, skepticism, and nihilism. Told with

stoicism and dignity, "Passage to Fudaraku" (1961) suggests that in

the absence of absolute certainty, the encounter with the sea yields the

ultimate reality principle by which the measure of life—and death—

may be taken.

not until the spring of 1565, the year in which he must him-self put out to sea, did Konko, Abbot of the Fudaraku-ji, meditate earnestly on the Buddhists who had set sail for the island of Fudaraku. True, he had occasionally thought of his predecessors whose sailings he had witnessed, but his musings now were pervaded with an unusual sense of urgency.

Konko had in fact never before given serious thought to the possi-bility of his embarking on such a voyage. His immediate predecessor as abbot had left these shores of Hama-no-miya in 1560, when he was sixty-one-years old, and the two abbots before him had done so when they were sixty-one, in November of 1545 and November of 1541. Although the three had set sail from Hama-nomiya on the south Kumano coast in November of their sixty-first year, with the Pure Land known as Fudaraku as their destination, there was no rule requiring the abbot of the monastery to do so.

The Fudaraku-ji, as its name suggests, was the fountainhead of the worship of Fudaraku. The monastery had long been known as a coun-terpart of Fudaraku Island—a realm in the southern region, the Pure Land of the deity of mercy, Kannon—and it had become a custom for devout worshippers to set sail from the Kumano coast for the mythical isle in the hope of being received by Kannon incarnate, in whose Pure Land they would be reborn. Hama-no-miya in time became the cus-tomary site for departure, and the Fudaraku-ji the monastery responsi-ble for overseeing the ritual sailing. Persons bound for the mythical isle customarily took lodging at this monastery because of its deep-rooted associations with the belief in Fudaraku. Moreover, several former abbots of the monastery were included among the nine revered as sages for having sailed to Fudaraku—the youngest, according to records kept at the monastery, at the age of eighteen, and the eldest at the age of eighty.

Because the three who had preceded Konko as abbot had put out to sea when they were sixty-one, people came to assume that every abbot of the Fudaraku-ji would embark upon a like voyage in November of his sixty-first year. The tradition associated with the monastery served rather naturally to reinforce the assumption, and Konko, now sixty-one, would have to submit to the dictates of popular expectation. That he had not fully understood the necessity was doubtless due to his innocence of worldly affairs, for he had known only the clergy since his youth.

Konko had at times reflected on the meaning of his role as abbot of the Fudaraku-ji, on the possibility of his presently feeling compelled to attempt the voyage; he regarded the prospect not wholly without anticipation. He was aware of a vague, self-imposed obligation. Dedicated to serving the Buddha, he regarded the eventual voyage with some fascination, yearning perhaps. He still recalled very vividly the dignity of Shokei at the time of his departure, and had long wished he might some day emulate this monk, who had been his teacher. Shokei had attained enlightenment when he was sixty-one, but Konko, aware of his own inadequacies, had never believed he could go so far without devoting himself to spiritual austerities over a long period of time—surely many more years than had been required of his teacher. He had been immersed in the traditions of the Fudaraku-ji for the better part of his life, and he longed desperately for a spiritual insight that would inspire him to embark upon the voyage.

The year 1565 was to be an unexpectedly baneful one for Konko. No sooner did the new year dawn than visitors began to ask him "When in November do you mean to sail?" or, solicitously, "Now that the long-awaited year has come, won't you tell me how I might be of assistance?"—questions they earlier would have considered indelicate. Now, however, all visitors seemed to feel obliged to touch on this matter—as if not to do so would be a discourtesy—and well-meant concern was reflected on their faces and in their voices as well.

No one would have addressed the abbot with malice. Since his youth Konko had disciplined himself severely. He had not achieved any great distinction, but he had an unassuming, pleasing manner. And in due course, after he was past his middle age, he came to be accorded a remarkable degree of trust and respect by the faithful. Over the past few years he had not once failed to notice the suggestion of reverence and affection in the eyes of whomever he chanced to meet—villager, Buddhist parishioner, even the ascetic Shinto priests of Nachi Falls. There was no questioning the respect and fondness he now inspired in everyone who knew him.

Konko was disconcerted by the growing expectations. He hoped to dispel them at an early opportunity: he would have it understood that his sailing would not take place until some future year when he was spiritually prepared for it, and that a voyage to Fudaraku undertaken without conviction or faith would likely be a failure. By spring, however, he came to despair of making his intentions known. Had there been only a few to convince, he might have prevailed. But he had to contend not with a mere dozen or even one or two hundred people, but the collective expectations of the whole region.

Whenever Konko ventured out from the monastery he would be showered with coins—offerings to His Reverence. Children, too, ran after him and threw coins. Beggars began to follow him through the streets to pick up the offerings for themselves. The monastery began receiving cenotaphs, customarily kept in homes, together with requests that they be taken by Konko and delivered to the Pure Land of Kannon. There were some who went so far as to entrust him with cenotaphs made for themselves.

In these circumstances Konko seemed to have little choice. Had he mentioned his reluctance to set sail or suggested a postponement until some future year, his words would have fallen on unsympathetic ears, and he might have provoked great disquiet and even violence.

The personal disgrace would not have mattered to Konko, but he could not have endured doing injury to the religion of Kannon. Insignificant though he might be, he was a member of the clergy. If by word or action he were to do injury to the faith, he could not possibly expect divine forgiveness even in death.

On the day of the vernal equinox, Konko announced formally that he would put out to sea in November. The announcement was accompanied by ancient rites at the Kumano Shrine. Having been a participant on seven previous occasions, he was best acquainted with the proceedings and gave instructions on the proper order of events, as well as all the details of the floral offerings and ritual music. Whatever he recited from memory was recorded dutifully by his disciple, a seventeen-year-old monk named Seigen.

At the sight of the youth, Konko thought of himself at twenty-seven, seated beside Yushin, then preparing to make his departure, and noting down Yushin's instructions. If Seigen was to remain at the Fudaraku-ji, then he, too, several decades hence must embark for Fudaraku. The young monk with freshly shaven head, Konko thought, was as pitiful as himself

THE DATE OF the first sailing for Fudaraku is not known. The old chronicles which Konko consulted state that the first to embark was

Keiryo, who left the Kumano coast on November 3 in the eleventh year of the Jogan Era, some six centuries before the Eiroku Era of Konko's time. The second was Ushin, who set sail fifty years later, in February of 919. A brief note suggests that he most likely was a monk who had left the far north in the hope of embarking upon the voyage, and had sojourned for some months or years at the Fudaraku-ji prior to his departure. The third was Kogan, in November of 1130, following an interval of more than two hundred years. Some three centuries later, in November of 1443, Yuson became the fourth to set sail for Fudaraku. In November of 1498, seven years before Konko was born, Seiyu put out to sea. Seiyu's exemplary erudition and virtuous attainments were yet well remembered when Konko first came to the Fudaraku-ji. A thirty-three year interval preceded the next sailing, of Yushin, whom Konko had known well—a monk with eccentric ways, better remembered as the blessed Ashida, a sobriquet he acquired because he habitually wore *ashida*, the common wooden clogs, instead of the sandals appropriate to his vocation.

The belief was commonly held that the Fudaraku-ji existed as a convenience for voyagers to the isle of Fudaraku; and that since early times all Buddhists with good sense had come there, had the appropriate rites conducted, and promptly put out to sea. But Konko knew well that such was not the case. Excluding the first four voyagers and the former abbots of Fudaraku-ji mentioned in early documents, only two or three among the many believed to have made the voyage seemed actually to have set sail. Notices of voyages undertaken by a warrior named Shimokobe Yukihide in 1233 and the priestly courtier Gido in 1475 appear also in records of other monasteries, and so these doubtless were authentic cases. As for the others, there was little or no evidence.

Though sailings for Fudaraku had come to be accepted as common-place, over a period of six hundred years no more than nine or ten persons had actually put out to sea. And this was only reasonable. Rarely would a man become prepared spiritually to covet dying at sea as the culmination of his faith. The ones who did were most uncommon monks, a scattering among thousands or myriads, unlikely to appear any oftener than once in decades, even hundreds of years.

There had all the same been an unaccountable increase in the number of voyagers; including Seishin, who had departed five years before, in all seven had left these shores during the sixty years of Konko's lifetime. Among the seven were two young men of twenty-one and eighteen. The zeal for discarding life in the hope of being reborn in the Pure

Land was itself the ultimate consummation—this was the essential teaching of the writ, in all its countless scrolls.

Never before, until the beginning of the stir in 1565, had Konko doubted the meaning of the ritual voyage. The voyager would be confined in a doorless wooden box nailed securely to the bottom of a boat; his only provisions would be an oil lamp that would burn out in a matter of days and a small quantity of food. To be cast off thus from the Kumano coast meant certain death at sea. The instant the voyager drew his last breath, the boat would begin carrying his body speedily southward, like a bamboo leaf skimming rapids, toward the isle of Fudaraku. There he would acquire new life, that he might live eternally in the service of Kannon.

A sailing from the shores of Kumano held the promise of an end to mortal life and the beginning of spiritual life. Not doubting this, Konko had noticed in the faces of past voyagers only the unusual serenity and composure that radiate from the hearts of those who have attained to absolute faith. He had seen joy in anticipation of new life, never sadness or fear. The voyagers had seemed tranquil and yet jubilant, and the onlookers, though understandably curious, had seemed wholly intent on glorifying them.

After he had announced his departure, Konko began to think differently of voyagers of the past. Waking and sleeping, he saw the several he had known, their faces somehow different.

Konko secluded himself in his cell through the spring and summer. Should he have stepped outside the monastery, people would have continued to throw coins his way, bow and pray to him as if he were a Buddha, and ask him, among other things, to take this or that to the Pure Land or lay his healing hand on the forehead of a dying man. This was so much bother for Konko, who was now preoccupied with somehow cultivating a genuine willingness to sail for Fudaraku when the time came, three or four months hence. Faced rather suddenly with the inevitability of putting out to sea, he was forced to acknowledge the utter inadequacy of his spiritual preparations. Now he spent his waking hours reciting the scriptures. Whenever an attendant went to his room, there he would be, facing a wall, reading from the scriptures.

Occasionally he would stop, and he would be staring blankly at some object in his room; seldom did he turn to face the attendant, who, when asked, had this same ready description: "They say that the saints are *yorori* the minute they put out to sea, but His Reverence already looks every inch a *yorori*."

There was indeed a saying that a saint at sea becomes the fish called the *yorori*. *Yorori* dwell only in the coastal waters between Cape Miki and the Cape of Shio. Fishermen of the region always release *yorori* caught in their nets; they never eat them.

Konko was tall and thin, as the *yorori* is long and slender. But it was not the physical resemblance that prompted the comparison. It was Konko's eyes, small and remote, dull and vacant, as if benumbed, the eyes of the *yorori*.

Konko spent his time either in recitation, his eyes closed, or in silence, staring blankly and vacantly. When his eyes resembled those of the *yorori*, he was thinking about one or another of the past voyagers. A few times in the course of a day, his eyes would regain, if briefly, their normal luster—moments when he suddenly became aware that he had been musing upon some voyager—and he would tell himself that he must not reminisce, that he must dispel whatever notion he had been dwelling upon, that he must instead be reciting the sutras, that all would end well if he continued to recite the sutras. And he would resume his reciting as if possessed.

No sooner had Konko finished another recitation, however, than his eyes were lifeless—a sign that in thought he was again dwelling upon some voyager of the past. He turned to pious recitation in order to keep his eyes from becoming those of a *yorori*, to banish from his vision the faces of past voyagers which appeared and reappeared. He devoted himself to this one purpose, and the effort took its toll of him.

The first time Konko witnessed a sailing for Fudaraku was on the occasion of the departure of Yushin, who was forty-three years old at the time. Konko, who only a half year earlier had moved to the monastery from a temple in his native village of Tanabe, was then twenty-seven. Yushin had been regarded as something of an oddity because of eccentric behavior—his insistence on wearing *ashida* instead of sandals, for instance. Suddenly he seemed to become a man possessed and, to everyone's surprise, declared that he would set sail for Fudaraku. And he embarked on the voyage three months later. Because his sailing was the first in thirty-three years, it attracted considerable notice. On the appointed day, the beach at Hama-no-miya was thronged with people who had come from places as far distant as Ise and Tsu to witness the inspiring event.

Konko and Yushin were both from Tanabe, and this association led to an acquaintance between them and opportunities for Konko to speak informally with him. Konko recalled how he often would remark that he could see Fudaraku Island. When asked its location, Yushin replied that on any clear day the island appeared distinctly on the horizon. Anyone, he added, who had freed himself of delusions and acquired faith in the Buddha could see it. Konko too would see it if he gave himself up wholly to faith in Fudaraku.

"It is level and high," said Yushin of this island, "rising on boulders that are pounded incessantly on all sides by the stormy sea. I can hear the pounding of the waves. This tableland with the sea all round it is an infinite expanse, calm, of untold beauty, covered with verdure that can never wither, abounding in springs that can never run dry. Great flocks of vermilion birds, their tails long and flowing, make their nests there. And I see people disporting themselves there—these people do not age as they serve the Buddha."

Yushin completed the customary ritual and boarded his boat near the first of several sacred gates in a line from the shore. He was oblivious to the presence of well-wishers who crowded the beach, and he spoke only to Konko, who attended him up to the moment of boarding. "Fudaraku is exceptionally clear today," Yushin said to him. "You must join me there someday." And he laughed softly. Konko, though he did not know why, was startled at Yushin's smile. Yushin's eyes, ever steady in their gaze, were suddenly piercing, and covered over by a kind of iridescence.

Yushin's boat was escorted as far as Tsunakiri Island, some seven miles from shore, by men on several vessels and there was sent off on its solitary voyage to distant waters.

Those who had escorted Yushin saw the boat moving directly south through the dark waves, speeding away as if it were being pulled in on a line. Perhaps the Buddha was leading it to the island that had dwelt so constantly in his vision. Monks at the Fudarakuji who earlier had treated him as an eccentric spoke ill of him no more. The curious actions of the monk who had worn askida were seen in a new light, and each became an episode to be recounted as a legacy of his high attainment.

Konko had been urged by Yushin to make the same voyage one day, and now, thirty-four years later, he was about to sail for Fudaraku. Whenever Konko thought of Yushin, he remembered the strange greenish iridescence in his eyes. There was no doubting Yushin's having seen the Pure Land. Were his eyes, as he studied the isle on the horizon, no different from the eyes of others? His voyage did not carry with it any promise of death. Quite probably he never thought about death. As he had failed to contemplate death, so had he failed to contemplate the renewal of life—these were not his concerns. His strangely glowing eyes had actually envisioned Fudaraku. The island became an obsession with him, and he simply decided to go there.

The sailing of Shokei took place ten years later. When Shokei first announced his intention to put out to sea, no one thought it remarkable. Had he lived his lifetime at the monastery, never associating himself with the belief in Fudaraku, he would have been revered no less. His decision, once it became known, was regarded by all as quite in accord with his character. This response attested to the great admiration with which people regarded this diminutive monk—so small that a child might easily pick him up—face wrinkled ten years beyond his age, eyes brimming with compassion.

Konko was filled with sadness when he learned of Shokei's decision, but only because he hated to say goodbye. When he remembered that he would not again hear those kind words of encouragement, those thoughtful and deeply felt admonitions, the sorrow became torment. Not even separation from the parents who had brought him into this world, he thought, could be sadder.

All through summer of that year, on now-forgotten occasions when Konko had gone to him, Shokei would say: "Meeting death on the blue expanse of the sea might be rather pleasant."

"Will you die?" Konko asked, for he had never before associated these sailings with death at sea. There would be death, to be sure, but was not the purpose of it all to acquire eternal life at the end of the voyage?

"Of course I shall die," Shokei replied. "I shall die at sea and sink to the bottom, which, by the way, is every bit as expansive as the surface, and I shall make friends with all the fishes." And he laughed merrily as if the thought gave him considerable pleasure.

When he boarded his vessel and when he sailed away, from Tsunakiri Island—at all times, indeed—Shokei was smiling as always. Earlier voyagers had had themselves shut in a box which was then fastened to the bottom of the boat. A similar box-like compartment was placed on his boat, but he did not go inside. He sat at the stern and the onlookers saw him waving goodbye. He shed no tears, but everyone else, young and old, was weeping.

Shokei envisioned drowning at sea, not passage to Fudaraku. Why, then, did he set out on a voyage to the mythical isle?

Konko could think of only one reason. Shokei must have believed that he would serve Kannon best by doing so. In the decade preceding his voyage, Kumano was beset with a succession of disasters—a great earthquake in January of 1538, a landslide in August of that year and, coinciding with it, the inexplicable splintering of every rafter in the

main Kumano Shrine, the typhoon of August, 1540, which swept down
to the sea every river boat of the commercial guilds and caused countless deaths all along the sea coast, and a destructive flood in August of
1541. To make matters worse, the civil war raging about the capital bred
violence in outlying districts. At night the region was the province of
brigands, and brutality and killing were the most common of occur-
rences. Religion was as good as forgotten to Shokei's unhappiness. He
must be an inspiration and bring people back to religion.

Konko was disturbed by the thought that a monk as wise as Shokei
believed in nothing about the voyage to Fudaraku save only dying at sea.
That was not enough for him. The eventuality of reaching Fudaraku
island might not have been of concern to one such as Shokei, who had
attained enlightenment. Konko knew, however, that he could not be
content with a voyage that carried no promise other than that of sinking to the floor of the sea.

Nichiyo put out to sea four years after Shokei, whom he had succeeded as abbot of the Fudaraku-ji. Nichiyo, sickly and short-tempered,
was a contrast to his predecessor. Konko felt as though he had not had a
moment's rest during the four years of his service to Nichiyo, who was
feared by everyone in the monastery. When he announced his intention
to set sail for Fudaraku—it was wholly unexpected—Konko was not
alone in breathing a sigh of relief. Life was very precious to Nichiyo; he
would have the monastery in an uproar if he so much as caught a cold.
In January of his final year his asthma was worse. Because medical treatment had no effect whatever, he concluded that he had not much longer
to live. Already sixty-one, he no doubt decided that a voyage to
Fudaraku was preferable to dying in a sickbed.

Surely Nichiyo was influenced very strongly by the hope of reaching
the Pure Land alive. Since autumn of the year before, he had talked more
frequently, and to anyone who would listen, about extraordinary
accounts in books he had read—typically, about a monk from such and
such province having set sail from Tosa in January of 1142 and having
lived to reach Fudaraku Island and to return to Japan with a knowledge
of the Pure Land. In arriving at his decision Nichiyo was encouraged
immeasurably by these confused accounts. Nevertheless from the time
he made the decision until the scheduled day of departure his deport-
ment was consistent with his exalted role. He seemed to acquire unusual confidence at the time the title of sage was conferred upon him and
throughout the summer and autumn months he was serene. To all
appearances he had no doubts about life, and death.

On the day before his departure, Nichiyo walked down to the shore to inspect his boat. He seemed displeased and asked Konko, who was with him, "Did Shokei ride out in a boat as small as this?" Konko replied that it had been an even smaller one.

The next day as Nichiyo was boarding the boat one foot slid into the water. He seemed very unhappy, indeed wretched. His expression was one of such despair as Konko had not known before. He stood motionless for a time, his dry foot on the boat and his wet foot on the gangplank, and then stepped aboard as if resigning himself to fate. The five who had accompanied him as far as Tsunakiri Island said later that he spoke not one word to them.

Though twenty years had passed, Konko could still see Nichiyo's expression clearly. It reflected, though he did not like to think so, his own feelings of the moment.

Bankei, who embarked upon the voyage when he was forty-two, had like Yushin often remarked that he could see Fudaraku Island. He was a tall, stout man, with a somewhat unruly disposition. Though Konko had never liked him, he was strangely moved when Bankei, ten years younger than he, announced that he would embark for Fudaraku. Bankei was a giant compared to the frail, diminutive voyagers of the past—much too large, it seemed, to be accommodated by the customary boat. His was not the image one could readily associate with the ritual voyage.

Bankei believed that he would live to see Fudaraku Island. "I don't want to die," he often said. "I'll get to the island safely because it beckons me. I can actually see it, and that most certainly means it beckons me there." He was inclined to ramble on in this vein.

No one gave Bankei the reassurance he sought—with the single exception of Nichiyo's successor, the abbot Seishin, who invariably responded with kind and reassuring words.

Seishin also embarked for Fudaraku when he was sixty-one, and Konko knew, for a reason distinctly different from the other voyagers. Seishin, who had no kin, was a lonely man. During the time he was abbot he was victim of a series of unhappy deceptions and betrayals. His feelings, like his frail body, were easily injured. He became hopelessly misanthropic, weary of society and of people and life.

Konko and Seishin got along well with each other, perhaps because they were so near the same age. The weariness that possessed Seishin in his old age was complete, and he longed for death above all else. He was not a man of firm religious conviction even though he had been a member of the order since his youth. He veiled his true thoughts, of course, and managed to complete the customary rites and earn the respect and reverence due a monk embarking upon the ritual voyage. Only Konko knew how he really felt.

Not long before the appointed day Seishin said that he would rather walk into the sea striking a bell, and continue walking until he sank beneath the deep waters; but he was dissuaded by his disciples. He departed with dignity as Shokei had.

"I want to reach Fudaraku as quickly as possible," he said. "Therefore I need no food or fuel. All I need is a boat with a mast and a sail that bears the inscription 'Praise to the Lord Amida.' " That was precisely as he had it.

Seishin carried a rosary, but in other respects he bore few of the marks of a Buddhist. He did not intone prayers or finger his beads as his predecessors had.

"At last," he said, as his boat was being cast off from Tsunakiri Island. "A man is a trial to others whether he's trying to live or die. But I suppose it must be so." He seemed happy to be finally alone, free of the many well-wishers.

There were yet two other voyagers: twenty-one-year-old Korin and eighteen-year-old Zenko, who put out to sea when Konko was in his thirties, the former in 1530 and the latter in 1533. The youths were sick and to all appearances on the verge of death when they came to the monastery, accompanied by their parents, to request passage to Fudaraku. Korin had been urged to do so by his parents, who believed that he might by some miracle live to see the island paradise. He apparently knew little about the ritual voyage. He knew, however, that his illness was mortal, and had chosen to abide by his parents' wishes. Zenko was carrying out his own wish. His parents had wanted him to live on and he sought to persuade them that he would die at sea and be carried by the currents to the Pure Land of Fudaraku; they were sadly troubled when they brought him to the monastery.

The youths were accompanied to Tsunakiri Island by large groups of well-wishers, and on both occasions the beach was crowded. Konko had been moved to tears at the sight of the emaciated Zenko putting out to sea, and at the recollection all the sorrow returned.

SUMMER WAS SPEEDING by. Konko each day would ask someone to tell him what day of the month it was, and each time doubt his ears. He continued to spend his waking hours reciting from the scriptures. After the autumnal equinox the days passed with astonishing speed. The light of dawn seemed instantly to fade into dusk.

Konko knew well that he was no better prepared spiritually than before. The faces of past voyagers continued to appear and reappear. However fondly he might regard them, they now seemed unrelated to Fudaraku. The grandeur that had fascinated him was gone.

THE FACES OF Yushin and Bankei—both had often said they could see Fudaraku Island—now seemed somehow aberrant. The voyage of Seishin, obviously undertaken in desperation by a thoroughly weary old man, could have had nothing to do with belief in Kannon or the Pure Land. He had only watched the dark waves running in turbulent succession upon the Kumano coast. In this respect he was no different from Konko's teacher, Shokei, who had displayed such remarkable dignity on his departure. Shokei had been certain of imminent death and had noticed only the surging sea on which his mortal remains would rest. He must not have been concerned with reaching Fudaraku and acquiring new life. His serene eyes were those of one who left such concerns behind.

Nichiyo was a man with a set purpose. At his departure, as he sailed, and days or even weeks later with no more than a plank to keep him afloat, perhaps he clung to life, still hoping to be rescued, to have Kannon reach out for him. He hoped for a miracle. He had, in the deepest sense, had no part of faith or of belief in Kannon or Fudaraku. He had seemed to believe, but had not believed.

Though both Korin and Zenko had moved the onlookers profoundly with an appearance of serenity, their voyages had in fact had nothing whatsoever to do with faith. Wasted from illness, they were able to resign themselves to death with less hesitation than most others.

When Konko became aware that he had been gazing at their several faces, he would hastily dismiss them. They were utterly dreary. He would not wish to resemble them, and yet he felt that his face would be any one of theirs the moment he slackened his hold upon himself.

If he was to embark on the voyage, Konko thought, he would not want to look like any of his predecessors. What would his expression be then? He did not quite know, but it must be one that would be appropriate to a truly devout monk setting sail for Fudaraku. If he must put out to sea, he would do so wearing an expression appropriate to his role.

In October, with the date of sailing just one month away, Konko began to think differently of the faces of past voyagers. He underwent another change. He would give anything to be like one of them—it did not matter which one. He had felt as if he could at will resemble any one of the faces, even though the thought was repugnant to him. Now that he longed to be like them, however, he knew that he had been indulging in wishfulness. He had set himself a hard task.

If only he might see the Pure Land! He recalled with envy the extra-ordinary glow in the eyes of Yushin and Bankei. He envied Seishin's expression of complete relief on gaining the solitude he had long sought. He regarded enviously even Nichiyo's expression, usually sullen as if to reflect some inner turmoil but capable of anger when he was disturbed, as when his foot slid into the water. There was little likelihood of attain-ing the calmness and dignity of Shokei. Konko even doubted that he could resemble either of the two youths. How were they able at such a tender age to assume expressions of such utter tranquility and resignation?

Kenko received callers, who were suddenly numerous. He did not know who they were or why they had come. He had neither the will nor the ability to remember. In the morning an attendant would lead him to the Thousand-armed Kannon in the main hall, and there he would sit until noon. Callers would come one after another into the hall. Konko did not speak to them. Having come to say goodbye, they seemed relieved that he did not. They seemed to conclude that in these circumstances words were an inappropriate means of farewell, and Konko's silence seemed not at all strange.

If a visitor spoke to him, Konko did not answer. He recited a holy text softly or sat in silence, his eyes like those of a *yorori*, fixed vacantly upon a darkened corner of the hall.

By November he had lost all awareness of time. When he awoke he would call Seigen. "Isn't this the day for my voyage?" he would ask. Told that it was not, he would lift his head in apparent relief, and look upon the white sands of the garden. He would gaze at the bright green plant-ings and listen to the lapping of waves on the beach of Hama-no-miya, which was like an extension of the garden. Only recently had he begun to notice trees and the sound of waves. He perceived things which he had not in many years.

On one of those bright, clear autumn days, Konko asked again if it was not the day for his voyage.

"You will be leaving this afternoon at four," Seigen replied. Konko stood up and sat down again. His strength seemed to have been drained quite away. He was perfectly still, quite incapable of motion.

An attendant came to say that a group of well-wishing Shinto priests had come from Nachi Falls. Another announced the arrival of a Zen abbot.

Konko at last seemed aware of the stir. With the assistance of several attendants he changed clothes. With several monks in the lead he went to the main hall, where he had sat in meditation every morning since first coming to the monastery. He glanced calmly at the Thousand-armed Kannon, Taishaku, Bonten, and other deities. Soon he was staring at them intently.

Every activity was now dictated by his attendants. He sat before the central image and recited from the scriptures, then returned to his assigned position and sat, gazing intently at the images. The air was thick with incense. The assemblage of monks flowed out of the small hall over the corridors to the garden. The hall itself seemed enfolded in the fullness of the chorus of prayer.

Shortly past noon, Konko retired from the main hall to the cloister, where he had tea with several monks. A sack containing one hundred and eight pebbles, each inscribed with one word from the scriptures, was brought to the veranda. Several sacred scrolls, a statuette of the Buddha, clothing, and a few other items—all to be placed in Konko's boat—were also gathered on the veranda and inspected by the attendants. And, finally, a wooden palanquin to carry these items was brought in and deposited in a manner which one might have thought unnecessarily casual. Though somewhat annoyed by the rough casualness, he did not feel inclined to protest.

The monks left the monastery shortly before the appointed hour. Unseasonably brilliant sunlight filled Konko's eyes. The strand was thronged with people. The party of monks, Konko at its center, moved along with the excited crowd, passed through the sacred gate, and came to the white sand along the shore.

As had Nichiyo years before him, Konko thought that his boat was the smallest of them all. He wondered why they had given him such a tiny boat. There was no boat landing. His boat and three others for those who would see him off lay at the water's edge, as if they had been washed ashore. The three were much larger than Konko's.

He was led aboard his boat at once. Workmen came aboard with a large wooden box which they placed over him. He was suddenly angry. The boat should have had a compartment which he could enter. Instead one had been brought afterwards.

There was a pounding as it was nailed to the boat. Presently the pounding stopped. It was dark inside the box. A door was opened, and various articles were pushed inside. Konko was asked to come out of the box and greet the onlookers, and he did so. The crowd stirred. Coins fell like rain on to the boat and along the shoreline and children fought to collect them. Konko fled back inside. He sat for some time in the dark while a mast and a sail bearing the formula 'Praise to the Lord Amida' were put up. Everything seemed clumsy and slow.

Almost two hours passed. With not a word of warning to him, the boat began to move. He felt it grinding against the pebble-strewn shore, and then there was the smoothness of the sea. He wanted to look out, but he could not open the box. It had been tightly sealed. However hard he pushed, he could not loosen a single one of the boards.

Then he heard the sound of an oar. He was not alone, then. The boatman would steer the vessel as far as Tsunakiri Island. There he would be cast off, alone.

He began to hear an intermittent chiming of bells through the sound of waves. Straining his ears, he heard a chanting of sacred words to the accompaniment of the chimes. But the chanting would be interrupted by the waves. Though at times it would assume a festive gaiety, it was soon obliterated by the roar of the sea.

As the boats made land at Tsunakiri Island, Konko found a slit and pressed his face to it. Night was approaching and the dark billowing sea seemed infinite.

"It's goodbye, Your Reverence!" the boatman called from above. Konko was confined. It was customary for voyagers to spend the night on Tsunakiri Island with the rest of the party and set sail in the morning.

"I'm to stay here tonight!" Konko shouted, so loudly in fact that he was surprised by his own voice.

"We're sending you off right now instead of waiting until tomorrow," the boatman answered. "The weather is bad, and we don't want to be stranded here."

Konko again cried out, but there was no answer. The boatman had already leapt ashore.

The boat was now pitching and rolling. Konko saw that the sea was much darker now, a broad expanse of turbulence.

At last he was alone. He sank to the floor. He felt the full weariness of the day and drifted helplessly into sleep.

Some hours later he awoke. In pitch darkness, he felt the boards beneath him rising and falling. He heard the crashing of waves below him, then overhead.

He quickly raised himself and with all his might threw himself against the side of the box. Never before had he resorted to such violence.

He repeated it in desperation five and six times. A board flew loose, and into the compartment came a blast of wind and spray. The box catching the wind sent the boat into a lurch. The next instant Konko felt himself being flung into the sea.

HE CLUNG TO a plank and stayed afloat through the night. At daybreak he saw Tsunakiri Island close at hand. As a child he had swum often in the coastal waters, and so he was able to save himself.

Around noon he was washed ashore, plank and all. He lay there until evening, when he was noticed by one of the monks who had accompanied him to the island the day before. The party of well-wishers had been detained there because of the high seas.

Konko was given a meal there on the bleak shore. The monks, meanwhile, were huddled together discussing at length what to do. They asked a fisherman for a boat and put Konko in it. Konko by then had regained some of his strength. "Spare me," he said, in a barely audible voice. Some of the monks must have heard him, but no one seemed to understand.

The boat was left on the beach for a while, and several men stood around it, regarding it in silence.

The young monk Seigen saw his teacher's lips apparently forming words, though surely not from the scriptures. He leaned close, but he heard nothing. He took out paper and brush and ink. With trembling hand, Konko strung together these words:

> Of mythical isles, of Horai,
> I have known two and ten.
> Believe only in the Pure Land.
> I shall believe in Lord Amida.

The words were barely legible. Again Konko wrote:

> Should you seek Kannon,
> Believe not in Fudaraku.
> Should you seek Fudaraku,
> Believe not in the sea.

Konko put down the brush and immediately closed his eyes. Seigen wondered if his teacher was dead, but he detected a pulse. He studied the words. Their meaning escaped him. They might perhaps be evidence of enlightenment and again they might indicate anger and frustration, no more.

A hastily made box was lowered over Konko and attached securely to the bottom of the boat. Then Konko and the boat were pushed out to sea.

THEREAFTER THE ABBOTS of the Fudaraku-ji were no longer expected to put out to sea when they reached sixty-one. There had been no such rule to begin with. As the account of Konko's voyage became known, it seems, people changed their minds about the role of the abbot of the Fudaraku-ji. Thereafter, when an abbot died, his body was sent out to sea from Hama-no-miya. The ritual voyage was called "passage to Fudaraku". There were seven such voyages over the next one hundred and fifty years. Because the sailing took place during the month in which the abbot died, it could be at any time of the year.

There was one more instance of a living embarkation for Fudaraku: Seigen's, thirteen years after Konko's, in November of 1578. Seigen was thirty at the time and the records of the Fudaraku-ji inform us that he put out to sea for the sake of his parents. As for the thoughts of this young monk, who had accompanied Konko to Tsunakiri Island, we have no means of knowing them.

harbor

W.S. MERWIN

W.S. MERWIN'S POETRY of borderline states explores the

thresholds between waking and sleeping, past and future, life and

death. In this superbly crafted prose poem, Merwin registers the sub-

tle atmospheric gradations and psycho-mythical resonances of land-

fall. More than anything, however, "Harbor" (1977) articulates the

particular kind of self-consciousness that steals upon us as we return

to land from the open sea: an overwhelmingly physical awareness of

ourselves as irrevocably transformed by our passage.

rarely is the night so clear on the crest at this time of year. All day we sailed in fog, floating through a pearl. The tide changed under us. We felt it slowly. The light went out of the pearl and we sailed on, through the back of a mirror, hearing the sound of a stream, which was ourselves, in the darkness. But we knew where we were as one remembers part of a story. We heard a buoy where it was supposed to be and we passed it according to the instructions published for the season, which means us. Then suddenly the fog cleared, and we saw the night: many stars and ahead of us and on either side an unbroken band of darkness. We were in the estuary. The sound of our passing through the water swallowed up the last low tones of the buoy behind us. Channel markers blinked, bells rang far off over the water as we made our way in.

We had not planned to arrive at night, but it makes no difference. I reach out over the stern and grasp the thick line that leads back to the patent log trailing behind us in the night, telling us our speed through the dark. I feel the pulsing of the line, the beat of the steady fish that is our time, and I reel in the heavy cord, hand over hand, stripping the water from it, hearing the metal fins break the surface and flounder over it until they come to hang upright, swinging in the night air, dripping into the babbling wake.

There are three of us: the old friend whose boat it is, the young woman, whom he scarcely knows, who came with me, and I. After the long passage we speak little, sailing up the estuary and when we do say something our voices are flushed and strained. We come to the end of a breakwater, where a small light is blinking on the top of a pole and we turn into the stillness beyond it.

I remember the harbor in the evening in another time: the glassy enclosure reflecting the cool sky full of yellow light after sunset and the one other vessel, a fishing boat moored alongside the looming fish-canning factory— a structure like an old colliery of wood and rusted tin, rising from the harbor's edge into the clear hour. One tall wharf ten or twelve houses around the shore: small, pointed white buildings from an age before any of us was born with grass running down to the water, and some windows full of sky, some with drawn white curtains, Hydrangea bushes in the twilight, fading.

We move slowly across the still harbor. I can make out the black shape of the factory, and then the high wharf jutting toward us on its stilts. My old friend walks forward and we take down the sails and glide on, propelled by nothing but our own momentum, in a long curve that ends with the wharf a few feet away. I take the painter and wait until I see, moving slowly toward me, the black form of a long ladder. I reach out to it and, with the line coiled on my arm, start to climb. Step by step the pilings of the wharf sink under the stars.

We will hear our feet walk along the wharf and onto the echoing land in the night. We will walk up the street between the few stores, past the speechless houses. Behind the curtains everyone is asleep. No one will know we are there. We will be standing in the street among the houses when the stars begin to fade, each of us seeing a different place. Unheard by us, someone will wake, on the other side of a curtain, and see us there, and not know who we are or where we have come from.

sailing away—

The high seas and waterways of the world have become a magnetic

piece of planetary real estate for those who want to "sail away" in

search of adventure, exotic encounters, and mystery. Today there are

more options than ever, from luxury cruise ships and chartered yachts

to bare boats (boats without captains or crews) and canoes, for navi-

gating the high seas and the great rivers of the world. What follows is

our list of handpicked cruise ships, yacht bare-boat brokers, and raft-

ing outfits that provide the best-in-class service for everyone who

wants a world-class experience from their sail away adventure.

oceanliners and cruise ships

Queen Elizabeth 2

The *QE2* is the darling of great ocean liners—there is simply no better way to sail away into the planet's most enchanted ports than aboard this luxurious ship. The *QE2's* annual world cruise is a voyage of oceanic exploration like no other. The *QE2* is a ship where you'll meet a unique group of "world cruisers," who have seen the globe from a seven-seas vantage several times over, and your every intellectual, cultural, and artistic desire will be satisfied.

> Cunard Line
> 6100 Blue Lagoon Drive, Suite 400
> Miami, Florida 33126
> Tel: 800-7-CUNARD
> www.cunardline.com

Seabourn Sun

The modernistic, sleek *Seabourn Sun* has been hailed (by the *Berlitz Complete Guide to Cruising and Cruise Ships*, among others) as the world's highest-rated cruise ship. Who can argue? Exciting itineraries, spa-on-the-sea indulgence, and ultra-luxury global cruising characterize voyages on the *Seabourn Sun* with its Scandinavian styling and sensibilities. The *Seabourn Sun* will join the Holland America Line in April 2002.

> Seabourn Cruise Line
> 6100 Blue Lagoon Drive
> Miami, Florida 33126
> Tel: 305-463-3000, 800-929-9391
> Fax: 305-463-3010
> www.seabourn.com

Seabourn Goddess I & Seabourn Goddess II

Only one hundred or so guests are accommodated on these ships, which means they can sail into exotic, unusual ports of call inaccessible to larger ships, from Greece to Australia. An unregimented atmosphere prevails (the usual jacket-and-tie requirements characteristic of other ships in its class are waived), which makes a trip on these ships akin to sailing on a luxury yacht with a group of close friends. Features like a water-sports platform, offering aquatic activities in many ports of call, give the *Seabourn Goddess* ships the feel of a tropical resort on the high seas—something unique to these adventures.

Seabourn Cruise Line
6100 Blue Lagoon Drive
Miami, Florida 33126
Tel: 305-463-3000, 800-929-9391
Fax: 305-463-3010
www.seabourn.com

Seabourn Pride, Spirit, and *Legend*

The elegant *Pride, Spirit,* and *Legend* are smaller than ocean liners such as the *QE2* but larger than boutique mega-yachts such as the *Seabourn Goddess.* They accommodate about two hundred passengers and cater to discriminating cruisers who look for sophistication, pampering, and distinguished cultural and educational opportunities. Imagine sailing the globe with a ballet-and-dinner gala in St. Petersburg's palace on one itinerary and a private visit to Peggy Guggenheim's Museum in Venice on another, and you'll get an idea of just how remarkable sailing on these best-in-class ships can be.

Seabourn Cruise Line
6100 Blue Lagoon Drive
Miami, Florida 33126
Tel: 305-463-3000, 800-929-9391
Fax: 305-463-3010
www.seabourn.com

the sail-away charter:
from bare boats to yachts

Admiralty Yacht Vacations

The beauty of Admiralty Yacht Vacations is that they charter sailing motor yachts for almost any worldwide destination. Admiralty specializes in Caribbean charters, but can also hook you up with charter specialists in the Mediterranean, England, and other locations. A wide range of boats, including mono-hull sailboats, catamarans, and power yachts are available for the discriminating sailor.

Admiral's Inn
Villa Olga, Frenchtown,
St. Thomas, VI 00802, USA
Tel. 800-423-0380, 340-774-1376
Fax: 340-774-8010
www.admirals.com

Sailaway Yacht Charter Consultants

Sailaway Yacht Charter Consultants provide bare boats almost anywhere in the world, including Greece, Florida, Polynesia, and Mexico. Saliboats and power yachts also are available for chartered excursions to exotic ports of call.

Bareboat Depot
15605 Southwest 92 Avenue
Miami, FL 33157
Tel.: 800-BAREBOAT
Fax: 305-251-4408
E-mail: info@bareboat.com

canoes, rivers, and the wilderness

Sunrise Expeditions

Sunrise Expeditions excels in unique and exotic river itineraries in such far-flung places as Arctic Canada, Maine, Australia, Scotland, and Iceland. Providing unique adventures for almost twenty-five years, Sunrise Expeditions emphasize exploring lesser-traveled rivers throughout Canada, as well as exotic river itineraries worldwide. Combining the best elements of traditional northern guiding and canoemanship, with contemporary whitewater and expedition techniques, Sunrise has over the years attracted some of the country's finest professional canoeists and veteran expedition river guides.

Sunrise International
4 Union Plaza, Suite 21
Bangor, ME 04401

1-800-RIVER-30
Tel: 207-942-9300
Fax: 207-942-9399
E-mail: info@expeditionlogistics.com

exotic expeditions and diving

Faraway Sail & Dive Expeditions Co. Ltd.
This outfit offers the opportunity to sail in Thailand, Burma, the Andaman Islands, and Malaysia, and offers the option of scuba diving expeditions. Mono-hull yachts, crewed charters, and private yacht charters are available. Faraway Expeditions specializes in uninhabited islands in the Andaman Sea, and scuba diving in Thailand, Burma, or the Andaman Islands.

Faraway Sail & Dive Expeditions Co. Ltd.
Soi Bangrae, 5/6 Moo 10
Chalong, Muang Phuket
Phuket 83130, Thailand
Tel: 011-66-76-200507
Tel/Fax: 011-66-76-280701
E-mail: info@far-away.net

Irene
Irene is a unique survivor from a bygone era. Built in the UK in 1907, she sailed with a rapidly dwindling fleet of British merchant vessels through two World Wars and a Great Recession, finally retiring from her trading service in 1960. She was abandoned for many years until discovered by her present owner. Captivated by her natural vitality and beauty, he set about her restoration. The *Irene* is available for yacht charter in the Caribbean.

Irene Yacht Charters
Bishops Lodge, Oakley Green
Windsor, Berkshire SL4 5UL
UK
Tel: 011-44-1753-868-989
Fax: 011-44-1753-842-852
E-mail: yachtcharter@ireness.com

Palawan

This fifty-eight foot yacht preserves the best traditions of American sailing craft. Yet as the first vessel of her type to use a fin keel, *Palawan* has broken with tradition to become a genuine landmark in yacht design. *Palawan* is Coast Guard certified for up to twenty-four passengers and offers a variety of support-craft. Tom Woodruff, the captain aboard *Palawan*, has many years sailing experience in both the Atlantic and Pacific oceans. An accomplished navigator and guide, Tom can be counted on to share stories, answer questions, and point out historic landmarks.

Tom Woodruff
P.O. Box 9715-240
Portland, ME 04104
Tel: 888-284-PAL1
E-mail: Palawan@nlis.net

Seatrek

The Bugis people of south Sulawesi, once feared as pirates, have always been the most skillful shipbuilders and sailors in Indonesia. Their boats, the "prahu" and "pinisi," were and still are hand-crafted entirely from timber. While the smallest prahu are fishing boats the proud pinisi have been used for centuries as cargo carriers, plying the old trade routes between the smaller islands of the Indonesian archipelago, carrying everything from lumber to coca-cola crates. The pinisi are elegant two-masted schooners with sails, top-sails and three jibs. Today, while still hand-built by native craftsmen and fully laid in teakwood with traditional riggings, they usually hold an engine in addition to the sails. These pinisi vessels, of course, don't carry cargo anymore. Rather, they have been refurbished for small group adventure cruising among the remote islands of Indonesia.

Seatrek - Anasia Cruises
Jalan Danau Tamblingan 77
Sanur, Bali
Indonesia
Tel: 011-62-361-283-192
Fax: 011-62-361-285-440
E-mail: contact@anasia-cruise.com

bibliography

the texts in this collection were taken from the editions listed below.

Brown, Jason. "Afternoon of the *Sassanoa*." New York: *The Atlantic Monthly*, April 1999.

Bunin, Ivan. *The Gentleman from San Francisco and Other Stories*. New York: Washington Square Press, 1987.

Burrough, Bryan. "Storm Warning." New York: *Vanity Fair*, May 1999.

Dahl, Roald. "A Dip in the Pool." In *Tales of the Unexpected*. New York: Vintage Books, 1990.

Davison, Ann. "My Ship is So Small." In *Great Voyages in Small Boats*. New York: John de Graff, Inc.,1982.

Duane, Daniel. *Caught Inside: A Surfer's Year on the California Coast*. New York: North Point Press, 1996.

Gardiner, John Rolfe. "The Voyage Out." In *Prize Stories 1994: The O'Henry Awards*. New York: Anchor Books, 1994.

Goss, Pete. *Close to the Wind*. New York: Carroll & Graf Publishers, Inc., 1998.

Heyerdahl, Thor. *Kon-Tiki: Across the Pacific by Raft*. Chicago: Rand McNally & Company, 1950.

Hughes, Langston. *The Langston Hughes Reader*. New York: George Braziller, Inc., 1965.

Lavin, Mary. "The Great Wave." New York: *The New Yorker*, June 1959.

Merwin, M.S. "Harbor." New York: *The New Yorker*, May 1977.

Parker, James Reid. " A Maritime People." New York: *The New Yorker*, November 1951.

Scherer, Migael. "Reading the Weather." In *Sailing to Simplicity: Life Lessons Learned at Sea*. New York: International Marine/McGraw-Hill, 2000.

Theroux, Paul. "The Seabourn Spirit to Istanbul." In *The Pillars of Hercules: A Grand Tour of the Mediterranean*. New York: G.P. Putnam's Sons, 1995.

Thompson, Earl. *Caldo Largo*. New York: Carroll & Graf Publishers, Inc., 1976.

Verne, Jules. "Twenty Thousand Leagues Under the Sea." In *The Works of Jules Verne*. New York and London: Vincent Park and Company, 1911.

Wallace, David Foster. *A Supposedly Fun Thing I'll Never Do Again*. Boston: Little, Brown and Company, 1997.

Winton, Tim. *Land's Edge*. Sydney: Pan Macmillan Australia, 1993.

Woolf, Virginia. "The Lighthouse." In *To the Lighthouse*. New York: Harcourt Brace Jovanovich, 1989.

Yasushi, Inoue. "Passage to Fudaraku." In *The Oxford Book of Japanese Short Stories*. Oxford and New York: Oxford University Press, 1997.

permissions

acknowledgments

have you noticed that there are very few places left—outside of libraries, airplanes, and sickrooms—where one can curl up with a good book long enough to be totally absorbed by it? At home the phone's always ready to rip into your concentration, and at bedtime sleep has a way of interrupting the best passages. That's why a ship is such a perfect place for reading: you can kick back and with minimal distractions, give yourself over, body and soul, to the pleasures of the text. Not surprisingly, the idea for this collection was both conceived and incubated on board ship, on the *Seabourn Spirit* and the *QE 2*, respectively.

For helping us chart the course of this seafaring collection, we want to thank Richard Pine, our agent, skipper, and muse, and Matthew Lore, our visionary editor and publisher. For inspiration, information, and illumination on things nautical and sailing lore, we are indebted to Captain Ronald W. Warwick, Master of the QE 2; Bruce Good of Seabourn Cruise Lines; Erin Overbey, in the library at *The New Yorker;* Dan O'Connor, associate publisher of the Avalon Publishing Group; Celeste Wesson of *The Savvy Traveler,* and PGW's Seattle-based sales rep Harry Kirchner, a first-class sailing literature devotee.

Over the months, we've importuned friends, family, and colleagues for leads that have taken us literally all over the map of literature in search of the perfect candidates for this book. We are grateful to Bianca Lenček Bosker, Catherine Glass, Christian Hubert, Ioanna Theocharopoulou, Michael Kunichika, Bibi Lenček, Jimmy Onstott, Roger Porter, Victoria Pustynsky, and Peter Steinberger. The staffs at Reed College Library, Multnomah County Public Library, and Powell's Books have been both patient and heroic in helping us with getting our hands on materials.

For their sterling professional help in "outfitting" the book: Shawneric Hachey for tracking down permissions, Sue McCloskey for taking care of business, Mittie Helmich for producing the photographic images, Pauline Neuwirth for her book design, and Howard Grossman for his cover—we are endlessly grateful. And though they might never see this collection, we thank the writers whose stories make it possible.

about the contributors and editors

Jason Brown teaches creative writing at Stanford University. His first collection of stories, *Driving the Heart and Other Stories*, was published in 1999.

Ivan Bunin (1870–1953) was born in Voronezh, Russia. A poet, short story writer, translator, and novelist, he wrote about the decay of Russian nobility and of peasant life, and in 1933 was the first Russian to receive the Nobel Prize for literature. Bunin immigrated to France in 1920 and was condemned by the Russian government as a traitor. He died impoverished in exile in the South of France in 1953.

Bryan Burrough is a special correspondent at *Vanity Fair* magazine. A former *Wall Street Journal* reporter, he is the coauthor of the *New York Times* bestseller *Barbarians at the Gate*. He lives in New Jersey with his wife and their two sons.

Roald Dahl (1916–1990), born in Llandaff, Wales, is best known as one of the most successful and popular of all children's writers. His books include *Charlie and the Chocolate Factory*, *Matilda*, and *James and the Giant Peach*.

Ann Davison is the author of several books on sailing expeditions, including *Last Voyage*, *My Ship Is So Small*, *Home Was an Island*, and *In the Wake of the Gemini*.

Daniel Duane, born in 1967 in Berkeley, California, is the author of three books and has distinguished himself as a writer of firsthand accounts of the thrills of dangerous outdoor sports. He lives in Santa Cruz, California.

John Rolfe Gardiner is the author of six books and his stories frequently appear in *The New Yorker*. He's the winner of the Lila Wallace Reader's Digest Writer's Award. Gardiner lives in Unison, Virginia, with his wife and daughter.

Pete Goss served in the Royal Marines for nine years prior to competing in the Vendee Globe Challenge. He's been awarded the Legion d'Honneur for gallantry as well as the Medal of the British Empire, and has been named Yachtsman of the Year. *Close to the Wind* is his first book.

Thor Heyerdahl was born in Larvik, Norway, in 1914. He's a naturalist and adventurist whose nonfiction adventure tales have captured the hearts of millions around the world and documented his scientific discoveries on the migration of people hundreds and thousands of years ago. *Kon-Tiki*, his first and best-known work, has been translated into sixty-six languages. He lives in Italy.

Langston Hughes (1902–1961), born in Joplin, Missouri, was a poet, novelist, lecturer, and playwright who wrote more than thirty-five books, including *The Weary Blues, Simple Speaks His Mind*, and the autobiographical *The Big Sea*. Among his honors are the Harmon Gold Medal for Literature and the Guggenheim fellowship for creative work.

Mary Lavin (1912–1996) was born in Walpole, Massachusetts, and immigrated to Ireland in her early childhood. She is the author of twenty novels and short story collections and is widely considered one of the most masterful short story writers in Irish history. She is the recipient of many awards, including the James Tait Black Memorial Prize for best book of fiction in the U.K., the Katherine Mansfield-Menton Prize and the Gregory Medal.

W.S. Merwin was born in New York, New York, in 1927. He is a major American writer whose poetry, translations and prose have won several awards, including the Pulitzer Prize for Poetry for *The Carrier of Ladders* in 1971. He lives in Hawaii.

James Reid Parker (1909–1984), born in Freehold, New Jersey, was the author of *The Merry Wives of Massachusetts*, a columnist for *Woman's Day* throughout the 1950s and 1960s, and contributed to *The New Yorker*.

Migael Scherer, born in Phoenix, Arizona, in 1947, is an award-winning writer of nonfiction. She is best known for *Still Loved by the Sun: A Rape Survivor's Journal*, for which she was awarded the PEN/Martha Albrand Special Citation for Nonfiction and the Pacific Northwest Booksellers Association Award for Literary Excellence. She lives in Seattle, Washington.

Paul Theroux, born in Medford, Massachusetts, in 1941, is the internationally acclaimed author of such travel books as *The Great Railway Bazaar, The*